UNDENIABLY MARRIED

J. SAMAN

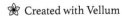 Created with Vellum

Boston World Family Tree

*This Does Not Contain Spoilers And Will Be Updated As The Series Progresses

Fritz Family

Octavia & Dr. Fritz

Rina & Brecken | Oliver & Amelia | Carter & Grace | Landon & Elle | Luca & Raven | Kaplan & Bianca

Layla, Keegan, Kenna | Owen, Wren | Stella, Sorel, Serena | | Stone, Forest

Rory

Central Square

Zaxton & Aurelia | Greyson & Fallon | Callan & Layla | Asher & Wynter | Lenox & Georgia

Hayes | Tinsley, Astor, Zoella | Katy, Wilder | Mason | Vander

Willow

The Edge

Jonah & Halle | Wes & Aria | Drew & Margot | Rina & Brecken

Jack, Estin

1

SOREL

I've played out today, this moment exactly, in my head so many times, that at this point, I feel like I'm acting out a script. Or perhaps watching from outside of my body, staring down as I see myself in a perfect white gown with my perfect hair and makeup. Maybe it's that I've spent the last year planning this wedding down to the last detail, and so far, it's everything I've dreamed it'd be.

It's a storybook. A fairy tale.

Too bad the groom is no Prince Charming.

Brody stands across from me, staring adoringly at me, his hands trembling and his eyes glassy as he recites his vows with heartfelt sincerity. He looks incredible in his black tux, and I take a moment to appreciate him like this. I fell in love with him in a tux. We met at an Abbot-Fritz gala I attended, and he was there looking just as handsome as he does now. We sat next to each other at dinner and spent the whole night talking and dancing.

That was it. Love.

Two years later, here we are.

Brody slides the plain gold band on my finger, and I stare

plaintively down at it. My engagement ring is platinum, and this is yellow gold. It doesn't match at all, and it speaks to how thoughtless he is. He didn't care enough to put energy or effort into picking out my wedding band.

Looking back, that was a common theme in our relationship. One I wish I had spotted earlier on. I was blind. A fool in love. Think of all the orgasms I've missed out on by being with him. I nearly snicker aloud at that.

The priest calls my attention, indicating that it's my turn to state my vows. We each wrote our own, and Brody's were beautiful. I'm sure part of him even meant them.

I turn around to my maid of honor, my best friend, my ride-or-die, and my twin sister, Serena, and signal her. She smiles knowingly and hands me the iPad she had waiting off to the side of the altar for just this moment. Brody's curious and surprised, perhaps even a little amused. He thinks I didn't memorize my vows, which shows how little he knows me.

He once teased me that I'd forget my head if it wasn't attached, and I remember hating the condescending barb. The man caught footballs for a living and barely made it through school. I save lives and graduated top of my class from both college and medical school. Not quite the same thing. Though Brody did recite his vows from memory, and here I am with an iPad. For how many times I've read and reread what I'm about to say, you would think I'd have memorized these by now too.

I clear my throat, my heart hammering in my chest as a fresh wave of nerves takes over. This is so not me to do this. I never cause scenes. I never make waves. I stay as far away from the spotlight as possible.

Brody is still holding my hand with the band on it, and he plays with the ring, rolling it a little with his fingers. I hope he's savoring this moment the way I am.

I smile, but it does little to stop the fluttering in my chest. "Brody, I had so many things I wanted to say to you today. So many heartfelt emotions to express how I felt about you. Then last night you slept at Noah's while I stayed in our apartment since it was important to us not to see each other before the ceremony. We thought it was bad luck." Now that laugh escapes, twisted with irony. "I'm not sure if you're aware that your phone is connected to your iPad." I hold it up, so he knows I'm referring to the device in my hand. "And with that, every time you get a text message, it also pops up in your messages here."

He freezes, his hand going still in mine, his face losing its expression and color.

I turn to the priest. "Please forgive me, Father, for I mean no disrespect. I'm simply reading from a text message stream I had the misfortune, or perhaps good fortune, of discovering and reading last night between one of my good friends and brides-maids, Eloise"—I pan the iPad in her direction—"and my fiancé, Brody."

I clear my throat again, unlock the iPad, and pull up the text stream.

"Sorel—" Brody starts only for me to cut him off with a sharp shake of my head.

"Shhh, sweetie. It's my turn to say my vows."

Another throat clear so I can project this directly across the church, all the way to the cheap seats in the back since it's a packed house. I wanted a small wedding but Brody wanted a big one. I'm positive he's about to regret that choice.

"From Brody: Do we need to talk about this? From Eloise: What's there to say? You're getting married tomorrow. From Brody: I know, and I love Sorel. I do. But I also love fucking you."

The loud cry of gasps can be heard throughout the church, echoing off the high ceilings and wood beams.

Brody is fuming—like he has any right to be—with red-hot fury crawling up his face. He's indignant that I'm so blatantly calling out his affair in front of our family, friends, and the priest.

"Give me the iPad, Sorel. Stop this. It isn't how it looks. I said it right there. I love you." He tries to steal the device from me, but I yank it back along with the hand he's been holding and take a step away from him.

Serena and my other sister, Stella, block Eloise, who isn't moving and is paler than Snow White after she bit into the poisoned apple, from trying to make a move for me. She's scrappy like that, so you never know what you're going to get with her. Obviously. But right now, I think she's too shocked to move, and I don't bother sparing her another glance.

It's not the first time a friend has betrayed me so egregiously.

I continue to walk backward down the steps, which isn't easy in my long dress. My father meets me halfway and takes me by my upper arm so I don't fall. He looks just as furious as Brody, but I'm not done with my speech yet.

"From Eloise: I love fucking you too, but I also love Sorel. She's been my best friend since college. Plus, I'm in love with James." James is her fiancé. He's standing now, and while I feel bad about hurting him, he needs to know. "From Brody: I don't want to stop. We've gone this long. Hell, we've been screwing each other all this time without an issue, so I don't see why we need to stop now. From Eloise: Good. Because that's what I want too. I love our dirty secret, lol. I love feeling you inside of me. I always need more. Like right now. From Brody: FaceTime me then. Show me your tits and pussy."

"Fuck," Brody hisses, scrubbing his hands up and down his face. "Sorel, I swear, I love you. I love you so much. I meant everything I just said to you. Every word of my vows. It's you I want to marry. It's you I want to be with. Eloise and I…" He trails off in frustration, his hands on top of his head as if he doesn't know what to say to make this better. "Please, stop this.

It didn't mean anything. Not to either of us. It was a fling. A stupid, meaningless fling. It's over now, okay? I swear. It'll only be you from now on."

I snicker. That's so ridiculous and insulting, I can't believe he even has the nerve to say it. "A little late for that don't you think considering you were both dating other people and it shouldn't have ever started. I suppose once a player, always a player. Even in retirement. Though you did me a big solid by being a cheating asshole last night. Imagine if I had gone through with our wedding and then found out?"

I fake shudder and shrug off my father, who lets me go, even as he stands in the aisle. My brothers join him along with a few of my male cousins. Brody is a big guy, but if he makes it out of this church without someone kicking his ass, I'd be shocked. I have a lot of uncles and cousins. They're big too.

I continue backward down the aisle, staring at Brody. I can't help my smile. I'm riding some sort of crazy adrenaline wave, and it's making me a little high. No one knows what to do. Everyone is frozen. Everyone except for me.

"From Eloise: Will you make me come? From Brody: Don't I always?" I laugh. It's kind of loud and a lot bitter. I meet his enraged eyes. "You see, and this is the sad part for me—and again, I apologize to my family and you, Father, for having to hear all of this—but you never cared if I got off. You always made it feel like an extra chore you didn't want to be bothered with. Why did she get all the special attention?"

Speaking of... I yank off my yellow gold ring and chuck it at him. I do the same with my engagement ring. Now he's even more pissed. Still, as a former wide receiver, you'd think he'd have better hands and try to catch them instead of letting them clatter to the floor. I've learned firsthand—pun intended—that he doesn't.

"Anyway, this whole awesome text stream ends with Eloise FaceTiming my fiancé for what I assume is video sex."

I throw his iPad on the ground, and it makes a delightful crunching sound.

"Even though I'm an avid lover of '90s music, I was never into NSYNC, but you just became one of their titles. 'Bye Bye Bye.' She's all yours now. I wish you both a lifetime of misery and hateful children."

With that, I turn and race out of the church, ignoring the cries from my family and friends and even Brody. I don't turn to see if he's chasing me or if he gets a fist or ten to the face. I'm a bride on the run.

I fly out of the church and slam the doors behind me. Ah, freedom. I suck in a breath of hot summer air and glance around at the world before me, unsure where I should go or how I should get there when someone comes straight into my sightline. I recognize him instantly, and relief swarms me like a pack of honeybees.

Mason Reyes. The hot, cocky, young quarterback for the Boston Rebels. He's Brody's former teammate, but he's been one of my closest friends since I moved back to Boston last year. He's also best friends with some of my cousins and friends. Cousins and friends who are still inside the church, hopefully severing Brody's spleen from his body.

He takes me in from head to toe, and I rip off the veil from the back of my head and toss it along with the comb to the ground. He frowns as it scatters away in the July wind and turns back to me.

"Is it over? Did I miss the ceremony?"

"Oh, it's over all right." The church door shakes as if it's about to open. Hmm. Time to go. "Can you do me a favor?"

He blinks at me, but the flash in his green eyes tells me exactly what his words confirm. "Anything."

"Can you get me out of here?"

A smile breaks free across his lips. "You've got it." He reaches out for my hand, and the moment our palms meet, a fresh shiver of warm tingles skates up my spine. It brings the first smile to my sli I've had all day to my lips and has me holding on tighter.

Without another word, we race down the steps and around a corner. He opens the door to a large SUV and helps me up while making sure my dress and train don't get caught. Then he scoots around to his side and starts the car, turning on the AC, which is nothing short of heavenly on my overheated skin.

"I feel like that scene from *The Graduate*." I look at him. "Where Benjamin comes in and steals Elaine from her wedding. Only this is so much better than that."

"Where can I take you, Mrs. Robinson?"

I snort-laugh at him calling me Mrs. Robinson. "I have no idea. I can't go to my place, and I don't want to go to my parents. I need to get away, you know?" I turn to face him. "Where would you go if you discovered the night before your wedding that your fiancé was cheating on you with your friend, and it seems had been for a while?"

He stares at me as his fists ball up, his jaw locks and twitches, and he shifts away from me, over toward his window, where he curses low and angry under his breath. He moves to get out of the car, and I grab his suit-clad arm to stop him.

"Wait! Where are you going?"

"To kill Brody," he states as if the answer should be obvious.

Just then I spot Brody sporting a red face and a swollen eye, turning the corner and looking for me. Shit! I don't think he's spotted us yet.

"Go!" I plead with urgency. "Please, go. I don't want you to fight him. I just want to get out of here."

Mason grunts, not happy about that at all. Without skipping a beat, he floors it, pulling seamlessly away from the curb and right into moving traffic. Brody completely misses us, which is a huge relief. I feel bad for dragging Mason along, and I'd hate for him to have to deal with Brody after being my getaway car, but there was never a lot of love between them, and neither was shy about letting me know it.

"What happened?" Mason asks softly after we're away from the church and my wedding which never happened. I'm so glad he was late. It was like fate doing me yet another solid.

I didn't know him all that well until I moved back to Boston last year. He was nice, and we hit it off instantly. Plus, his people are my people, which made me trust him when I don't always trust others so easily.

Then again, I trusted Brody and Eloise.

Mason is cute too. I mean, Mason Reyes is fucking gorgeous, young, but fucking gorgeous. But he's so cute when he smiles like this. Almost like he's innocent when you know he secretly plays with the devil. You can't help but be endeared with him.

"I discovered last night that Brody has been screwing my college bestie, Eloise, for a long time. Probably before I started dating him since she introduced me to him. I thought about calling off the wedding this morning, but as the hours passed and the day progressed, I was a bit shell-shocked and knew I wasn't going to have a chance to see him until the ceremony. Serena and Stella suggested that I call him out on what a bastard he is in public. They said it was nothing short of what he and Eloise deserved, so I went with it because I didn't have a better idea."

"Call him out how?"

"I read aloud their sexting from his iPad—which is how I discovered their cheating in the first place—when it was my turn to say my vows."

Mason laughs. Like head thrown back, full-on belly laughs as he drives us around the city.

"That's seriously brilliant and badass. Shit, now I'm pissed I was late and missed it." He shakes his head incredulously. "God, he's the dumbest motherfucker I've ever met." He sobers quickly. "How could anyone ever cheat on you?" He shakes his head again as if such a thing is impossible. "You're a dream girl." He rubs his hand across his jaw but quickly returns it to the wheel, but if I didn't know better, I'd swear he was blushing.

"A dream girl?" Now it's my turn to be incredulous.

He shrugs. "All I'm saying is, he's a fool and doesn't deserve you. I'm sorry if that hurts to hear or isn't what you want me to say. I don't mean to sound trite or throw platitudes at you about what you're going through. But..." He stops. Shifts. Turns back to me as we approach a red light. "He's a fool. You're smart, beautiful, and insanely sexy. Any man would kill for his shot with you."

My brows scrunch. "I'm seven years older than you."

He shrugs. "Doesn't make it less true." He drives us through the light and takes a random right, curling us around Back Bay. "Besides, I was speaking about men in general. Not necessarily me. Where am I taking you?"

"I don't know," I tell him honestly, shifting away from him toward my window. I didn't mean to drag him into this, but here we are. "I'm not sure where to go. I don't want to be anywhere he can find me."

"Do you just want a place to hide out, or do you want to get out of the city for a while?"

Good question. "Out of the city, maybe." I scrunch my nose as I think about it. "We were set to go on our honeymoon tomorrow, which I'm obviously not going on, but the last thing I want to do is sit around and mope or feel sorry for myself, and I don't have to be back to work for more than a week."

"I know a place we could go. It's perfect for this sort of thing."

"We?"

He shoots me an impish grin. "I'm in this now too. Your accomplice. And I have a way out if you want it."

Huh. A way out if I want one. That sounds pretty good.

Possibly even great. I should say no, but find myself asking, "Where?" I'm far too curious about what he has in mind, and so very tempted to say fuck you to Brody and the world for a bit.

His lips twitch as he answers, "Vegas." Almost as if he knows how ridiculous that idea is.

I laugh. "Vegas? I haven't been to Vegas... well... ever."

"It's the perfect place to get over your heartache," he continues. "Fun hotels and casinos, spas, the Strip, great shopping, amazing shows, restaurants, and bars. I'd love to help you get over Brody, and I know a way to keep it quiet if that's what you want. What do you say? As luck would have it, I have a week with not a whole lot planned either."

"You want to come away for a week with me?"

"I never thought you'd ask. Sure, I'd be happy to go away for a week with you."

I roll my eyes with a smile. "I'm serious."

"I am too. If you want to go, I'd love to go with you."

Vegas. I play that over in my head, going through his list item by item, and yeah, it sounds perfect. Like a hell of a lot of carefree, careless fun. With Mason, whom I adore and trust. But still... Vegas. Oh my god, this is crazy. I can't believe I'm entertaining this.

"Vegas," I repeat, this time with a bit more inflection and thought.

I'm jilted. I'm a mess. None of this has even sunk in for me yet. I mean, hell, I'm a runaway bride. This is so not me. None of this is. But maybe getting away for a bit is exactly what I need. A change of scenery. A way to clear my head.

I grin at him, excited. "Screw it. I'm in. Let's do it."

2
MASON

I've been keeping a secret for the last year. I have a serious thing for Sorel Fritz. It's why I was late to the church today, hoping I'd miss the ceremony entirely. The last thing I wanted was to see her marry Brody. I get it. It's all sorts of complicated. She's older than me. Cousins of my best friends. One of my closest friends. And until this moment, engaged to my teammate. Well, former teammate now.

But one by one, those complications are starting to fall away. Except for the friend part and the fact that she just ran out on her wedding. That's a bit of a motherfucker, but not insurmountable. I have no plans to make a move anyway. Not when she just ended things with Brody. It's too soon for that. But I do plan to make her notice me in a different light than she has before.

Little by little, I'll make her as crazy about me as I am about her.

Starting with an impromptu trip to Vegas.

I can't believe she said yes. I thought for sure she'd laugh it off and have me take her to Stella's or her parents' place. Sorel isn't spontaneous.

We race to her apartment, which I know belongs to Brody and not her. He rented the apartment when they moved to Boston a year ago because he didn't want to buy. He's been hoping to secure a broadcasting position with a large network, but so far, that hasn't happened.

Considering he cheated on one of Boston's princesses, a Fritz, he'll have to move out of the city for sure.

Sorel used to complain about the apartment. He picked it out without her there, and like a thoughtless, inconsiderate prick, he signed the paperwork for it before she could see it. She hated how it was close to the stadium and far from her work. How it was old, a three-story walk-up with no AC, and they weren't able to make a lot of the updates she'd want to make. Most of the time, I held my tongue about him. Sometimes I didn't.

My knuckles crack. I wish she had let me get at least one hit on him.

She stares out the windshield as we approach her building. "Oh my god. I'm crazy. I'm totally losing it, right? I'm Green Day's 'Basket Case.'"

That makes me pause for a moment as I try to remember the lyrics. Sorel is huge into alternative '90s music. Like has a massive CD collection and is always throwing out titles or lyrics to songs. For Christmas, I bought her a shirt that said, *The 90s called...they want their music back* with a cassette tape titled *Sorel's Mixed Tape*. She loved it.

"You're not crazy, and you're not a basket case or whatever," I reassure her. "You're... well, I'm blanking on relatable 90s hits, but I'm sure we can think of something better later."

"Because we're on the clock?"

I nod. "We're on the clock."

"Right. Let me move my ass then. At some point, I'm going to have to pack up my stuff and move it out of here," she muses as we pull up along the curb and I park. "But for now, I'll be quick. He could show up here at any minute. I already have a suitcase packed for our honeymoon, so I'll bring that."

"I'll stand guard outside and wait," I offer.

"We're like Bonnie and Clyde. Outlaws. Fugitives on the run."

I smirk, not mentioning how Bonnie and Clyde were also lovers. "Hopefully with a better ending than them."

She smiles, her hazel eyes sparkling at me. "Thank you, Mason. I'm not sure what I would have done if you weren't in the perfect place at the perfect time." She races out of the car and upstairs, and I get out too and start to pace. I'm not sure what I'm doing, but there's no way in hell I'm backing out now. Not unless she does, and then I'll have to find another way.

I pull up my text stream with my best friends, Vander, Stone, and Owen. Owen and Stone are Sorel's cousins, so this should be interesting.

Me: I'm doing something crazy, and I need to tell you about it, so you won't kick my ass later.

Stone: Dude, now is not the time for your shenanigans. Sorel just ran out on her wedding because Brody cheated. Uncle Landon punched him in the face, and then Brody ran out before any of us could get to him. We have no clue where Sorel went, but she's not picking up her phone.

Me: I'm with Sorel. That's the crazy thing I need to tell you.

Owen: What? How are you with Sorel?

Me: I ran into her right outside the church, and gave her a ride. And I'm taking her to Vegas.

I continue to pace, my gaze vacillating between watching the street for Brody and my screen.

My phone rings in my hand. Stone. I slide my finger across the screen and answer, but before I can say anything, Stone yells, "Are you insane?!" into my ear.

"I might be," I admit, only now I'm grinning.

"Asshole, you can't take Sorel to *Vegas*." That's Owen, and I'm guessing they're all together somewhere.

"Yes, you can!" a voice that sounds like my cousin, Katy, yells from the background.

"Don't listen to her," Stone states firmly. "We're all at the reception getting drunk since there is no reception, and no one wanted the food or booze to go to waste. We were hoping Sorel would show up here. Serena texted her to come since Brody and his family wouldn't dare come here. You need to bring Sorel here. She needs her family right now."

"I'm her friend. She needs those too."

"Right. Exactly," Owen agrees. "So act like her friend and bring her here. Where are you anyway?"

"She's in her apartment, changing out of her wedding gown and grabbing her suitcase. I'm thinking we'll charter a jet to stay on the DL."

"How did this happen, Mason, and what the fuck is going on?" Vander questions, though I can hear the amusement in his voice. Vander isn't related to Sorel, so his stake in this is different from Stone and Owen's.

"I didn't drug her or anything. I offered, and she said yes."

"*Sorel did*? Sorel said yes to going to *Las Vegas* with you?" Owen's skeptical. I was too, so I get it.

"Yep." I glance around and rub the back of my head. "She's my instalove," I say in a low tone. "Do you remember I mentioned that when you told me about how fast you fell for Tinsley, Stone? Well, that's Sorel for me," I state not even caring if that makes me sound like a pussy. The second I saw Sorel, my heart went wild in my chest, and my head spun. Then she started talking, and I was done for. Hell, I agreed to be friends with her. Friends! What sane, heterosexual man is friends with a woman they find as attractive as I find Sorel? None. It was that or nothing, and nothing felt like a death sentence. That feeling has only grown over the last year. I tried to get rid of it. I tried to ignore it. I tried not to want her or think about her, but I couldn't help it, and I couldn't stop it.

It's been a hell of a crush or infatuation, or whatever you want to call it, and not in a fun way. Wanting someone I couldn't have has been agony, but now it's exactly as she said: I was in the right place at the right time. I mentioned that I had a thing for a woman to Stone last fall. Since then, he's pressed me a bit, and the other guys know about it too, but I kept my mouth shut on who the woman was for obvious reasons.

"You're fucking kidding me?!" Stone shouts. "Sorel is your instalove? Bro, she's a lot older than you."

"Only seven years. Besides, Owen is a lot older than Estlin, and Bennett is seven years older than Katy. Don't judge that shit. Age is just a number. Are you saying she's too good for me and that I don't deserve my chance with her?"

"No. We'd never say that," Vander asserts. "If she's the one you want, you deserve her, but more than that, she deserves you."

"Thanks, brother. I'm mentally fist-pumping you." I lean my back against the brick façade of the building and shrug out of my suit jacket, then toss it over my forearm. I'm sweating like a politician.

"I don't know about this," Owen states pensively. "This isn't a small thing."

"And I've been nothing but supportive of you assholes when you were screwing around with your best friend's little sister, Owen, and when you were screwing around with your brother's ex, Stone. How about a little reciprocity here? I'm telling you I've had a serious thing for Sorel for a year. Think about it. I haven't touched another woman since I met her."

"Shit," Stone hisses, and I hear murmuring in the background. "Fine. Yes. We support you. But you know, she's our cousin, and if—"

"I'm not even going to dignify that with a response because

you should know me better than that, but it's not like that between us. At least from her end. She just walked out on her wedding, and I'm her friend. I'm simply taking her away to get her mind off everything, and well, if something happens between us in the process, all the better."

I rub at my Cheshire grin. I need to get that wily fucker in check.

"Christ, this is going to be messy," Vander growls in a low voice.

"We're here for you, Mase!" Katy shouts again. "You get her. She needs a guy like you. Someone young and fun who will pull her out of her shell. I'm happy for you."

"Thanks, Katy! Love you, babe." The door to the building opens, and I quickly murmur before Sorel can hear, "I've gotta go. Wish me luck."

I disconnect the call and turn to face her. She's wearing jeans and a white linen top with some kind of girly frills on it. Her blonde hair is down, swinging around the tops of her shoulders, but she still has a full face of bride makeup.

"Hi," I say, unable to help myself as I take her in. Damn, she's pretty.

"Hi. Um, everyone is at the reception venue."

I nod. "Yeah, I just talked to the guys." I rub the back of my head as a weird, awkwardness that wasn't there before looms between us. Fuck. She's having second thoughts. "Do you want me to take you there?"

She peers at me for a very long minute, visibly mulling this over. "It sounds a bit depressing, right? Going to my wedding reception when the wedding didn't happen. Plus, everyone will be all over me, checking on me, talking about it, suggesting where I should go and what I should do next. Don't you think?"

I nod. "Probably."

"Can you think of anything more depressing than sleeping on your older sister's couch or even worse, going back home to your parents' house when you're thirty-five and have been living on your own since you were eighteen?"

"Is that rhetorical?"

She tilts her head, the sun catching her hazel eyes and accentuating the warm brown in them. "Vegas doesn't sound like that."

A smile cracks across my face, and yeah, I do need to work on keeping it in check. "I'll make sure it's not."

She gnaws her lips, but she's smiling against it. I can see it. "Then let's go pack you a bag."

3

MASON

Two hours later, we're sitting on a private plane, sipping champagne and soaring away from Boston and up into the blue, cloudless sky. Sorel has been quiet since we went to my place. She's been there plenty of times before, but instead of coming in and sitting down while I packed, she hovered by the front entryway. I'm not sure she knows what to make of the turn her life has taken.

Her phone rests on her lap as she stares out the small oval window. She's been texting a lot, as you'd expect, but her expression has been stoic, so I don't know what's going on or who she's texting with, and it feels intrusive to ask.

Studying her glass of champagne, she watches the bubbles float to the top. With a tip of her hand, the glass meets her lips, and she swallows the rest. "That's good." She laughs, but there's no humor to it as she sets the empty glass down on the thin table between us and returns her gaze to the window. "I picked out good champagne for the reception too. I love champagne, and I figured when's a more appropriate time to drink the good stuff than at your wedding? Eloise thought it was a great idea, and we spent an afternoon taste-testing champagnes until we found the one we both liked best."

She nibbles on her lip and stops talking for a few moments before she sighs and continues.

"I'm sort of shocked I haven't heard from her yet. I mean, I realize it's only been a couple of hours, if that, but she's not one to let things lie. Serena always called her the yang to my yin. Maybe that's why our friendship was so easy. She and Serena are a lot alike, though Serena would never betray me. This wasn't the first time someone who I thought was my close friend did that. My high school bestie made the mean girls in *Mean Girls* look saintly. You'd think I would have learned my lesson about trusting outside people after that, but three years later, I met Eloise, so there you go."

She pauses. Blows out a breath, but all of her thoughts seem to be pouring out one after the other, and I don't dare move or speak as she does this.

"Is it weird that I'm not sad?" she asks but doesn't turn away from the window. "Serena thinks it's weird. She also thinks it's crazy that I'm on a plane heading to Vegas. My parents do too. My little brothers think it's awesome, but they would. They live in London and bounce around Europe all the time. It probably is crazy. All of it. Calling out Eloise and Brody the way I did and then running off to Vegas."

I set my phone down and look at her since she's sitting opposite me.

"You're likely still in shock. And yes, it probably is a bit crazy, but sometimes the best things in life start as the craziest of ideas."

"Let's hope." She smiles and brings her bare feet onto the seat and her knees up by her chest. "But I'm not sad," she continues. "I'm angry. I feel duped and unbelievably stupid for not realizing it sooner. James, Eloise's fiancé, texted to tell me that he broke up with her. He said she and Brody had been screwing around with each other since before he and I moved to Boston. Brody had a lot of 'business trips'"—she puts air quotes around the words— "back in New York over the last year. He was trying to work out contracts with networks, or so he claimed, and per James, Eloise just so happened to have them at the same time. I can think of at least a dozen in the last year, and before that, when we were living in New York, it was clearly a regular thing between them. They were sneaking around and fucking each other right under our noses." Now she turns to me. "How did I not know? How did I not suspect a thing? He was sleeping with my friend, and I had no clue."

Shit, that's rough. Once again, it makes me wish she had let me out of the car to hit him. I wouldn't have stopped there. Not until he was bleeding and broken and unable to go near her ever again. Landon must feel good that he got a solid punch in on him. I'm insanely jealous.

I run a hand along my clenched jaw, trying to relax it. "Because you loved him." I pause here, trying to gauge her reaction to that. "You trusted him. And her. Those are two very powerful weapons they used against you."

"Tell me about it. It's how I had videos and recorded conversations of me posted all over school and social media. Trust is dumb."

I'm assuming that's the high school friend who betrayed her. I stand and retrieve the bottle of champagne, top off her glass and set the bottle on the table beside it. I think she could use it.

"Thank you." She lifts her glass and gulps half of it down. "What pisses me off the most is that in the texts between the two of them, she talked about how he always makes her come. Or maybe he said it. Whatever." She waves that away. "He never made me come. Hardly ever. And if I said anything about it, he'd get all huffy and defensive and make it seem like I was the problem and not him." She laughs mirthlessly and swallows down the rest of her champagne before she refills the glass again. "I don't know why I'm telling you that. I'm just bitter, and it feels good to vent."

I kick up my ankle to my opposite knee and lean back in my seat, throwing my hands behind my head. I wish I were wearing my hearing aids because the white noise of the plane and her soft-spoken words are making it tougher to hear her than it otherwise would be. Thankfully, her lips are pretty easy to read.

"You have every right to be bitter, and don't feel weird or self-conscious about telling me whatever you need to get off your chest. For the record though, as far as I'm concerned, men only have one responsibility in bed, and that's to make sure our partner gets off. There is nothing better or more of a turn-on than that. The ones who don't get that are selfish and lazy."

"He was both of those things. And inconsiderate. Everything was about him and not me. Everything from where we lived to his career being more important than mine to little things like where we'd go for dinner or what music we'd listen to or what we'd watch on TV. Even my fucking wedding band was wrong because he didn't think for more than two seconds about it when he bought it."

"He was like that as a player too," I tell her. "He hated it when I'd throw to someone else or didn't throw to him what he felt like was enough. He wanted his airtime and to always be the superstar, even if it didn't benefit the team. He even used to mock my hearing deficit and how my dad and I would sign with each other sometimes."

Horror floods her face and stains her cheeks red. "I didn't know that."

I grin. "Because I never told you."

"I wish you had. That's disgusting, and I likely would have left him then and there." She shakes her head indignantly. "He used to complain about you, though he never mentioned your hearing deficit to me. He said you can't be a superstar if you put the team above yourself. He also said you only got that position because of your dad."

I shrug. "You know I never liked him much, so I don't care. My dad did draft me, so he's not the first to say that, and again, I don't care because having my dad as my coach has been everything. No one believes in me the way he does."

Truthfully, I always thought Brody was a dick, but I hated him because he had her, and now I hate him even more for having her and taking her for granted all that time.

"I don't want them to break me, but at the same time, I'm not sure how I'll trust beyond my family again."

"What about friends of your family? You can trust them."

"I do trust you, Mason. I wouldn't be here with you if I didn't."

She drops her gaze, and it pulls at my heart, my chest inflating like a hot air balloon.

"I can't believe I'm doing this." She laughs incredulously, brushing her bangs back from her forehead. "What the hell are you doing here with me, Mason? We're on a private plane going to Las Vegas."

"Like I said, I didn't have much going on this week."

Her eyes narrow. "Don't you have training camp?"

"Next week. Rookies start this week."

She points a finger in my direction. "You're stuck with me and my crazy now. You know that, right?"

"Back at you." I give her a long once-over, unable to help myself. "Though from where I'm sitting, that doesn't seem so bad."

Her eyebrows pop up and her lips part in shock. "Are you flirting with me?"

I wipe my thumb along my bottom lip. "Maybe."

Her jaw unhinges further. "Are you going to flirt with me all week?"

"Would you like me to?"

She bites into her lip to hide her smile and turns back to the window. "Maybe."

"WELCOME TO LAS VEGAS, MR. LICKE," the concierge greets us, not even skipping a beat when he says my fake name as he shakes our hands the moment we step out of the car. "It is a pleasure to have you with us. We have secured the villa you requested for both you and Dr. Herass."

Sorel snorts under her breath, but quickly masks it as she clears her throat.

"If you'll come with me, it would be my pleasure to take you directly there and show you around."

"Mr. Licke can make Dr. Herass come with pleasure too," I murmur in Sorel's ear, and she nudges me with her elbow and rolls her eyes. She hinted I could flirt, whether she meant it or not, so why not test the waters I've never tested with her before?

"Behave, Mr. Licke."

"I'll try, Dr. Herass."

With that, we're led onto an elevator off the private entrance we were brought through and whisked up forty-four floors. I haven't touched Sorel since she ran out of the church, and I'm tempted to take her hand but refrain. She was quiet for the rest of the flight. I have to imagine she was questioning and rethinking everything, including this, and I don't want to push her.

Our bags were already taken by the valet, and they'll likely bring them through another elevator. Some might say this is a bit too excessive, but I don't care. I've always wanted to stay in this villa, and now I have the perfect excuse. I want to wow

Sorel. The girl of my dreams doesn't know she's the girl of my dreams. That means I have to pull out all the stops even if she is a Fritz and, with that, a billionaire heiress.

She doesn't live like that, though, and if you didn't know about her family, you'd never guess the kind of money she has other than from her bags. The girl likes her handbags.

The elevator opens, and we step out, guided by our concierge. "This is a three thousand square foot villa that features a living room with a full bar, a library, and a billiard room, as well as two king-sized bedrooms and two and a half bathrooms. But the real showstopper is this..." He trails off as he walks directly across the main living room to the balcony doors. He opens them with gusto, and both Sorel and I step onto the large terrace complete with a gas firepit, a plunge pool, and a hot tub, all overlooking the Strip from high above.

Sorel gasps and clutches my hand. "What in the hell are you doing?"

"Making sure Dr. Herass does Vegas the right way and has the time of her life."

She turns to me, her hazel eyes challenging, and something warm courses under my skin. "And you, Mr. Licke? What's in this for you?"

You. You're the only thing I'm here for.

I shrug, trying for nonchalance. "Mr. Licke is all about Dr. Herass. And I think it's pretty obvious what's in it for me." I pan my hand around the patio and then back toward the villa. "This is Vegas, baby. I love it here. I haven't had a vacation in a long time either, so it's a break for me too."

She seems satisfied with that answer and doesn't press me further.

I get it. It doesn't make sense that I'd drop my life on a whim, take her away for a week to Las Vegas, and put up the cash for a private plane and a dope-ass villa. On the plane, she offered to split everything with me, and I refused. Not happening. But I think that confused her more. I saw her relief when the concierge mentioned two bedrooms, so I know she wants to keep this arrangement purely platonic as we've always been.

I'm playing the long game here, but so far, she's still with me, and now she's holding my hand.

The concierge finishes showing us around, informing us that our butler will take care of unpacking our luggage for us. Once he's gone, I lead Sorel over to the bar. She drops her elbows on the wood top and stares expectantly at me.

"Would you like a drink, Dr. Herass?"

Sorel cracks up and then emits a little screech. "Oh, my hell, this is like Cocteau Twins' 'Heaven Or Las Vegas,' and so not me. Sure. Why not? When life hands you lemons, make lemon drop martinis."

"Coming up." I go about fixing both of us a lemon drop and slide hers over to her. "I haven't heard that song before."

"You're missing out. I'll have to play it for you tonight." She takes a slip and licks her lips. "Mmm. That's good. Okay. What do we do first? Remember, I'm a Vegas virgin and I want the full experience."

"A virgin, huh?"

She blushes ever so slightly.

"Don't worry. I'll give you the full experience. Let's shower and get changed. Then we'll go get some dinner and have a lot of drinks and fun. After that, we'll see where the night takes us."

"Hmm." She takes another sip of her drink, and I have to imagine she's still half-drunk from all the champagne on the plane and the wild day she's had. "That sounds fun, but I don't know what to wear." She covers her face with her hands. "Christ, I don't even know how to feel. This is so surreal."

"Feel free because you are. Wear whatever you feel beautiful and sexy in because you are both of those things. And get used to being on my arm tonight because unless you tell me no, there is no way I won't want you there."

The reason I picked this villa, other than its exclusivity, is the pool. I want to get Sorel in her bikini or less in that pool before this trip is over. I want to imprint myself inside of her so all she feels and knows is me. I want to make her come and come and fucking come until she's so blind with pleasure that she has no clue that any other man existed before me. I want to make her smile and happy and show her that not all men— including football players—are assholes who cheat.

Even if I don't get the sex, I still want her to feel like that. How her ex not only cheated on her but never made her come is mind-boggling. I want all of those things with her, but I know I can't have them yet. Still, it doesn't stop the desire.

The corner of her mouth tilts up, and her eyes gleam. "Let's do it then."

We each retreat to our rooms with our drinks to freshen up. I never drink like this. During football season, I don't drink at all, and once March hits, I'm in training, so I don't drink much after that. Training camp starts next week, and while I want Sorel to relax and have fun, there is only so much fun I can have too.

Plus, one of us has to keep our wits about us.

I dump the rest of my drink down the bathroom sink and hit the shower. By the time I'm ready, Sorel is waiting for me on the patio in a short, white dress that is all tits and back and thighs.

Jesus, hell. I run a hand over my face and through the back of my hair. I can't help but wonder what her skin smells like with my nose buried against her neck and what her mouth tastes like with my lips pressed to hers. Will she be as warm as she's making me?

"Wow," I tell her, not even pretending to hide the wonder in my voice or expression. "You look incredible."

She turns and smiles at me, giving me a once-over. "You look pretty good yourself, Mr. Licke."

"Are you ready?"

"For what?" she asks softly as she holds onto the railing behind her.

I reach out my hand for her. "For all this night has in store for us."

4

"Hmm. Should I stay or should I hit now?" I sing a parody of the Clash's "Should I Stay or Should I Go." Not a 90s song, but still some of the best punk out there. I'm staring at the five of diamonds that's face up and I take a sip of my martini as I debate. I went from the lemon drop that Mason made me to wine at dinner, which felt boring, to a Cosmo back to a lemon drop, and I think this one was the right call. It's delicious, and there's a saying, right? Something about sticking with the same drink and not mixing alcohols or something? I don't know. I can't remember it now, but lemon drops are yum.

"You should hit, honey," the cowboy next to me drawls with a heavy twang. "You always wanna hit that."

I snort. "That's what he said."

The guy throws me a funny look, but Mason is smirking at me. "You do you," he tells me. "Hit or stay. Your call."

"Except it fucks up the deck for us," the serious guy on the end with the neck and hand tattoos sneers, wearing sunglasses and all black like he's a mob boss. Oh, maybe he is! This high-roller table is a bit intimidating. And fun. I like gambling. I've never done it before, but it's great.

And we passed by some fabulous shops I want to go into later or tomorrow. I like Vegas. Vegas is fun.

Mason simply shrugs like he doesn't care, but he stares the guy down, letting him know he's not intimidated. "She can play however she wants to."

"She wants to hit it before she quits it." I snort-laugh, but for real, that dude is a bit scary, and while I love protective Mason, I don't want him to end up in a body bag at the hands of Don Tattoos. Plus, I'm going to go with the fact that these guys know how to play blackjack more than I do since this is my first time.

Yet another thing I'm a virgin with.

The dealer slaps a six in front of me, and I cheer, my hands shooting up in the air like I just don't care. "Woohoo!"

"Nice move, Dr. Herass!" Mason gives me a high-five.

"Thank you, Mr. Licker."

"It's Licke," he teases with a wink. "Though I have no problems being a licker."

I crack up. "Is that so?"

"Absolutely, Dr. Herass. I can assure you that I am a professional Herass Licker, but I'm also happy to Licke Herass."

I laugh harder, falling into him a bit. "That I believe. Your reputation precedes you."

He leans into me and brings his mouth by my ear, his hot breath making me shudder and my nipples harden. That's unexpected. This is why I don't drink a lot that often. My body has strange reactions to things it shouldn't.

"As I told you this afternoon, it would be my pleasure to combine Mr. Licke and Dr. Herass and get you to come with me whenever you want."

Oh boy. Now it's not just my nipples getting in on the action.

My empty core is about to pull a muscle, it's clenching so hard. I'm going to blame the alcohol for my reaction to him. And my shaky emotional state. And the fact that he's Mason Reyes, and that's like female Kryptonite or catnip or whatever the voodoo is that makes women go after and spread their legs for hot professional athletes.

Even when they belong to someone else. I frown. I hate Eloise.

I shove him away—so I don't do anything stupid like kiss him to make myself feel better—and nearly fall off my chair in the process. "You're a flirty flirt. Friends don't flirt with friends. Who have been drinking." I tilt my head and scrunch my face up as I think that through. "Wait. That's not how that goes."

He gives me a crooked grin and a wink. "But it could be. No harm in flirting, princess, unless I decide to act on it."

Whoa is he cute when he does that. He has this chin dimple that I sort of want to lick or at least play with. It's always been a tempting asset of his.

"Princess?"

"Works for you."

"It kind of does," I concede. I'm a Fritz, and we're known as Boston's royalty since our grandmother is essentially the queen of the town. Wait. I had a point.

"What was I saying?"

"Flirting."

"Right!" I smack the table and nearly tip over my drink. That would have been tragic. "Um, I think I was going to tell you not to act or to flirt or something, but the moment is over. I'm having so much fun. Vegas was totally the right call. It's so fun!"

Mason is amused by me, I can tell. Brody used to hate it when I'd get drunk because he thought I was annoying. Mason doesn't think I'm annoying. He's the best like that. He took me out to this incredible French restaurant that had a view of the fountains and the Strip because he knows I love French food.

Then we walked around for a bit and found ourselves here. This casino is pretty. It's a little girly with a lot of pink lighting. I love it.

I'm also up five hundred dollars, so that's fun too.

Plus, Mason is fun. Am I saying fun too much? I don't know. Probably. But that's totally what I'm having and totally what he is. He's also so hot. Like seriously hot. And has muscles. Big muscles that I enjoy touching when I can since I've been holding onto his arm a lot whenever we walk. I never thought of him that way, but it's impossible not to notice now. There is nothing about Mason that isn't irresistibly risky, but I'm here for it all the same.

I'm so glad I did this. It's so much better than being back home and moping or, even worse, sleeping with a cheating husband who I didn't know was cheating.

I feel like I escaped prison or cheated death.

It's a freaking rush.

Somehow another hand went around, but the dealer had a blackjack, so we all lost. This round, I have a two, which is useless. I hit and hit and then bust. Boo. Mason busts too, and the dealer moves on to the woman on his left. Mason has been trying to keep a low profile. He's recognizable, or at the very least, head turnable. Is that a word? Whatever. He's tall and broad and simply has the build and look of a professional athlete. Even coming from a family of famous billionaires, I'm far from recognizable outside of Boston. No one knows me here, but Mason has definitely been getting looks.

I scrunch my brow at him. "Is princess my new first name now?"

"More of a pet name than a first name."

"Should we come up with first names, then?"

"Nah. Who needs them?"

True. He has a point. Our fake last names are far too awesome to mess with.

His hand meets the back of my chair, and his thumb grazes ever so subtly against the top of my back. For a moment, I freeze. Was that intentional? I don't know. I can't tell. If it was, I'm sure he's simply being comforting. Despite his joking, I can't picture Mason actually making a move.

It's never been like that between us.

He flirts, but that's just who Mason is. A flirt. He's incredible, really. Sweet, funny, charming, and quick-witted. So much smarter than people give him credit for. They look at him and see a dumb jock, but he's not that at all.

If I were a single girl—which I know I technically am, but you get the point—and a little younger, I'd be all over that. Who wouldn't be? His attention is intoxicating. His flirting makes me giddy and a little high and definitely a lot turned on because he's not shy with his innuendos. I'd be lying if I said I wasn't thinking about what he said to me on the plane about being a generous lover.

Because hell, could I use a screaming orgasm or two and a good hard fuck to go with them right about now. But I won't risk our friendship. I won't go near that, not when I'm too emotionally fragile, frazzled, and unstable. My friendship with him is stable, solid, and makes me feel grounded, which is exactly what I need. It's why I'm here with him.

The hand ends and another is dealt when suddenly Mason freezes, and his gaze locks on something. When I follow it, I notice it's the TV above the center of the pit.

"What in the hell?" I shoot to my feet, the room dipping and swaying, and I nearly topple again as my ankle rolls in my heel. Mason is on his feet too, his hands on my hips to steady me. "Can you turn that up?" I ask the dealer, pointing to the screen.

"We can't. I'm sorry. But I can turn on the subtitles."

I nod, and she clicks a button on a remote beneath the television.

Brody is doing an interview with a major sports network.

It's hard to read the screen, especially after all these drinks, but I manage. "It was a simple misunderstanding that will be easily cleared up," it reads.

"He's out of his tux. And... is he wearing makeup?" I ask.

Mason simply shakes his head, continuing to stare at the screen.

"What about the accounts stating that you cheated on your fiancée with her friend and that's why she called off the wedding?" the reporter asks, not beating around the bush for a second.

Brody gives a sad sort of smile, blinking his puppy dog eyes at the camera like he's heartbroken, even as he keeps his left eye slightly averted from the camera to hide his bruise. "As I said, it was a misunderstanding that will be cleared up soon. All the fans need to know is that I love Sorel Fritz with all my heart and would never do anything to hurt her. My phone was hacked, and someone played a vicious trick that hurt her terribly. Once we get this figured out, we'll set a new wedding date. I know the Boston fans are especially anxious for that."

"Oh, my freaking bastard." I peer back at the dealer. "Thanks. You can turn that off now. I'm all good." Or not. Not even close. A hacker?! What in the land of bullshit is he playing at?

I should have gone all Carrie Underwood on his ass. I didn't even mess up the apartment, though it's all his furniture and not mine, because when I moved in with him a year and a half ago, I sold all of my stuff. I should have flushed his keys down the toilet, ripped up his beloved couch, and put a chair through his massive television. Oh, and shredded his old jerseys and pawned his Super Bowl ring.

Why didn't I do any of that?

How am I supposed to find peace or solace when he goes and runs his mouth like that? He's making himself look like the scorned, sad, *wronged* man, and me like the unstable, wild one.

I grab all my chips and slide them into my purse. The thing is bulging, but it'll survive. It's what we women always do. We survive. I pick up my martini, drink the rest down, and storm off. I don't know where I'm going, but I'm too furious to sit still. I've had my phone on Do Not Disturb since we landed because it was blowing up like the climax of an action film. Climax. Ha!

Not funny, Sorel.

Still, I was tired of everyone telling me what I should and should not do. I'm thirty-five. I can make my own choices, and I don't have to listen to anyone else. I blocked Brody and Eloise then too because I didn't want either to call or text me. I didn't want them to try to explain away what they did.

But now I'm tempted to call my prick of an ex and ask what he's up to.

"Hey." Mason catches up with me. "You okay?"

I shake my head and plop myself down at a bar. I pull out my phone and search through my Instagram.

"Holy shit! It's all over his social media talking about how he's devastated that our wedding was canceled, but that it's just a minor misunderstanding over a hacked phone, and we'll be back together soon. *A minor misunderstanding? A hacked phone?*"

"*Intertainment* is reporting that sources close to you say he was cheating and admitted to it," Mason declares. "His bullshit story won't go far."

My hand waves frantically in the air to flag down the bartender. Mason comes up beside me, standing close by, his back to the casino around us and the ballcap he's been wearing low on his brow.

"What can I get you?" the bartender asks.

"Four shots of tequila, please."

Mason chokes.

"Two are for you," I explain. "I'm not trying to die tonight. I just want to erase my morning and my ex."

"Are you sure you want to drink that much?"

I glance up into his greeny-green eyes. "Absolutely." I start humming "Bitter Sweet Symphony" by the Verve.

Mason smirks, recognizing the song. "Okay, okay." He nods toward the bartender while keeping his head down. "Four shots of Patrón, please. And two glasses of water."

Water. That's a good call.

The shots are poured, and we're left with limes and salt, but I don't want any of that fluff. I want to get drunk. Drunker. I want to forget all about the way my life took a sharp derail this morning and now feels almost unrecognizable. Or maybe I'm the unrecognizable one.

"He put on makeup, but it was still daylight, and it looked like the front of the church," I muse as I twirl the small shot glass around with my fingers. "Brody wanted press at our wedding, but I refused. I wonder if he had set up interviews anyway without telling me. I wouldn't be shocked. He's been desperate for a booth gig, and marrying a Fritz made him look good. I bet Eloise did the makeup for him. She's a bitch like that."

"Having your fiancée run out on your wedding after calling you a cheater in front of all his family and friends won't get him that."

"No. It won't." I pick up the first shot and gulp it down, quickly followed by the second. I barely taste them, which seems odd because anytime I ever drink tequila, I always need a lot of chasers because it's strong and it hits me hard. That's why I chose it. Tequila will see me through. Serena would be proud. I get feisty with tequila. Maybe I'll do my own interview. Ha. Never.

Mason drinks his first shot, but slides his second away. I go to reach for it when he picks it up and drinks it so I can't. Boo. Though it's cute he's so protective of me. He's been such a good friend to me. He hasn't left my side all night. Why aren't there more Masons and fewer Brodys in this world?

"That's why he said all that bullshit, you know," I lament, plopping my arms on the bar and dropping my forehead onto them. "He doesn't care about me. He never loved me. How could he when he didn't just cheat, he screwed *my friend* for what is likely our entire relationship with no plans to stop? He only cares about how he looks to the public and what's best for him. Fucking bastard."

"He'll look stupid when you don't reconcile and marry him."

"He'll come after me and do what he can to win me back. He as much as said so because now he's trying to save face." The thought makes the alcohol in my stomach revolt against me. "I don't want to see him again. I don't want to deal with him, but I don't know how to stop that if he's this determined," I murmur. The room starts to spin a little, and I close my eyes to slow it down. "I wish I could do something to hurt and humiliate him the way he hurt and humiliated me. A little revenge would be nice, and I don't even care if that makes me sound petty. He deserves it. But more than that, I'd like his lies to go away along with him, and I don't know how to make that happen when he's telling the press nonsense."

"You left. You walked out. You did it all publicly, which was badass, and a pretty sweet revenge. The press will realize his story is garbage and move on, and for now, you're in the party capital of the world having a great time."

I snort. "I thought it was the wedding capital of the world." The words hit like lightning, and I sit up straight to meet Mason's eyes. "I'm having the best dumbest idea ever."

5

MASON

"Mason, let's get married."

I almost laugh at that. Almost. Except her expression tells me she's dead-ass serious.

"No," I state flatly. "And you're officially cut off."

Her hands meet the bar top, and she leans into me like she's about to negotiate this. "One, why not? Two, you can't cut me off, you're not the bartender, and three, I'm older than you."

"What does your being older than me have to do with me cutting you off or anything else?"

"I don't know," she rants. "It just sounded good in my head. But you didn't answer number one. I'm serious. I want us to get married. It'll be fun."

I drop my elbow on the bar in front of her and lean in. I get close. Real close. So close our noses practically touch, and I can see every swirl and fleck of green and brown in her drunk eyes. My hand goes to the back of her chair, and I keep her good and locked in place.

"I know why you're asking. I get it. You want to make him look ridiculous to the press for saying it was a simple misunderstanding, and if you're married to me, he can't try to win you back. I get it, Sorel. I kind of like it even."

"Yes! Exactly. It's perfect, right? Only I don't want the press or anyone else to know. Just him. It'll be a zing he can't rub off or lie away."

"But being married means we're *married*. As in legally bound to each other."

She rolls her eyes. "I'm not looking to saddle you with a long-term commitment here. There will be no white picket fence or two-point-five kids for us, though maybe I'll get a dog. I've always wanted one." She shakes her head. "I digress. We'll get it annulled after a couple of weeks once Brody stops trying to fight city hall in the media. I promise it won't disrupt your life or your bachelorhood."

My bachelorhood has become a joke thanks to her, but that's hardly the point. She's only partially making sense, which is yet another reason why I say, "No."

"Oh, come on." She pouts, slouching dramatically. "I thought you were the fun and adventurous guy."

I grin. "That doesn't make me stupid, princess. I'd get my ass kicked by your family if I married you."

"Is the big, tough football player afraid of my cousins, father, and uncles?" she mocks.

I nod. "Yes. Absolutely. Because I'd kick my own ass for this."

"I just said I don't want anyone to know. That means they won't know. Genius, right?"

"Except I don't keep things from my guys. That's not how we roll. Plus, it's *marriage*, Sorel. As in, you'd be my wife and I'd be your husband. It's the same thing you almost did this morning with love on the brain. Annulling it or not, it's still a real thing, and I'm not sure annulments are as simple as you're making them out to be."

"They can't be that difficult. Celebrities have them done

with the same frequency as plastic surgery and rehab. Besides, that's what makes it so perfect. You're my friend. Friends get married all the time, and having love on my brain didn't exactly help me this morning. If anything, it hurt, and how much could I have been in love with him anyway if I haven't even shed a tear over him? Let's do it, Mason." She tugs on my shirt. "Let's get married. I want to. I want to erase everything that happened this morning, and this is the perfect way. We're here in Vegas." She pans her hands around us. "I want to be this Sorel. The one who runs out on her wedding and the asshole she was about to marry and hops on a plane to Vegas on a whim. I don't want to be smart, sensible Sorel. That's all I ever am. I'm thirty-five, and I've never lived. It's been college, med school, residency, attending physician, and Brody. Blah." She throws her hands up, and I have to save her from falling off the chair. "Ah! Oh, shit. Thanks for the save there, QB. Anyway, my life has been boring, and what do I have to show for it? I've been safe. I've been so safe, and I still got screwed over. I want to carpe diem. I want to take risks and do stupid things. I want to look back on my life when I'm a hundred and fifty and say *look at that. Look at the wild thing I did once.*"

I'm running out of arguments. Maybe it's the tequila and the drinks before that talking, or maybe it's that she trusts me and wants to marry me that's softening me, but I'm pretty much putty in her hands and have been for a year. I haven't been able to look at another woman since she walked into my life. I want to make her happy. Isn't that what I said about this from the start? That I was going to take her out of her shell. Or maybe Katy said that, but she was right. Plus, I kind of like the idea of marrying her even if it's just a revenge wedding and a temporary gig. It binds her to me in a way. It puts me in her life as more than simply her friend.

I squint. "On a scale of one to ten, how drunk are you?"

She tilts her head and pinches her eyes shut. Her body

sways as if the room tilted the wrong way when she did that, and once again I put my hands on her shoulders to steady her.

"I might be like a six or a seven. Definitely not a ten."

"Ten, and you're in the hospital with alcohol poisoning."

She snorts and holds her hands out wide before she alternates touching the tip of her nose with each pointer finger. She misses twice and pokes herself in the eye. "Ouch. That hurt. Yeah, I'm probably a seven. But I still really, really want to get married. Please, Mason. Help me walk on the wild side and stick it to my ex at the same time. I know you want to." Her eyebrows bounce suggestively, and I can't help my chuckle.

"You're serious?"

She sits up a little straighter because she can tell I'm melting like an ice cream in the Vegas sun. "Like a preacher on Sunday."

I squint at her. "No."

"What?" she squawks, her hands flailing about as she searches around the bar as if to find someone to commiserate with, like, *can you believe this guy?* "I so thought I had you there. What can I do to get you to say yes? Unless." She fake sniffles, giving me the saddest of sad eyes. "You don't want to marry me."

I fold my arms and lean back against the bar. "Nice try, princess. That's not it."

Her eyebrows shoot up. "See! You do want to do this. There's nothing holding us back."

"You can't marry someone you've never kissed before. That's against the law here in Nevada. So, you see, we can't get married."

"Argh." She grabs me by the back of the head and slams my face to hers. Our lips mash together, and our teeth smack painfully, but that only lasts a half-second until my brain catches up to the fact that Sorel is kissing me. I don't even care about the reason for it. I didn't think she'd do it. I thought that would be the thing that had her retreating.

But since this might be my only shot, my hands capture her face, and I tilt her jaw so I can deepen the kiss. Her lips are soft and warm and sweet, but as I begin to part her lips, she pushes me back.

"There. We kissed." Only her eyes are dark, and she's staring at my lips as if she wants another taste. A deeper taste. It's what I want too, and like a magnet, I lean back in, but she holds me at bay. "Save it for the wedding, baller. I'm a lady on the streets and a hopeful freak in the sheets." Her eyes widen, and she sits up straighter. "Oh, that can be a fun part of this. Sexy lessons. Searching for my unrealized kink. I must have one. Everyone does, right? Serena used to tease me that I'm a secret dirty slut, but thus far I haven't been, and it's yet another disappointment in my life."

Jesus, this girl. "We'll table that discussion until you're sober, even if there is nothing I want more than to help you explore your every fantasy and kink and turn you into the dirty slut you've always wanted to be."

"You do?"

How can she be dumbfounded by that? I drag my thumb along her cheek and stare straight into her eyes. I'm desperate to kiss her again, especially with all this talk of sexy lessons and kink and wanting to be a dirty slut, but I hold back. For now. Because she'll only ever be a dirty slut for me. That I can fucking guarantee.

"You really want to do this? You want to get married to me? As in legally binding married."

She beams a smile that is the equivalent of the first light of dawn after a sunless winter. "Yes."

I shouldn't. I shouldn't. I fucking shouldn't!

"Okay. Let's do it. But when you're sober tomorrow and regret having my ring on your hand and my last name as yours, please remember I said no at least twice and tried to talk you out of it."

"Fritz-Reyes has a nice ring to it. Speaking of, let's go shopping! And not yellow gold. Ugh! I can't believe that asshat did that."

She jumps out of her chair and stumbles on her feet, and I think she was right about this being the best dumbest idea ever. There is no way getting married in Vegas to my friend, my best friends' cousin, and my former teammate's ex-fiancée won't come back to bite me in the ass. She's lucky I love her.

I pause. Freeze. Even as my heart starts to go haywire. I gaze at my princess before me. Love? Do I actually love her? Not just a crush. Not simply an infatuation.

Can you truly be in love with someone when they don't love you back? I think about this last year. About the fact that I haven't wanted to be with anyone else. How I kept telling myself that once she got married and I no longer had any shot with her, I'd get back on the horse. How I'd call her to hear her voice when ninety-nine percent of the world texts. I'd find ways to hang out with her just so I could see her and talk to her and be near her. I wake up every morning with her on my mind and fall asleep after jerking off only to thoughts of her.

Yeah, I think I do love her.

Shit. Now I'm really screwed.

I drop some cash on the bar for our drinks and lead the way because if we're doing this, we're fucking doing it, and I know exactly what I'm getting her for a ring. It'll be worth the ass-beating from Owen and Stone. Vander won't jump in because that's not his style, but Sorel's other cousins, her brothers, and likely her dad and uncles will want in on it. They'll want my blood for sure.

Fuck it. Nothing ventured, nothing gained, I remind myself. It's been the motto of my life, but never has it been more relevant than now.

I check the time. "It's going to be tight."

She winks at me. "That's what she said."

My lips bounce with amusement. "Secret dirty slut indeed."

With her hand in mine, I lead her out of the casino we're in and head back toward our hotel. It's hot as hell out here, even at night, and a sheen of sweat covers me as we walk briskly up the Strip.

"Where are we going?" Sorel asks, struggling in her heels to keep up with my pace.

"Back to our place. I need to change because I'm not getting married in this, but we need rings and to get to the clerk's office for a license."

She throws me a side-eye, her smile unstoppable. "You've got this all figured out, don't you?"

"We'll see." I call our butler, who picks up immediately. I tell him everything that we need, and he informs me he'll have it taken care of. The moment we reach our elevator, I spin her around and press her into the wall, crowding her and leaning some of my weight against her. My hands run across her face and play with the strands of her soft, flaxen hair. "You hated the ring Brody got you?"

"I didn't hate it. I was disappointed. I know that makes me sound snobbish, but he bought me a yellow gold band when my engagement ring was platinum. It clashed. It was thoughtless. That's what bothered me. It was simply the icing on the wedding cake I never got to eat."

I shake my head. "Every bride should have the ring they want from their groom. What did you want?"

She nibbles on her lip and shakes her head. "I wanted him to pick out the ring he thought was perfect for me. The one he saw and thought, *that's the one.* The band he'd want me to get married to him in and would wear for the rest of our lives. I didn't care if it had diamonds or was a plain band. Hell, I didn't care if it was real or fake, but I wanted some-

thing that at the very least matched the engagement ring he
got me."

"We don't have an engagement ring."

"Mason, I don't care about the ring. This marriage isn't like
that. You can pull something out of a vending machine off the
lobby and I'll be fine with it."

My heart thunders because this marriage might not be that
to her, but it also might be my only chance to put a ring on her
and call her mine. "What's your ring size?"

"Mason—"

"Tell me, Sorel."

She stares up at me with wide, pretty eyes. "Five."

The elevator doors part and our butler is there to greet us.
Sorel runs off to get ready, but I tell her to keep on the dress
she's already wearing. Our butler hands her another glass of
champagne. Great. More alcohol in her system. I tell him the
rings I need him to get for me—because, like she said, I know
the ring I want her to have—and that we want to get married
on our patio.

I ask him to make it as romantic as possible. This is Vegas. If
ever there's a town I can make ridiculous after-hours requests,
this is it. The ceremony needs to be private. I'm not doing this
in a chapel downstairs, and I tell him phones and cameras are
not allowed anywhere near the ceremony or us. He's already
signed an NDA as part of our stay, and this is what he does, so I
know he'll manage it however we need him to.

Then I go and change into black slacks and a white button-
down. Simple and classic.

By the time I'm done, Sorel is by the elevator wearing the
white dress that I'm mildly obsessed with as it shows off a hell
of a lot of smooth, creamy skin. She's changed her hair and
makeup, fastening shoulder-length hair on top of her head in a
simple bun with her heavy bangs still across her forehead and a
few whisps framing her face. Her makeup is sweet and shim-

mery, with pink lips that are so gorgeous I'm counting the seconds until I can kiss them again.

For a moment, I can't do anything other than take in every perfect inch of her. Nerves tickle me. I'm going to get my heart broken before this is all done.

I swallow thickly and utter, "You're a goddess."

"You look great too." She takes my hand. "Let's go get married."

A car is waiting for us out front, and we're sped down to the county clerk's office. That doesn't take long. No more than an hour, and shockingly enough, we're the only ones here. Sorel thinks this entire thing is hysterical, though she tries to act as sober as she can while they ask us questions. No one seems to be a football fan, or at least they don't recognize me or my name when we fill out the license form.

I'm jumpy during the short car ride back. My knee bounces and my stomach plays with all the alcohol I shouldn't have had. I'm not trashed, but I'm not sober either, and I wish I were. Still, I already know I won't forget a thing about tonight. Especially as we walk into the villa and Sorel gasps.

"Mason," she utters in a low, shaky breath. "Did you do this?"

Red rose petals are scattered in a concentrated trail guiding us out toward the balcony. Flameless candles line the path. Their glow is the only light in the villa. Two glasses of champagne along with a bottle in a bucket of ice are on the table that leads out to the terrace, and I snatch one for each of us because, at this point, it doesn't make a difference.

I take a sip and then a big gulp, more of those nerves hitting me. I'm about to marry Sorel Fritz. And though she can talk annulments and revenge, to me, it means more. To me it means everything because even though I told myself all this time it was just a big crush, I think I've been in love with her for a while now and never let myself admit it. I called her my instalove, which was more of a joke with my guys, but looking at her now, the joke's on me.

I empty my glass and set it down on the table. She does the same with hers, her eyes heavy-lidded and glassy. I shouldn't be doing this. She's insanely drunk, and I know it.

I debate this. "You can still change your mind. You don't have to do this."

"Oh, come on. Don't be a downer. It's been so fun. I want to do this."

She's a liar. She just doesn't know it yet.

I take her hand. "Are you ready to get married?"

From outside, "Crash Into Me" by Dave Matthews Band starts to play, and she gasps again, her eyes glassing over. She thinks I'm playing 90s music for her, and I am, but the lyrics are for her too. She doesn't know it.

"It's funny," she muses as we kick off our shoes and walk barefoot along the velvety petals. "I made this whole thing about not seeing Brody before the wedding because it's considered bad luck. It was because of that I discovered his infidelity. But this, so far, I think seeing you before the wedding is the best luck. And this wedding is already more the wedding of my dreams than the one this morning ever was."

My chest clenches painfully. "Really?"

"It's so romantic." She looks up at me with a drunk, shy smile. "I get it. It's not real or forever between us. But right now, this is magic, and I'm excited we're doing it."

I ignore the part about this not being real or forever between us and walk us out onto the patio. There is an officiant, our butler, and a woman who works for the hotel in guest services, or so her name tag indicates. We go right up to the balcony, the porch also glowing with flameless candles and scattered with rose petals everywhere, including in the dipping pool.

The butler hands us each the rings I purchased and then the ceremony begins.

It's brief. Not a lot of words are exchanged except the standard fare you see in movies or on TV. My heart is pounding out of my chest, and my palm is sweating against the ring and her hand.

And when it's my turn to speak, I answer, knowing I mean it. "I do."

Sorel says the same magic words, and I slide the band I got her onto her finger, and when I'm told I can, I lean in and kiss her.

I kiss my wife.

I kiss her like this is real, with a lot of lips and tongue, a little teasing, and a lot of sweetness. I take her in my arms, dip her back, and kiss her again, much to her amusement, because somewhere in the back of my head, I know this might be the last chance I get before the reality of tonight comes crashing down on us tomorrow.

6

MASON

I wake up early despite the late night. It's like this for me anytime I travel to the West Coast. The time change is always a motherfucker. I crack open an eye, my head feeling a little muddled from the two shots and the extra champagne I didn't need to drink. And with thoughts of those shots and all that champagne, a jolt of adrenaline hits my blood. I lift my left hand in the air, and even in the dark I can see the flat, black band twisted around my ring finger.

I glance to my left and find Sorel still passed out. I have no idea how she's going to wake up today. In fairness, I tried to talk her out of it. I told her she'd regret it. She swore she wouldn't. She was drunk. Very drunk. So drunk she was staggering a bit in her heels and had to hold on to me.

I gave her about ten different outs, and she plowed past each one, determined to do something wild. Something crazy. Something that would show Brody up and get rid of him once and for all. It's not how I pictured this would go between us, and though I'm not so thrilled to be her revenge, I didn't know how to say no and have it stick either.

Let me rephrase. I didn't *want* to say no.

In the moment, it seemed like an adventure. Something that would tie her to me as more than her friend, even temporarily. But now I'm not so sure that was the way to do it. How can I win her heart when, with the first sober breath she takes, she'll be trying to figure out how fast we can get this marriage annulled?

I peel myself out of bed and quickly throw on my gym clothes and sneakers. Sorel's phone has been kept on Do Not Disturb, so I find a piece of hotel stationary and write her a note telling her where I'm going and that she needs to make it so that my number can reach her. I'm pretty sure she already has that for Serena.

For a moment, I take in the pretty lines of her face. The dark sweep of her lashes as they flutter ever so slightly as she dreams. How her full pink lips are parted and her hand sporting the princess-cut diamond eternity band I bought her is tucked up by her face.

I had her sleep in my room last night even though I didn't touch her. She was too drunk to sleep alone, and by the time the ceremony was over, I had to carry her. I didn't go near her clothes. She's still in the dress she wore out last night.

Fuck.

I run a hand over my face and through my hair, edgy and anxious about how this day is going to play out. There will be repercussions. That's for damn sure.

I leave the room, needing to burn off this unsettled energy, and I find my way to the gym they have exclusively for the villas and presidential suites. It's not even six in the morning on a Sunday in Vegas, so it's no shocker that I'm the only one here. I hit the treadmill hard, running at nearly a sprint for a mile and then backing off to a fast jog.

Sweat drips from my face and runs down my neck and back. I need to talk to the guys. I need to tell them what happened and what I did. But first I need to talk to Sorel and see where her head is. I can feel the ring on my finger—heavy, but far from uncomfortable. I like its weight. I like feeling it there.

I married Sorel, and I'm not freaking out about it the way I should be. Not even a little. I said my vows, and I meant them. She's it for me. The woman I *want* to be married to. Not just for today, but forever.

"Do you think you'll ever get married?" she asked me once about five or so months ago. She was upset. She'd had her cake tasting and Brody didn't show up. I happened to be in the neighborhood, and by luck, we ran into each other. I talked her into grabbing a coffee with me and we sat there in a café chatting while I tried to make her smile and laugh. At the time, I blew her question off. I told her that one day after I met the right girl, I would.

"When you find that girl, make sure to remember the little things like wedding cake tasting," she grumbled bitterly as she stared down at her cappuccino. "It's the little things that matter most to us."

"Like being there with coffee and corny jokes when your person is sad?"

She glanced up at me and rested her hand on mine. "Exactly like that."

I startle out of my memory, nearly falling off the treadmill when my phone rings and cuts out the music blaring through my AirPods. It's Brody, and now I laugh as I answer through my watch with a tap of my fingers while I slow my pace on the treadmill to a walk.

"Hey, man. Good to hear from you. How's it going?"

"How's it going?" he barks incredulously in my ears. "Are you fucking kidding me with that, Reyes?"

I grab my towel, stop the treadmill, climb off, and walk over to the weight bench. The towel drags across my face, forehead, and the back of my neck as I sit down. "Not so good then?"

"Fuck you with that."

I smile. "Okay, I'll rephrase. I take it you got the picture Sorel sent you."

Sorel and I took a selfie with our ringed hands showing. She unblocked Brody just long enough to send it to him and then immediately blocked him again. It was a savage move, and I think Sorel is pretty badass for doing it.

"Tell me it's fake."

"It's not. I'm looking at my wedding band now."

"What the fuck?!" he bellows, and I stand to pull two seventy-five-pound barbells off the rack. "How are you even involved in this? How are you with her?"

"I was in the right place at the right time," I explain as I lie back on the bench, get into position, and start to do bench presses with them. "But I can tell you that you're easily the dumbest motherfucker on the planet. How you could cheat on a woman like her is beyond me. And then to run your mouth to the press about how it's a simple misunderstanding and lie about your phone being hacked while keeping your shiner averted from the camera is deplorable. It's condescending and disrespectful to the woman you already disrespected. How did you think she'd react after seeing that?"

"I was giving her a way to come back to me without it looking bad for either of us."

"You're so full of shit, man. That move was one hundred percent about you and your image and had nothing to do with her. You don't deserve her, and you never did. Not even close. You have no right to your anger. You put yourself in this position. Now Sorel is *my wife* and not yours. Get over it and move on."

"Move on?" He breathes out a laugh. "You think this is going to be easy for you? You're a fool. Let me guess, she got drunk, and you took advantage."

I grin. "Drunk, for sure. Other than that, you've got it all wrong, but whatever makes you feel cute and cozy at night when you think about me with her."

"I will ruin you," he seethes.

"If you weren't such a selfish, self-serving prick, you'd realize the only person you ruined is yourself. Your loss equals my gain. Thanks for that. But while we're trading threats, stay away from Sorel. She's no longer yours."

I disconnect the call with another tap of my fingers and continue my bench presses, pushing myself harder and wishing I picked up the hundred-pound weights instead of these. After I finish my set, I put them down and pull my phone from my pocket. I text Sorel, curious to see if she's awake and did what I asked her to in my note.

Me: Let me know when you're awake and how you're feeling.

Much to my surprise, she replies immediately.

Sorel: I'm awake and feeling like someone put me in a blender and turned it on to full speed.

Me: I'm going to send someone up to give you an IV.

Sorel: For real? They'll do that? I'm almost ashamed to call myself a doctor for how unprepared I am for this.

Me: Yep. They do. Brody called me.

My phone rings in my hand, and I swipe my finger across the screen to answer it, her soft voice filling my ears.

"He did? Why?" she immediately asks only to follow that up with, "Oh Mylanta, I sent him a picture of us last night."

I snicker. "Yes, you did. We had a nice little chat where I told him to fuck off." I wipe more sweat from my face and drop to the floor to start pushups. "I explained that he was an idiot for cheating and running his mouth and that you're my wife now and not his."

"You said that to him? That I'm your wife?"

I freeze in a plank. I can't tell by her voice if that bothers her or not. "Yes."

"Hmm. Um, okay. Why do you sound like that? You're grunting and out of breath."

"I'm doing pushups. I left a note telling you I was at the gym."

"Right. Sorry. My brain is like scrambled eggs frying in a pan."

"What did you think I was doing?" I smirk because now I know why her voice sounded like that. I like that her mind went there.

"I'm not commenting." She giggles lightly and then groans. "Ugh. My brain hurts, and my stomach feels like it's dancing a bad version of the Macarena. Oh, and I have a diamond band on my hand."

I chuckle. "That's because I put it there."

"I remember. Sort of. I don't think I appreciated it last night, though. Mason, what were you thinking with this? I mean, it's gorgeous, but holy hell. You didn't have to do this."

"I was thinking that's what you deserve to be wearing, and I wanted to be the one to put it there, princess." I pause, wondering if maybe that was too much. If she even gets the symbolism of the ring. Princess-cut diamonds in an eternity band. "Do you remember the ceremony at all? You pretty much passed out on me after it."

"Is that how I ended up in your bed? I'm going to assume since I woke up in my dress nothing happened?"

"Nothing happened," I tell her, pushing my body up and down a little faster. "I put you in my bed because I didn't feel comfortable letting you sleep alone."

She groans. "Oh my god, Mason, we're married. What the hell was I thinking? I talked you into it. I all but begged. Do you hate me?"

"Not even a bit. Do you regret it?"

"I don't know. I don't think so, but I won't lie and say I'm not freaking out too. This is why I don't drink a lot. Alcohol, especially tequila, makes me do wild things when I otherwise wouldn't, but I believe that was the point last night."

"It was. So here we are."

"We have a lot to talk about."

"We do," I agree.

"First, I need that IV. I can't have a real conversation about anything serious when I feel like this. I won't even tell you what I threw up twenty minutes ago."

"Ugh. Sorry, princess. That sounds rough. I'll get that set up for you and return with coffee and breakfast."

"That would be incredible. You're incredible." She pauses. "Mason?"

"Yeah?" I stop in a plank again at the sound of her soft, hesitant voice.

"Thank you."

I smile, feeling my chest flutter. "No problem. I'll see you in a bit."

I shoot off a text to our butler and personal concierge asking if someone can get Sorel set up with an IV, and they tell me they can have their in-house medical team up to start one in ten minutes. I return to my pushups, feeling a little better that she didn't sound angry or upset. Hell, I was worried she wouldn't remember any of it considering how drunk she was.

This is uncharted waters for me. I've never been in love with anyone before, let alone someone who doesn't want me back. But now we're married. I've already kissed her twice. Our friendship is on a new path—at least I hope it is—and I need to get my footing.

I finish my workout and linger in the gym a little longer because it's quiet and I need to assemble my thoughts. I wanted to date Sorel, not marry her—at least not yet and certainly not like this—but I need a strategy. A game plan. Because I don't hate the idea of being married to her. Not even a little.

I call my dad because I'm going to have to tell him and my mom sooner or later, and I trust my parents like no one else.

"Hey!" my dad greets me. "How's it going?" There's a noise in the background, and I hear him yell, "That's good defense, Jorkin. Keep it up. Sorry," he says, coming back to me. "These rookies are greener than the ones last year."

I smirk. "You said that about the ones last year."

"True. I meant it then, and I mean it now. Anyway, I was going to call you in a bit to see if you wanted to meet up and get some reps in this afternoon."

"I'm in Vegas."

"Vegas?" Shock laces his tone. "How'd that happen? Training camp starts next week, Mason."

"I know. I'm, well, I'm in the gym now if that makes you feel better, but I'm actually calling to give you the news." I go through the entire story from soup to nuts, and when I'm done, he's not saying anything.

"Dad?"

"Yeah, I'm here. I'm thinking." He laughs. "Jesus, Mason, I can't believe you got fucking married in Vegas last night. And to Sorel Fritz."

"I know, but I..." I trail off, my forehead in my hand.

"You want her."

I stare down at my band. "Yes. I want her."

"Coach or dad?" he asks me, and I grin. On the field, he's my coach and never my dad. At home, he's my dad and never my coach.

"Both."

"You have a hearing deficit. Something you've had to work with and against your entire life. You were in speech lessons to help with your pronunciation and learned to speak sign language. You sat in the front of the classroom because you didn't always want to wear your hearing aids. You still don't."

"Dad, don't start with—"

"Shut up and listen, son. What I'm saying is, you're no stranger to fighting against something you don't have a lot of control over. You learned how to move on the field and trust your other instincts when your hearing wasn't enough. People said I drafted you because you're my son, but that's not why I drafted you. I drafted you because you work harder than anyone else. I knew it and saw it. Yes, you're talented, but you have that something else. That grit. That drive. Nothing beats you, you beat it. Do the work. Put in the effort. And if it's meant to be, it'll happen. If it's not, then at least you know you gave it your all."

"Like you did with Mom?"

"She put me through my paces and made me earn her. She had a lot of distrust too. Especially with football players. In the end, I made her fall as hard for me as I fell for her."

I grin. "Thanks. I needed that."

"Good luck." He laughs. "You're going to need it with what you just did."

Yeah, no shit.

I disconnect the call and go down to the café off the lobby to order breakfast for both of us. A protein smoothie for me, and coffee for her. I could have ordered room service, but I want to give her a bit more time to finish her IV and start to feel better before I see her.

And I needed a bit more time to think all of this through.

When I walk into our villa, I notice the patio door is open, letting warm desert air trickle in and making me sweat all over again. Remnants of rose petals are still scattered about, and I set our food down on the dining room table and follow them. The soft music floating over to me that I recognize as "Glycerine" by Bush makes me smile, only to have the sight when I step outside rob me of my breath.

Sorel is in the pool, her arms folded on the patio hardscape as she stares out at the Strip beyond. From here all I can see are two red strings, one at the back of her neck and the other tied off around her back, and a hell of a lot of skin in between.

My mouth waters and my cock instantly hardens. This is exactly what I had fantasized about when I got this villa. This exact moment.

She hears me coming and turns her head over her shoulder, her hair wet and slicked back from her face. She doesn't smile. Instead, she watches me with an indecipherable expression, and my heart starts to pound.

Without thinking twice about it, I kick off my shoes, peel off my sweaty gym shirt, and enter the pool in my shorts. The water is just cool enough that it feels good without being cold, and I sink beneath it quickly to wash off my sweat before I walk the few steps to her. She watches me approach, but before I reach her, she turns back to the view beyond the balcony. My hands meet the lip of the pool on either side of her, my chest close to her back without touching.

I pick up a floating rose petal and drag it along her shoulder and down her arm. Goose bumps erupt on her skin, and I suppress a smile, knowing I'm pushing her a bit beyond her comfort zone. Immediately, she snags on the ring adorning my left hand, and I note she's not wearing hers. My gut sinks.

"Did the IV help?" I ask, trying not to feel as crushed as I am.

"It did, thank you. I feel a lot better." She sighs. "I've been running through last night in my head. Going over what I remember and what pieces are either foggy or absent. I think I dreamt about the wedding too, so now I'm not sure what is real and what was my dream."

"Do you need me to fill in any of those pieces for you?" I drag the petal back up and around her shoulders to the other arm.

Her voice shakes as she asks, "It's real, right? The marriage. We went and filled out the license."

"Yes."

She nods and swallows audibly. "And the ring?"

"It's real, too."

"I thought so." Her breath hitches, and her chin drops toward her other hand. That's when I spot the ring in it. I take it from her and put it back on her left hand. She doesn't stop me, but I know part of her wants to. I know she's questioning and mentally challenging everything about this.

"It's yours, princess. You should wear it."

"Princess," she whispers, her tone unsure as she finally notes the cut of the diamonds and pieces together why I bought it for her. She falls silent, the air thick and tense with our unspoken questions and confessions.

"Did I... did I ask you for... sexy lessons?" Her voice is so soft I have to strain to hear her.

I smirk and drag the petal around her shoulder blades. "You did. And to help you find your unexplored kinks."

"Oh god." Her face hits her hand. "I love it when I'm smooth like that."

"You were funny, but I told you we'd revisit that when you're sober."

She stills. "So we didn't do that? I didn't make a move, and you didn't make one either?"

"You were drunk," I reply and shift some of her hair away so I can touch her neck with the petal. I don't know why I'm doing this other than I don't know how to stop myself. "I'd never touch you like that. Was that part of your dream?"

She emits a breathy laugh. "I'm not answering that."

Desire shoots through my veins like a tonic, and I bring the petal up higher. "You were quick to take that selfie, and then you all but passed out. No moves were made last night. But we're both sober now."

I drop the petal in the water, and she shivers when the tips of my wet fingers meet the back of her neck where the string of her suit rests. "What are you doing?" she asks shakily.

"Thinking about that conversation. Do you remember what I said?"

"You um, you said you'd love to help me do that."

"I meant it. I would. If you wanted me to." My lips meet her shoulder, and she exhales heavily.

"Mason."

"I can help you explore anything you want to explore. Do anything you want to do." My lips drag up beneath her hairline, and I take a deep inhale of her.

"What are you doing?" she asks again, her voice unsteady.

"Trying to give my wife the sexy wedding night she deserves," I reply softly, my tongue sneaking out to steal a taste. "Since I didn't get a chance to last night."

"Mason..."

"Yes, Sorel?"

"I... we... we need to talk. We have to figure out how to get this annulled."

"I know. You told me that last night when I agreed. I'm not arguing that. But since we're here in Vegas and married for the time being, I'd like to kiss my wife again." My hands move to her hips beneath the water. "Everywhere this time. If she'll let me."

"We have more to discuss."

"We will," I promise her. "But I can't handle how sexy you look right now in your bikini." *And wearing my ring*, I don't add.

My hands drag up her body and cover her tits that are full and soft and feel incredible even with the small triangle barrier. Her nipples are hard, poking through her suit, and I rub them with my palms as I cup and squeeze her.

She moans, her head falling back to my shoulder.

"Say yes." I nip along her jaw to the corner of her mouth. "Tell me to keep going. Tell me not to stop."

7

SOREL

Smart decisions I've made since I walked out on my wedding to Brody yesterday? Zero. I think at this point it's safe to say I've made zero smart decisions in the last twenty-four hours. It's as if finding out Brody had been leading a double life with Eloise short-circuited my brain. Serena's always been the wild one of the two of us. Not me.

I'm the level-headed, practical, always-does-as-she-should doctor.

Yet somehow, I'm in Las Vegas with Mason, a younger man, a professional football player at that, and after a drunken night, we're now married. I wanted revenge on Brody, and I suppose I got it. Hell, I begged for it. I talked Mason into this, and I was worried he would be mad or upset with me, but that certainly doesn't seem to be the case.

I wanted to be wild and crazy and do something reckless and impulsive.

I got what I asked for. And a whole lot more.

Smashing Pumpkins' "Today" plays through the speaker on my phone almost as if it's mocking me.

Oh my god, I'm *married* to Mason Reyes. I married him the

same day I broke off a two-year relationship with someone else I was going to marry. There is nothing smart or rational about that, and I'll have a lot of explaining to do, but do I even care right now when Mason is touching me while practically begging to make me come?

When Mason *wants* me?

This younger, cocky, hot quarterback, who is wholly desired by models and actresses wants me. The girl who is... well, just a normal girl. A girl with one boob that is slightly bigger than the other and stretchmarks on her hips and cellulite on her ass.

He brought me to Vegas. He's made me feel like this from the first moment my hand met his. He married me when I asked him to, despite the fucked-up, ridiculous reasons. Maybe he's simply being a good friend to me or feels an obligation to my cousins—I know he's insanely loyal—but that's not what this feels like. Not at all.

This feels like wicked heat and a hell of a lot of lust.

His hands are doing incredible things to my breasts as his mouth flirts with the corner of my lips. I find the back of his head and hold him against me, and yet I say, "We're friends, Mason. Friends don't do this."

Though I'd be lying if I said I didn't remember what his kisses felt like last night and how good what he's doing to me now feels. Better than anything I can remember in a very long time. I dreamed about him doing this very thing to me last night, only he was peeling a white gown off me and not a bikini.

Desire burns hot in my blood, once again clouding my better judgment. I want to come at the hands of someone other than myself. It's been so long since that's happened that I was starting to believe there was something wrong with me because I couldn't get off with Brody.

Especially after reading how Brody made Eloise come.

I want Mason to prove that wrong. I want him to shatter that self-doubt.

"Friends do this, Sorel. They absolutely do."

My eyes pinch shut. "It's going to complicate this more."

"Not if we don't let it. I kissed you, and it hasn't changed us. I married you, and it hasn't changed us. It's Vegas, remember? No regrets, only adventure. I want to make you come. I want to make you come so fucking hard. Just tell me it's okay. Please, baby, tell me you want that as much as I want it."

Oh, god. I shouldn't do this. I really, seriously, truly shouldn't do this.

But I want it.

As much as he does.

He's saying it won't change us. And it won't. Not if I don't let it.

"Keep going. Don't stop."

I've come this far. No sense in stopping now.

Mason growls against me and rips the triangles of my bikini to the sides so he can feel me unobstructed. "You have no idea how much I want you."

"Show me," I whimper when he pinches and pulls my nipples. "Make me feel it, Mason. I need to feel it."

He spins me around, and his mouth crashes down on mine, his tongue immediately diving in as he gives me a long, drugging kiss. He groans, his hand fisting my hair at the nape of my neck so he can control me. My hands are everywhere, through his short hair, down his shoulders to his back, and around to his chest. Mason is a work of art. Brody had a nice body, but it's got nothing on Mason's. His skin is hot and wet, and he feels incredible as I explore. His tongue plays with mine, his kisses alternating between deep plunges and sweet, playful nips.

One of his hands rubs along my ass, playing with it over my bikini before he pushes that aside and squeezes my flesh.

"Fuck you feel good." He presses me against him, the hard ridge of his cock rubbing my lower belly as his hand on my ass dips lower and rubs my pussy from behind. The water adds an extra layer of friction, and I gasp into him and rip myself back.

Mason's eyes are dark, twin pools of black ringed with green circles, and his reddish-brown hair is wet and all over the place from my hands. His expression is reticent, caught between the desire to kiss me again and the struggle to hold himself back. He glances down, his chest rising and falling with his exaggerated breaths as he stares at my tits like a man on the edge of his sanity.

He's feral, and it makes my empty core clench and my clit throb.

I might regret this later, but right now, my body is running the show.

Wordlessly we reach for each other at the same time, his hand going back to the nape of my neck and mine to his hips. We slam together, an ionic bond chemically reacting as we cling tightly, any space too much space, and our mouths are no different, whimpering and grunting, rubbing and kissing. I scrape my nails up his abs, and he bites my lips, sucking and dragging them with his teeth. A moan hits the air, and I grind into him while he plays with my pussy and tits.

I need more friction, more contact.

He must sense this because, in a flash, he picks me up by my hips and drops me on the edge of the pool. His eyes are hot on mine, burning me from the inside out as he removes my bikini string by string, and when he glances down, when he sees all that's before him, he licks his lips, and his eyes grow darker than I've ever seen them.

"Jesus," he rasps, adjusting me so my legs are spread wider. I'm breathing so hard, I'm dizzy from it. Scared and excited like I've never been before. "You are so fucking sexy I can't even think straight. You have the prettiest pussy."

He shakes his head, runs his hands over the top of his head, and sinks to his knees in the water. The pool is only about three and a half feet deep, and Mason is tall. Certainly tall enough that his chest is above the waterline, and he's practically eye-level with my pussy. The urge to close my legs is compelling, but there is no way I can. Not with how he's looking at me.

"We're not running from here," he tells me, his gaze darting up to mine and locking firm. "We're going to enjoy our week with each other. I'm going to enjoy every inch of you, everywhere I can, whenever I can. I'm going to do unholy things to your body, Sorel Fritz-Reyes. The rest we'll figure out. That's what long plane rides are for. You feel me?"

I'm about to, I think, but simply nod because, while I should argue, I don't want to. Not when he's laying that sort of promise at my feet. Not when he's saying all the right things. It's just sex, just this week, nothing more.

"Yes. I feel you. I *want* to feel you."

He grins. "Then spread your thighs wider for me, princess. I want to lick my wife's cunt until she comes all over my face."

OMFG! Oh my fucking god!

"Stop calling me your wife." *But keep talking dirty.*

"Because you like it or because it reminds you of exactly what you are?"

"No! Neither," I protest.

Except he knows I'm lying. What is it about him calling me his wife that makes me hot? Or is it simply the way he says it? So possessive with a dominant edge that makes me wet.

With his eyes on mine, he spreads me wider, and his middle finger drags up and down my slit. "So pretty." His finger slips inside. "So wet." He pumps in and out of me. "So tight." He adds a second finger. "So mine."

I watch the slide of his digits as pleasure unfurls through me from inside while making me even more turned on by the erotic voyeurism of it. His lips come down on me and suck my clit straight into his mouth. He groans loudly, and I gasp, my back arching and my hand shooting up to his hair as my eyes close and my head falls back. Holy fuck is this man not gentle. His tongue is a tornado, wicked and violent and taking no prisoners.

A third finger slips inside me, and his pace slows, almost agonizingly so.

"You drive me so crazy. Open your eyes. Watch me eat your pretty pussy. See how much I want you. See how much I love the way you taste and feel and smell." As if to prove that, he takes a deep inhale of me and licks at my opening where his fingers are still slowly fucking me.

My eyes snap open, and I stare down, almost shocked by all that I see.

Flushed skin. Tits pointed up and out with hard, pink nipples. Thighs spread wide with Mason Reyes positioned directly between them.

"Oh." A moan surprises me as it flees my lips. Because I wasn't moaning at what he's doing to me—though it's pretty fucking incredible—I moaned at what I'm seeing. At how hot and sexy and dirty and almost wrong it is. The watching is almost just as good as what he's doing to me. The fact that we're outside, on our patio, where people nearby could hear us or even possibly see us... "Oh, fuck!"

He peeks up at me with a dark, devilish grin. His large hand holds my hips, rocking me forward and fucking me up into his face. I plant one hand on the hardscape behind me, the other on my breast, unable to get enough of the sight of him like this. I've never watched before. Hell, I've never been given oral sex in the middle of the day with daylight streaming all over me. I'm completely open and exposed, so utterly visible to him.

It's getting me high. Drugged.

Somewhere nearby we can hear people laughing and making noise, and I moan again, louder. I don't even know how it happens. It's like once again, I'm outside my body.

He chuckles against me. "Naughty girl, you want them to hear you. You want to get caught."

It's as if he's reading my mind. But how can I want to get caught? That doesn't even make sense, and yet the thought of someone seeing this, watching it the way I am...

I can already feel the first signs of an orgasm building deep in my core.

Before Brody, I went for the smart, quiet, sensible, nerdy type. Decent sex, but nothing mind-blowing. Nothing more than average sex with some mild foreplay thrown in there. Brody changed that in terms of the type of guy he was, but I believe it's already been established that his bedroom proclivities weren't to my benefit.

Mason and I haven't even had sex yet, but I can already tell sex with him is going to be more than simply mind-blowing. It's going to be epic. Life-changing. Body-ruining. That thought scares me for a second until he distracts me by dragging the pad of his tongue up my pussy and I can't think about anything else other than the driving need to come.

As if sensing this, he picks up his pace, rubbing the inner front wall of my pussy as he circles and flicks at my clit.

"Ah, Mason." Oh my god, I'm going to come.

"That's it, baby. You're so close. I can feel it. Come for me. I want to taste it. Make me taste it." He doubles his efforts, licking and sucking and French fucking kissing the hell out of my pussy while his fingers bang into me right on the spot I need them to.

"Oh, god!" I cry out as I rock into him, my pussy clenching as my orgasm rolls through me. I grip the edge of the pool, my other hand holding me up as spasms shake me. Wild hot heat courses through my blood and across my skin, making my toes curl and my thighs tremble.

Yes. Thank God.

I slump and fall against him as I try to catch my breath and not pass out again. My head is spinning as it is. *Woof.* Silly emotion hits me, and tears sting the backs of my closed eyes. Relief consumes me, and I bite my lip to temper this down. How ridiculous. I'm crying over having an orgasm. But it's not just the orgasm. It's what it signifies.

I feel him move and shift, and then the head of his thick cock is at my entrance. Before I can get my bearings, or even open my eyes, he thrusts inside of me all the way to the hilt, and now all of Las Vegas knows I'm getting fucked by a man with a huge dick. Holy shit!

"Mason!"

"Fucking hell, you're tight." He pants out a breath, his forehead on my shoulder where he kisses and sucks on my skin, trickling down to take my nipple in his mouth. "But damn do you feel *so good.* Shit. I'm not wearing anything."

He starts to pull out, but I hold him tight. "It's okay. I'm on the pill."

"You sure? I've never... I mean, I didn't mean to just... I haven't been with anyone in a very long time and I'm—"

"I'm good. Don't stop."

He draws back and cups my face, inching in closer until our chests touch. He rocks his hips ever so subtly, driving himself in just a little deeper. "You look so beautiful with me inside you. You wanted me to make you feel it." He pushes in. "You feel that, right? You feel how hard I am for you?" He groans, his face red and his pupils totally blown out. He's so hot like this. So dangerous. "Are you ready to take my cock? Out here in the open of our balcony where anyone could hear me fucking you?"

Oh, Jesus.

I clench, and he smirks, almost triumphantly.

Without waiting on a reply I'm positive I couldn't give him, he slides out, his gaze now glued to his glistening cock before he slams back into me. My lungs empty, and a moan falls through the air between us. My hands move back behind me, and my legs wrap around his waist. I roll up, seeking to take him back in, wanting him deeper, needing to feel this, because fuck does it feel good.

"Fuck yeah. That's it. Take it from me."

With his hands on my hips, he brings my ass to the edge of the pool, and he starts to fuck me. His cock drives into me with precision on smooth, even strokes that rattle my already rattled brain. Taking one of my bouncing tits in his hand, he holds it up for his mouth to catch. His teeth scrape my soft skin before he bites my nipple. Not hard. But enough to have me whimpering and writhing on him.

He grunts and thrusts into me, swiveling his hips when he's bottomed out and so deep, I practically feel him in my stomach. My head falls back, and I groan, grinding and fucking against him. I get lost in this. In the push and slides of his dick, in the unbridled grunts and groans he's emitting. In the heat that's everywhere, from the July desert air to the man fucking me to the sound of people on a not-so-distant balcony listening to how good I'm getting it.

My tits bounce and sway as he drives into me, his pace growing faster. He smacks one, and I cry out at the zap of pain that's nothing short of sweet with how it immediately turns to pleasure.

"Sorel," he moans, his voice shredded. "You. This."

I nod because yes. This. And this becomes everything when a wet finger rubs and rolls my clit.

"Oh, god," I whimper, holding him tighter with my thighs, moving my hips faster to meet him thrust for thrust, pound for pound. "I'm coming. Fuck, I'm coming." It's almost a surprise how it takes me. Mason growls as I shoot forward and clutch onto him, practically bent in half. I jerk and twitch and whimper, unable to stop myself or control my movements as he fucks me through it.

Strong arms wrap around me, and he holds me tight as he pumps harder and faster up into me, right on that magic spot that now has me screaming, especially when his thumb presses in on my clit, and he whispers, "They're quiet. They're listening to you come. Do you think they're fucking now too?"

It sends my orgasm to the next level, continuing something that would have otherwise already been over. And when he can't take it anymore, when he reaches his breaking point, he grunts, stills, buries his face in my neck, and with a couple of twitches, spills himself inside of me. He holds on tight, and for a few minutes, it's just us breathing, the sound resonant now that we're still.

I'm no longer listening for the people. That thrill has passed, and all I hear is him and the music still coming from my phone.

Slowly he pulls back and brushes a thumb along my cheek as his gaze flickers around my face. Wordlessly, he leans in and kisses me, and I don't know what this kiss is. I can hardly describe it or make sense of it in my head. Thankfully, it's brief, and he pulls out of me.

"Let's get cleaned up and have something to eat so we can talk."

That sounds perfect, and I nod, gathering the scraps of my bathing suit and putting it back on, doing a quick tie so I'm covered. I don't know what I just did out here in the open like that, and I need to get out of this heat. Reality is crashing down on me and I need to be alone.

I grab my phone and pull myself up, ready to dart back inside when he calls out, stopping me. "And Sorel?" I don't turn around. "That was just an appetizer for things to come, princess."

I race into my bedroom and go straight into the bathroom. I lock the door and flip on the shower. My legs are wobbly, and I throw myself a quick glance in the mirror only to laugh. I look like I had a wild night in Vegas followed by a rough morning and a hard fuck. Jesus. I just did that. With Mason.

But with that what I said to him in the pool makes my stomach roll. My gaze snags on the thin compact half sticking out of my makeup bag. My pill. Crap! Did I take it last night? I honestly can't remember. I slept in Mason's room. I all but passed out. I've never missed my pill. Not once.

I flip open the lid and sure enough, I didn't. Double crap.

I snap two pills out of the blister pack and shift them around in my palm. It's only one missed pill, and I can double up without needing backup contraception, even with a proges-terone-only pill. Medically, I know this. Still, it's not something you like to see after you just fucked a man you're not involved with bare.

I fill a glass with water and down both pills before I sit on the edge of the bathtub and call Serena.

"Hey!" she shouts into the phone. "Finally, she calls. What's up, sugar plum? How's it going?"

I can hear people in the background. "Where are you?"

"We're at the compound, hanging out by the pool. What's wrong? Are you okay? You sound funny."

By compound, she means our grandparents' massive estate just outside of Boston. "Who's with you?"

"A bunch of us are here, but at the pool, it's just Katy, Layla, Tinsley, Stella, Wren, Keegan, and Kenna." My older sister Stel-la's best friend Layla is my cousin by marriage and Katy's adop-tive mother, and Wren, Keegan, and Kenna are my cousins. Tinsley is engaged to Stone, but her dad is best friends with Mason's dad. Even still, she's not going to talk about anything. It's only family, more or less. Plus, these women are more than that to me. They're my people, and right now, I need some serious girl talk or advice or something.

"I um... I'm fine. Well, sort of. I had a rough night last night with too much alcohol."

"Uh-oh. What'd you do?"

I choke on a humorless laugh and get up to turn off the shower before I sink to the bathroom floor and draw my knees up to my chest.

"Oh, boy. This is bad, I can tell. Do you want this private or a group chat?"

"Group. I think. Grandma and Mom aren't there, right?"

"No. It's just us. They're all inside."

Perfect.

"I have Sorel on the phone," Serena announces, and I get a round of hes and hi and how's it going.

I laugh. It's not even funny, or maybe it is, but I can't help it, especially as I blurt out, "Last night I got married to Mason, and this morning, just now actually, we consummated said marriage."

My forehead hits my knees, and I keep my phone by my ear instead of putting it on speaker because I know what's coming next.

"Oh my fucking god!" That's almost in unison from everyone there. "Are you serious, Sorel?! What the actual fuck were you thinking?" That end part is a combination of Serena and Stella.

"Did you see the mini press conference Brody did?" I throw back at them.

Katy, Tinsley, and Wren are cracking up. They're good friends with Mason, so that's no surprise.

"You revenge married Mason Reyes?" Serena questions like I've lost my goddamn mind. I have. I totally have. I don't even know who I am right now.

"And then slept with him?" That's Layla. "I mean, he's hot. I'm a hundred years too old for him and good friends with his dad, but we all know he is."

"So hot," Stella agrees. "I don't even like dick, and I know he's hot."

"He's also an amazing guy," Katy jumps in. "Like one of the best guys I know."

"I agree," Tinsley states. "There are few guys who are better than he is."

I swallow and close my eyes. I can freaking feel Mason's cum leaking into my bikini bottoms. "I know he's the best. But I don't do this. I don't do crazy and impulsive—"

"Unless you're drunk," Serena snorts. "Remember that time you came to visit me in Paris and we—"

"Ah! Shut up. Okay, yes, alcohol isn't always my friend. But I don't randomly get revenge married and then fuck my new revenge husband. He's my friend. My freaking friend. Who marries and fucks their friend on the same day they were going to marry someone else?!"

"Whoa, calm down," Serena soothes. "It's okay. One thing at a time."

I cover my face with my hand and try to take slow, even breaths. I'm losing it a bit. I can feel it. The events of the past twenty-four hours are finally starting to hit me.

"What am I going to tell people?" I start to cry, and I feel so stupid for it. I'm a mess of my own making.

"Why do you have to tell anyone anything?" Tinsley questions. "For real?"

I wipe a tear from my face. "I don't know. Maybe I don't have to. I told Mason last night I wanted it to stay between us and Brody."

"Are you sad about Brody?" Katy asks. "Are you wishing it were him instead of Mason?"

"No," I whisper, but it's no less true. "I don't. That's the odd part. I'm angry, and maybe I just haven't started the grieving side of this, but I don't miss Brody. I'm relieved I didn't marry him. I just... I wanted to hurt him for all that he put me through. For all that he was doing behind my back. For the countless lies he told me. For touching and kissing and holding me after he fucked my friend. For never putting me first and always making me feel last. I wanted him to know what that feels like. What that sort of betrayal is like, and that's why I married Mason. But now Mason is talking like we're going to have this fling, and I don't know. I don't know what to do."

"How was the sex?" Layla questions.

"Mom!" Katy gripes. "Gross. I don't need to hear this about Mason."

"Then cover your ears because I want to know."

"I kind of want to know too." Tinsley giggles. "What? Don't give me that look. It's Mason. Have you seen that man? He has that I'm-a-sex-god vibe thing."

I snicker because she's not wrong about that, and it lightens the heaviness sitting on me a little. "The sex was incredible. Best I've ever had. Sorry, Katy, but it was."

She makes a vomiting noise in the background.

"That's great!" Wren states emphatically. "Enjoy it then. Enjoy it as much and as often as you can. If the sex is hot, then don't stop having it simply because you had a drunken escapade down the aisle."

"Wren, I love you, but you're like twenty-five," I say. "I'm in a totally different space of life than that. I ran out on my wedding *yesterday* and married Mason the same night. I'm no longer a girl in my twenties who can throw caution to the wind and do this sort of thing."

"But why not?" she presses. "I get it, you're older than me, and viva la twenties, but again, why not? You're thirty-five, not ninety-five. You have no plans to make your nuptials public. If not now, when? As you said, you ran out on your bad wedding and your bad guy, but that's even more of a reason to do this. You can do whatever the hell you want now, babe. It's your life, and you only get one. So truly, why can't you have a hot fling in Vegas with your hot husband?"

Silence. I'm met with silence after that.

If not now, when? It's your life, and you only get one.

That's a sucker punch because I've never lived my life like that. I'm a planner. A future-thinker. I've never been an in-the-moment girl. But... if not now, when? And wasn't that my whole speech to Mason last night? How I didn't want to look back on my life and regret I never lived it.

"The girl has a point," Stella concedes. "Since I assume you already have annulment or divorce plans set up and neither of you is looking for anything real to come of this?" she questions.

"Yes," I acknowledge, leaning back against the edge of the tub, my chin pointed up toward the ceiling. My hand covers my eyes. "We talked about all that last night before we got married. Besides, this is Mason. It's just sex to him. Just some Vegas fun. He as much as said so."

"Then enjoy it," Serena asserts. "Sorel, there is nothing wrong with having some fun, especially if the guy you're having fun with is into it and in the same mental and emotional place you are. You deserve this. Hell, you *need* this. It's just a week, right? What's the worst that could happen?"

8

MASON

I can't stop smiling. All through my shower and the entire time while I get dressed. Even as I sip my smoothie and reheat our now-cold breakfast in the kitchen, I can't stop smiling. I need to make it stop. But it's the goofy, happy sort of grin I get. The one I had the night of the draft when I went second overall or when I won the Super Bowl a few years ago—at only the age of twenty-five, I might add.

It's my *I'm a happy motherfucker* smile.

I already know Sorel is about to wipe it off my face, but for a moment, I enjoy it. This feeling. This high. I haven't had a woman get to me in a long time, and never to this extent. She's in my head—she's been there for a year—but now I think she owns my heart too, and while that should scare me because she's not even remotely interested in being there, in this second, it doesn't.

I'm riding the wave she comes with.

I used to sleep around. I was a bit of an admitted player. I like sex and I like women, and I've never had trouble getting either. Being the son of a famous NFL star and becoming one yourself leads to that.

But none of them have been Sorel. No one knows I haven't been with anyone since I met her. I don't talk about it, and they probably just assume I still get some. I felt a bit pathetic, but now it makes this so much better.

It's with that thought in mind that I finish my smoothie and leave her reheated breakfast on the table. I go back out to the balcony to try not to look as desperate as I feel. I want her to come to me, but maybe she's not ready for that. Maybe it's going to be a week of me chasing and coming after her. That's fine. I can handle that. If there's a chance of her staying with me on the other side of this, I'll chase her anywhere.

"How can you stand this heat?" she asks, and I turn, trying to curb my damn stupid smile.

"It oddly feels good."

She lingers along the doorway. "Did you eat?"

I shake my head.

"Come eat with me." Without waiting for me, she turns and walks back inside. I follow her because, like I said, I'm willing to chase, but when I get inside, she's sitting on top of the table instead of in one of the chairs. "The table is too long and formal," she explains. "Sit up here. It'll be like a picnic." She pats the spot across from her. "I can't have this type of chat at a table like this. I'll feel like a Mafia bride being offered up as part of some deal."

I move a chair out of the way, grab the side, and haul myself up and onto it. She raises an impressed eyebrow, and I wink at her.

"Athlete, not don."

"That's not a selling point for me."

I shake my head and lean across the small space between us to whisper in her ear. "That's because you were with the wrong one."

She laughs and shoves me back. "No distracting me. Not until we talk. After that, you can distract me all you want."

That catches my attention, and my eyebrows shoot up. "Really?"

She smiles and pulls her bottom lip between her teeth, gliding her teeth along the soft flesh. "Might be fun to fool around while we're here, don't you think?"

I snag on the middle part of that, caught on the line like a fish dangling from a hook. Fool around while we're here. Meaning not after that and definitely not anything beyond fucking. A fling. She wants me to be her rebound, Vegas fling. My heart sinks, but I brush it off. I shouldn't have expected she'd want more. How could she? It's too soon.

"I might be okay with that." *With the caveat that I plan to try to make you mine by the end of this week.*

"Good." She glances down again, and it still shocks me that this sexy, beautiful, smart, funny woman is so demure. So bold yet vulnerable. It's not even a Brody thing, though I have to imagine that didn't help, and it's not even a confidence thing because I know she has that. She's shy. She's an introvert. She keeps herself along with her heart and thoughts held tight.

The mystery of her is part of what drew me to her initially. It felt like trying to put together a five-thousand-piece puzzle without a picture to help guide you. I wanted to know every thought she refused to share, and even now, it's like that. A challenge. Something I have to work for.

She's different, that's for sure. So unlike the women I encounter.

"Go on," I encourage when she ends it there.

She unwraps her breakfast sandwich and takes a bite, chewing thoughtfully. "I complicated this. I dragged you into my drama and mess and then upped the ante and married you."

"As I recall, I suggested Vegas."

"I talked you into marrying me."

"I knew what I was getting into." I swallow. "Are you regretting that now?"

"No!" she exclaims, setting her sandwich down. "To be honest, I'm not regretting either. I mean, the fact that we're married is over the top, and we'll obviously have to have it taken care of at our first opportunity, and yes, I momentarily freaked out this morning and perhaps just now a bit after the sex." She shrugs and laughs in a cute, self-deprecating way. "What can I say, none of this is me. At least not sober me."

"Last night was the drunkest I've seen you. I was trying to remember this morning, but I think other than that time we all drank those bottles of wine at my place after I lost in the play-offs, I've never seen you trashed."

"Because I rarely get trashed. Another shrug. "Now I have no choice but to roll with it and let fate deal me another hand."

"Now you know why I said yes to you."

She picks at the bagel of her sandwich, twisting the bread between her fingers. "But I keep feeling like it's an uneven exchange. You've done all these things for me, and I've given you nothing but a headache and a load of bullshit you now have to deal with in return."

"You gave me a hell of a lot more than that this morning."

She blushes and stares down at her bagel as she mangles the poor thing. "You know what I meant."

"And I meant what I said." I take a breath. "Sorel, you don't have to worry about me. I wasn't that drunk last night, and I knew what I was getting into when I agreed. I'm here. I'm in this. I care a lot about you, and your happiness means everything to me. I don't regret a second of any of it. I like being the one to help you through this. I like being someone you can trust and rely on. And I fucking love being the guy you need me to be. Sex. Lust. Friendship. Trust. Honestly. No fucking regrets. All of it, I'm here for."

Her hazel eyes are warm and piercing. "I'm glad, Mason. I'm

so used to worrying about everyone else's feelings all the time. It's a habit I'm working on trying to break since it's never served me well. This morning..." She trails off with a laugh. "But I've never had to do that with you. You tell me things straight up and are always there right when I need you to be. Hell, you've even been handbag shopping with me and that's like running a gauntlet."

I chuckle lightly. "That was an experience, but let's just say it brought us closer together."

"Katy and Tinsley said you're one of the best guys they know. They're not wrong. I've felt that way about you since I first met you." She looks up at me through her lashes. "I'm glad I'm here with you. I'm glad we're doing this. Thank you, Mason. For everything."

I lean in and kiss her. The truth is, I don't know what to say. You're welcome feels trite. I'm hiding things from her. I want to be the guy she needs, but I also want to be the guy she wants. The guy she falls for. The guy she can't get enough of and maybe even considers staying with even if the marriage ends.

With that thought sticking in my head, I kiss her deeper and push our food to the side.

She giggles against my lips. "We're not done talking. Or eating."

"We can talk later. And I'll take you to a buffet after this and feed you whatever you want. Or maybe I'll simply feed you my cock while I feast on your pussy, and we'll survive by eating each other."

She pants. "Your mouth—"

"Makes you come."

"Yes. It does. But every time you say we'll talk later, this happens."

"Not a bad pattern to start." I drag my hands through her hair and hold her tighter to me, playing with her lips. "Stop worrying so much, Sorel. You don't have to do that with me. I won't be your regret. I'll be your adventure."

She moans against me and climbs onto my lap, her knees pressing into the table as she tilts her head to drive our kiss deeper. "I like that," she purrs against my lips. "You being my adventure. I might just let you do whatever you want to me."

My teeth graze her jaw. "Is that so?"

"You said it yourself," she pants, her nails scraping through my hair and along my scalp. "You've been such a good boy. You deserve it. I'm thinking we both do."

I groan as her tongue flicks my lips. "Hard to argue that. What does whatever I want mean? Anything?"

She smirks against me. "Anything. Surprise me. I'm all for those sexy lessons we talked about." She pulls back ever so slightly, but I can see the blush all over her. She's covered in nerves but musters on. "I want you to fuck me like a dirty slut, but I need to be treated like a princess too."

I'm not going to survive her. I already know it.

The bravery and trust it took for her to say that to me absolutely floors me.

"You're my princess," I whisper against her lips as I pull her top off and toss it to the side. Her bra goes with it, and I undo her shorts and slip my hand inside her panties. "But I'm going to love fucking you like my dirty slut."

"Yes," she whines, moving into me. "That's exactly what I want."

She's soaked for me. I don't know if it's because she's incredibly turned on or if it's still some of my cum from earlier dripping out. But the thought of fucking my cum back into her takes me from hard to steel.

I slip two fingers straight into her tight pussy and start pumping up.

"Grind against me, baby. Rub your sweet little clit on my palm."

Her hands settle on my shoulders, and she starts to do just that, moving forward and backward against my hand and up and down on my fingers. She's unbelievably sexy like this, breathless with dark, heavy-lidded eyes trained on me as she takes what she wants from me.

I lean in and suck her nipple into my mouth, and she emits a shaky breath.

"Ah, I don't remember my nipples being this sensitive. Or maybe it's just you. I like that. Whatever you're doing, I like."

"What else? What's something you've always wanted someone to do to you, but you were too afraid to ask?" I have a suspicion of something I picked up on earlier. Something that I think even caught her by surprise.

Her eyes pinch shut as she picks up her pace. She's getting close. I can feel it. Her cunt is soaking me. "I don't know." Her forehead falls to mine as she continues to ride me like this.

"You know, Sorel. You haven't let yourself live it out in your mind, but it's in there. I bet, even when you're alone and you're using your vibrator or fingers, occasionally you let your mind wander to those dark, dirty, slutty places."

She keeps her eyes shut as she continues to fuck my fingers and hand. I'm testing her. I know I am. She had meh sex with mediocre partners, and her latest betrayed her. But the girl who climbed onto my lap on a dining room table just now and asked me to fuck her like a slut, the girl who let me fuck her in a pool on an outdoor balcony, has a dirty mind. She has a wild side she's never allowed out for one reason or another, but she's tempted by it.

The devil calls to her. She just has to be willing to answer.

She's panting harder now, but her lips are sealed.

"We're going to be that for each other," I tell her, licking a circle around her nipple. "It's going to be a week of fulfilling each other's fantasies, one by one."

"Oh, god, Mason." She moans, and her pussy clenches

fiercely around my fingers as she continues to ride me. Her orgasm hits making her hips jerk wildly as they buck and mindlessly dig against my palm. Her arms wrap around my neck, and she holds me as if I'm the only thing keeping her upright. I kiss her neck, her skin tacky and warm and fucking delicious.

Just like her.

Speaking of...

The moment her body sighs and relaxes against me, I slip my fingers out of her shorts and into my mouth one by one. I can taste her, but I can also taste myself, and while that's not normally something that would ever turn me on, mixed with her, it's fucking heady. It makes me want to rip off her shorts and splay her out on this table so I can see my cum inside her.

I've never fucked a woman without a condom before, and I didn't even think twice about it earlier. At that moment, I felt like I was going to die if I wasn't inside her that very second, desperation like I've never known taking the reins, and I acted instinctively. I tried to pull out, but the fact that she let me take her bare is doing all kinds of cartwheels in my mind.

I have to see it. I fucking have to.

"Take off your shorts," I tell her. Wordlessly, she climbs off me, obeying me immediately. She rises to her knees and slips her shorts and panties off until she's completely naked on top of the table. "Jesus, Sorel." I shake my head, letting her hear the wonder in my voice and see it across my face. "You are the sexiest woman I've ever seen."

She stares down at me, and I catch it. The flash of disbelief. I climb up onto my knees to join her, removing my shirt as I go. She looks away for a beat, and I drag her face back to mine.

"You don't believe me?"

"I'm seven years older than you, Mason. You screw women at least ten years younger than me who earn a living based on their bodies. I'm not being insecure. That just feels impossible to believe given who you are and the women I'm sure you've been with. I eat real food and exercise when I can, but I'm normal. I have a roll on my belly when I sit and some cute puckering on my ass. I'm okay with that, but I liked the honesty we had going. I don't need unnecessary compliments."

I cup her breasts in my hands, quietly groaning at the feel of her, and run my thumbs back and forth over her nipples while I stare into her eyes. "You. Are. The. *Sexiest*. Woman. I've. Ever. Seen." I punctate each word, making it a sharp staccato so she doesn't miss a syllable. "It's not just your body, which is fucking sensational, puckering or rolls or whatever it is that you have. I'm here for it, and that's no lie. But it's more than that. It's all of you. I like you exactly as you are. I wouldn't change a thing. There shouldn't be an ounce of doubt in your head about that. I don't give a shit if you're older than me or eat real food—because thank fuck for both of those. If my words don't sell it, how hard I am for you should."

I take off my shorts and climb off the table. I help her to do the same, and when her feet hit the floor, she grabs my cock and gives it a firm squeeze. I wheeze out a growl, her touch on me like fire in the best of ways. She starts pumping me, and I stare, mesmerized by the sight of her small hand working my big dick.

"You keep doing that, I'm not going to last much longer."

Her hand runs up my abs and chest, and she steps into me, pressing up on the balls of her feet so she can kiss me. The velvet slide of her lips and tongue against my own while she builds me up is almost euphoric.

"Enough." I push her hand away, and she pouts. "Stop being so cute. I want to fuck you."

"Fine. But only because that's what I want too."

"You're getting very bossy."

A playful gleam lights her face. "I'm older than you."

"But I want you to be my little slut, so be a good girl and do as I tell you."

My hands meet her hips, and I spin her around before I push her chest flat against the table. She shudders when her warm skin meets the cold table, and I kiss my way up her spine to her ear.

"Spread your legs for me, princess. Show me the wet cunt I just made come."

Her lungs empty, and she bites into her lip. I suck it free from her teeth, but I don't linger. My hands trickle down her body, over the sides of her breasts crushed against the table, and down to her hips, where I hold her steady. Crouching behind her, I just about lose my mind at the sight before me.

Her pussy is pink and swollen and so perfectly wet. I lick my lips, her smell and taste everywhere, and I can't hold back from licking her. Just once. Just enough to make her moan and wiggle. Bouncing back up, I line my cock up with her opening and slide into her. Slowly this time. Last time I was too riled, too impatient, but this time I want to feel every inch of her.

Her hands shoot up over her head to grip the edge of the table. She holds on, already close. So am I. She feels unbelievable. Better than anything. I don't know how I can do this with her for only a week. I won't be able to give her up.

I'm already getting greedy.

My forehead meets her spine, and I blow out a breath as I slowly pull out and push back in. I do it again and again, maintaining the same agonizing pace. She's growing impatient as she presses back, seeking more, wanting me to fill her faster and harder. I'm busy trying to burn everything about this into memory. Especially how my ring looks on her hand as she grips the table while she gets fucked by me.

"Mason, please," she begs. "I need it. I need you. Make me feel it."

My dick surges, thickening against her tight walls.

I smack her ass as I drive into her, loving the sounds she makes. Like relief and ecstasy mixed with yearning. Like it's so good, everything she wants, but she still needs more. My arms snake under her shoulders, and I press down on her spine, giving her some of my weight but holding her in a way that protects her face from the wood of the table.

It's perfect.

The angle is fucking perfect.

My hips ram into her, slapping into her ass and thighs with each roll of my body. The table moves, sliding along the floor and shaking with the power of how hard I'm giving it to her. A chair falls over and thwacks to the floor, followed by another.

"I want to break every room in this villa with you," I breathe into her ear. "I want to sit you up on top of the bar, spread your legs, and eat your pretty pussy while you sip champagne. I want to bend you over the railing and fuck you so hard the entire Strip will see how good my cock feels inside of you."

"Oh my god. Oh my god. More," she moans. "Don't stop. Please, oh god, don't stop."

Stop? Who the fuck plans to stop?

"You make the prettiest noises, princess. I want everyone to hear them, and I'm happy to let others hear them too, but this body is mine and only mine. No one else can see it, and sure as hell, no one else gets it."

I give it to her to prove that point. I give it all to her. Lost in the slippery feel of her pussy as it clenches and squeezes around my cock. I'm so deep in her like this. As deep as I can possibly go, but it still doesn't feel like enough. It still feels like any second she'll slip through my fingers, and I'll lose her.

I'm on borrowed time as it is.

I cup the side of her face and lift it to angle her so my lips can capture hers. It's messy and uncoordinated and I'm saying a million things into her mouth. Things like *I can't get enough* and *you're so tight* and *you feel too good* and *I love fucking you* and *I want to feel you come all over my cock.*

"Do it, Sorel. Do it now, baby. Make my cock fucking messy."

Because I'm so close. So fucking close, and I'm not sure how much longer I can hold off because I meant everything I said. She feels too good. She's perfect for me.

"My girl. My wife." They both slip out before I can stop them, and it's too late. She hears me. Even when I don't want her to.

"Fuck. Mason."

I shake my head against her spine. *Don't do it, Sorel. Don't ruin this.*

I don't give her the chance. I fuck her like a man losing his mind inside his woman.

She gasps as I work into her harder, swiveling my hips so I hit her front wall. She grinds against the table, rubbing her outside while I work her inside. Her using the table to help get herself off throws me over the edge. My balls tighten and my abs clench, and nothing I do will stop it. Thankfully she's right there with me, coming with a loud cry and a harsh whimper. I give a few final thrusts, and with a roar, I still as she milks every throbbing drop out of me.

I collapse against her back and hold her for a beat, breathing so hard I might pass out before I force myself to stand and pull out of her. My cum drips down the inside of her thighs, and I swear, I'm fucking primal with that. I run my fingers through it with one hand as I use my other to help her up.

She giggles lightly and gives a playful roll of her eyes as she pushes my hand away.

"I need to get cleaned up. Again."

I shake my head. "No point when I'm just going to make you

messy again." Before she can protest, I scoop her up in my arms and carry her to her bed. Not planning on leaving it until she makes me. Already knowing that our time is coming to an end faster than I want it to.

9

SOREL

With a yawn, I roll over in bed and find Mason asleep beside me. He took me again, and then I think we both passed out. My body is sore in all the best ways, but my stomach is too empty to go unnoticed. I'm starving. We still haven't talked about anything beyond sex, and at this point, I'm not even sure what there is to say. We both know what this is and how it will work.

And when we get home, I'll call an attorney and get the marriage end of this sorted.

That will be that.

Fling over.

I frown at the thought as I stare down at him. I like Mason. He's everything I need him to be right now, but that doesn't mean it can turn into more. Or that I want it to. I'm not even close to being able to think about another relationship right now. I need to figure out where I'm going to live. I need to spend some time thinking about what Brody and Eloise did and allow myself to feel because I haven't done that yet and that can't be healthy.

You don't walk away from a two-year relationship and a

twelve-year friendship without feeling something. It's impossible. The lyrics to "Under the Bridge" by the Red Hot Chili Peppers float through my head, and I push them away along with Brody and Eloise.

The ring on my hand sparkles, catching my attention, and guilt tickles the back of my neck. I still can't get over all he's done for me. This ring is next level. It's real, and I won't think about the fact that he bought me princess-cut diamonds after I told him about the band Brody got me.

Mason isn't looking for more. He wants it to be a fling. He said nothing would change between us. He said a week from the start. Those were his words. His idea.

My guilt is my own, and I need to move past it.

Climbing out of bed, I slip on the hotel robe and walk into the bathroom to brush my teeth when Mason's reflection comes into view. He rubs the back of his sleep-mussed head, and I can't help but admire the muscles of his arms and shoulders as they bunch. He's naked and completely unbothered by it. Why should he be? He's flawless. Honed muscles and tan skin and large cock—even when it's not hard.

"I'm starving," he mumbles as he presses his lips to the crook of my neck and wraps his arms around my waist from behind.

"Same. I believe you promised me a buffet."

He grins against me and meets my gaze in the mirror. "I believe I did. We can do that, or we can get dressed up and go out. Maybe do some more gambling. Up to you."

"I don't think I can do dressed up. Or alcohol, for that matter. But gambling sounds fun."

"No more alcohol for me either. We could do room service if you prefer that," he offers, and while that's tempting, I think I need to get out for a bit. Walk around. Clear my head. Not immediately climb back into bed, or onto the table, or into the pool with him. I need to keep my mental boundaries with this straight.

"Let's go out. It doesn't have to be a buffet, just something good. Then I want to play more blackjack. I killed it last night." I bounce my eyebrows at him in the mirror.

He nibbles my neck. "You did. You were a card shark, Mrs. Fritz-Reyes."

He sets his chin on my shoulder, his cheek beside mine, and I try very hard not to think about what he just called me. It makes my belly flutter uncomfortably. He holds me, rocking us gently, and that flutter grows, tickling up through my chest and down my limbs.

"Are you okay?"

I look up at his reflection, straight into his green eyes. "I am." I think. Maybe. I don't know. "You?"

He winks at me. "I'm great. Best weekend of my life."

I giggle lightly. "How are you always this charming?"

"I'm only this charming with people I'm trying to impress. Is it finally working?"

I scrunch my nose. "Not really."

He tickles me, and I jump forward and spin around, trying to ward him away, when he picks me up, drops me over his shoulder, and walks me back to bed.

"No!" I cry. "I'm hungry."

He laughs as he tosses me down on the bed so he can jump on top of me. He's still naked and now the tie of my robe has pulled a little and is opening up. He's helping it along, his eyes glued to what he's unwrapping like it's a present.

His hands shift inside the plush white fabric and slide across my belly. He dips in to kiss me just as his phone rings. With a groan, he climbs off and walks on his knees toward the nightstand where his phone is sitting. He groans again when he sees who's calling.

He flips the phone around so I can see it. Stone. They're

best friends. Stone is Mason's age, and I wasn't as close with him growing up as I was with Owen since Owen is only about six months older than I am. I can only imagine what his friends, my cousins, have to say about all of this.

"Hey, man," he says as he picks up. "Can I call you back?"

He sucks in a sharp breath when I take his semi-hard cock deep down my throat. His eyes bulge, and I giggle lightly under my breath. "I told you I was hungry."

He chuckles and slips his hands into my hair, but he doesn't encourage me. Nor does he stop me. "Wait, what? Sorry, I was distracted." His hand cinches in my hair to stop me, but he releases me immediately when he catches me wincing. He sits up straight, pulling himself away from me, and I can tell that whatever he's hearing isn't good. "Hold on, hold on. No, that's not..." He runs a hand through his hair. "Shit," he mutters. "Yes, I was going to tell you. All of you. It's why I texted this morning saying that we needed to talk." He listens for a beat. "I figured you were at work, and that's why you didn't get back to me. Same with Owen. I'm sorry you heard this way, but can you go over that again with me because it's not making any sense."

He pulls the phone back slightly from his ear, and I hear Stone shouting.

My brows furrow, and he reaches out his hand for me. Without hesitation, I shift in beside him and climb under the blanket along with him as he does.

"Stone, slow the fuck down. I'm putting you on speaker so Sorel can hear what you're telling me, so stop yelling at me for two minutes. I'm hearing impaired, and you're still hurting my ears. You can bitch me out after." He sets the phone down on his lap and hits the speaker button. "Okay, she can hear you, so be nice and explain this again."

"What I was telling you is that your fucking wedding picture is all over the goddamn internet."

I gasp and cover my mouth as I face Mason.

"I heard that, but did Brody leak it?" Mason sounds incredulous, and frankly, I would be too. I can't imagine Brody would want our drunk, smiling selfie out there. It'll make him look stupid.

"I don't know who leaked it." Stone is not happy. "All I know is that it's everywhere, and that's how I found out you're married. That's how we all found out. Her parents. My parents. Your parents. My *grandparents*, and you know what that means now that Grandma knows, Sorel."

"Grandma knows?!" My hands cover my face. Crap. Octavia Abbot-Fritz is going to be all over me about this. It's a scandal, and the Fritz family doesn't love scandals, though we do weather them well, so there's that. But me being married is going to be her drug. She loves love, but she *loves* weddings. I'm thirty-five years old and not afraid to admit I am afraid of my grandmother and how she'll respond to this.

"Yes. She knows. So now I want you to explain how this happened. Are you actually married? Did this really happen?"

"Jesus," Mason hisses. "Stone, I'll explain everything. Just give me a second to see what picture you're talking about."

"Here. I'll help you out. I'm sending it your way now," he snaps. "Mase, brother, we talked about this. You promised."

"I know what I promised, but—" A text comes through on Mason's phone, and he pulls it up so we can both see. "What the hell is that?" he bellows.

I grab the phone from his hand so I can see it better. I enlarge it with my fingers and then hand it back to Mason. "That's not the selfie we took. We didn't allow photos at the ceremony."

"No," Mason agrees with a shake of his head as he examines it. "It's not our photo, and no, we didn't."

It's dark and a little grainy because it was taken during our ceremony, and the only light we got married by was fake candlelight. It's us kissing after we said *I do*, my hand on his arm and his on my face, but you can see my ring glinting on my left hand.

"Who took this?" I whisper because that's not even the worst part of this. The worst part of this is a screenshot Stone sent, and it's on the front page of *Intertainment's* website along with a caption, ***Brody Clear's Ex-fiancée, Sorel Fritz, Marries His Former Teammate and Rebels QB, Mason Reyes, in a Secret Wedding Hours After She Ran Out On Clear.***

"It was either our trusted butler or the person who was there as an extra witness," Mason states flatly, his lips pulled in a thin line, fury emanating from his pores.

"It's true, though? That's you?"

It's a little tough to see our faces in the darkness with the way we're kissing.

Mason sighs. "Yeah, man. It's us."

"What. The. Fuck, Mason? This is not what we talked about, brother. Not even a little."

"Yeah, but now we're actually cousins and not just brothers from other mothers."

Stone is not amused.

"It was my idea," I explain to Stone. "I begged Mason to do it. I wanted revenge on Brody. I was drunk, and Mason was just trying to help me out so Brody would feel the sting of betrayal back."

"*By marrying you?*" Stone is incredulous.

I sigh, sinking down into the bed a bit further, feeling more foolish than ever. My photo is on freaking *Intertainment*. "By marrying me," I parrot. "We were going to get it annulled when we get back." I take in the photo. "It was crazy and impulsive. It was meant to be my way of hurting Brody for what he did and then what he felt the need to come out and say publicly about it."

Only now Brody looks like the wounded, scorned party and not the other way around. He must love that. I look like an unstable whore who jumps from one football player to the next and picks up rings like championship souvenirs along the way. My name is on the cover of *Intertainment*. What will this do to my practice? My reputation as a serious doctor?

Anxiety starts to hit me like a barrage of bullets. My empty stomach churns violently, and my chest quakes. I don't like the spotlight. I'm the quiet one. The introvert. The one who doesn't have my face in tabloids. That's Serena's thing, not mine, and she's never been stupid enough to pull a stunt like this. I never should have called him out at the ceremony. I never should have run off to Vegas.

"Maybe we can say it's not us. Maybe this doesn't have to go beyond what it is." My voice climbs frantically as panic surges through me.

Mason holds my hand and tries to calm me down. "Except there's a wedding license that's easy to look up," he tells me, his eyes soft and sympathetic. "We maybe could have gotten away with that, but a little digging and it's out there. I'll call my PR team and speak with them, and we'll talk with your family's people and come up with something."

My hand covers my face. "It's going to look so bad," I murmur. "I ran out on my wedding because my fiancé was cheating, but I ran right into the arms of another man and married him the same freaking day. I'm so sorry, Mason. I dragged you into this." Emotion clogs my throat and burns my eyes. "I didn't think about it this way. I never intended for the press to get wind of it. I figured it'd be my fuck you to Brody, and then we'd go home and quietly take care of it and it'd be like it never happened. I'm so stupid."

"Hey," Mason soothes, moving the phone and shifting me until I'm sitting sideways in his lap. He runs his hand down my hair before he rubs my arm reassuringly. "Don't do that. It wouldn't have been a thing if this person hadn't snapped a picture without our consent. In fact, they weren't supposed to have a phone in there at all. I had everyone put them by the front door of the villa for this very reason. She must have had a second one on her. She knew what she was doing, and there will be hell to pay, I can promise you that. But this crap will fade after a few days. It's a headline and some buzz, and then it'll pass when the next thing hits."

Stone has been quiet. Maybe he doesn't know what to say, or maybe he's still angry that his best friend did this with his cousin. I don't know. Guys are weird with their bro code crap.

My phone has been on and off Do Not Disturb since I left Boston. I've talked to my parents, and I spoke to my girls this morning, but I wanted a reprieve from the rest of the real world. Now the real world is getting ready to bitch slap me in the face.

It's only been a day. How can so much happen in one day? How did my life go from one thing to something completely different in the blink of an eye?

"Mason's right," Stone says in a low voice, still unhappy but reconciled. "This buzz won't last long unless something perpetuates it. Talk to Mason's PR people. Talk to the family's. Come up with a plan that minimizes damage to everyone. It'll get worked out. It'll be fine."

Only nothing about this feels like it's going to be fine. And what started as something easy just got a whole hell of a lot more complicated.

10

MASON

I hang up with Stone, and everything that was fun and sexy and perfect not even ten minutes ago has taken a complete nosedive. It sucks. I don't know what to say to make her feel better. I'm not sure there's anything I can say in this situation. The headline is accurate. The truth is what it is. All I can do is be here and hold her a little tighter, so that's what I'm doing.

A little press doesn't bother me. I smile, act cocky, and throw a ball for a living. Generally, that works for me. Yes, I've gotten my share of crap over the years. Reporters saying I only went as high as I did in the draft because my father drafted me or that I'm an overinflated quarterback or that my hearing deficit makes me a liability on the field.

Whatever. I don't let that shit get to me. I focus on what I can control.

But Sorel, despite being a Fritz, has never lived that side of her famous family. That was intentional on her part. She was living in New York, not Boston. She flies under the radar. Even when she moved back to Boston with Brody, she kept it that way. Plus, as far as Fritzes go, her father is probably the quietest and least famous of them—like Sorel.

I liked that about her.

She doesn't seek the limelight or use people to up her fame the way so many women I encounter do.

Which only makes this worse because this headline doesn't paint her in a good light. Me neither, honestly. It makes it look like I stole a bride, another man's woman, and it makes Brody look like the hero. We didn't consider any of this last night, and I hate how careless I was. I should have known better. I should have double-checked people for their phones. At that point, my mind simply wasn't on that.

Sorel rests her head on my chest and falls quiet for a few minutes.

"We'll get it figured out," I promise her, kissing the top of her head.

I don't want to let her go, but I can already feel her slipping away from me. It was too soon. I made my move too soon, and the weight of that foolish decision is sitting heavy on my chest. I went after her the way I go after everything else in my life— single-mindedly. I didn't stop myself, and I didn't follow my original game plan of going slow with her.

I can't take it back. I can't change it.

And I know she's regretting everything with me.

"How are you still talking to me after all I've put you through? You're married to me, and now this."

"Shit happens. I'll survive it. We both will, and when it blows over, it'll be like it never happened."

With a heavy breath, she climbs off my lap and goes for her phone. She turns off the Do Not Disturb, and the thing erupts like a volcano, spewing texts and voice messages out like lava.

"I'm going to go call my parents," she says softly, her voice dejected as she sifts through some of what's on there. She climbs out of bed, tightens her robe, and walks out. I watch the empty doorway for a minute. I can feel it. The wall that's coming back up around her. The shell she feels comfortable hiding behind.

It was too fast. Not even a full day, and she's already gone.

Wow, that really sucks.

I sink back against the headboard and chuck my phone across the bed, no longer wanting to deal with that side of this. She's all I've cared about since this started. Making her smile. Making her happy. Bringing life back into her when others stripped her of it. Sure, the marriage was dumb. It was foolish.

But if I wasn't Mason Reyes and she wasn't Sorel Fritz and she wasn't formerly engaged to Brody Douchebag, none of that would matter.

My heart pounds out a steady, tireless beat. I married her. That makes her mine. Mine to protect. Mine to fight for.

I don't care if she sees it as fake. I've never been a quitter. Even when the odds were stacked against me and life wasn't always in my control, I fought for the win. I've never failed at anything, and I sure as shit won't fail at this. Not when the stakes are this high and what I've wanted for the last year is on the line.

Resolved to that, I crawl out of bed, and go to my room to take a quick shower and get dressed. My motions are mechanical, my brain running circuits as I think through how to go about this.

After that's done, I text my guys, including Stone.

Me: I'm sorry about all this. I know it's going to cause drama and headaches and you're likely pissed at me. But remember what I said about her being my instalove. I know that was hyperbole at the time, but now, I'm starting to think it's been real all along. I'm in love with her, it's unrequited, so cut me slack on this.

Then I text my parents and let them know what's up and

that I'll call them later. My dad is going to have a lot to say. This sort of thing could be a distraction for the team. Brody was one of us, and our season last year was far from our best. I need to come out strong and as a solid leader for the team, but Brody made some friends, and there could be backlash. But that's a training camp and preseason problem and not something I'm going to worry about now.

What I am going to worry about right now is my wife because she's hungry.

Going out to eat is no longer an option for us. I order something from every restaurant on the property instead, and just as I'm hanging up with room service, our butler calls me. For five minutes, I sit on the edge of the bed and listen as he explains what happened. Evidently, the woman he brought in to witness our nuptials was the woman he was seeing. A woman he trusted. A woman who worked as a concierge for the main hotel. Worked. As in, she quit this morning after she sold our picture to *Intertainment* for who knows how much. He apologized profusely and begged us not to demand his job over this.

How could I?

Poor bastard fell for the wrong woman who used him for her own gain. The long and the short of it is, no matter what fight I put up, the picture is out there. I have no choice now but to embrace it and deal with it. And find out more about the woman who sold it and determine what action I need to take.

Speaking of that, I dial up Vander who is a cyber security CEO for Monroe Technologies by day and one of the best hackers on the planet by night. But only a select few of us know about his alter ego.

"Ah," he says as a greeting. "I was wondering when you'd call."

"I need everything you can get on the woman who sold the picture to *Intertainment*. I don't make it a rule to ruin people's lives, and if she needed the money that badly, so be it. But I want her phone wiped of anything else she could potentially have on there."

"On it," he says. "Actually, I was already on it without you having to ask." I can hear the smile in his voice as he clicks around on his keyboards in his bat cave or whatever he works in.

"Perfect. Thanks, man. I owe you. What can you do for me with Brody?"

"Anything. What are you looking for?"

"I want eyes on him. I know this motherfucker. He's not a guy who goes quietly. He's a guy who wants to not only be the best but *look* like he's the best. No matter the cost to anyone else. I don't trust him, and I don't want him to do something to hurt Sorel more than he already has."

"Easy enough. I can monitor him and let you know if anything comes up."

"Awesome. Thanks."

"You really married her?"

I smirk. "I really married her."

"My parents did it that way, you know. My mom needed to get married to inherit Monroe Technologies, and my dad stepped up. Now look at them. They're like your parents. Happy and blissfully in love."

"She hated him, right? Your mom?"

Vander chuckles. "Well, he did break her heart, but he made it up to her."

I stand and start to pace. "I needed to hear that."

"I figured you did."

"Except Sorel was never in love with me. Hell, she's not even in like with me. I'm her friend. A guy she let screw her a few times, but that's all."

"You'll have to change her mind about that."

"That's the plan."

Only he can hear I'm posturing, and his tone sobers. "Mase, she's there with you. She married you. You're sleeping together. She might not know it, and she might even resist it given the circumstances, but she's more in like with you than you think."

I pause, my smile growing. "Thanks, brother. Wish me luck. I'm going to need it."

"Good luck. And if you need any more help along the way, just call."

We disconnect the call, and I go to find Sorel, Vander's words sparking renewed vigor in me. She's sitting on the sofa in the living room, still in her robe, staring down at her phone as if the thing betrayed her.

"I ordered room service," I speak softly, not wanting to startle her.

She glances up at me and nods, her expression vacant and her eyes lost.

I don't know if she knows what Vander does, but it's not something we talk about with anyone. I could tell her because she's Sorel Fritz and not just anyone, but right now there's nothing to say, and I'm not sure I want her to know that I'm having Brody looked into just yet.

"I was going to call my PR team," I continue. "I thought you might want to be part of that conversation."

She pats the seat beside her. "My dad reminded me that my uncle Oliver was fake engaged to my aunt Amelia. Their fake engagement started out as a fuck you to his ex and to the people who bullied her in high school, and it went viral on them."

I smirk. I'm not sure I knew that. "Sort of like us."

She smiles back, and relief hits my bones. "Sort of like us. At least the first part. Oliver fell hard for Amelia pretty quickly, so I don't think our fate will be the same as theirs. Still, it was nice to hear I'm not the only Fritz to do something crazy."

I ignore the part where she says our fate won't be the same as theirs. "Stone and Tinsley were fake engaged."

Her eyes sparkle. "For the press and her safety. Yes. Keep going. What else do you have?"

"Vander's parents had a fake marriage, and the media fed on it. It all turned out okay."

She sighs, rolling her shoulders and her head on her neck until it cracks. "I've never been good at the unexpected or not knowing what comes next. I'm sorry I freaked out." She gives me a wilted smile and nudges my arm with her shoulder. "I feel like all I'm saying is I'm sorry to you today, but I am."

I shake my head. "Stop apologizing. I swear, I'm good, and if I'm not, I'll tell you."

She nods, liking that answer. "Okay. Let's call your people and figure this out."

∼

"THREE MONTHS?" She tucks her robe a little tighter against her chest, closing herself off from me again. I have a bad feeling this is going to be a pattern with her. I shouldn't be surprised. This is who she is. Cautious and reserved. Well, most of the time.

"Yes. Three months." That's Bruce, my main PR rep. "You admit you got married on a whim, but say there's something there between you. Brody cheated, and you ended that relationship before you left for Las Vegas. You and Mason have been close friends for a while and care about each other. We leave it at that. And you agree to stay married for three months. That's long enough for the press to move on to something else."

Sorel shoots to her feet. "Are we supposed to live together?"

"That's what we'd recommend," Bruce tells her plainly, his voice deadpan because I don't think Bruce has ever had any emotion. That is why I hired him and his company. "Three months is enough time for everything to play out. Including a divorce or annulment, but at this point, an annulment is unlikely."

She stares heavily at me as if he's speaking to her in Italian and she needs a refresher course in romantic languages. One I'm all too happy to give her, but now's not the time for that.

"Mason?"

I shrug. "I can't argue it, Sorel." Mostly because the idea of it makes me happy like a six-year-old on Christmas morning. "What he's saying makes sense. It's safe. It makes it quiet instead of loud. If we go straight to an annulment right now, the press will be all over us. If we say we're trying to make it work, the press will find that boring and move on."

Her hands fly, as do her eyebrows. "You want me to not only stay married to you for the next *three months* but *move in with you* for that time."

It's not a question. It's an *are you crazy* statement.

"Bruce, hold on." I put the phone on mute so I can speak directly to her. "If you don't like what my people are saying, ask your PR people and see if they suggest anything else. I understand it's not what you want or what we originally discussed, but right now, you don't have a place to live anyway. This takes some of the stress off of that for you. This is safe. It's clean. And by the time the world moves on, we can file for divorce or figure out an annulment without it being front page news."

Sorel stares down at my phone. Then looks up at me. "Three months?"

"Three months," I confirm.

"I move in with you?"

"You do."

She starts to pace, needing a second with that, so I take Bruce off mute and ask him what's next. He launches into a diatribe about legalities and contracts and things we should do, press conferences we should never hold, and things we should absolutely never ever speak about. I'm not stupid. I may be a baller, but I'm not. I know what to say and what not to say, and believe it or not, I read. I had a three-point-seven GPA in college with a major in economics, and that was not because I had a cheerleader do my work for me.

I may not look smart, and I make act like a goof a lot, but I'm smarter than people think. With that, there is an advantage to playing dumb. It gives you an upper hand in this world.

"I guess I don't have a choice, and I understand the logic of it. Thank you for your time." Sorel walks over and hits the end button on my phone, disconnecting the call before she folds her arms, all business. "No sex, Mason. And I'm not sleeping in your bed."

The fuck is that?

I toss my phone on the couch beside me and stand. "What do you mean no sex and you're not sharing my bed?"

Her hands meet her hips, and I hate that I know she's completely naked under that robe. A robe I started stripping off her only an hour ago.

"I mean no sex," she tells me in no uncertain terms, her hazel eyes fierce and unwavering. "I mean, we both planned on a week of fun here, but now that doesn't make sense for us, and if I'm living with you, acting as your wife, we can't sleep together."

I stare at her, all of her pretty features one by one. I tilt my head, taking them in from a different angle. Nope. It still doesn't make sense to me.

"Why not?"

"Because sex confuses everything. If we're married, if we're acting as a married couple and I'm living with you, it's not a fling anymore. It's business, and I won't mix business and plea-sure, and I won't mess up our friendship more than I already have. We said this wouldn't change us, and continuing to sleep together will do exactly that."

Right. I might understand that part of it. Maybe. Or not.

The word friends just became one of my least favorite words. Up there with moist, ointment, and curd.

"Why do we have to leave now? We have the week here. We can still have that."

She gives me a dubious look. "Come on, Mason. You know we can't. It was fun. A lot of fun. A little too much fun. But we have to go home and deal with this. We can't hide out here and pretend it's not happening."

"Sorel..." I trail off. I don't have an argument. I don't have my own words to give her. I'm the sad part of every romance movie. The third-act breakup, as Katy calls it. There is no convincing her to stay when she's right about why we need to leave. I can't tell her that I've wanted her for a year and that now that Brody is finally out of the picture, I can admit to myself that somewhere in that time, I fell in love with her. I can't tell her that I don't want a divorce or to call our marriage fake because I want it to be real.

I want to tell her that I can't see anything I don't like about her. I don't simply just want her, she completes me. I burn for her. I wanted it to be her. I wanted it to be her so badly. I want to do this with her, all of her, forever, her and me. I'm a man, standing in front of a woman, asking her to love me. I wish I knew how to quit her. I think I'd miss her even if we never met. I sigh and chuckle as Sorel stares at me like I've lost my mind because I have.

Thanks, Katy, for making me watch every chick flick ever made because now I've become a cliché. Mentally spouting lines I didn't write one after the other.

I take her by the arms, sit her on the couch, and get on my knees in front of her.

"Kiss me. Kiss me as if it were the last time."

She stares at me as if I'm nuts. I might be. Again, I'll blame Katy for this later. But we're talking *Casablanca* here. Has there ever been a more romantic movie where the guy has the girl and then loses her? But the truth is, I could spout a million lines written by other people, filled in movies about love, but those are useless. They're lines. Meaningless. This thing between us is not, she's just afraid to see its potential.

Or maybe it's just not a consideration for her yet. But it will be. I have to make it so.

"Do it, Sorel. Kiss me as if it were the last time."

Her eyes flicker back and forth between mine. I think she's going to say no, but she surprises me when she cups my face in her hands, tilts her head, and leans in to kiss me.

It's magic. It's heaven. It's sin.

It's a perfection that sears a path of heartbreak through my veins. I wanted more time with her. I don't want this to be it. I might even have to swallow the truth that she'll never be mine. Not for real. Not in any space she wants to be. She wants out of this and away from me as fast as she can get it.

So I kiss her back.

I hold her face as she's holding mine, and I split her lips and set my tongue free inside her mouth. I feast on her. I devour her. I *consume* her. I kiss her because this might very well be the last time, and I make it count.

Only in my head, I have three months.

Three months I intend to use to my advantage. I might have fucked this up early, I might have been overzealous and jumped in too quickly, but what if I get her to love me back? Hell, I got her to agree to hop on a plane and come to Vegas with me. Who knows what I can do in three months?

I pull back. "That was great." I grin. "Now I'm good."

"Good?" she murmurs, almost confused, her eyes glazed.

"One last kiss." I shrug. "You just told me no sex for three months."

I get a hard blink. Maybe a touch of perturbed. "Yep. That's what I said."

This line is mine. "With kisses like yours, there's no way I'm not going to do everything I can to break that rule. You know that, right?" Before she can respond, I stand and wink at her. "Here's looking at you, Mrs. Fritz-Reyes."

11

SOREL

Kiss me like it's the last time.

My eyes close, and I blow out a breath as I turn the corner and collapse against the wall. Je-sus, that was a kiss. A kiss I don't want to be the last. I want more kisses that make my toes curl. More sex that blows my mind into the next realm. But that's why it needs to be the last one, isn't it?

Weezer's "Say It Ain't So" flickers through my head, and my hand covers my racing heart while I try to slow my breathing.

I'm not in a good headspace for this. I knew it going in, and I ran toward that instead of away from it as I should have. Now look at what I've done. I'm married to Mason. I have to move in with him. We have to stay married for three months. And I have to pretend like it's real when pretending like it's real is dangerous.

I blink open my eyes and raise my left hand. Fuck, that man bought me a pretty ring.

I have to trust that his PR people know what they're doing. What other choice do I have if I want this to go away quickly? I mean, right now, it's as bad as it gets. The fact that I ran off and married Mason after walking out on Brody is everywhere.

Brody is Mason's former teammate, so there's that added element to the story.

It's not good. Not good at all.

I hear Mason doing something in the living room, and I quickly scoot down the hall to my room. It smells like him in here, and the bed is sex rumpled. I shoot into the bathroom and slam the door. I can't breathe. My hands meet my thighs, and I bow my head, trying to calm myself down as a burgeoning panic shoots up through me like a geyser.

I laugh. It's a bit—or maybe a lot—hysterical.

Oh, god. My hands cover my face. What have I done?

Three months. That's all it is. I can use that time to look for an apartment. Some place *I* want to live. Some place just for me. It's Mason. He's the problem. He's exactly what Katy and Tinsley said. Despite his threat to break my rule, I know he cares about and respects me. He was just being his usual charming, flirty self. He's a guy. He likes sex. That's just Mason.

I blow out a breath, turn on *OK Computer*, which is my favorite Radiohead album to full blast through my phone, and just as "Paranoid Android" comes on, I climb in the shower I so desperately need. The food will be here any minute, at least I hope, and I need a few minutes alone to digest everything before I shove food in my stomach.

I start to break this down, focusing on what these months will entail. I'll have to lie to people. Lie to work colleagues and nosy patients. The press will likely follow us for a bit, and my face and name will appear in places I don't want it to, likely not portrayed in the best light. I've dealt with that before, just on a different scale.

My high school best friend took all our silly videos and recorded chats I didn't know she was recording and posted them on the internet and social media for everyone to see, laugh at, and ridicule. All my private thoughts that I shared with her. All my secrets. All my weird moments of letting go and being completely me with someone.

I was sixteen and felt like my world had just ended.

We had them taken down, but by the time I learned of it and acted, it was too late. Everyone saw them.

I survived. I turned inward. Years later, I stupidly trusted outside of my circle again, first with Eloise and then with Brody.

Speaking of Brody, I will have to deal with him at some point. At the very least, to get the rest of my stuff. Plus, I think I'm ready to know why. Why get involved with me if he was sleeping with my friend? Why pursue me as hard as he did if it wasn't genuine? He told me he loved me after a month of dating and wanted me to move in with him shortly after that. When the Rebels picked up his free agency, he asked me to move to Boston with him—which felt like a no-brainer since all of my family with the exception of Serena and my brothers are there —and he proposed the moment I said I would.

But why?

How could he claim to love me when he was sleeping with Eloise?

My back hits the tile wall of the shower, and I sink to the floor, drawing my knees up and bowing my head between my outstretched arms. I told Mason when I asked him to marry me that I didn't want to look back on my life with regrets, but it's difficult sitting here like this to have anything but those. Brody might be the biggest of them.

Why isn't my heart broken?

I was going to *marry* him. I should be devastated.

If I'm honest with myself, truly searching my soul, I think part of me knew Brody wasn't right for me. I don't think he ever understood how I work, but more than that, he never tried to. He wanted a big, flashy wedding when I wanted a small and intimate one. He didn't care about my work as a doctor and was never supportive when I'd leave to go visit Serena and my brothers, especially if it interfered with football season. Hell, he wouldn't even let me play my music if he was home. That's not even the half of it, but it speaks to our entire relationship. I chalked it up to opposites attract, but the reality is, it wasn't that we were opposites, it's that our fundamentals weren't aligned.

When he proposed, I didn't feel... excited. Or excited enough maybe is a better way to say it. I didn't burst into tears or feel overwhelming love swim through me. I was happy. That was about it. I didn't wake up Serena in Paris in the middle of the night to scream into the phone that I was engaged. I never referred to Brody as the love of my life, and I can't remember a time I ever thought of him that way. I didn't cry when I saw the texts between him and Eloise. My heart didn't act like it was being stabbed to death.

It was just another person who I trusted to betray me. Maybe part of me was expecting it or was emotionally detached after what I went through in high school. With that, maybe I'll never truly fall in love because I don't know how to trust anyone enough to fully open myself up to them.

I scrub my hands up my face and push back my heavy, wet bangs that are dripping warm water into my eyes, and once again snag on the sparkling diamond band on my left hand. A band that doesn't seem like it's going anywhere anytime soon. So now that I've gotten myself into this mess and learned how I'll get out of it, I have to figure out how I'll manage the in-between of being married to Mason.

Married.

He called me his wife this morning while he touched and kissed me. He called me his girl. Hell, he called me Mrs. Fritz-Reyes.

A shudder rolls through me as the memory surfaces, but I quickly push it away. I meant what I said. No more sex and absolutely no sleeping in the same bed with him because, clearly, I am not to be trusted where he's concerned. I lose my head and my better sense whenever I'm around him. He short-circuits my brain, and I become someone I'm not. Someone who gets themselves into a hell of a lot of trouble.

So that's how I'll survive the in-between. By avoiding him whenever possible. By not sleeping with him in any fashion. No more slip-ups. No more giving in to temptation. Sane, rational Sorel is leading this charge once again, and she will not be side-tracked. I am steadfast. I am resolute. From now on, I will only make smart choices for myself.

With that solid plan and mental declaration, I stand and finish showering. I put on the least sexy thing I brought with me—joggers and my old college T-shirt—brush my hair, forgo makeup, and go in search of the food Mason promised me. I find him sitting on the table he fucked me on earlier with a spread of food Henry the Eighth would drool over. As it is, my stomach growls loudly. He has the television on to some sports network without the sound but with the subtitles going.

I've never thought much about Mason's hearing deficit, but I have seen him on occasion wear his hearing aids, and whenever I've been at his place and the TV is on, so are subtitles.

"Another picnic?" I question as I climb up onto the table to join him.

Using chopsticks, he slides some noodles from a container into his mouth, his lips coated with a small sheen of grease. He turns to me almost apologetically. "I felt like Henry the Eighth sitting in one of the chairs with all this food before me."

I blink at him, a little taken aback that I thought nearly the same thing.

"Help yourself," he continues without missing a beat. "I went a little overboard. That's what happens when you let a football player order when he's hungry." He points to a few boxes on his left with the chopsticks, going over them one by one. "Tacos, pizza, Asian fusion, truffle fries that are some of the best I've ever had, some kind of zucchini and corn fritter with pulled chicken on it, a salad with steak that I already ate half of, a spicy lobster pasta thing that looks and smells amazing that I thought you'd like, and dessert." He smirks. "I got a lot of desserts."

I grab a rolled-up fabric napkin and unravel it so I can get to a fork. Mason has plates out, but I'm still stuck on the lobster pasta and pick up the container to set it on my lap on top of the napkin.

"How did you know I'd like this?" I remove the plastic lid and inhale the garlic, herbs and spices. Yum.

He shrugs, slurping more noodles into his mouth with his attention back on the television. "I remember you ordered something similar once when we went out."

"You do?" The words slip past my lips before I can stop them.

His eyes shoot back to mine. "Yes." He flashes down to the pasta on my lap and then back up at me. "Was I wrong? Bad choice?"

I shake my head, at a loss for words. Brody would never have known what to order for me and I lived with him for almost two years. "No. It's perfect. Thank you for getting it for me. It's exactly what I would have ordered for myself given a menu."

Another shrug. "Cool. Good. Eat up. Once I started, I couldn't stop. I think I have a touch of a hangover stomach. I never eat like this." He chuckles. "I'll regret it in about an hour, but right now, it's all so good I even plan to indulge in the peanut butter and chocolate cheesecake that's in there."

That catches my attention. "Peanut butter and chocolate cheesecake?"

He smirks, licking the grease from his lips. "Yup."

"And what if I want that?"

"I'll fight you for it. That's how badly I want it."

I haven't even taken a bite of my pasta yet, but now the threat is there. I cover the pasta and set it aside. He sets the container with his noodles down, the chopsticks sticking out of the open lid. The glimmer in his eyes and the challenge on his face gets my heart racing. I look at the only bag on the table. The one he indicated when he mentioned dessert.

"No way you're faster than me, princess."

I cock an eyebrow. "Care to place a wager on it, baller?"

"Always."

I reach for his chopsticks, scoop up a mountain of noodles, and shove them in my mouth. I'm starving, and they looked really good, but I'm also distracting him. "Oh, those are delicious." Now I'm distracted. They're spicy and garlicky and crunch with pieces of peanuts.

"Now you know why I was eating them."

"Here." I splice a slippery bunch of noodles and feed them to him. Just as he opens for me, I shove the noodles in his mouth, drop the chopsticks, spin around, and go for the bag.

"No fair!" he bellows around a mouthful of noodles that he's trying to chew at the same time he's trying to stop me. He grabs my foot, yanks me back, and I kick at him, missing but shirking his grip. "That cheesecake is mine."

"Not if I get to it first." I scramble down the table on my hands and knees, nudging to-go containers out of my way. My hand wraps around the handle of the bag at the same time he gets a handful of brown paper. Bastard got off the table and ran, which gave him an unexpected advantage. "Let go!"

"Not gonna happen, princess. That cheesecake is mine. You can have the crème brûlée and cookies."

"Crème brûlée and cookies are for pussies who lose."

"Agreed, which is why you'll be the one eating them and not me."

Both of us tug back and forth on the bag, the paper crinkling as it rustles on the table with our struggle. Frustrated, he plants a large hand on my chest and pushes me back with his freakishly strong muscles.

"Ah! Hands off! That's cheating." I jerk the bag hard in my direction while trying to extricate his hand, and the bag tears in the process. Containers filled with various desserts spill out onto the table, scattering around us. I dive for the one that looks like cheesecake and snatch it away, nearly toppling off the table in the process.

I right myself—but just barely—and gleam in victory at him.

He rolls his eyes dismissively and folds his arms. "Fine. You want it that badly, you can have it."

"Oh, I want it. If you're a good boy, maybe I'll share a bite with you. Maybe." I pop the top, dip my finger in a dollop of whipped cream, and lick it clean. "Mmm. This is so good. Maybe I won't share it with you after all." I smirk and bat my eyelashes tauntingly at him. "Enjoy the cookies and crème brûlée."

"Now you're the one not fighting fair." His eyes darken, but a mischievous smirk is starting to curl on his lips. One I don't like. "You've got one problem, princess."

I narrow my eyes. "What's that?"

"Your fork is all the way down there." He points to his left, and I glance down at the end of the absurdly long table. Crap. He's right.

"What the hell?" I snap when the container is ripped from my hand. "Bastard! That's cheating."

He jumps back when I swipe at him, making my hand catch nothing but air. With his eyes on mine, he sticks his tongue out and licks some whipped cream. Holy wow, that was unexpectedly sexy. Especially since I know just how good that tongue is in action.

"I licked it, so now it's mine. You don't like it," he plays, his voice low and seductive. "Come and take it from me."

I squint. "Not everything you lick is yours."

He smirks, and his gaze shifts to the band I'm still wearing on my left hand. "I beg to differ."

I slide off the table and stand before him. "Now I don't want it anymore. In fact, I have a better idea." I take two fingers, smear them into the cheesecake, and smash it across his lips and chin. "There. That's for being a dirty cheat."

I suck my messy fingers into my mouth and watch as he licks his lips and uses his thumb to wipe the rest off before he licks it clean. "I'm all for playing dirty with you, princess. That move you just did there is going to cost you."

I shake my head and start to run when he stops me mid-stride by banding an arm around my waist. He spins me around, and somehow I end up with my back on the table and him leaning over me. We're both breathing hard, and his eyes are molten fire as he holds me down with his weight. The thick, hard ridge of his cock digs into my thigh, making my breath hitch.

I try not to squirm or bite my lip or show any sort of reaction to being in this position with him and feeling him so turned on. It's nearly impossible. As it is, my traitorous nipples are sharper than pins, and my empty core clenches almost painfully. I hate how sexy he is, and I wish I could go back to a time when I wasn't so aware of it.

Wordlessly, he swivels a finger in the cheesecake, and when he lifts it, it's covered in peanut butter cake and chocolate. He paints my lips with it, tit-for-tat, and I lick them as he goes, catching his finger in the process. He hisses out a wounded breath, and I suck his finger between my lips and massage it against my tongue. Reflexively, I lick it, sucking him deeper, grinning around him, because I know I've got him now.

"You keep doing that, and I'm going to fuck your pretty mouth *and* your sweet pussy. No more games. That's not a threat. It's a promise." He grinds his cock into me, rubbing it up and down along my hip, letting me feel him. "Tell me no. I dare you."

I need to stop. I told him no more sex, and I meant it. I did. I have a plan I need to stick with. But I didn't know that last time was the last time. And we're still here in Vegas. Our flight home isn't until tomorrow morning. What's the harm in one last night? Tomorrow it'll be a new situation for us. One I will stick to.

"No. But I dare you to do something about that."

His gaze grows dark. Sinister.

He rips my shirt up and over my head, clearly already aware I wasn't wearing a bra, and with his hooded eyes locked on mine, he dips his finger back in the container, gathers chocolate sauce and whipped cream, and circles it all over my nipples. I gasp at the cold wetness, already so keyed up I can no longer help but squirm against him, needing friction, needing... *something.*

"Looks like you need to get cleaned up again, princess." He takes both of my wrists in one of his hands and locks them above my head. With his weight on me and my arms pinned, I'm completely at his mercy. And from the look of him, he has every intention of keeping me that way. Right now, I don't have the strength or desire to stop him.

"One last time. One last night."

His mouth captures my nipple, then licks the chocolate and whipped cream up before he sucks it deep into his mouth and releases it with a wet pop. "Is that another dare?"

12

MASON

With her wrists held tight in one hand, I use the other to rip her joggers and panties down her legs. My shorts and boxer briefs follow, pooling around my ankles, and I kick one of my legs free. We didn't even make it an hour together before we're at each other, and if she thinks this is the last time we're doing this, she's nuts.

Nothing that feels this good and this right should end.

I don't linger on any of that. The details and bullshit lines she's manifested in her head can chill out for a little while longer. I'm not going anywhere.

I lick my fingers, only to think better of it, and shove them in her mouth to do that job for me. "Get me nice and clean, princess. I want to put these inside your pussy."

Her eyes flare, and I can see she wants to fight me more, but she also wants me to use them to fuck her, so like a good girl, she does as I ask her to. For once. It's going to be months of offense and defense with her. Trick plays and quarterback sneaks.

My fingers slip from her mouth, and I immediately push

them inside of her. Her back arches against me, and she hikes her legs up until her feet are on the edge of the table.

Even better.

I shift between her thighs and bring my face inches from hers, so I can watch her as I finger fuck her. She's so pretty. So fucking pretty I can hardly stand it.

And I tell her that just to watch her reaction when I say, "My wife is so beautiful. Absolutely stunning. Whether you're beneath me or on top of me or simply across the room. I could watch you watching paint dry, and I still wouldn't be bored looking at you. But you're especially exquisite when you're getting fucked by me."

Her face pinches up, and she turns her head to the side. "Don't. Please don't."

I smirk. "What? Tell you the truth? I thought you liked my honesty."

"Mason—"

I suck her lip into my mouth and kiss her because I don't want to hear it. Not the protest she was about to spew or that this is whatever it is she's turning it into.

Right now, she's my wife. And that's all I care about.

To punctuate that I'm the one in control and not her, I remove my fingers from inside her and use my cock instead, gliding it up and down her wet cunt from her opening up to her clit and back. I dip inside her a little, barely enough, but she writhes and whimpers into me, moving and shifting to try to force me deeper.

"Not yet, my impatient little princess."

I want her to start to come so I can fuck her as she's coming and then fuck her into another orgasm. Because no one has made her come the way I do. And that's how it's going to stay.

I slide against her, rubbing my cock faster, hitting her firm clit with every pass, and massaging the head of my cock against it just to get her there a little faster. She's warm and so wet, and her full, soft tits are pressed against my chest and I'm kissing her. It's goddamn heaven. So sweet and incredible and intoxicating. Just like her.

"Christ, you feel good," I mumble against her lips. "You have me so wet, I bet my cock could slip right into your ass."

She moans. and her eyes pinch tighter as she gets closer. I wonder if she's ever done that before. If she likes it as much as I think she would.

"Do you want that? Me in your ass?"

She pants against my lips, balls her hands still held by mine into fists, and shakes her head no. She does. She just doesn't want to get that intimate, though what we've already done is about as intimate as it gets.

Fine. That can wait.

Her pussy quivers around my cock, her body growing tense and jerky, and I up my pace, focusing on her clit with the head of my cock.

"Oh!" Her back bows and her hands thrash against my grip as she starts to come all over my cock. Perfect. With her like this, I slam straight into her, wrenching a scream from her lungs. "Fuck! Mason!"

That's it. That's what I was after.

I start pounding into her, holding her down, rubbing my pubic bone against her clit, and setting a relentless pace. She's thrashing against me, trying to fuck me back, but it's nearly impossible with how hard she's coming right now. And fuck is it tight. Such a snug fit as her pussy works my cock.

I fuck her through her orgasm, keeping the same brutalizing pace. Honestly, it feels too good to stop or slow down, I'm not sure I even can. Didn't I say this from the start? I was going to fuck her until I left the imprint of myself inside her. Until I'm all she can feel and remember. She will be sore after this. I know she will be. I'm not being gentle.

I'm punishing her. Punishing her for stopping and ignoring all that we could have.

It's with that thought in mind that I take my other hand that's been on her hip and bring it up to her throat. Her eyes burst open when she feels the collar I'm placing on her, and I stare down at her, holding her wrists above her head and her throat in my hand as I fuck her into next week. I test the waters, giving her neck a little squeeze, and her eyes roll back in her head as she emits a breathy cry.

Well then.

It seems we've uncovered yet another kink.

She likes the idea of being watched, of being caught, and it seems she also likes it when I take from her and choke her.

Mindful of her breathing, I continue to apply pressure to her neck as I pound into her with hard, deep strokes. Sweat tickles my brow, and I wish I weren't wearing my shirt so I could feel her skin against mine, but at the moment, my hands are too busy to remove it. That'll come later. That'll be for rounds two through fifty or until my dick falls off, whichever comes first. She told me I have tonight, which means neither of us is sleeping anytime soon.

I fuck her straight into another orgasm, and the moment I feel her start to spasm around me and see the euphoria on her face, I let go and explode inside of her, coming harder than I think I ever have.

The moment my forehead meets her chest, I release her wrists and neck and pull her against me so I can drag both of us to the floor. Her weight feels good in my arms, and I hold her close, not letting go even when she starts to squirm.

"You told me I had tonight," I remind her.

"And we shouldn't have done that." She sighs. "I'm sending mixed signals. I know I am. I get swept up in the moment and then the after hits me, and I don't know what to do with it."

"Stop overthinking it, Sorel. You already laid your rules

down before me. We have tonight. Reality can come back to us tomorrow. Okay?" I pull away from her neck and meet her face. "Okay?" I ask again because she still looks uncertain.

She swallows and nods. "Okay." Then she laughs. "I need to get cleaned up again. And freaking eat dinner."

I smile and kiss the tip of her nose, then help us both to stand. We get dressed, and she runs off to use the restroom before she returns with a sweet smile and climbs back up on the table. She digs into her pasta with gusto, and we talk about her work and even mine.

Much to my surprise, after she's done eating and we've cleaned up our mess, she snuggles with me on the sofa as I put on some chick flick that would make Katy proud.

"You didn't have to put this on."

I tilt my head to meet her gaze, my brow pinched. "What do you mean?"

"It's a chick flick." She points to the screen as she shifts deeper into the sofa.

I squint at her. "So?"

"So you don't have to put that on to impress me. I'd watch almost anything."

I sit up a little straighter. "Do you like this movie? Have you seen it?"

She shakes her head. "No."

"Would you like to?"

She shrugs. "I mean, sure, but you don't have to put it on for me. I get that it's not really a guy movie. We can watch something else. Sports are fine if that's what you'd rather go with."

Wow. Her ex is a real piece of shit. I don't think she realizes what she's saying or doing. It's not being kind or considerate. It's putting herself second because she's too worried about pleasing me. I think back and realize we've never just hung out at my place to watch anything. When we've hung out, we mostly talked and ate food and even tried to kick each other's asses at Trivial Pursuit and Scrabble, but I don't think in the year we've been friends that we've ever simply watched a movie or TV together other than what was on in the background.

I wish I had known about this sooner.

"I'm going to assume Brody never watched these types of movies with you."

She flushes ever so slightly. "No. They're not his thing."

"So you always watched what he wanted to watch and he never reciprocated?"

She looks away, but the answer is obvious. Yeah, I should have punched him when I had the chance. What a selfish asshole. Half the fun of watching movies like these is snuggling up with your woman and watching her smile and laugh and then showing her how you can fuck her better than the hero in the movie fucks his girl. Fool didn't understand the assignment.

"Sorel, I want to watch this movie with you. It's a good one, and I think you'll enjoy it."

She rolls her eyes at me. "Oh, and you've seen it?" Her sarcasm makes me chuckle.

I hold in my smug grin. "Yep. I can even tell you the ending, though you can probably guess on your own since it's a bit formulaic and predictable." I hold up a hand. "Not that I have anything against that."

She stares at me as if such a thing is entirely unheard of by the male species.

"Katy and I have a standing date when we can make it work," I explain. "At least once a month we hang out and watch a movie together at my place or hers. It gives me time to see baby Willow, which is always a bonus, and Katy has this thing where she doesn't like swearing in front of the baby. With that, we watch classics, chick flicks, or cute rom-coms. I've sort of gotten into them."

Sorel does a slow, owl blink at me, her lips parted slightly as if she doesn't know what to do with that information.

"For real? How did I not know this?"

I wrap my arm around her and snuggle her in close. "I don't know. We don't advertise it much because we don't want others jumping in on our movie sessions, which they would have, along with their opinions about what to watch. We're very specific. Now enjoy the fun of watching a chick flick with a guy who likes touching you and making you come."

She places a soft kiss on my neck and rests her head on my shoulder as we curl up, and the movie starts. This is perfection. This is everything I wanted. *Everything*. And in a few short hours, I'm going to lose it all.

Tomorrow is going to suck.

13

SOREL

The plane starts to descend into Boston, and my stomach lifts like I'm flying down a rollercoaster. It's not just the plane doing that. It's what's waiting for me at home that's leading that charge.

Me: I need to come to your apartment and gather the rest of my things.

Brody: Oh, are you unblocking and speaking to me now?

Me: Only until I get my stuff. Then I'm blocking you again.

Brody: Real mature, Sorel. In fact, that's how you've been through all of this.

Is he kidding me with that?

Me: You want to talk maturity? How about when you're in a monogamous relationship, you're actually monogamous?

Brody: I get that you're hurt, and I know I fucked up, but I meant what I said to you. I love you. I never loved Eloise. It wasn't like that between us. It was purely physical. She's not who I want. You are. And instead of talking to me about it, you read those texts during our wedding and then ran off with Reyes. And then FUCKING MARRIED HIM!

Me: What are you upset about? Getting caught, losing me, or being publicly embarrassed by me getting married? Because if I had to guess, I'd say it's the latter.

Brody: When are you returning home?

I smirk. Gotcha there, didn't I? Though I am remiss to admit that getting married to Mason as a fuck you was immature. What can I say? I wasn't of sound mind or body, and I'm certainly not the first person to do something dumb when they're drunk. But I never would have been there in that position if it wasn't for Brody's cheating. And the fact that he's not taking any responsibility for any of this is so telling.

Everything in our relationship was about him. It was me making concession after concession. I know I have culpability in that. I allowed it to happen. I didn't see it for what it was. I thought because I loved him, that's just what you do. But you only make those sacrifices if your partner does too. Mason sort of threw that in my face last night, but he wasn't wrong.

And Brody never did that with me. Not once.

Me: My flight is landing now.

Brody: Then come and get your stuff after you land.

Me: Will you be there?

Brody: I haven't decided yet. I'm not sure I'm ready to see you after what you did.

Me: Good. Same goes for me. If you give me two hours, it'll be like I never lived there.

"Why do you look like you're about to crack a molar?"

"Huh?" I start. Mason had been asleep. He kept me up half the night with a lot of hot, dirty sex. Today that's all done with and Operation Three Months Until Annulment begins.

He sits up with a yawn and rubs at the top of his hair. Shifting toward the window, he glances out, noting that we've started our descent. "I can see your jaw clenching from here."

"Oh. I was texting with Brody. I need to get my things from him."

Now Mason's jaw clenches, and he gives an absent nod. "I'll go with you."

I shake my head. "Serena is picking me up, and we're going to do that together. She returns to Paris in a few days, and I want to spend time with her. Plus, I'm not looking for you to get arrested or mess up your throwing hand." I raise a pointed eyebrow at him.

He leans forward and drops his elbows on his thighs. "One, it'd be worth messing up my hand for. Two, I don't want you to see him. Three, I get that you want time with your sister before she goes back to Paris, but you're still moving in with me."

I mimic his pose, putting us closer together but still far enough apart with the thin table between us. "One, I don't need you to fight my battles for me, though I do think it's sweet and even a little sexy that you would. Two, I don't want to see him either, and from the sound of his last text, he's in the same boat with me, so I don't think it'll be an issue. Three, I know I'm still moving in with you, but if you think that means you get to call the shots with me and tell me what I can and cannot do, you've got another thing coming."

He smirks at me. Freaking smirks. And his eyes wander all over me in a way I've grown familiar with over the last few days.

"Okay."

My eyes bulge. "Okay?" I laugh incredulously. "That's not what I thought you were going to say."

"Would you like me to put up more of a fight? I can. Hell, I'm dying to. You already know how much I love picking you up, tossing you over my shoulder, and taking you how I want you. But you're telling me you've got this, and I believe you."

"You do?" I squeak. That's how shocked I am.

"I do. I may not like it. I may want to jump all over it and call the shots as I do with everything else, but that's not what you need from me right now. That said, I definitely want to kick his ass because he deserves it and then some, and if the opportunity presents itself, I still might. But okay. Do what you have to do, and if you need me, I'm here."

I don't know why he is, though. I don't know what he's getting out of this. It doesn't make sense to me, but I don't want to question it either. I can't figure out Mason's angle, and I don't want to be distrustful of that. Mason feels like a gift I didn't know I deserved. Is this what real friendship is? It's terrifying and a lot annoying that I automatically question and distrust his intentions.

Except I think Mason is honest. I think he's the real deal.

He's younger than me. He's cocky and arrogant and sexy as sin. On the surface, he's everything I should stay away from. And I plan to. More because I'm not ready for anything else with anyone new, and that's not what he's after either, but who he is on the inside makes it easy to see him as more when seeing him as more isn't an option.

"But remember this," he continues. "You and I are undeniably married, and that makes you my wife and not his. You gave me the rule of no sex and not sleeping in my bed. My rule is no Brody. Or anyone else."

Hmm. I sit back and fold my arms over my chest, ignoring the flutter I feel there. "Are you being territorial?"

"Damn right I am."

"Does that rule extend to you?"

"No Brody? He's not exactly my type. But his ex-fiancée definitely is."

"Stop flirting and answer me."

He stares straight into my eyes. "No one else."

I shouldn't care and I shouldn't feel relief from that answer, but I do.

"Any other rules you have?" I ask.

He rubs at the back of his head and shrugs, the gesture

making the muscles in his arms bunch in an annoyingly hot way. "Not that I can think of. You?"

"No."

"You understand the press might stalk my building for a bit and follow us around. We have to appear like a couple. At least a couple trying to make something new work."

"Yes. I know. I'll manage even if the press is my least favorite thing."

"How have you survived as a Fritz this long without them up your ass?"

"I'm boring. I don't know." I throw a cocktail napkin at him, making him chuckle. "Don't look at me like that. I am."

He shakes his head. "See, there I beg to differ. I've spent the last year hanging out with you and the forty-eight hours with you in several ways and in several positions. You're not boring, princess."

"Ugh. You and your sexy sex."

"Nothing wrong with sexy sex. It's my favorite kind."

Mine too, but it's also a troublemaker.

"I think you just need to get out of that mindset of labeling yourself as boring or uptight or however you like to frame yourself that isn't necessarily positive. You can just be you without the labels, especially if you teach yourself to shrug off the fear that's holding you back. You were close there for a moment, and then someone leaking one photo set you back a bit."

I ignore what he's saying because I can't with that. I just can't. He's too perceptive, but he doesn't get it. He's twenty-eight. A football player. His life is so different from mine. Though I can't help the tickle in the back of my throat his words provoke. Especially the part about being afraid.

Can you blame me? springs to my mind. Being quiet, being boring, being an introvert is safe, and safe is comfortable.

"To answer your original, non-sexually provocative question, I've been photographed with my family before. Especially at Abbot-Fritz events. You know this. You were in one with me a few months ago. That comes with being a Fritz." I swallow as my ears pop. We're close. The city is right outside the window. "I love my family and I love supporting them, but we're famous because we're billionaires, and that's a crappy reason to be famous in my opinion. Nothing good comes from people solely having an interest in you because you're rich. At least that's my experience. It's easy to stay away from the limelight, especially when Serena is your twin. She loves wearing couture she designs, being quoted in fashion magazines, and having her picture taken every chance she gets."

"I'm shocked Brody didn't go for her with all of that."

The way he says that makes my stomach churn if for no other reason than what he's implying is something I've already considered. Brody was only with me because I'm a Fritz. Because my family is next-level wealthy and famous, and with that, we have pull and connections. Pull and connections he wanted to utilize for his career.

He asked if I could pull strings for him. He asked if I could get him interviews with top network executives. I did a couple of times as my uncle Kaplan's wife, Bianca, has a lot of friends and acquaintances in that world through the Abbot-Fritz charity she runs for us. I never thought much about it and didn't hesitate to help him whenever I could.

"When I met Brody, Serena was with me. And so was her boyfriend of the moment. She also lives in Paris and has no plans to return to the States anytime soon other than for trips. Eloise and her fiancé introduced me to him at one of the Abbot-Fritz events, since her fiancé was friends with him." I laugh. It's bitter. "Think of that. Eloise's fiancé was friends with Brody, and she introduced me to him and it's possible they were already fucking each other."

"He's a dirtbag, and so is she. They deserve each other, and I'm glad you didn't marry him."

Mason's not very good at keeping the vitriol out of his voice when he says that.

I grin. "Me too."

His eyes linger on me with something unspoken behind them. Something I'm not sure I'm reading right. Something that almost looks like, *I'm glad you married me instead*, but that can't be right.

The plane lands, and the moment it comes to a stop and the doors open, we both stand and stretch. It was a long flight home. Serena is over by the entrance of the private terminal, and she's not alone. Wren and Tinsley are flanking her, waving at us.

"She brought back up," I muse because Wren and Tinsley are scrappy, and between the three of them, they take zero shit from anyone.

Mason climbs down the narrow ladder to the ground and turns to offer me his hand to help me do the same. We retrieve our bags and exit through the terminal to greet them. Immediately, the three of them envelop me in hugs that already make me feel better.

"We have it all worked out. We're all going with you to Brody's," Tinsley explains. "And then I'll drive you back to our building and act as a bit of a cover."

For a moment, I scrunch my nose only to remember that Mason and Stone are neighbors, which means that he and Tinsley are now my neighbors too. Even if just temporarily.

"I take it the press are hanging out once again in front of our building?" Mason questions.

"Yep," Tinsley tells him. "But we're on it. We've got it all covered."

"Excellent. I'm going to meet Stone for a run. That should be fun, but it'll be yet another diversion, so you should be fine getting into the building, especially if you go through the garage."

I reach up on my toes and wrap my arms around him. I don't even care about the spectators. He deserves a hug. He deserves a lot more than a hug, but right now, a hug is all I can give him. He hugs me back, though I can feel the question in his slightly stiff posture.

"Thank you, Mason. Thank you for being in the right place at the right time. Thank you for taking me to Vegas and for saying no and then saying yes. Thank you for not being a jerk when the shit hit the fan and messed up your life because of me. Thank you for getting me through what could have easily been one of the worst forty-eight hours of my life. Just thank you. For everything."

He plants a tender kiss on my neck. "Mrs. Fritz-Reyes, I'm starting to realize there isn't anything I wouldn't do for you."

I step back, ignoring, well, all of that. "Let's go get this over with," I tell the girls.

"Remember what I said about Brody," Mason reminds me, shifting his weight and appearing edgy as he cracks his knuckles. "Or, you know, I could come too."

I shake my head. "I've got this. Remember?"

He sighs, visibly unhappy about that, but finally, he steps back. "Okay."

I climb into Tinsley's car. Time to end things with Brody once and for all.

14

SOREL

"I feel like we're breaking in and stealing." Serena is all smiles as we climb the stairs to the apartment I shared with Brody.

I start to sing the first few lines of "The Old Apartment" by Barenaked Ladies, making everyone giggle. "I have the key, he knows I'm coming, and it's my stuff we're getting."

"Don't ruin this for me with your level-headed approach, Sorel."

"We should totally go all gangbusters on his stuff," Wren suggests. "My mom did that when she discovered her fiancé was cheating on her."

I smirk at her. "When I saw his press conferences, that was the first thought that went through my head. How I wished I had pulled a Carrie Underwood on him."

"I think marrying Mason was sort of that move," Tinsley offers smugly. "That was way better than trashing his stuff. It was the chef's kiss after the mic drop at the wedding."

"I still feel weird that I did that in the first place. None of it was really me."

"Or maybe it was you. Did you ever consider that?" Serena cocks an eyebrow at me.

"Have you been talking to my husband?" I quip only to freeze, and everyone else freezes along with me. My hand claps over my mouth, and I stare at my sister with wide, unblinking eyes.

"Did you just..."

I nod at Tinsley. "I think I did."

Wren snorts out a laugh. "Sorel and Mason, sitting in a tree. K-I-S-S-I-N-G. First comes marriage—oh wait, that's not how that goes."

"Shut up." I laugh, smacking her arm. "No more of that. It was a slipup. He's been calling me his wife. I'm sure that's the only reason I said it. Now let's get my stuff and get the hell out of here."

I can feel the women behind me exchanging looks, but I push on and continue up the steps to the landing and then over to the apartment. Using my key, I unlock the door and cautiously open it. Everything looks the same as it did when I left here two days ago. Well, minus the pile of dishes in the sink and the pizza box half-open on the counter.

I glance around, my ears searching, but I don't hear anything. Thank God. He left like he said he might. I sag in relief, not realizing how tense I was.

Blowing out a breath, I shut the door behind us. "I have two suitcases that are mine in the hall closet. Let's grab those, and anything you think might be mine, toss it in. None of the furniture is mine. Only my clothes, books, CDs, and some trinkets."

We set to work, but when I enter the bedroom, I scream at the top of my lungs when I find Brody silently sitting on the edge of the bed, his head in his hands. I fall back against the door, my hand over my racing heart, and everyone comes flying in.

Brody slowly raises his head, and I note the large purple welt around his eye. My dad got a good hit in.

Serena grabs my forearm, and I know she's looking at me to see what I want to do, but I can't take my eyes off him. He looks like shit. I should feel relief in that, but I'm not sure I do. This is all about him feeling sorry for himself. It has nothing to do with me at all.

"Hey, Brody," Wren calls out to him. "I hope you get C. diff and neurosyphilis."

Serena snorts out a laugh. "Actually, I hope his dick shrivels up and falls off. That's more poetic justice, in my opinion."

"Sorel?" Tinsley questions.

"I'm fine," I tell them. "Would you mind giving us a few minutes?"

"You're sure?" Serena checks.

"Positive."

They leave the bedroom, and I hear the front door open and close a minute later. Brody's gaze snags on my left hand hanging by my side, and his expression immediately hardens.

"Are they real?"

I nod, and he blows out a breathy chuckle, utterly incredulous. "He bought you real diamonds for a fake marriage. Fucking asshole. He did that to spite me."

See what I mean? All about him.

It's funny, looking at him now, I'm not sure what I ever saw in him to begin with. It's amazing how you can finally see someone's true colors after they hurt you but are blind or make excuses for them until that happens.

"You didn't enter into his thoughts at all. Mason did what he did for me because he's my friend and not to spite you. That's why *I* did it." I fold my arms and lean farther against the wall. "How long have you and Eloise been a thing?"

He practically snarls at that question. "We were never a thing."

I hold up a consolatory hand. "My apologies. How long have the two of you been fucking?"

He drags a hand across his face and winces ever so slightly as he says, "On and off for about three or so years."

It's a slapshot to the chest. I knew it. I mean, I didn't know the full length of time, but I figured it was the entire time he and I were together. But to hear it confirmed isn't pleasant. Eloise and I were as close as anyone. Her callousness is gut-wrenching.

I clear my throat and the sting of that along with it. "Were there others?"

"Sorel—"

"Answer me. The truth."

He swallows thickly. "One or two here or there, but nothing more than one time each."

Wow. It's a good thing I got tested at my annual a week before the wedding and haven't slept with him since. Who knows what he could have given me?

"Got it. Thanks for clarifying that for me. I officially hate you more than I already did, and now any guilt I felt over my master class fuck you is gone."

"Do you know how difficult this is for me?" he questions, and I want to laugh at his statement's pure selfishness and irony but refrain. "You discover I've been screwing around, and instead of coming to me and hearing the truth about it, you splatter it in front of all our family and friends and then not only run out on our wedding but off to Vegas with fucking Mason Reyes, of all people, and marry him. What am I supposed to do with that, Sorel?"

"How do you think me coming to you and learning 'the truth,'" I put air quotes around that, "as you put it, would have changed anything?"

"Because it was just sex!" he yells, throwing his hands up in frustration as if I'm missing the key issue here and being overly dramatic and emotional about the situation. "Just sex and nothing more. Meaningless."

"Meaningless to you." I point at him and refold my arms. "You having sex with my friend *the entire time we were together* and then one or two others isn't meaningless to me. Hell, if it only happened once, we'd still have this outcome. Did that ever occur to you? I mean, it must have since you both went to great lengths to hide it, but how you think explaining that you were simply fucking her and not in love with her changes anything is beyond me. I'd almost feel better if you were in love with her. At least then your infidelity would have a purpose I could wrap my head around. You telling me it was meaningless sex to you hurts more because that means you didn't care enough about me to stop it."

He growls under his breath and stands, his arms shooting out wide. "How much are you going to punish me over this? I fucked up. I'm sorry. Let me make it up to you. That's what all the guys on my team do with their wives, and they forgive them."

Ah. That's why he doesn't get my reaction. "You mean I should ask you to buy me a big diamond or something to make up for it?" I squint at him. "Do you even know me at all?"

"You should at least think about trying to forgive me. I forgive you, and what you did is so much worse."

"Worse than screwing around on me with my friend and random strangers?" I stare, disbelieving. Is he high? How could anyone think that?

"Right," he scoffs derisively. "And you didn't fuck Reyes. Someone you know I hate."

"You and I weren't together when that happened. In fact, I had every right to fuck him since he's now my husband."

It's a low blow, and it hits him hard.

"You ruined my life," he barks, his hands going to the top of his head, his expression distraught. "You took everything from me. I had a shot with a network in New York, and now they tell me they're no longer interested. That was my dream job. The future I had mapped out for us. Now I have no choice but to take a low-level coaching position with my former team."

"Um, boo-hoo for you? I think you're missing the point here, Tiger. *I* didn't ruin anything for you. You dicking around on me and still going to marry me is what ruined it. You mouthing off to the press and lying about your phone being hacked and it all being a misunderstanding is what ruined it. You thought I'd never find out because you're an arrogant, spoiled son of a bitch. But I did, and with that, I showed the world who you are. That's what you don't like."

He shakes his head. "Jesus, Sorel. Do you not get it? I love you. I love you so much. I'm in agony here. I never wanted this for us. I don't care about Eloise. I'll never see her again. Not ever. And I'll never touch another woman again either if you give me another chance. I don't even care that you married Reyes. That's bullshit revenge, and I know it. The world knows it too. What you and I have is real."

At the mention of Mason, his rule about no Brody pops into my head. Oddly, I feel like I'm betraying him, but I'm not. There is no Brody to me anymore. This is simply the business of ending something.

"No. What you and I had was not real." I push away from the wall and stand before him, telling him the truth we both need to hear. "I'm not sure it ever was. How could it have been when you were doing that with my friend and keeping it from me? It's more than the sex. That's what I don't think you realize. Real relationships are built on honesty, trust, and communication. We didn't have any of those things. I just didn't know it until it was almost too late."

"That's not how it was for me. I was... I don't know." His hands fall heavily to his sides. "I was scared by what we had. It came on so fast and so strong. I didn't know how to stop it, nor did I want to. I wanted you like I'd never wanted anyone else, but I panicked. You were my first serious relationship, and the thought of forever with one woman seemed daunting. It doesn't anymore, though. Not even close now that I know what it feels like to lose you. I'm so sorry. I regret what I did and how I treated you. You deserved better than that, but you got your revenge. We're even now."

Are we though? I'm not so sold on that. Regardless, he's not someone I want to go back to.

He breathes out a heavy breath when I don't say anything in response. "I'm moving back to New York. The Thunder offered me a defensive secondary coaching position."

I nod. "I gathered that."

"I want you to come with me. We can start over. I'll be a better guy for you."

"No, thanks."

He grits his teeth and charges toward me. His hands meet my shoulders, but his touch feels like acid on my skin, and I shirk it. "Just like that, you quit? That's not who you are."

"Do you know who I am?" I repeat because the first time it was rhetorical, but suddenly, I'm realizing I don't think he does. Mason has said stuff. Serena has said stuff. And I've blown them off because that's easier and safer and there's less fear involved with it. But did Brody ever know me? Did he ever see me? Or did I become someone he wanted me to be?

"I thought I did. I thought you were the woman of my dreams. Sweet and kind and patient and endlessly giving. You laughed at my corny jokes and didn't care whether I was a football player, a broadcaster, or anything else. None of that mattered to you."

"It still doesn't. But while I was endlessly giving of myself to you, you weren't endlessly giving of yourself in return. It was all about you, Brody, and I let it happen for reasons I can't even figure out now."

"That's not fair. You don't make it easy. Eloise was easy. She told me her thoughts. I didn't have to try to figure them out or piece together an unsolvable puzzle. What I saw with her is what I got. With you, it wasn't that way. You don't trust anyone enough to fully let go with them. Do you know how frustrating that is?"

I swallow thickly, emotion thickening my throat and burning my eyes as I fight it back. He's not wrong on that. Considering I was betrayed by my best friend in high school and then again by him and Eloise, can you blame me?

"That's not an excuse. Why should I have trusted you with my thoughts and feelings when you were betraying me the entire time?"

His expression crumbles. "I know I blew it. I know I did. Just..." He pauses. Pants out a breath. "Think about my offer. Please. Just please think about it, Sorel. Don't automatically dismiss it. I love you, and I want you to come back to New York with me." His eyes search mine, and he takes a step back. "I'll go so you can get your stuff, but you should know, I'm offering you a future. The one we both talked about and wanted. One with just us. I'll only focus on you and where we want our lives to go."

I don't know what to say that I haven't already, so I stay silent, a bit thunderstruck by it all.

He kisses the corner of my lips. "Think about it." Then he leaves and walks out of the apartment with a hard click of the door. I've heard of couples reconciling after infidelity. I've heard about that sort of forgiveness. I'm just not sure I have it in me. How could I ever trust him? Do I even want to try?

I have no compelling voice in my gut telling me to run after him or pull a *Notebook* moment where I yell and kiss him, and he lifts me into his arms despite the fact that I'm married to someone else. Though I think she was only engaged to the other dude and not married.

Whatever. You get my meaning here.

There are no letters written every day since I left him, and no house he constructed just for me. There are only his words, and his words don't hold a lot of merit. He's a cheater. A liar. A user.

I go for the suitcases and straight into my closet. I text Serena, and a few minutes later, I hear the door open and the ladies stay in the other room. They give me space. My sister knows me well.

Packing up my things is bittersweet. I thought by thirty-five I would have it all figured out. I thought I'd have the perfect guy and the perfect job and the perfect life and maybe be pregnant with a kid or two. Nothing is going as I planned, and I'm not sure how to pivot.

Ugh. Now I feel like Ross with the couch from *Friends*.

I take my time and go through the place. If he's moving back to New York, then this is likely my last chance to get everything that's mine. Thankfully, my ladies do their job. We get my stuff together, and in under an hour, everything is packed up into Tinsley's car.

"So, here's the real question," my sister asks. "Are we going to Mason's or are we calling in the squad and going out?"

"Squad!" Tinsley and Wren exclaim at the same time, and Serena looks at me.

Fuck it. "I have no argument. Let's do it."

But, because I just spouted all kinds of stuff to Brody about honesty and communication, I text Mason to let him know. Not that we're together. Not even close. But still, he's been so amazing, I don't want to take advantage of that.

Me: The girls want to go out for dinner and drinks.

He responds almost immediately.

Mason: Sounds fun. Enjoy. Just be safe and mindful of the press. What about Brody?

Me: I'll tell you about it tomorrow.

Mason: I don't like the way that sounds. And if you're going out drinking, can I ask Tins to bring her car home? I'll pay for a car service for you.

I reread his text. "Mason wants us to bring the car home and he'll supply a car service tonight, so we don't drive."

All chatter falls quiet, and I catch Tinsley's wry smile from the rearview mirror.

"That's sweet of him," she says.

"Yes," Wren agrees, also smiling in a way I'm ignoring.

Serena turns around to face me from the front seat. "You cool with that?"

I shrug. "I was actually thinking of telling him we're badass bitches who earn our own money and can afford our own car service."

She grins coyly. "That's sort of what I was thinking."

I get a round of cheers for that and text it back to Mason.

Mason: Stop being so sexy. I'm not allowed to make moves on my hot, badass wife. I just want to make sure you're safe. That's all I care about. Have fun. But know that I won't always be so easy with you. I liked punishing you when you deserved it, and I already know you spoke to Brody.

Me: No sexy sex. Remember?

Mason: I'll never be able to forget or not want your sexy sex. It makes me hard just thinking about it. But I'll be a good boy. Just for you. Just for now.

Shit.

I'm not sure there is any other word to say or think after that.

"Stella's!" Serena cries out. "Let's go change first. I want to wear something cute and moving clothes are not cute. She has the back room waiting for us." Our older sister Stella owns a chain of top-tier restaurants in Boston with her wife, Delphine. Stella's is her landmark one, though. "And I've got all the ladies coming!"

Oh, boy. I can only imagine what this night will turn into.

15

MASON

With my hearing aids in, I can hear the elevator door ping from inside the apartment. Like a puppy awaiting its owner, I'm tempted to stand by the door with my tail wagging excitedly. But because I'm more of a man than that, not only will I not pee on the floor, I'll act indifferent as I stand in front of my TV that's being fucked with thanks to Stone's on-demand cable guy. For some reason, when I returned home, the cable was not working.

The front door opens, and Sorel and Serena waltz in each with two large suitcases rolling behind them. Tinsley and Wren likely went to Stone's place next door, and like the puppy *he* is, he scrambles off the couch and runs straight over there.

"Way to play it cool, brother."

He flips me off, and I grin just as my girl comes into view.

"Hey," I say, trying to be nonchalant. "Everything go okay?" And can you tell me every second of your interaction with Brody?

She doesn't.

She simply shrugs. "It went well enough. Um." She eyes the cable guy, and I can tell she doesn't want to say anything. I can't exactly ask if I can show her to her room either since, outwardly, she's my wife and supposed to be sleeping with me.

Serena has a look in her eyes as if she can read my every damn thought. It's unsettling. "I'm taking your wife out tonight."

"Awesome," I reply. "As long as you bring her back home to me, I think that's great."

Serena pauses and studies me. I haven't spent a lot of time with her since she's been living in Paris. "You do?" Her skepticism is warranted. I ran off and married her sister on a whim, and she doesn't know me very well other than what she's heard about me from everyone else.

"Absolutely. I think you should go out and have some fun."

And she smirks. Again, reading me better than I'd like her to.

"Right then. I promise I'll bring her home to you."

"Excellent. I appreciate that. My wife is my world." Sorel is already down the hall in her new room, which is why I said that aloud. It didn't take her long to find it either. She headed in that direction and went to the biggest room at the end of the hall, suitcases rolling behind her. Smart girl.

"That so?"

I tilt my head. "Do I strike you as the half-assed type?"

I get a smirk as she swirls her pointer finger in circles through the air in return. "Play on, player."

She spins on the balls of her feet and follows after her sister, and I feel like I just got a high-five and a *you've got this* from the most important person in Sorel's world. So that's something.

The cable guy acts as if he's not hanging on our every word, but I have zero doubts he's all over everything. Whatever. As long as he fixes my cable and keeps his phone locked by my front door, I don't care.

Half an hour later, there's a knock on my door and an

unhappy Stone waltzes in, quickly followed by Tinsley, who is wearing a black cocktail napkin as a dress. I look away immediately. It's more skin than I'm comfortable seeing on her. Tinsley is more or less a little sister or cousin to me. Our parents are best friends, and we grew up together. All of the Central Square crew did. Central Square was a famous rock band back in the day that was on top of the world for four years before tragedy tore them apart, and they all went their separate ways, doing their own things while remaining impossibly close. When Callan Barrows—drummer turned ER doctor—married Layla Fritz, the Fritz crew came along, and now we're all connected and close.

Wren is dressed similarly, and now my cable guy doesn't just take notice, he chokes. On nothing. Likely his tongue, and I shoot him a *don't fucking try it* glare.

"My cable box is the only place your eyes should be," I warn him, and he throws an apologetic hand up over his shoulder and gets back to work.

"They've got a car service lined up." Stone scowls. He isn't happy with Tinsley dressed like sex on legs, but Tinsley doesn't care. My props to her. Just as I think that, the door down the hall opens, and after a series of high-pitched clicks and clacks, my wife comes into view wearing a short, tight, pink dress that doesn't cover much.

I shoot to my feet, and Stone throws me a, *see, asshole*, smirk.

"Hi," I say, then inwardly wince because, really? *Hi?* I rub the back of my head and neck. "Um. You look..." I stop. Beautiful, sexy, stunning, gorgeous, cock-hardening. They all work. "Nice" is what slips out, and I wince again. "You're going to Stella's?"

Sorel smiles at me, clicking and clacking some more in her high heels and tiny dress. She's still a few inches shorter than me, but her curves in this fucking dress are what make men cross deserts and oceans for.

"I am."

I smirk and grasp her waist because I feel like I can, even though I probably can't. I bring her left hand up to my lips to kiss her knuckle just below her ring and lean in to whisper into her ear. "So sexy, Mrs. Fritz-Reyes. My wife is fucking gorgeous. A lot of men are intimidated by their awesome, kickass, brilliant, take-charge, money-earning women, but I'm not one of those pathetic bastards. I think it's hot, not emasculating. Remember that."

Then, because I'm still pushing luck I shouldn't be, and frankly, I can no longer resist, I turn my head and kiss her. Just a simple kiss. A peck on the lips. But it's firm and it has meaning, and I want her to know I'm still so goddamn into her.

"I'll see you later." I tell her that like it's a threat. A promise. It makes her frown ever so slightly, and I'm like a fish out of water here. Women never frown when I kiss them or try to charm their panties off. Not ever. I'm coming on too strong, and I know it, but I don't know how to slow down now. I've never had to backpedal before. Not with anything. How can someone go from having everything they want to it being gone but still within their grasp and not go after it?

It's torture.

I'm also desperate to know about what happened when she saw Brody and if she likes her room here and if she secretly needs me to kill her ex because he sucks at life. I will. Gladly. Maybe I should just do it and not tell her. Stone will help me get rid of the body, and Vander will cover up anything we miss. We'll protect Owen because he he has Rory, though he'd be there if I asked. That's how my guys work.

I keep my mouth shut. That'll have to wait till tomorrow. She's taking all my control away, yet oddly, I'm not the least bit annoyed she's flipped my whole world upside down.

Still, that doesn't mean I'm not going to fight to gain some of it back.

"Behave," she reprimands with a meaningful look of her own.

Oh, princess, I vow to make you putty in my hands before this is all done.

I grin and wave as the door shuts behind them. Both Stone and I glance at each other like *what the fuck do we do now* when the sound system kicks on blaring SportsCenter at full volume. It's loud as hell, and why did I put in my hearing aids?

"We're going out!" I shout against the pounding bass.

"Out where?!" Stone shouts back.

I pan a hand toward the door. "Where our fucking women are going, douche."

He hears me and shakes his head. "No way. My little rose will kick my ass if I show up."

"Or she'll think it's sexy."

Stone pauses, and both he and the TV dude turn to give me an *are you fucking with us on that* look.

"Guy, if you have to follow her around, she's getting dick, and it's yours," the guy says. Is he trying to die? I mean, he must be. Stone's gaze is almost comical. I'm equally unimpressed.

"Thanks for your oh-so-intelligent advice," I deadpan as the sound finally cuts out. "I'll take that into consideration along with the advice from guys who have never played football in their lives but know exactly how I should run each and every play."

Stone laughs. The dude does not.

Instead, he gets defensive. "Sometimes fans know how to do that better than players."

"Right. I'm sure they do."

Mr. Defensive isn't going to listen. He's gearing up for a fight I have no intention of participating in. I shoot Stone a *can we get rid of the cable guy* glare. If SportsCenter is on, that means the cable is working again. Job done.

"Thanks for your help. If we need more, I'll call you, Joe." Stone starts to guide him to the door.

"But I haven't fixed the whole problem."

"You've had over an hour. If you can't fix it at this point, then it must be fucked." I'm trying to be nice. I'm not saying what I'm actually thinking. Stone ushers the cable guy out, and the moment the door closes behind him, I fall apart.

"Joe?"

"That's his name."

I shake my head. "No, it's not. You brought that dude into my house amid a social media frenzy? There is press lining our sidewalk. Get Vander to check the people you allow into my home next time before you allow them in. No actual cable guy is named *Joe*, and how do you know he didn't just plant a camera or a microphone?"

Stone glares plaintively. "Have we really gotten this paranoid? You told me your cable wasn't working. I brought in the dude who's fixed mine in the past." However, he does turn back to the new cable box in question and studies it skeptically. He walks over to it and yanks it out before setting the thing on the floor. "Fine. I'll have Vander check it—"

"Check what?" Vander asks as he strolls into my place.

I crack up at the sight of him. "Grizzly Adams, when was the last time you trimmed the roadkill on your face?"

Vander rubs at his jaw that's one giant beard of brown hair despite his blond head. "I don't know. A week or so? I've been busy. Why are you being a dick?"

I sigh. He's right. I'm being a dick. To everyone. The ground beneath my feet suddenly doesn't feel steady, and I'm the guy who is always surefooted. I don't know how to interact with her now. What's allowed and what's not. Hell, I don't even know how to be her friend anymore.

"Because he's in love with a woman who doesn't want him

back. Keep up. But for real, how do they let you into the office looking like that?" Stone questions. "Have you showered?"

Vander has to think about this for a moment. "I think I showered yesterday morning. Or was it the morning before that?" He pauses and tilts his head. "No, it was definitely yesterday. And I own the company, asshole. They have to let me in. There was a massive cyber event, and I was working both sides of it. Sorry if I'm not as pretty as you two at the moment. You called and asked me to come over. I'm here."

"Did you figure out who the threat actor was?" Stone presses.

Vander grins like an evil genius and shrugs. He never tells us any details about his nighttime hacking activities, though he does point to his colorful arm where he has a string of small dot tattoos. He adds a new dot for every hacker he takes down.

"Well, now that we've established this, we're going out to Stella's."

Vander glances down at himself and then narrows his eyes suspiciously at me. "Why?"

"Because Sorel is heading there and Mason doesn't know how to play it cool," Stone supplies. "I'm also getting the impression he's the nervous, jealous type. Who knew."

Who knew, indeed? I've never been jealous before. Likely because I never cared enough to be jealous until now.

"Oh, brother," Vander remarks with an admonishing shake of his head and quirk of his lips. "We're not going to Stella's. You can't."

"That's what I told him." Stone grins smugly at me. "Settle in, we'll watch a movie or baseball or something while we wait up for them."

I glare at my two best friends. "You're telling me the women go out and we stay in and watch a movie?"

They both shrug. "Owen and Bennett are babysitting Rory

and Willow tonight while Estlin and Katy go out, so they're not coming over. We could call—"

I hold up my hand to shut Stone up. "Stop. I'm fine. Sorta. Somehow this was easier when she was with the douchebag because I knew she belonged to him and not me. I trust her. We set rules. But men are going to be looking at her because she looks so goddamn hot I can hardly stand here without losing my mind and I'm not there to tell them to fuck off. She's also not *actually* mine, so there's that side of this for me." Ch-rist. My hands drag through my hair. "How do you handle this?"

"Wow, you've got it bad for her," Stone muses, sitting on the sofa and tossing his arm back along it.

I glare balefully. "Um, what was it that tipped you off? Me calling her my instalove for a *year* or running her off to Vegas or me *marrying* her?" This sucks.

"The guest services chick who spilled your picture has a family in Guatemala, including two small children with special needs she's trying to bring up. Money gets them safely across the border," Vander tells me.

I fall into my recliner, my elbows on my parted thighs.

"Fuck. Okay. Fine." I shake my head. "Leave her be."

"I was already going to, but I did wipe her phone, including any pictures she took of you."

That's good, at least.

"Brody got a job with New York as a secondary coach," he continues. "Per his texts and emails, he's not happy about it. He's also been privately-not-privately trashing you everywhere he can, including to other players and teams as well as a few journalists. He's been telling them you're a showboat, nepotism baby, half-assed player who is selfish on and off the field and likes to touch things that don't belong to him. Seems a bit like a pot-and-kettle situation, but that's just my opinion. He's also trying to rally support to his side by asking friends to be your foes, so be on the lookout."

"That's good about the job," I comment. "It means he'll be out of Boston and away from Sorel. Are his ramblings hurting me or my reputation?"

I don't care that much, but I do care a little. It's my career that I've worked my ass off for, and I don't want it to go down the toilet because Brody feels like throwing a temper tantrum. What I did with Sorel probably doesn't look good to the public. I know this. It's why the press is outside right now. It's scandalous, and I look like a woman-stealing asshole.

Sorel's worth it, though.

"Nah," he tells me, taking a seat on the sofa and scratching his Grizzly Adams beard. "Oddly enough, there's a lot of online buzz and chatter about what a great guy and an amazing player you are. They're also talking about how you came to Sorel's rescue after she learned about Brody's cheating. All of that is somehow circulating everywhere, not just in Boston."

"*Somehow*?" I question, raising my eyebrows at him.

He grins and shrugs. "No one questions how a magician does his magic. They simply enjoy his show in awe at the spectacle and wonder of it all."

"Fuck," I hiss, my forehead falling into my hands. "Shut up. I love you. Don't tell me more."

Vander chuckles, and I blow out a breath.

"I play Brody's team this season. That should be interesting." Another breath tumbles from my lungs.

"Best advice?"

I glance up at Stone. "Shoot."

"Stop pushing Sorel. Give her time and space, and let her grow comfortable here and around you. Be her friend again. While slowly showing her you want more and all the reasons you're the perfect guy for her."

I sigh. "I can do that." Or at least I can try. What other choice do I have? Even if it sucks.

16

SOREL

I wake up in an unfamiliar bed in an unfamiliar room to an unfamiliar life. It takes me a second to realize where I am, and when I do, I roll over and grab my phone. It's after eight. Wow. I never sleep that late. We didn't get home until about two, and though I didn't drink much, my head is still foggy. Mason was already asleep, and it felt weird walking in here. I live here now. It's strange and foreign and not quite comfortable.

Despite that, the room is very nice. It has a large bed, a walk-in closet, and a private bathroom that's pretty, if not a little girly, since it has a small crystal chandelier over the soaking tub. The apartment is also clean and smells nice. It smells like Mason, and that scent has new meaning to me now. One I shouldn't like as much as I do.

It's been like this every time I've come over to hang out. I remember being surprised the first time. It's not what I thought I'd find in a football player's house. A younger football player at that. Brody is a year older than I am, and when I first went to his place, it felt like a frat house complete with the toilet seat up, dishes in the sink, and the bed unmade. He didn't even try to impress me, and why I continued to date him after that is still a mystery to me.

I love that Mason is so different from Brody.

I love that Mason tries and cares to put in an effort.

Speaking of, I know Mason has questions and I need to talk to him. I also need to ask him not to flirt or push the whole *my wife* thing so much when it's not necessary. I need boundaries. Lines he won't cross. I like his flirting, and I like how he looks at me. I like how he feels and smells. I like how he touches me and seems to know what I want even before I do.

On the surface, he's the perfect guy.

Easy to get lost in, but that's not something I can do with him. My head isn't on straight, and the last thing I want is to get hurt again.

And Mason would hurt me.

He'd never intend to, but it would happen.

Mason likes women, and I can't deal with another player. Not ever.

Wren showed me pictures of the woman he went out with last year before I moved back to Boston. A model. He dated a freaking twenty-two-year-old model. Before her, he's been photographed with dozens of women. All young. All beautiful. None lasted more than a couple of months.

That's who Mason is, and it's easy to forget that when he makes me feel like the center of his universe, but I refuse to ignore the reality of what's in front of me. I've been blind long enough.

After climbing out of bed, I use the bathroom, brush my teeth, and take a quick shower. I feel out of sorts here. None of this is actually mine, and I can't wait for these three months to be up so I can find a place of my own again. Mason's apartment is huge, and though I've hung out here about a dozen times over the last year, I haven't explored much beyond the great room, kitchen, and media room.

I hear a noise coming from a room a few doors down from mine, and I pad along the soft, neutral hardwood floors until I stumble upon an exercise room that might be bigger than my last apartment. Then again, he's a professional athlete, so I shouldn't be surprised. Mason is running at a hard pace on one of his treadmills—he has two—with sweat running down the tanned skin of his back, his honed muscles moving and flexing in a practiced rhythm. He's only wearing gym shorts, and damn does he make that look good.

For a minute, I can't stop staring at him as heat rises within me. He picks up a towel draped over the side of the treadmill and wipes his face, chest, and neck without breaking stride.

I do yoga, Pilates, and speed walking, but I can't run like that.

"Hey," I call out, entering the gym and looking around at all the equipment he has in here. An elliptical, a stair climber, free weights, several weight machines, yoga balls, and mats—the man legit has everything. I'm going to use this space. It's like walking into Home Depot and getting inspired to build something when you've never built much before. Still, I can feel its energy and buzz.

Mason has his AirPods in, but he must catch me out of the corner of his eye because he glances back over his shoulder and grins, his green eyes warm and piercing on me before he turns back to the treadmill, slows it down to a walk, and then stops it.

"You don't have to stop for me."

He pops the AirPods out of his ear. "What?"

I repeat myself so he can hear me.

"I'm not. You're simply giving me the excuse I was looking for."

He jumps off and wipes at more sweat, his eyes all over me

before they linger on my mouth for a split moment. A flutter hits my stomach, and I quickly look away, suddenly having as much trouble catching my breath as he is.

"How was your night?"

"Fun," I tell him, because it was. "It was nice to hang out with the girls and be with my sisters. It's been a while."

"How long since Serena was home last?"

"About six months, though she'll be back for fashion week this fall. My brothers left while I was in Vegas. They needed to get back to work."

"They're doctors in London, right?"

I nod.

He whistles through his teeth as he walks over to one of the weight benches, drops his towel on it, and goes for two one-hundred-pound weights. "I have to imagine that's tough considering how close you all are." He picks them up with a small grunt and walks them back over to the bench. Holy shit. It's like watching porn the way his muscles bunch and ripple as he moves. He's not even trying to show off.

It takes me a second to remember he said something. What was it? Oh, right. "It's the worst, and with my work schedule, I don't get to Paris as often as I'd like."

His lips twitch, catching me in the act of ogling. "Or London?"

"Right. Or London."

I mentally smack my forehead. As it is, I feel a blush creep over me.

He sits on the bench, a barbell in each hand, before he lies back and starts to thrust them up in the air. And if I thought I was blushing seconds ago... whoa! I need a fan at full blast on my face and vagina. I try not to bite my lip as I watch him.

Holy Moses in a basket. I can't remember if I grabbed my vibrator from Brody's, but if I didn't, Amazon has same-day delivery here in Boston.

Mason is pressing more than I weigh. Does that mean that he could—

"And yesterday with Brody?" he questions with a small grunt as he thrusts up, and Jesus, now I'm sweating. And my nipples are painfully hard, which I'm sure is visible through my thin T-shirt. My panties are totally soaked, but thankfully that's hidden from him.

"Huh?"

"Brody?"

"Oh. Right." I laugh. It's awkward. My weight shifts, and I don't know where to look because the only place I want to look is the one place I totally shouldn't. I force my gaze away and attempt to calm myself down, but there's a mirror lining one wall, and it's like a magnet for my eyes, and I find myself watching him from this angle.

I clear my throat. "Fine. We talked." I emit a humorless laugh and stare down at the black rubber floor. "I think it was the most honest and straightforward we've ever been with each other. It felt good to get all of that off my chest. He didn't get it. I'm not sure he still does."

"How do you mean?"

"It was like he figured if he ever got caught, he'd just apologize and buy me something to make it up to me, and we'd move on. He couldn't wrap his head around the fact that I was so upset and called it quits."

"That's because he's selfish," Mason asserts with more grunting that reminds me of exactly what he sounds like when he's inside of me. It's getting more difficult to stay in here and have this conversation with him. I'm two seconds from straddling him and making him bench-press me.

"Yes. I agree. He's moving back to New York."

He nods, his expression giving nothing away.

I take a step back toward the door, desperate to flee when

he stops me with, "I heard about New York. How do you feel about that?"

"I'm glad he's going," I tell him truthfully. "It takes a lot of pressure off me worrying if he'll come around or I'll run into him."

He throws me a quick glance before returning to the weights. "And he didn't try to get you to go with him?"

I shift my weight again, feeling strange about answering this, though I don't know why. It was twenty-four hours of sex with Mason. Nothing more, and he's my friend. Friends ask each other these types of questions.

"He did. I didn't say yes." I'm not sure I said no either, but that's irrelevant. I'm not going back to New York, and I already told Brody that it's over.

"Were you tempted?"

"No, I wasn't." I laugh because that hits me. "I wasn't tempted at all. I'm glad he's going. It wasn't just Eloise he was fucking, but it's more than that. He wasn't right for me. I just didn't see it before."

He smirks, rolls up to a sitting position—an act that does amazing things to his abs—and sets the weights down. "I knew he wasn't."

I roll my eyes. "You're just saying that because you hate him."

He shakes his head. "No. I knew." Standing, he returns the weights to the metal shelf. "I had an idea for today if you're up for hanging out with me. We might be photographed, but it'll be easy and relaxed, and with that and the statement my PR people made yesterday, it might start getting the press off our backs."

I hesitate. Spending alone time with Mason goes against my trying to keep my distance plan. I also haven't mentioned the flirty stuff, but so far this morning, he's not flirting. In fact, he's acting like the Mason of old. The one I knew and hung out with before Vegas happened.

So maybe what happens in Vegas actually stays there. Other than marriage, of course. I'm relieved, I tell myself. It makes this so much easier. Less stressful.

I find myself smiling for the first time all morning. "What did you have in mind?"

17

SOREL

"This is not what I had in mind. You said the beach!" I yell over the wind whipping through my hair and pounding my ears. I'm jostled about in the front seat of Mason's souped-up Bronco Raptor, which has no doors or roof and took a forklift to get me up into the seat because the tires are so big and the truck is so high off the ground. Still, it's a very cool car. Truck. Whatever.

An excited "Eep" flees my lungs as we go over another big bump, and I fly up in my seat only to snag sharply on the harness and slam back down.

My stomach is doing somersaults, and I'm glad Mason suggested we wait to eat until we get to the beach. I've never done anything like this before. It's exhilarating and terrifying all at once.

"We're almost there," he calls back to me. "Just hold on. We're going to hit the dunes in a minute."

"Ah!" I cry as he quickly jerks the wheel to fishtail the back of the truck. It flings me left and then right, and I come so close to falling out the side, it's not even funny. My hair is filled with sand, and no doubt I'm going to look like I've been electrocuted. If I survive this, that is. At least my glasses are protecting my eyes. The car swerves again, and I scream. He's been doing that a lot to get that same reaction out of me. "Oh my god! I hate you!"

"You love me. Trust me. I've got you, princess. This is supposed to be fun. Let yourself enjoy it."

Let myself enjoy it.

I close my eyes for a beat and feel the harness tight against my chest. Mason told me that even if we roll, which he promised me we wouldn't, the harness as well as the support beams of the truck would keep us from falling out or getting hurt.

Trust him, he says.

Fine. I'll trust him, but only because he seems to know what he's doing and hasn't let me down yet.

My eyes open, and I allow a smile to crack my lips.

"There's my girl. Let's do this!" he yells as we go over another dune, and I throw my left hand up in the air while holding on for dear life with my right.

And when I allow myself to relax and get into it, he's right. This is fun. Better than any roller coaster I've ever been on.

I never knew Cape Cod had driving beaches. I'm holding onto the oh-shit bar as the warm sun and salty air surround me. It's a perfect day, and a little escape is exactly what I needed.

"Here we go!"

Oh my god. Oh my god! I bite into my lip as a nervous bubble hits me square in the chest at the sight before me. "Mason, that's huge! It's too big."

"Don't worry, you can take it, princess. I've experienced that firsthand."

I laugh despite myself and grip the inside rim of the seat and the oh-shit bar. Mason speeds up and heads straight for the large mountain of sand and grass. We hit it at top speed and

go flying up and even catching some freaking air under the
tires before we come down on the other side of the dune with a
hard, jostling landing that robs me of my breath.

Mason twists the wheel and brings us to a stop on the
north end of the beach, high above the soft sand and waves.
It's absolutely stunning, with the sun shimmering off the
midnight-blue water and the white froth of crashing waves as
they trickle up the sandy beach. I take a deep breath, still
breathing hard from the wild ride, and a calm comes
over me.

"Fun, right?" He gleams at me, looking like a little boy with
adrenaline-flushed cheeks and excitement in his eyes.

"So fun," I concede. "I'm glad you kidnapped me into it."

That smile, if possible, glows even brighter. "If I had told
you my plan from the start, you never would have done it."

He's probably right. "You get me to do a lot of stuff I
wouldn't otherwise do. The beach was the right call," I tell him.
"Maybe we should have done this instead of Vegas." I give him
a wry smirk.

He chuckles. "Too late now. Here. Let me help you." He
starts to undo my harness, his fingers working around my lower
belly, and his hand brushes the top of my mound. I bite into my
lip again, staring at his face as he concentrates on what he's
doing. It's really unfair how good-looking he is. What
happened in Vegas was my fault, but it's difficult not to wish we
had never gone. Then I wouldn't be thinking about him
this way.

Then I wouldn't be stuck living with Mason Reyes as my
husband.

"There." He pulls back with a victorious smile and a wink.
"See. I knew you could take it." He undoes his harness and
hops out of the truck. With easy strides, he runs around to help
me down. The warmth of the sand heats through my flip-flops,
and I pull my hand immediately away from his. He doesn't

seem to care as he goes around to the trunk and pops it open. "Here. Take these."

I come around and grab my tote bag, and the bag with our towels and things in it. He's got the cooler and the umbrella, and after closing up the trunk, we carefully walk down the side of the dune to the beach, which is a bit more crowded than I was expecting.

Then again, it's a gorgeous summer day in July on Cape Cod.

I think he wanted it this way. I think this was all part of his plan. As he said, we'll be photographed, but it's just a simple day at the beach. Nothing exciting about that.

"You sure you can park there?"

He glances back at his car and then over at me with a shrug. "I've done it before, and no one has ever said anything. This is a public beach, and people will notice us," he tells me as he drops the cooler in the sand and gets to work on setting up the umbrella.

"And that's a good thing?" I question as I lay out the beach blanket that could easily fit four and secure it at the corners, so it doesn't blow away with a couple of rocks I find hidden in the sand.

"Yes. We want people to see us together, princess. But we're just hanging out at the beach. Having a good time together. It's not sordid or taboo. We're going for outwardly boring right now, remember?"

Getting on my knees, I pull off my top but decide to leave on my shorts for now. I am not wearing the red bikini. Instead, I'm wearing a baby-pink seashell one that twists in the center of my breasts and ties around my neck.

Mason stares, his jaw slightly slack with his hands frozen on the umbrella. His gaze drags along every inch of skin and fabric, and something warm courses under my skin and heats my face. I dig through my bag and locate my spray sunscreen.

Doing my best to ignore Mason, I set to work. I burn and not tan, and while Mason teased me about bringing the umbrella, I'll be living under it today. Speaking of, I grab my Rebels hat and put it on, looping my ponytail through the back.

His lips twitch. "Nice hat."

"Thanks." I wink at him. "I stole it from some baller I recently hooked up with."

"That so? Is he deliriously gorgeous and fantastic in bed?"

"Aw, does the young baller need reassurance?"

He rubs his bottom lip and finishes with the umbrella. "Just making sure that's my hat and not someone else's."

"'Hey Jealousy,'" I say, mentioning the Gin Blossoms song.

He picks up his phone, and a second later, the angsty '90s ballad comes on, and despite myself, I grin. Just a little.

"What can I say? I want my wife to wear my hat and no one else's. If you had said he sucked in bed and was as gross-looking as a bathroom floor at an underground boxing match, I'd know for sure you were talking about something else."

"So modest, Mason. Spray my back for me, would you?"

"What? I don't get to rub it in?"

"Now you know why I brought spray instead of cream. Behave. And no more *my wife* stuff. I think I already told you that."

"Yes, ma'am. Even if it makes your nipples hard and your pussy wet, I'll refrain, though it's damn near impossible with you in this knock-out bikini—to continue the boxing metaphors."

Damn perceptive bastard.

"It doesn't do that."

"Uh-huh."

I sigh. "Mason—"

"Just being honest while keeping my hands to myself. That was the deal we made."

I let it go as he sprays mist all over my back and shoulders. "Ah!" I shiver and push away.

"Cold?" he teases.

"Here." I snatch the bottle from his hand and go after his back.

He screeches like a little girl and instinctively flinches away from me. "Fine. Yes, that's cold. Ah, shit. Stop. I'll do it myself."

"Wimp," I tease and hand him the bottle. Sinking down onto the blanket, my face shielded by my hat, I relax for the first time in days as I watch the ocean roll in and out. Vegas was not relaxing. Not like this, and before that it was all wedding madness. "I needed this," I murmur.

Mason lies beside me, his arms butterflied under his head and his eyes closed. "I did too. Training camp starts Monday for me."

I roll on my side to face him. "Do you play for you or for your dad and his family?" Mason comes from a family of football royalty. Not just his dad, but his uncle and grandfather played, as well as his mom's estranged father.

"Both. Sports is in our blood, especially football. My brother, Crew, is playing for Alabama and will hit the draft in the spring and my sister, Quinn, is a figure skater like my mom was." He shrugs. "I guess it's just what we do, but I fucking love it and can't imagine doing anything else." He rolls on his side, mimicking my position. "What about you, Doctor?" An eyebrow slides up from beneath his sunglasses.

"Both." I throw his word back at him. "It's also what we do. But I love family medicine. I love treating everyone, from newborns to the elderly. I also love floating down to the ER, which I do more frequently now that they've been short-staffed down there."

"My mom is a doctor, as you know. I think what you all do is incredible."

"Thank you." And I mean it. Brody always thought my

career got in the way of his because of my long hours. It'd annoy him that he'd get home from practice, and I wouldn't be waiting there like Betty Crocker with dinner for him.

"Would you rather skinny dip here with all these people around or streak down the Strip?"

I snort. "Neither. Do you know me?"

"I'd take the ocean. Though the cold New England water might have me rethinking that."

I snort out an unladylike sound. "Domestic or international?"

He falls onto his back, his golden skin glowing in the sun as he tosses his arms behind his head. "International. I've been all over this country for games, and I've been to London a couple of times, but that's about it. I went to college and then straight into the NFL, and I'm always training. I never take breaks." He turns and looks at me. "I wasn't kidding when I told you Vegas was my first vacation in a while."

"Sorry I cut it short."

He smirks. "I'm not." He picks up his phone and sets it to a mix I catch named Sorel's Playlist. "Kool Thing" by Sonic Youth comes out of his phone, and my heart picks up a couple of beats.

"I have a playlist?"

"You do. I like it. I had fun picking out songs to add to it."

My breath hitches, and those extra beats of my heart turn into a heavy drum bass to match the raucous notes of Sonic Youth. He didn't say that to earn brownie points or win a medal. He said that because it was the truth. Because he actually enjoyed making me a playlist of my weird music so few people get or even enjoy.

What am I supposed to do with that?

"Nightswimming" by REM comes on next, and I practically fall into tears.

"This is my all-time favorite song."

I feel his hands in my hair. "You told me that once."

I blink back tears behind my sunglasses. "I did? When?" It's the song that got me through the hardest nights of my life after what happened to me in high school. It just felt like the world wasn't always going to be so dark, and yet it was okay to hide a bit at the same time. Like a rebirth. Like something new that wouldn't always hurt the way it did.

I would sing all of the lyrics word by word until I believed them.

"I can't remember. Maybe one time when I admitted I liked country music, and you tried very hard not to judge me for it."

I grin. "I'm still judging you for it."

"For someone who only listens to '90s alternative, you're in no place to do that." He rolls back to me. "I'd like you to come to some of my games."

"I'd like that too. I love football."

"Sabotage" by the Beastie Boys comes on next, and I start to rap the lyrics to lighten the mood.

He chuckles. "You're that girl? The one who raps terribly and doesn't care?"

"I'm *so* that girl."

"Good thing I'm hearing impaired."

I smack his arm, and he laughs harder, teasing me. "No. For real, it's hot."

"You've got no idea."

"Believe me, I do. Lover or friend? I think it'd be fun to be both."

"What?" My eyebrows knit together, not understanding the question.

Without waiting for my answer, he leans in and kisses me. And I don't know what to do. Part of me wants to keep it going. To deepen it. Because man, can he kiss. But it's not the lines we drew up. It's not the boundaries I need for this to stay platonic and easy and free of heartache.

I pull back and wipe my lips. "Mason, what are you doing?"

"Sorry. I saw someone taking a picture of us, and I was trying to act the part of your loving husband."

"Then why did you kiss me? I thought we were supposed to be boring."

"Oh, right. Oops." He rolls onto his back again. "I forgot."

"Don't do that again. That's not what we discussed." I don't intend for my voice to come out as sharp as it does. It just happens, and I regret it instantly.

He sits up and goes for the cooler to pull out two bottles of water before he hands me one.

"I'm sorry," he states, looking contrite. "It won't happen again. I got a little lost for a moment."

My eyes close. I can't tell if I'm playing it smart or stupid. If I'm letting go of all that could hurt me or of the one man who could save me.

"I'm sorry," I whisper. "It wasn't personal, and I didn't mean to snap at you like that. I'm not good at trusting anyone."

He looks down at me with eyes that tell me a thousand things I've always wanted to hear. "You trust me."

He leaves it there, and I'm without an argument.

I do trust him.

The realization leaves me thunderstruck.

"Stop stressing about it, princess," he comes back with, and I can't tell how he means it by his tone of voice since it's so flat, which is so unlike Mason. "I know it's only for three months. I know you want to get out of this marriage the first chance you get. I know you want to escape the bullshit being with me the past few days has put you in. But I'm not bummed you moved in. It's been a weird few days, but I like you. I like spending all this time with you. For whatever that's worth. That said, you don't have to panic or read too much into it. I won't kiss you again. Not until you want me to."

He shoots to his feet and heads down to the water,

removing my ability to say anything in response. I'm not sure what I would have said. I'm positive he meant it as a friend or a means to fight off cameras, but my belly swoops and dives like one of the seagulls going after a fish.

It'll be easier to avoid him and drawback once he starts football and I return to work.

But part of me knows I'll miss this with him.

What should have been crying and miserable has been smiles, laughter, hot sex, and some inner strength I needed to rediscover. But more than that, Mason cares, and that shouldn't feel as foreign to me as it does. It's been messy and chaotic, sure, but I've gotten through it smoother than I would have on my own.

Mason is the reason for that.

But now it's time to let that go and stand on my own two feet. Without him stirring up thoughts and feelings I can't afford to have.

18

SOREL

"Press are not allowed in the patient area of the emergency department," I tell the reporter who snuck in here.

It's been three weeks of this. Three freaking weeks. Why won't they simply move on already? They still hang out outside the apartment building. Pictures of Mason and I kissing at the beach swept across the internet like a brushfire, but after that, there's been nothing because I've made it so we haven't been out together in public.

And he hasn't fought to change it.

Only the press doesn't seem so bored with us yet.

I think that beach kiss fed fuel to the fire and, well, possibly my own. I miss his kisses. I miss the way he'd hold my face and look into my eyes and then, only after he was satisfied, would he kiss me like it meant something. It was like his reward, and I reveled in it. And pushed it away because I can't think of him as something more. Mason Reyes. Ha. That's almost comical.

But all of this is affecting my work because now this asshole is here.

"I'm a patient," he explains, pointing toward his stomach. "I'm simply trying to get to know my doctor."

"By asking me personal questions with your phone out after requesting me specifically?" I retort.

He doesn't so much as bat an eye. Okay. Two can play that game.

"Both your ultrasound and CAT scan are perfectly normal, as well as the exam my intern did. Your stomach does not require any further intervention. The one test we did not perform other than endoscopy or colonoscopy was a guac test."

"A what?"

"It's an exam where we stick a finger up your rectum and test the smear of stool we collect for blood."

He grows whiter than a sheet. "Is that... um, I'm feeling a lot better. My stomach pain is all but gone. I don't think that's necessary."

I give him my most concerned doctor expression. "Hmm. Are you sure? I'd hate to miss something and have you die overnight. I can have my intern return and do that. I mean, he hasn't performed many of those yet, but this is a teaching hospital. How better to learn, right?"

He shoots off the gurney. "No. I'm good. I swear."

"Perfect. So happy to hear you're better." I give him a saccharine-sweet smile. "Follow up with your primary care doctor as needed. I will have Dr. Erik return with your discharge paperwork."

I turn to leave when he tries to stop me with, "How do you feel about Mason being photographed with Erin Mann? Is your hot new marriage already over, and will you go back to Brody now that it failed?"

I keep going. Erin Mann works for a local Boston sports network and the night she was photographed with Mason, he was attending a team charity event, and she was covering it. He came home that night, and we ended up watching a movie together on the sofa. No touching this time. Not even cuddling. And when Mason saw the photograph the next day, he cursed for about five minutes, complaining how they were trying to stir up bullshit before he swore to me that nothing happened with her.

I believed him. It wasn't even difficult to, which feels weird for me to admit, but I could see his sincerity, and since he came home right after the event and didn't smell like anyone other than himself, I knew nothing happened without him having to reassure me. Not that I own him. Other than our rules of no sex and no other people during these three months, I have no hold on him when it comes to other women after that.

Which is why I don't like to think about it.

Especially because I did see the way they were looking at each other in the picture.

All the sexiness that Mason and I had going—well, most of it, he still makes innuendo-laced comments and watches me when he doesn't think I notice—was left in Vegas and on the beach. We've gone back to being friends, and I've settled into his apartment. Other than the press, things have been great between us.

We both find ourselves coming home after work to be with each other. We watch movies and have dinner together—always something healthy because he's serious about that when he's in season—and hang out on weekends with our friends and family. He even came with me to see my grandparents over the weekend because he told me he loves talking with my grandmother. Even right now, I'm headed out to the field to watch his first preseason game with a few friends, though he told me he likely wasn't going to be starting in it.

"Hey." Jack, a fellow attending, and Owen's lifelong best friend comes up to me. Now that I've been working down here somewhat regularly, Jack and I have gotten close. Like when he discovered Owen was secretly dating Jack's younger sister

Estlin—who Owen is now engaged to—he unloaded on me, and when I returned to work after everything that happened with Brody and the wedding, he listened to me vent for over an hour. "Are you off?"

"Yep. I'm heading to the game tonight after I discharge the reporter in curtain four. What about you?"

"I'm on tonight." He sighs and shifts his weight, searching around to make sure we're alone. "You know we get a new round of med students down here in a few weeks."

I snicker. "Such joy. Remind me not to float down here that week."

"Owen told me Wren is going to be one of them."

I blink at him. He seems bothered by this. "Is that a bad thing?"

"We just don't get along," he explains simply, but it feels like there's more to it than that. "Callan is already talking about putting her with me since she's Owen's little sister." Callan Barrows is the emergency department chief, and is married to my cousin Layla, and is also Katy's adoptive father. Layla works down here as well, but not as many hours as she used to.

"Don't sweat it. It's a six-week rotation, and I'm sure she'll be on her best behavior, and you will be too. Wren's a bit... feisty, but—"

Jack snorts, cutting me off. "You think?" he grouses sarcastically.

"So pass her to someone else."

He grits his teeth and looks away. "I'll deal with her, but if your cousin is in a bad mood for those six weeks, you'll know why."

I breathe out a laugh and pat his arm. "I think I'll know why you're both cranky. Good luck with that. I'll see you tomorrow morning. I'm here for another shift."

"See you. Have fun tonight at your husband's game."

I covertly flip him off and walk away, listening as he

chuckles behind me. I sign out the rest of my patients and then meet up with Keegan and Katy, who also work in this hospital, to head over to the game.

"I'm so excited!" Keegan exclaims. "I love the start of a new season. My fantasy team is on point."

"I'm still pissed you got Mason," Katy laments.

"How could I not? You would have gotten him given the chance."

The two of them go back and forth over their fantasy teams as we hit some traffic the closer we get to the stadium. I'm busy checking my email but pause when I see another one from Brody. He's taken to emailing since he can't call me, and his emails are filled with everything from asking about how I'm doing and how work is going to pictures of his new place and how it's missing me to how lonely he is without me and that he can't stand this anymore.

He even sent me an article on sex addiction as if to say that's his issue and the cheating wasn't his fault because it was an addiction. Give me a fucking break. Brody doesn't have a sex addiction. He has an *I like to have my cake and eat it too* addiction. For the most part, though, I think this is simply routine for Brody. He's not exactly putting in a ton of effort, and I'm grateful for that.

This email is much of the same as the others, and like the others, I don't reply.

We arrive at Rebels Stadium with plenty of time before the game. I'm starving and looking forward to eating my weight in the spread they have in the booth, when a team employee intercepts me.

"Mrs. Fritz-Reyes?"

I want to groan at that, but I hold it in. As it is, Keegan and Katy are quietly snickering.

"Yes?"

"Mr. Reyes asked for you to join him on the field before the game."

I throw the girls a *WTF* look, and they simply shrug. I don't know what Mason is up to, but I won't turn it down. I've never been down on the field before a game, and I won't start to think about why that is.

"Great."

I follow the attendant through the back pathways and underground of the stadium until I'm led out by the player entrance. The game starts in about ten minutes or so, and all the players are already on the field. I hang close to the stands, working my way along and taking in all the staff and players. I spot Mason's dad, Asher, talking to his wife, Wynter, who is the chief orthopedic doctor for the team. They're talking seriously about something, and just as I turn back to try to find Mason, he intercepts me.

"Hey," he says, startling me a bit. "You made it."

"I made it," I tell him, keeping my eyes on the field and away from his, though I know he's watching my face. It's so he can't see how my heart is strangely pounding, creating a warmth that flows effortlessly through my veins. It's happened almost every time I see him lately. But right now, for some odd reason, I'm nervous. Likely because I'm out here as his wife and not his friend. As if to prove my original thought, he leans in and kisses the corner of my lips. Not my cheek. In fact, he gets more lips than cheek with that move, and I turn back to him.

As if that was his goal all along, he smirks triumphantly. "I'll let you get upstairs with everyone else, but I wanted to give you something before the game starts."

"Oh." My eyes widen when I realize he's holding a red and gold jersey in his hand with his number on it.

"Will you wear it?" Without waiting for a response, he tugs the fabric over my head, and I slip my arms through. It's a little long on me, but I'll tuck it into my jeans when I get upstairs.

"I guess I have to now, but I like it. Thank you. I've never owned a jersey before."

"For real?"

"Honest and true."

He grins like that made his entire night, but his eyes are volcanic as he takes me in wearing his number. He tugs on the hem. "Shit," he hisses. "It looks better on you than I imagined it would." He leans in to kiss me, and fresh nerves swarm my stomach. I can't push him away. Not out here. Not when we're so visible.

"Mason, what are you doing?"

"Staking my claim. Pressing my luck. Kissing my wife even though she hates it when I call her that."

His lips press softly to mine, and I can feel the smile on his just as his hands come up and go around my neck. For a moment I think he's just holding me, but then I feel his fingers move at the nape of my neck and a heavy weight presses against the top of my breastbone.

He pulls back, and I glance down. I'm wearing a platinum chain with the number eleven with diamonds dangling from it. It's not large or gaudy, but it's still his freaking number around my neck in diamonds.

I look up at him, and the smugness I thought I'd find isn't there. Instead, it's a serious expression, and his hands slowly come up, almost as if he knows he shouldn't and is trying to stop himself but can't, to cup my face. They glide back through my hair to hold me like that.

"Don't be mad," he mumbles so softly I'm not even sure I hear him correctly over the roaring crowd. His lips come back down on mine, this kiss a bit deeper, and then he's whispering in my ear, "You have no idea how incredible you look wearing my number. It's a good thing I'm not playing tonight, I'm too distracted now. Not to mention all I can picture is you wearing these." His fingers glide across the pendant and down the jersey. He steps back, and now I see that smirk. "Enjoy the game, Mrs. Fritz-Reyes."

I glare. It's not a kind glare.

He stands a few feet away, the sound and lighting in the stadium changing, indicating the game is about to start.

"That wasn't boring!" I yell over the cheers and cries of the crowd. "You could have just left these up in the booth for me or given them to me this morning before I left for work."

He shakes his head. "And miss my opportunity to see you in them like this and get to kiss you? Never."

Christ. This is going to be everywhere.

As if reading my thoughts, he comes back in and murmurs over my lips so only I can hear, "And don't worry, I've taken care of it. Other than a few fan photographs that might leak through, you won't see these pictures anywhere. Promise. We were at a commercial break the entire time, and any professional photographs won't be usable." Another kiss. "That one was for luck."

He jogs off, and I'm left standing here for a quiet moment, not understanding how he can take care of something like that. And what's with the staking his claim and all the damn kissing? Frustration and ire along with something warm and gooey battle within me. I want to be mad. I want to hate his kisses and have them not mean anything. I want to not care that he wanted me to wear his number.

But that's just it. I'm learning that with Mason, I don't want to care. But that doesn't mean I'm not starting to.

19

MASON

"Hey, Reyes," Tony Clark, not to be confused with Tony Stark, even if he thinks he's fucking Iron Man, calls out to me. I ignore him as I head for my locker. I'm in team clothes, track pants, and a hoodie since this is the second preseason game I didn't play. I don't need a shower, but I do have to change for post-game interviews. "Maybe you can give me your wife's number. I hear she likes it up the ass from football players."

I grit my teeth while trying to maintain my smooth mask of indifference. Even if I want to pound his face in until he's unrecognizable and his cocky grin is toothless.

"Funny, I heard the same thing about you," I retort and leave it at that.

Alistair, our openly gay punter, snorts under his breath, and I shoot him a covert wink, letting him know I have nothing against people being gay or taking it up the ass. I said it to be a dick—pun intended—and get a rise back out of Tony. Tony is a bit of what I like to call a football dinosaur. He likes to talk shit about things he shouldn't, and he enjoys throwing dirty hits on the field. As far as I'm concerned, he can retire or get himself traded.

He's been slow to get to the receiver and the ball lately, and that concerns me more than anything else.

I pull my phone out of my locker and immediately see the text from Vander.

Vander: Watch your back. Brody is fishing around with his former teammates.

Damn. It's like Vander has a crystal ball or something.

"You weaselly motherfucker," Tony barks affronted, and I can hear him charging my way. A shove hits my back but it's not hard and it's hardly threatening. It doesn't even knock me into the locker, because he's all bark and very little bite. He's trying to provoke me, clearly at Brody's request, but I have a long fuse, and he's barely lit it.

I was wondering how long it'd take Brody to make his move.

I turn. Slowly. Standing up to my full height, which is about the same as his, I stare straight into his eyes, not wavering for a second. "Something you need, or is your roid-rage getting the better of you?"

He's all alone with this. No one is jumping in, though they're all clearly watching.

"Listen here, asshole. I don't like what you did to Brody."

"And it took you a month to say that to me, or was this just when Brody asked you to take up his charge since he's too much of a pussy to do it himself?"

And right there. That flicker in his eyes tells me everything. Well, that and Vander's message. "That bullshit you pulled is bothering a lot of us, and what you did on the field last week with her was crossing the line."

That might have been, but I had this dream of her wearing my jersey, and after that, I couldn't get it out of my head. For the last four weeks since returning, I've stayed in line, kept my hands to myself, and followed the rules she set for us while keeping us strictly in the friend zone. Well, anytime we haven't been in public, that is. When we're in public, there's no stopping me.

I hold her hand and whisper things into her ear to make her blush and smile. I kiss her when I think I can mostly get away with it. And when we're at home, I do everything I can to spend as much time with her as possible. Even if this past week since my little stunt that's proven more difficult.

Still, there is only so much a man can take for so long, and after that dream, I bought the necklace and the jersey, and she wore both all game. I've even caught her wearing the jersey around the house because the other morning I saw her come out of her room to start her coffee, but I was already in the gym when she walked by. She slept in it. Or at least seemed to have, so I have no regrets about what I did last week on the field.

Besides, only a few fan photos leaked. Nothing major. If Brody saw one, sucks to be him, but he needed to know who Sorel belongs to, and it isn't him.

"Like you don't bring your wife out onto the field before the game?" I throw back at him. "She's there before everyone. You practically hold her hand right up until kickoff because you're so obsessed with her."

He doesn't have a response other than to give me another shove, as if what I said was out of line. I know why he picked today to start something with me. He thinks I'll fight back and get myself kicked out of next week's game because it's preseason and not regular season, which makes it perfect for everyone because it won't impact the team or our season.

But again, not gonna happen. I intend to play the entire game next week.

"That's different. She's my actual wife. Not some showy bullshit to get back at Brody."

"So you're cool with him cheating on her, then?" I continue, making sure my voice carries. "Even up to the night before their wedding with her friend, who was also a bridesmaid. He had no plans to stop either. None. He said it all in the texts, which I know you heard because you were in the church that day."

"His phone—"

"Don't," I warn. "Don't perpetuate a lie like that. His phone wasn't hacked. You heard what he said in the church. He admitted it."

He shifts his weight and glances around at the other players. Again, no one is stepping in to join the Brody brigade. Tony's on his own with this. "It still wasn't right to run off with her and marry her on the same day."

"Maybe, maybe not." I shrug indifferently. "Still doesn't mean my marriage isn't real and that what Brody did wasn't wrong." I tilt my head, ready to give it back to him. "Maybe before you allow him to talk you into taking up his personal shit, you should make sure it's a cause worth fighting."

Two fingers punch my shoulder. "You think you're God's fucking gift because your dad is the coach. You're not. You're just a deaf motherfucker who can barely throw the ball."

Hmm.

"Funny, since I can hear your yapping well enough and set a team record the year I led us to the Super Bowl for the most throwing yards." I slap my thigh and snap my fingers in an aw-shucks way. "Oh right. You weren't on that team. You've never won a Super Bowl."

He grunts. His fight was half-baked at best, but if he thought I was going to jump the first second he said boo, then he's as dumb as his friend who asked him to pick a fight for him.

"Brody doesn't need you fighting his battles for him," I continue. "He can be a real man and come speak to me himself if he has a problem. I don't owe him or you an explanation for what I did. If you don't like it, tough shit. My personal life isn't why we're here. Take out your anger on the field and not with

me. Brody's not your brother, your father, your current teammate, or your son, and as far as I'm concerned, he doesn't
deserve her, and I do. End of fucking story."

Although as I say the words, I'm hit with a glaring reality. I
may deserve her, but that doesn't mean I'll get her, and I can say
whatever I want, but that doesn't actually make her mine.

It's so quiet you could hear a pin drop.

"Anyone else have anything they'd like to add?" I glance
around the locker room, going from face to face, but focusing in
on Brody's buddies. I knew this would happen at some point.
Brody played for a year with us, and there is a comradery to a
certain extent in this sport. We can be dirty assholes on the
field, mouth off, and throw our testosterone around, but off the
field, there's an element of respect and brotherhood.

Or should be. That often doesn't carry over.

Like right now with him coming after me on Brody's behalf.

I look back at Tony. "I'm not going to fight you, but if you
ever talk about my wife again, I'll make sure you fucking regret
it. I don't have to throw fists to make you feel my weight. Others
might be afraid of you, but I'm not. Remember that."

I turn my back to him and start getting ready for the stupid
press conference I'm now running late for. He storms off, again
all bark and no bite, and I finish up and leave the locker room.
But I'm edgy. Salty. His tantrum came at a bad time. I put my
jersey and my number on Sorel, and she looked at me as if not
only she could not understand what I was doing, but she hated
me for doing it.

Even if she wears it, it doesn't mean she's wearing it for me.
It's the same with the ring.

I'm tired of pretending this thing with her isn't real. Because
it is. It fucking is. Time is slipping away from me—a third of
our arrangement is already over—and I know Stone told me to
be patient and do this slowly, but it's not working. Even worse,

she's started keeping her distance from me. At first, I saw her when I'd come home, or she would.

Now, it's like she's avoiding me, and I don't know what to do.

I'm struggling to concentrate because she's all I think about. I want to feel her and taste her and smell her hair and make her smile and watch as she comes for me. It's affecting my game. My home life. Even my friends because they're her people too.

The only person who doesn't know I'm in love with Sorel Fritz is Sorel Fritz.

Every move I make, every word I say, every look I give her, I find myself second-guessing, and it's not who I am. At this point, I can't tell if it's a lost cause or if she simply needs more time. I don't know, but next week is my first game, and after that, it's season time. This is why I never dated any woman for very long. My head needs to focus on one thing and one thing only, and that's football and making sure this season is better than last year's.

That's my job.

And Sorel Fritz is fucking with my head. And my heart.

Two things she wants no part of.

I put on my smile and do the press conference with the same passion and excitement as I do every week. But the moment that's done and I get into my car, my chest caves. It's the first time in four weeks I don't want to go home. I'm not sure how much longer I can pretend, and I already know tonight I won't be able to. She needs time and space, and tonight, I do too.

I call Vander since he's single and has a very nice guest room. I would actually consider calling Owen or even my dad because I could use some sage advice, but I'm tired and just want to zone out for a bit and then crash.

"Hey, man," he answers immediately. "What's up? You got my text?"

"Yep. Thanks for the heads-up. Tony Clark started shit, but it didn't go anywhere. Can I crash there tonight?"

He pauses and then asks, "Things that bad at home?"

I release a heavy breath. "I don't even know what things are at home. I just know I can't be there tonight."

"You're always welcome. Come on over."

"Thanks, brother. I'll see you in a bit."

I put my car in drive and head straight out to Cambridge. Vander lives in his dad's childhood home since his parents mostly live up in Maine and only come to Boston once a month or so. The house sits on a pretty tree-lined street, and I pull into the driveway and turn off the car. I end up sitting for another moment, feeling like I'm failing and giving up for the first time in my life.

I don't do either of those things, and it's eating at me like a festering wound. This isn't who I am or how I was raised. But it's more than that. I finally found the woman of my dreams. I even went and married her. Only before I know it, she'll be gone, and the marriage will be a thing of the past. And I don't know how to stop it.

I sigh dejectedly and get out of the car.

I just need a night to figure it all out and perhaps sleep this feeling off. Maybe kick Vander's ass at *Madden*.

The back door opens, and Vander is inside holding a beer. I really, seriously want one, but I won't. "I always knew you'd come knocking at my door again."

I roll my eyes at my friend but chuckle all the same. "Miss me, sweetheart?"

He claps a hand on my back. "Like a raging case of herpes." He offers me a beer, and I shake my head. "I get to be you for the first game."

I grunt. "Fine. I'll still kick your ass even if I don't get to play as me."

"Wanna bet on it?"

Fuck yeah, I do. "Loser has to make breakfast."

MONDAYS ARE MY DAYS OFF, though today is the first one I'm not looking forward to. Typically, I'm sore as hell. Bruised and aching and the only thing I want to do is sit on the sofa, watch game film, and not move again until I have to. Today I'm not sore, and while I could watch game footage, I didn't play, and we're not playing against that team again this year.

I could watch other games, but I've done that already, so there isn't much I'm missing, and I know my playbook inside and out.

So basically, I have a full day with not a whole lot to do. Worse yet, tonight I have one of the Abbot-Fritz galas to attend. Yet another ruse when I show up with Sorel Fritz posing as my wife on my arm. I don't even know what her schedule is for the day, so I'm not sure if I'm meeting her there or if we're going together, and I simply don't have it in me to text her and ask only to have her blow me off in one fashion or another on her crusade of avoidance.

I decide to go for a long run around the city since it's still very early, not even seven, but when I unlock the door to my apartment to get changed into running clothes, I'm shocked by what I find. Sorel isn't at work. She's asleep on the sofa, wrapped up in a throw blanket. She looks so sweet like this, all curled up and small with her blonde hair all over the place and her dark lashes fluttering.

I'm almost tempted not to wake her. She must need the sleep, but I can't imagine what she's doing on the sofa. The TV is on, the sound so low I can't hear it, but that doesn't mean it isn't on. It's set to HGTV, and I realize there's still so much about her that I don't know. Does she always watch this station when she watches TV alone? Is she secretly into home décor and renovations?

I watch her sleep for a moment, warmth spreading through my chest. She's the first good thing I've seen in over twelve hours and easily holds my attention. Without thinking twice, I cross the room and shut off the TV. She doesn't stir, and I lower myself to my knees. I debate leaving her like this or picking her up and carrying her to her bed. She clearly needs the sleep if she's this out, but I think she has work today and is likely late.

Before I can come to a conclusion, her eyes flutter, and her marbled hazel eyes, swirling with color, framed by dark lashes and light eyebrows blink at me. And then narrow. She sits up quickly, immediately putting space between us.

That's... unexpected.

I sit back on my haunches, my brows furrowed. "What's wrong?"

She brings her knees and the blanket up to her chest. A barrier. I'm starting to need a manual for how to deal with her without fucking something up. She certainly keeps me on my toes and is never boring, I'll say that much.

"Nothing's wrong. I must have fallen asleep out here is all."

"If nothing's wrong, then why are you looking at me like you're disappointed to see me?"

Her expression clears and becomes unreadable. Unfazed. "Why would I be disappointed to see you, Mason? It's not as if you've been out all night and didn't bother to text or call only to return home when it's barely dawn out wearing the same clothes you wore during your press conference last night."

I tilt my head. In my attempt to pump the brakes and give her the space I thought she needed, I've made her... what? Worried, jealous, uncertain.

"I'm sorry I didn't call or text," I tell her because, yeah, that was pretty inconsiderate of me. I shouldn't have done that. For a year, I've watched Sorel knowing she was untouchable to me.

Forbidden. I'm still getting used to her being here. "I haven't had to check in with anyone since before college. It wasn't intentional to be rude or dismissive. I went and crashed at Vander's last night."

She scoffs and shoots off the couch, going around the other side of the coffee table to avoid me completely. "Don't lie to me, Mason. I've had enough of that to fill a lifetime. If you were out fucking someone all night, just own it."

I stand, watching as she marches down the hall toward her bedroom. "You're so goddamn blind," I yell after her, losing my patience. "Christ, when will you open your eyes and see what's right in front of you?" She pauses, and I take advantage. "I didn't fuck anyone last night. Truth be told, I haven't fucked anyone else since you walked into my life. I want *you*, Sorel. I slept at Vander's because it's been killing me to come home night after night with you here and know that I can't touch you or be with you. This last week since I put my number around your neck and kissed you on the field, you've erected a wall to keep yourself safe from me. When will you realize there is no one your heart is safer with than me because no one will ever take better care of it than I will?"

She doesn't turn around, though her voice shakes with emotion as she rasps out, "I have to get ready for work. I'm late."

And then she runs off, her door slams shut behind her, and she leaves me here to feel like the biggest chump in the world.

20

SOREL

I stayed in with Tinsley and Stone to watch the game and the post-game conference on TV. That part was fine. Fun even. We ordered pizza, which I haven't been eating since Mason eats super healthy during the season and had margaritas with it. I've loved living next door to Tinsley and Stone. Stone and I have grown closer as cousins and Tinsley and I have become good friends even though she's about ten years younger than I am. She leaves this week to go on location to film a movie and will be gone for about two months. I'll miss her, but Stone is next level with it, so I didn't linger.

I came back next door and got ready for bed. I was tempted to call Serena, but it was the middle of the night in Paris, and I didn't want to wake her. Instead, I waited.

And waited.

I wanted to see Mason before I went to bed. I've been avoiding him all week, and it's been weighing on me. The necklace, the jersey, and all those kisses, especially in public, threw me. I wasn't sure about his motive for doing it other than it felt a bit like a dig at Brody, who Mason knew was going to see the pictures. It was a publicity stunt.

One I didn't especially appreciate.

It didn't feel like he did it for me or even for himself necessarily.

Except on that field, I found myself wishing it weren't just for show. That he meant it, and it was real. With that, I needed distance. I still look forward to seeing him, and I make sure I at least get a *hey, how was your day* before I go to sleep.

Only he didn't come home.

At first, I was worried and debated calling him, but I stopped myself. If there was an issue, I'd hear about it. I'd get a call or Stone would and he'd come and tell me. That's how these things work when you're a celebrity. Bad news travels fast. Obviously.

And the young, beautiful female reporter he was photographed with at that charity thing a couple of weeks back was at the post-game conference with him. I know because she asked him a question, to which he smiled and answered. He hadn't smiled at any of the other reporters. Not the way he smiled at her.

I put on HGTV and sat there feeling sick and jealous and fucking mad.

He broke his rule by going home with her since I knew that must have been where he was. *His* rule. That one wasn't even mine. Then I started to question if that photograph of the two of them together, the one the reporter mentioned to me when he snuck into the ER to talk to me, *was* showing something and Mason lied to me about it.

He could have fucked her in a random bathroom or in a limo for all I know and then come home to me. Hell, Brody did it all the time, and I had no clue. I kept telling myself that it didn't matter. That our marriage isn't real. That there is nothing more between us and that I should go to bed.

But I couldn't.

I couldn't force myself to get up and walk down the hall to my bedroom.

I wanted to leave. I hated being in his house with his ring on my finger. I had even slept in that damn jersey for half the week. Feeling stupid and ridiculous, I decided I no longer cared about the press or how things looked to the public. We were going to talk about annulments, and I was moving out at first light.

The worst part? My heart hurt. It was more than my pride or even my jealousy.

It shocked me how much I was hurting. I would have thought after Brody and Eloise, nothing could ever get to me again, but there I was, sitting on Mason's couch, struggling to hold back tears and fighting pain with every breath.

I must have fallen asleep because when I opened my eyes, there he was. Only it wasn't midnight. It was six thirty in the morning, and he had a jaw lined in stubble and last night's clothes on his back. It felt like someone had rooted into my chest, dug out my heart, and set it on fire. It was done. Cooked. Charred beyond recognition. It was the final straw because at that moment, I realized somewhere along the way, feelings for Mason hadn't just crept up, they'd poured a foundation and built a home just for him.

I was shocked too because it hurt worse than finding out Brody was messing around on me with Eloise, and how on earth could that make sense? Brody was my fiancé. We had been in a relationship for over two years. Mason and I had a two-day Vegas fling. I mean, I realize we were friends before that, but still, it made no sense until I realized I broke my cardinal rule.

I trusted him. Or had before that. The pain I felt at him being out all night was more than just the cherry on top of a lot of emotional hell. I had feelings for him. Real feelings.

And I hated it.

It made me just as furious as Mason looking the way he did. Until I stormed off, and he blew up my world.

Did he mean it? Or was he just saying that?

The fact that my trust is so shaky tells me I'm in no place to be with him or anyone else right now. I need to get out. I need to get away from him and this fake marriage and everything that comes with it. How can I even trust that the feelings I have for him are real and not a byproduct of everything else?

What I need is space, distance, and time.

That thought propels me through the day, coupled with waves of nausea and chest flutters. I have to talk to Mason. This all has to stop.

After my shift in the family medicine clinic, I take a shower and slip into the gown I brought with me. Hair, makeup, and heels after that, and by the time I walk out of the women's locker room, I look like a Fritz ready for the ball.

Or gala in this case since we have about three or four of these a year, not including Stone's charity. I have my check ready in my purse and slip into the limo that's waiting out front. Keegan, Katy, Bennett, Katy's husband, who works as a trauma surgeon along with her, my aunt Rina, my uncle Carter, and aunt Grace, who are Owen and Wren's parents, are already here. Evidently, I'm the last to arrive.

It's a car full of doctors and a nurse, so naturally we talk about our patients as we make our way across town to the Four Seasons, where tonight's event is being held. I contribute to the conversation as best I can but quickly fall into a lot of smiles and head nods as my mind spirals through seeing Mason after our morning blowout and what I'm going to say to him.

The limo pulls up front, and we're helped out. My gown is a soft pink chiffon with a sweetheart neck and a low-cut back. The dress rustles as I walk and feels cool against my skin, or perhaps that's simply the cold sweat I'm breaking into. I don't know why I'm so nervous. It's just Mason. It was just a fight. It's just a conversation.

Katy, Bennett, Keegan, and I head over to one of the bars in the event space, and I order myself a glass of champagne. I want something strong, but I also want to keep my wits about me. Just as I turn to head to one of the gaming tables since tonight's theme is Vegas—I shit you not, and the irony isn't lost on anyone, especially me—I spot Mason through the crowd. He's facing me as if he saw me before I spotted him. His eyes drag down my gown and over every inch of visible skin.

I gulp and my pulse spikes.

He's sinfully gorgeous in his black tuxedo, looking tall and formidable with his broad shoulders and simple, black bowtie twisted at his neck. He has a light pink handkerchief folded expertly and tucked into his breast pocket. Somehow, he must have known what color gown I was planning to wear because it matches almost perfectly. A sliver of an expensive watch peeks out as his hand comes up to brush back some of his styled reddish-brown hair.

Without hesitation, he walks toward me, and I swallow my nerves and meet him halfway. With a smile that doesn't quite meet his eyes, he leans in and kisses my cheek. The scent of his delicious cologne and the heat of his large body hits me just right—or wrong—and I hold my breath until it subsides.

"You look beautiful," he says simply. And since he's never one to miss an opportunity, he captures my wrist, pulls me in, and kisses my lips. He lingers for a moment, but when he pulls back, his gaze is sharp and intense on mine. Even when he casually asks, "How was your shift?"

"Mason, what are you—"

He pivots right in front of me. "We need to talk."

Only a man with silver hair, an expensive tuxedo, and an unlit cigar hanging from his mouth intercepts us. "Mason!" he exclaims. "I was hoping you'd be here."

"Mr. Limpcock, how nice to see you."

Limpcock? For real?

Mason turns to me with that glint in his eyes. "Have you met my wife, Dr. Sorel Fritz-Reyes? Sorel, this is Dick Limpcock, the new owner of the Rebels. He's been with us for about three years now."

My wife. I swear, he does that just to mess with me. He knows I both love and hate it. Thankfully I'm stuck on how Mason can call this man Dick Limpcock with a straight face when, like a child, I want to giggle.

The man appraises me. "I haven't, but I did see the press on you two. It's nice to see you together and to finally meet you, Dr. Fritz-Reyes." He extends his hand, his sausage fingers gripping me firmly.

"It's very nice to meet you as well."

The two of them start talking football, and I try to extricate my arm from Mason's grip so I can make an excuse and retreat. Only Mason isn't having it. He's holding on tight while keeping me close. It's not for show. It's his way of saying I'm not going anywhere until we've talked.

Finally, Dick Limpcock excuses himself, and Mason is once again all business. The hand on my wrist pulls me along, and I quickly glance back over my shoulder, though no one is paying much attention to us. That is until we practically slam right into my parents.

"There you are," my mother says with a warm smile. I look a lot like my mother. Same hair and eyes, but she's always had a lightness to her that I've never quite been able to master. "We were hoping we'd get to see you here." She leans in and kisses my cheek, and my father follows.

"Dr. and Mrs. Fritz. It's so nice to see you again." Mason shakes both of their hands while still holding onto me. Something my father doesn't miss as his gaze drops to where Mason's hand is holding my wrist.

"I suppose you're technically my son-in-law," my mother teases, but with that, she gives him a hug and I can hear her whispering something directly into his ear, though I can't make out what it is.

"Yes, ma'am," he says with a charming smile when she pulls back. "I fully intend to."

"Good!" She's smiling too, but my always overprotective father isn't having it.

"Yes, Mason. It's nice to see you," he says smoothly. "But you don't mind if we have a moment alone with our daughter, do you?" It's not exactly a question, but Mason handles it with tact.

"Of course not." He releases me and steps away, though I can tell he's not pleased about it. Only before he retreats completely, he comes back into my ear and whispers, "Later." One word with a million possibilities and outcomes.

"Are you all right?" my dad asks once Mason walks away.

"I'm fine." I smile, blowing it off with another sip of champagne. "We had a fight this morning is all."

My mother searches my face. "But you're not together. Are you?"

"No. We're not. What did you say to him?"

"I told him that he better take good care of my daughter if he wanted to keep her."

"Mom! You did not."

She gives me a dismissive eye roll and tsk of her tongue. "Sorel, that man has been searching this ballroom for you since the moment he walked in, and when he saw you, well..." She fans her face. "All I can say is that boy has it bad for you."

"That's..." Only words suddenly fail me as what he said this morning rings loudly through my ears. *Christ, when will you open your eyes and see what's right in front of you? I didn't fuck anyone last night. Truth be told, I haven't fucked anyone else since you walked into my life. I want you, Sorel. I slept at Vander's because it's been killing me to come home night after night with you here and know that I can't touch you or be with you. This last week since I put my number around your neck and kissed you on the field, you've erected a wall to keep yourself safe from me. When will you realize there is no one your heart is safer with than me because no one will ever take better care of it than I will?*

I shake my head to clear it away.

"I hate to admit it, but it's true," my father agrees. "Just make sure he's the right guy instead of just a guy jumping in at the right time."

"I don't want to talk about Mason or anything that's happening in my life. How's the start of the school year going?" I ask my mom, who is a middle school teacher, even though I'm not fooling her for a second. Thankfully, she indulges me. Once upon a time, she was my older sister Stella's teacher and neighbor before she got together with my dad.

The night continues through the cocktail hour, and I spot Mason here and there, his gaze almost always on mine or quick to seek me out as if he were scanning the crowd for me. There's a lot on his mind, and after my second glass of champagne, I not only need to use the restroom but could use a breather from his relentless stare.

Shortly before we're about to sit for dinner, I walk out of the ballroom, through the foyer, and down the hallway toward the grand staircase that leads to the first floor. There are smaller event and conference rooms on my left, and right and just as I reach the edge of the foyer, a hand grabs my wrist and yanks me straight into one.

The room is dark and cool with the air conditioner blasting. There are three rows of tables and chairs, but my vision is obscured by the man breathing heavily in front of me.

"People will wonder where we are," I tell him, but he crowds me, not giving me any room to move.

"I don't give a shit. You and I have to talk." His hand meets the bare skin of my back before it trails down to the space just above my ass and loops around to my hip, where he holds me close. "You've been avoiding me."

"Mason..." I sigh. "This isn't the time or place. Not now."

"Yes, here, and yes now. I can't..." He breathes out a torrent of air, his sweet breath tickling my lips as his forehead falls to mine. "I can't take this anymore. I wasn't with another woman last night. I haven't been with another woman in so long I can't even remember the last time."

I try to push him back, but he doesn't let me. Instead, his arms wrap around me, holding me against him, refusing to let me go and forcing me to hear him.

"Quit pushing me away," he growls. "Both literally and figuratively. I'm fucking sick of it. I..." He pauses. Hesitates. And blurts out, "I am crazy about you, Sorel. I've tried. I've tried so hard to be the guy you need. I've tried to be your friend. I've tried to give you space. I've tried to build your trust. But no matter what I do, you push me away, and I can't take it anymore. I'm drowning without you, and all I want is for you to throw me a life raft and tell me there's a chance. I'm not looking for more than that, and I'll take it as slow as you need, but please." His lips sear down on mine. "Please," he mumbles against them, drawing me in until our bodies are flush. "Please." His teeth capture my lip.

My instinct is to flee, and I attempt to by planting my hands on his chest over his heart and push. Except I can feel the burning heat of him and how his heart is racing like I've never felt it before. I fight to get the words I had served up in my head out for him to volley with, but nothing comes, and he doesn't give me the choice. He's got me caged in with his lips crushing mine, punishing and unforgivingly fierce.

"Kiss me back," he whispers urgently, and I shake my head, fighting this. "You're scared. I know you're scared. I understand why. But you've turned me inside out," he rasps. "I'm in this. I've been in this from the start. I've been in this with you for a year.

Christ, Sorel, how I've wanted you. All this time, I've wanted you. Since the moment I saw you, you are undeniable to me. It's always been you."

He slides down to the curve of my ass and with one hand, lifts me off the ground, swings us around, kicks two chairs out of the way, and sets me down on one of the conference tables. He pulls back, breathing hard. His face is barely visible in the dark room, but my eyes adjust quickly.

My chest caves as I stare at him, filled with things I can no longer say. Because I want him too. I do. It hit me last night and again this morning, but it's hitting me like a wrecking ball now. His words fill me with more hope than I'd dared allow myself to believe.

"You mean that? No one else? It's been me?"

He smiles, but it's almost sad as his fingers glide across my cheek and his eyes search mine. "It's been you. A year of you and a year of watching you with someone else. I was your friend because that's all I had of you, but I can't be just your friend anymore. Not with how I feel about you. Not with how I think about you constantly. I can't take it anymore."

My body racks with a violent shudder, and he rips off his jacket and throws it over my shoulders, immediately enveloping me in his scent and heat.

"Trust me," he implores. "Please, Sorel. Please, baby. Trust me. I'll never hurt you. Not ever. I'll never betray you. You are safe with me. I swear it."

My voice is embarrassingly unsteady as I whisper, "Okay."

His eyes flutter before his head tilts as if the word isn't computing. "Okay?"

It's become our word. One of trust. One of understanding. It's what he said to me on the plane when I told him I was going to my apartment to get my things and that I had this, and he said okay as his way of telling me he trusted me. His lips twitch and then bloom into a full smile as the memory hits him.

I nod, feeling lighter than I think I ever have. "Okay."

Because I can keep fighting this. I can keep walking away and ignoring it. But at some point, when the dust of the last month settles, I'll be back here with him. I know it in my heart. I'm scared. This feeling of giving in, of letting go is a tight fist around my neck squeezing the breath from me. Taking this leap is so far outside my comfort zone I'm practically having palpitations and an anxiety attack over it.

What if I get hurt again? What if he cheats? What if, despite his promises, he does betray me? How will I ever recover again if he does?

But I keep coming back to two universal truths. If not now, when? And if I don't try, what am I potentially giving up?

In a flash, he's on me, his hands capturing my face and his lips toppling over mine, and I'm doomed. This is it. There's no going back now.

21

MASON

If happiness were a color, it would be the color of the dress I'm about to remove from my princess. Light, fluffy, cotton candy, sunset pink. She said okay. That means she's in this. It means she's going to trust me and try with me. I don't know what that entails for her. I don't know if it's simply sex or dating or a relationship. But for now, I'll take whatever she's willing to give me and win the rest.

I wanted to tell her that I'm hopelessly in love with her, but I can't. Not yet. Even I have a limit for rejection and how far I'm willing to put myself on the line.

My tongue swirls with hers, going deeper and taking as much of her mouth as I can. She tastes like the champagne she's been sipping all night and smells like heaven. I want to bury my nose in her neck to inhale more of her, and I do before I kiss my way down her jaw and repeat the motion just beneath it. Her pulse thrums against my lips, and I lick at it, making her gasp and her hands shoot up to my chest.

My jacket on her shoulders has to go, and she helps me out by twisting and shrugging out of it while I kiss and suck on her heated skin. I toss the coat at one of the chairs, and then I'm back on her, searching for the zipper of her dress. At any moment someone could walk in here needing to make a phone call or simply to escape the festivities in the ballroom only a few doors down.

With a smirk on my lips, I pull back and watch her face as I unzip her dress. "We could get caught in here, you know."

She shivers and her eyes round as my thumb glides down her spine along with her zipper. Once it's undone, the straps slip from her narrow shoulders to reveal the tops of her perfect breasts. My hands slide up her calves, taking the stiff material of her dress with me as I lift it up and up until it's bunched around her waist.

Then I step back and take in the sight before me.

Sorel is breathing hard, causing more of the top of her dress to fall. If possible, I swear her tits are bigger, fuller. Her hair is mussed from having my hands in it, and her thighs are spread wide, showing me the paradise I've been denied for far too long. The tiny scrap of lace covering her pussy matches her dress, and I fucking love how sweet and girly Sorel is. Her nails are always painted pink in one shade or another, and her clothes when she's not in scrubs always have some sort of girly embellishment.

And she likes sexy panties.

I lick my lips and drop to my knees, taking her inner thighs in my hands to spread her wider for me. She kicks off her shoes, and her feet hike up onto the table. I drag a finger along the wet seam, pushing in a little when I reach her clit.

She whimpers, and her teeth catch her lip.

"Can you be quiet for me, my princess, or do I have to gag you with these?" I run my fingers across the lace again, so she knows what I'm referring to.

"I..." She swallows audibly, visibly turned on by the thought of being gagged with her own panties. I won't lie. The thought has me harder than I've ever been. "I don't think I can be quiet."

Fuck do I love this woman.

"Then we'll have to fix that." My fist balls up the crotch, and with my eyes on hers, I rip them in one fast motion. She gasps but also rocks forward into my knuckles, so turned on she can hardly hold herself up with her trembling hands. I quirk a finger and make her bend down to accept her panties. "Open for me."

She does, though I catch the defiant flash in her eyes. Without acknowledging it, I wad up the lace and slip it between her parted lips.

"Your cunt tastes good, doesn't it?"

She hums against it, and I can't stop my smile. She never fails to surprise me.

"You need to stay quiet now or we'll get caught. You don't want that, do you?"

She gives me a long look and slowly shakes her head. She does want that. I know she does. She likes the idea of someone seeing her or catching her or hearing her. I figured that out in Vegas on the veranda. It's why we're playing this game. Only the reality is, we're at an Abbot-Fritz gala, and half the people in that ballroom are her family, so we don't *actually* want to get caught. Just play with the idea of it.

I grasp her hips, yank her to the edge of the table, and cover her pussy with my mouth. A loud noise vibrates from her, muffled slightly by the thong in her mouth. That's because I'm not being gentle. I don't know how to slow down. I'm ravenous for her. An animal let out of his cage.

She's mine, but I barely have a grasp on her. She's still that water flowing to her own wake and slipping through my fingers whenever she feels like it.

With that, I don't hold back, even with the location we find ourselves in. She peers down at me, her heavy lids, wild hair, and overflow of cleavage spilling out of her dress making her look entirely too sexy. She moans through the lace, and her shallow breathing shoots straight to my cock.

I can't keep my hands off her. I need her like a man needs air, and having her once now and then having to go back to the event will be torture. All night long I'll be thinking about doing this to her again.

Her hand clutches my head, her other holding her up as I suck on her clit, pull it between my lips, and use my tongue to play with it. Her sounds get louder, and I can't help my own grunts and groans. I fucking love eating her out. It's one of the things I've jerked off to most over the last month. Probably because she comes so hard when I do this.

I dive back in, alternating my tongue and fingers, fucking her and licking her up and down, swirling my tongue and getting high on her scent and taste. It drives me over the edge, and I lose control, getting rougher than I intended.

Her back arches, and her hand in my hair grows tighter. The zap of pain only urges me on. Reaching up, I wrench her dress down, exposing her pretty tits. I palm one in my hand, pinching and rolling her nipple, and she cries out so loud, it almost shocks me.

I peer up to make sure I didn't hurt her, but her eyes are in the back of her head as I work her tits while I hold her cunt against my face with my other hand.

"Ah! Mason," she garbles, losing it. Have her tits always been this sensitive? Christ, I want to devour them to see if she can come just from me playing with them. She rolls up into me, aching for more of my lips and tongue and teeth while driving me deeper into her body. I can feel her orgasm start to take over, and when it hits, there's no controlling her, gag or not. She's fucking my face and holding me where she wants me and crying out into the dark conference room as I twist and pull on her hard nipples.

I continue to tongue fuck her until she's all but spent and

her body sags. Her hands try to rip me away from her sensitive clit, but I don't give in that easily. I pull away with one last kiss and stand, extricating the wet lace from her mouth. She licks her lips and clears her throat, and I stare down at my girl as I undo the tight knot of my bowtie and let the ends hang loosely around my neck. She sits up, her hands going to the belt and zipper of my tux pants.

"Forget the shirt," she tells me. "We don't have time. I need you now."

"What's up with these?" I ask, cupping her tits and pressing them together.

She moans and shakes her head. "I don't know, but I hope they stay like that because whatever you're doing to them feels so fucking good. But please, Mason. I need it."

Her impatience has me winded, and I dip down to capture her mouth in a soul-stealing kiss. I take over on my pants, lowering them enough to free my cock. This is going to have to be faster than I want it to be because she wasn't wrong when she said people will notice we're gone. Sliding her to the very edge of the table, I tilt her back and crouch a bit given the messy angle and short table.

I line myself up and push in.

We continue kissing—we never stopped—and this is one of my favorite parts about fucking Sorel. The gasps she makes every time I first enter her. It's a combination of pleasure and pain. Of me being a bit too big for her, but she loves the stretch all the same. I grip her hip and press our bodies together, going in as deep as I can. The world spins behind my eyes, and my lungs empty at the warm, velvety feel of her.

Home. Heaven. Bliss. *Mine.*

My girl. My wife. My Sorel.

The words pound through me and urge my body into motion. Pulling almost all the way out, I immediately press back in to the hilt.

"Oh, hell, that's deep," she curses under her breath and angles herself further back to accommodate me. The action causes more of her dress to slip down, and I help it the rest of the way until it's around her waist, wanting to see all of her tits when I fuck her.

Her breaths pant past her lips on a shaky exhale as I dip down to capture a nipple in my mouth. I'm deliriously happy right now. It's not just being inside of her again. It's her saying okay to me. I nearly laugh at the irony of that.

I'm trying to date my wife. I'm trying to make her fall in love with me.

She moans, and I pop away from her nipple to bite into her bottom lip. "Try to be quiet, princess."

"It feels so good," she whines.

"I know," I whisper, because it does. "But be my good girl and try for me."

"I thought you were my good boy."

I smirk against her lips. "I'll always be your good boy, but since you're so rarely my good girl, I'm gonna need you to work on it so you don't get caught getting fucked on a conference room table." Thrust. "Is that what you want?" Thrust. "You want someone to walk in and see your pretty face all flushed as I make you come on my cock?" Thrust.

"Your wickedly dirty mouth isn't helping me stay quiet," she pants, and her eyes close as I fuck her harder.

I pump faster, setting a rhythm with quick, shallow fucks. I'm too tall for this angle, but I make it work. I can't stop touching her everywhere I can, alternating watching my cock slide in and out of her tight heat and her face as she gets fucked. She's urging me on, meeting me thrust for thrust, hiking her legs up and over my forearms as I pick up my pace, needing to bring us both over the edge. I kiss her and swallow her sounds and my own as I move faster and harder, the smacking of our bodies together making my balls draw up and my abs tighten.

I want to wrap my hand around her neck, but that'll show for sure, and we still have dinner with her family after this.

"Dirty. Fucking. Slut."

"Oh, god!" She's barely hanging on, one arm wrapped around my neck and the other struggling to support her weight. "Mason," she cries, getting closer, her thighs trembling against my forearms.

"You're so tight, princess. I can't..." I grit my teeth. "I can't hold off much longer. Tell me you're there too."

All she can do is nod as her head falls back and her lips part. "Yes. God, please, right... there."

I pound her exactly where she's begging me to, and it sends her flying into a sweet abyss. She grips me tighter, and I adjust her, so I take on her weight and hold her tightly against me. Her pussy spasms, clenching my cock in the most beautifully painful way, and I explode into her, pistoning my hips and filling her with my cum.

For a moment all I can do is hold her and breathe because if I move, I might pass out. I'm having a headrush to beat all headrushes as it is.

I love you. In my daze, the words almost slip out. They're right there on my tongue, jumping up and down like anxious little fuckers, trying to break free. Dammit, this needs to stop happening every time I have sex with her. She's not ready, and I'll only sound like an obsessed asshole. Which, in fairness, I am but still.

Slowly I pull out of her and pick up my jacket to remove the satin handkerchief so I can clean her up with it.

"Ah! Oh my god, stop." She swats my hands away, and I chuckle.

"Sensitive or too intimate?"

"Both!"

I roll my eyes. "Here." I hand her the cloth. "It's all yours, but you should get used to being intimate with me. That's not going anywhere anytime soon."

"You're not supposed to be like this. I'm unprepared."

"What?" I laugh the word.

"Perfect." She lands a kiss on my lips. "I'll run to the restroom. Help me zip up first."

She stands and turns around, and I place a kiss on her spine as I rezip her dress, feeling like a hero, like a million bucks, like I can fly.

When that's done, I redo my bowtie, put back on my jacket, and run my fingers through my hair. We're both flushed, and no doubt if anyone saw us together right now, what we were just doing would be obvious. I take her panties and my cum-soiled handkerchief and stuff them both in my pocket.

"Ready, Mrs. Fitz-Reyes?" I hold out my arm for her as she finishes with her hair, using her camera app to help her along. Smart girl. Only women think of these things.

She slips her phone back into her purse and takes my arm. "I'm ready, but you need to stop calling me that."

I open the door and grin over at her. "Never. You're my wife." I kiss her cheek. "Get used to it. I don't plan to change that now."

She opens her mouth to lay into me when someone steps in front of us, blocking our clean escape. *Oh shit.* My heart starts to pound at the sight of the elderly woman with a perfect blonde bob, regal features, and fiery green eyes that miss nothing.

Sorel gasps, and her face flames. "Grandma. Hi."

22

"Seriously? Your grandmother caught you?" Jack laughs raucously as if that's the best thing he's ever heard. He knows my grandmother well. Fiona Apple's "Criminal" has been in my head, mocking me since she gave me a once-over and proceeded to purse her lips disapprovingly. Serena planted the song in my thoughts when she couldn't stop laughing for ten minutes straight on the phone last night, and now it won't die. Neither will Jack, who's still laughing.

"Fuck off."

"Isn't that what you got caught doing?"

"She caught us after the fact." I don't know why I'm telling him this other than Jack is pretty much a vault, and sometimes it's nice to have a non-family member or a non-Mason person I can talk to. After my grandmother gave me a very knowing, very chastising look last night, we were essentially escorted into dinner and forced to sit there with my entire family—including my parents—at our table.

I got a lot of questioning looks, scowls, and wry smirks.

It was a tense night, let's just say that.

I think my father and his twin brother, my uncle Luca, were plotting how Mason's body could wash up in the Charles River without them being implicated.

But when Mason and I got home, he scooped me up and carried me down the hall to his room, giving me no choice in the matter. He laid me down on his bed and made me scream his name six ways to Christmas, and by the end of it, I was agreeing to move into his room and not quit our marriage. I don't even know how it happened. The man pulled some orgasmic witchcraft on me.

But I guess now we're trying, and if we're trying, I don't have much of an argument against it.

"That's great." He laughs harder, and there is no stopping my small giggle even as I try to appear annoyed or indignant or whatever I'm going for. It is pretty funny, and I'm thirty-five, not fifteen. My grandmother can guess I have sex, but still, it's my grandmother, Boston's queen, and Mrs. Proper and Manners herself.

"Shush it." I smack his arm playfully. "But what do I do about the..." I glance around and lower my voice. "What do I do about the marriage part of it?"

"You mean because Mason Reyes wants you to have his babies and stay married to him for life?" he deadpans, and I roll my eyes.

"It's not quite that extreme."

He gives me a look. "Men don't want to stay married unless it is."

Before I can formulate a response, the overhead PA system goes off with "Code White, Emergency Department. Code White, Emergency Department."

Jack and I exchange wide-eyed glances and look around. We're in the back part of the Emergency Department where fast-tracks take place since those are primarily what I float down here to do, but we don't see or hear anything. Code White is a violent situation, but—

Boom. Out of absolutely nowhere, I'm hit from behind and body-checked straight into the corner of the wall. White-hot searing pain shoots up my jaw and through my cheek, and I drop to the floor in a crumpled heap. Reflexively, I cover my face, whimpering and trying to stave off automatic tears when I feel blood.

"Fuck you, fuckers, I'm out of here!" the person who smashed into me cries out, and I catch a woman wearing only a patient gown and nothing else since her ass is on full display, running zigzag past us. A nurse and an intern are hot on her heels, chasing her like two puppies chasing a car, and Jack springs into action, going after the patient. Only before she can reach the back exit or be properly subdued by the trail of hospital employees after her, she slams into a code cart in the hall, sending it careening against the wall with a loud bang, and subsequently, she goes down like a ton of bricks.

Jack slides to the floor next to her, and I hear the wheezing intern who is splinting his side explain how the patient came in high on something they think might be meth and that before they could examine her or get a full, detailed history, she hit him with a bedpan—thankfully an unused one—and made a run for it.

"Give her 100 mg of Haldol IM and put her in restraints until we know she's calm. And get a full set of labs, including a tox screen," Jack orders sharply, and the intern and nurse spew a thousand promises and apologies as they work on the patient. Jack climbs to his feet and comes back over to me, snapping on gloves and crouching before me.

"Are you okay, Dr. Fritz-Reyes?" a passing nurse asks, and I grunt, but this time not from pain. Not her too.

"I'm fine. And It's Dr. Fritz." She's already gone, not having waited for my answer as the patient is starting to regain consciousness and her energy, requiring more hands to attend to her.

Jack smirks for a half-second before it slips, and he's right in my face. "*Are* you okay?"

I nod, though I'm not sure I am. It was a hell of a blindsided hit, and my face hurts like hell.

"Can you stand, or do you need me to get you a wheelchair?"

"I can stand." Because I'd rather die than get into a wheelchair in front of the entire emergency department.

Jack shields me with his body, one hand taking mine, the other looping under my arm to help me up. He tucks me against him and walks us slowly toward an empty patient room where he shuts the glass door behind us, jerks the curtain closed, and helps me onto a clean gurney.

"It's not that big of a deal," I tell him.

He gives me a look. "Why are Fritz women always so stubborn? You were just attacked and knocked into a wall. Your cheek is bleeding and swollen and you winced about sixty times just getting up on the gurney. I'm going to check you out unless you want me to call in someone else to do it. I think Layla is on soon, and I can see if she's already here, or do you want me to page Katy?"

I shake my head. "No. Just do it."

"Okay. I'm going to have you lie back for me."

I do, squinting against the harsh LEDs overhead. He uses some saline-soaked gauze to clean the wound on my face and starts to examine it, pressing around on the bones and skin. I wince as a fresh wave of pain zaps across my cheek.

"We're definitely getting an X-ray of that," he tells me. "And possibly some glue unless you want plastics to come down and stitch you up."

"Glue is fine unless it'll make me look like Frankenstein."

"It won't. It's a tiny cut, just deep and a bit of a bleeder."

"Glue away."

"Ribs first. Are you okay with me lifting your shirt?"

"Yes, Jack. I'm fine."

He cocks an eyebrow. "I have to make sure. You have a thing for ruining your friendships with men."

"Har, har. That was a low—" I hiss out a breath. Jesus, that hurts. "Blow," I finish, holding my breath and releasing it slowly as the pressure of his fingers leaves.

"Those are getting an X-ray too, though there's no redness or bruising."

"The pain wasn't terrible, just a bit of a shock."

"That's good at least. Hopefully, they're not cracked."

He pulls his stethoscope from around his neck and checks my breathing to make sure I don't have a collapsed lung or, worse, a hemothorax or hemopneumothorax, which is blood or blood and air in my pleural space.

"Lung sounds are clear. I'm going to get the portable X-ray. Any chance you're pregnant?"

"Nope," I answer automatically, but for some reason, he holds his gaze on my face. "What? I'm not. I'm on the pill."

He gives me an unimpressed look, and I huff. How many times has a patient come in and told us they were on the pill only to turn up pregnant? Too many to count is the answer.

"When was your last period?"

I sigh, already knowing where this is headed. "I don't get one. I'm on a progesterone-only pill."

"Great. Pregnancy test it is. Can you go to the bathroom and leave a specimen, or should I get you a bedpan?"

Ugh. "You're an asshole. Help me up."

He chuckles, grasping my hand and back to sit me up, though it feels like someone is stabbing me with razor blades. Gingerly, I make my way down the hall and into the bathroom, holding my stupid specimen cup in hand. It takes me forever just to be able to sit on the toilet and then even longer to be able to pee into the cup because, fluffernutters, injuring your ribs is no joke.

Once that's done, I screw the cap on the cup, flush, and go to wash— "Oh, shit, my face."

I look like I just lost a boxing match. People will get the wrong impression about this, and I couldn't blame them for it. I'll have to talk to Mason. The press is finally starting to quiet down, and Brody's emails are less and less frequent. I think he's starting to get the message it's over, though he's still trying, I guess.

Now this happens.

With the pace of a snail, I come back to the patient room I was in and set my lovely cup of urine down on the metal tray. Humiliation has nothing on me now. Thankfully, Jack is all business as he snaps on fresh gloves.

"Nothing says friendship like doing a dipstick on your female friend's urine."

He throws me a sideways grin. "If anything, it'll bring us closer."

"Closer like you and Owen closer or closer like you and Wren closer?" I bounce my eyebrows and regret that too. I need to stop moving. Or breathing.

"I don't know what you're talking about."

"Riiight. That's why I heard you're trying to switch students with Montgomery."

"Shut up."

I smirk and lie back down. Sitting sucks.

He dips the stick in the urine and sets it down on a paper towel, leaving it as he sets up the X-ray.

"Face or ribs first?" he asks.

"Doctor's choice."

He cleans my cut with Betadine and applies a small amount of Dermabond to the cut. It stings a bit, but it doesn't last long.

Once he's satisfied with the wound's approximation, he goes back over to the waiting stick. "Do you have someone to drive you—" His voice cuts off as he stares down at the stick, and a spike of alarm shoots through my blood, making my muscles tense.

My lips part to ask him why he looks as though the Grim Reaper is doubling as my pee, but I can't make the words let alone any sound come out. *It's impossible*, I immediately think, only my body seems to know better as a tidal wave of nausea hits me.

"Jack?" I finally utter, and he turns remorsefully to me. Without a word, he walks the stick over to me so I can see it. Two pink lines, clear as fucking day. *No!* I shake my head, my mouth opening and closing like a fish. I stare at the lines, my heart racing and my thoughts swirling. "Do another," I whisper so low I'm not sure he heard me, but he must have because he returns to the tray, pulls another out of the box, and repeats the process.

He stands over it, watching, and I can't get up because my fucking ribs hurt like hell, and oh my god, I'm pregnant. I'm pregnant with... fuck. *FUCK!*

With a sigh, he wheels the tray over to me and sits down on the gurney beside me, taking my hand and helping me to sit up so I can see it for myself. A tear slips out quickly, followed by another, and I sniffle.

"Glad we checked."

I nod, licking my lips and tasting my salty tears on them. I wipe my face and let out a humorless laugh. "I don't know..." My voice catches, and I swallow to clear it. "I don't know who the father is," I admit and break down, only crying makes the pain racking my body excruciating.

He squeezes my hand tighter.

"I don't get a period," I continue, battling hysterics. "I don't know how pregnant I am. The last time I slept with Brody was a week or so before the wedding, and I slept with Mason the day after I ran out on Brody and married him." Oh, Jesus, this is bad. So freaking bad. I'm the ultimate cliché. And it sounds even worse when I say it all out loud. I was tested a week before the wedding, and Brody and I last slept together the night before that. Either it was too soon to tell I was pregnant, or I wasn't pregnant yet. Then I remember the pill. "I missed a pill and doubled up when I was in Vegas."

"That shouldn't necessarily do it, but on progesterone-only pills..." He trails off, and I know. You have to be especially careful with those. They have to be taken at the same time every day religiously. So maybe, hopefully, it's Mason's and not Brody's.

"Oh god, Jack. I can't be pregnant. My life is a mess. My ex ruthlessly cheated on me, and my husband isn't even my real husband. We're not... I mean, we're not even fully together. I told him only *last night* I'd try, but trying isn't the sort of thing that lends itself to pregnancy, and I just got out of my relationship with Brody a month ago."

Hysteria starts to consume me, making my limbs shake with adrenaline.

"Shh," Jack soothes, running his hand down my hair. "It's okay. It's going to be okay. First things first, you need an ultrasound to determine how far along you are. That should tell you who the father is."

"Right." More tears, and there is no stopping them. I wish Serena were here. Why does she have to live in Paris? I could call Stella or hell, even Layla or Katy, but I'm not ready to have this passed through my family yet. Speaking of, I laugh and then wince and cry some more.

"I could do the ultrasound, but it needs to be transvaginal and—"

"No." I blow out a tight breath and force myself to get my shit back together. "I'll go up and see Keegan. Thank you, though. You're an incredible friend, and I'm so grateful you're here right now. I swear, I'll never tease you about Wren again."

He gives me a sad sort of smile. I can't even tease him well right now.

Pregnant. How can I be pregnant?

23

SOREL

There are pluses and minuses to having a large portion of your family work at the same hospital as you do. Case in point...

"Hi, is Dr. Fritz available?" I ask the receptionist in OB while making a small attempt to keep my face tilted down. I look like shit. Worse than shit.

She glances up at me, and her eyes go wide. I have a Lidoderm patch on my ribs because I refused anything heavier for pain, but my face is a circus, and clearly there is no hiding that right now despite my meager attempt. Good to know. Not to mention my eyes are probably red from all the crying I did downstairs.

"Um." She blinks at me only to finally remember what I asked her. "Which one?"

Right. Because my uncle Carter and my aunt Grace also work here in OB. Awesome. Or not.

"Keegan Fritz." I cannot deal with my uncle or aunt, though maybe I should because, as memory serves, they got pregnant with Owen before they were together, and it wasn't planned.

Maybe Grace is the way to go. "Actually, either Keegan or Grace would be fine, please."

She clears her throat and leans in toward me though we're separated by a partition. "Are you okay, Dr. Fritz-Reyes? Do you need help immediately? As in, would you like me to notify the police?"

Oh. I smile and shake my head, ignoring the Fritz-Reyes thing. "No, it's not like that, but thank you for asking because that's important. A patient down in the ER did this to me." I point to my face.

Relief strikes her features, and she clicks in her system, only to come back to me with an apologetic look. "I'm sorry. Grace isn't here today, and Keegan is fully booked. Would you like to make an appointment?"

I start to tremble, but quickly push that away. "Um. No thanks. It's nothing urgent. I can talk to them later." I give her a smile I don't feel and start to walk out when she stops me.

"Just give me one second."

More clicking, and the sound is like fingernails on a chalkboard. *Click, click, click.* They're playing happy music in here, and all around me are women, many of them at various stages of pregnancy. It's like another shot to the ribs. What am I going to say to Mason? *Hey, it seems I'm pregnant, but I'm not sure you're the father.* I can't do that. I can't tell him that.

Hiding it doesn't sit right either, and I'm not sure what to do.

"I can fit you in with Keegan tomorrow morning at seven. She doesn't have a patient opening then, but she's always here that early."

Oh, thank Christ. "Perfect. Put me in. Thank you."

I leave the office, and Jack is waiting for me in the hall with his keys in his hand. "Don't argue," he starts, noting my shocked expression. "I'm driving you home."

I start to cry again because I think Jack might be my new favorite superhero. "I'm not going to argue."

He moves in closely beside me, and we go down the elevator and through the building. I keep my face averted as best I can, hoping and praying I don't run into anyone I don't want to. We make it to his car, and he helps me in, starting it up and pulling out. My ribs aren't that bad. Sore, for sure, but I don't think I broke any.

"What do I tell Mason?" I ask quietly.

He glances quickly in my direction before turning back to the street as we exit the garage and head in the direction of Mason's place. "You mean because you don't know if it's his?"

I nod, thankful he's driving, and I don't have to look him in the eye. "What if I don't tell him yet?"

He's quiet for a very long beat. "I don't know, Sorel. That's a tough one."

"I have an appointment with Keegan tomorrow morning at seven."

He runs his hand along his jaw to the back of his neck where he holds it before returning it to the wheel. Blowing out a breath, he says, "Then tell him after. It doesn't help Mason or you to tell him you're pregnant until you know for sure it's his. Or not. Especially if you're trying to build something together for real."

Are we? I think we are. His words last night and the way he's been with me have shown that's exactly what he wants. It's what I want too if I'm being honest with myself. It's why I said okay. Before all this began. My heart sinks.

"Assuming it's his, would you be mad if the woman you were trying to date didn't tell you immediately?"

"You just found out and are allowed time to process and figure things out for yourself, especially given the circumstances. Twenty-four hours, I'd understand. Keeping it from me after that, no."

"Twenty-four hours to figure this out," I murmur. "That's not nearly enough time." But he's right. I couldn't keep it from Mason longer than that. Whether it's his or not. Brody lied and withheld things from me, and I'd never return the favor to anyone. "But it'll have to be."

"Your face!" Mason drops his heavy gym bag on the floor and sprints over to me, falls to his knees and grabs me.

"Ah!" I scream at the top of my lungs as pain slices through my body like a series of bullets.

He releases me immediately, springing back with fear and horror on his face. "I'm sorry! What did I do and what happened?"

"It's fine," I wheeze, trying not to cry. Again. "You didn't know. My ribs are a little banged up along with my face, but not bad. Well, until your bear grip." I smirk, trying for light and teasing. He frowns, not interested in that at all. Especially when I'm positive I'm not selling it well.

"You didn't call me." He takes in every inch of me, but I don't miss the hurt on his face.

"You were at practice."

Adamantly, he shakes his head. "I don't give a shit, Sorel. I would have come the second you called. Practice isn't nearly as important as you are."

He means it. Sincerity is bleeding from him, and my eyes burn with unshed tears. I've been sitting on the sofa covered in a blanket with HGTV on because it comforts me to watch other people make something beautiful and happy with their lives and homes. Forget retail therapy or chocolate, HGTV works way better. But I've also been thinking about everything, and that was something I had to do alone.

"A patient slammed me into the wall and gave me this"—I point to my face—"as well as a couple of bruised ribs."

"Baby." He comes in and kisses the spot beside my cut with so much tenderness I instantly choke up. I don't know if it's pregnancy hormones or Mason being this guy to me or the fact that I'm holding this secret back from him and I feel like shit about it. "What can I do?"

"Nothing." I shrug. "These things happen. I'm fine."

"But you're crying. You're in pain. I need to do something." He looks so helpless and wrecked, and why couldn't I have met him before I met Brody? Why couldn't it have all started and ended with him? "Can I make you a drink?"

"Um, no. Not good with, um, my face and stuff."

His eyebrows pinch as if that's not making any sense. Probably because it's not.

"The swelling," I tack on, and he moves past it.

"What about dinner? Are you hungry?"

"Not really."

"You need to eat though. How about I make us some spaghetti?"

A disgusted noise crawls up my throat, and I scrunch my nose only to immediately relax my face when my cheek stings. "With the plant-based pasta?"

His lips twitch. "It's not that bad. You get used to it."

"Bacon cheeseburger?"

He chuckles and kisses the tip of my nose. "You got it. Do you want to take a bath or anything?"

"Nah. I showered when I came home. I'm honestly not in too much pain." I cup his face in my hand. I think I'm starting to fall for him, which feels wild and too soon given how I was about to marry another man a month ago. Is it a rebound? It feels like it should be, but at the same time, it doesn't feel like that at all.

It feels like he's the guy I was always meant to be with.

I want this baby to be his. I want it to be his so badly. Because if it's not... I don't see how he'll want to stick around, and I don't want to lose him.

"Thank you," I whisper, kissing his lips.

He smiles against me. "For what? I didn't do anything."

"Mason, you've done so much. And you didn't recoil from my face, which I know is no joke."

"Hey, none of that." He kisses me again. "You're beautiful to me. You're always beautiful to me. No matter what."

My heart thuds against my bruised ribs. The pain is so acute, I can hardly catch my breath.

"I don't deserve you."

"You do," he tells me adamantly. "We both deserve this, so learn to live with it and enjoy it." He slides in next to me, so fucking gentle I can't keep my tears at bay. I've never wanted something this much and been so afraid to lose it.

Burgers are ordered—mine a bacon cheeseburger with fries and his a chicken burger with no cheese or bread and a salad for a side—and he watches HGTV with me all night without a complaint. He even starts to get into it, asking if he should redo this or that or if he should buy a beach house somewhere.

I'm terrified of what tomorrow will bring, but for tonight, this is perfect, and perfect might equal Mason.

24

SOREL

"No, that's not possible," I tell Keegan, who is sitting beside me, holding a probe inside my vagina and giving it to me straight. No pun intended. I feel like my world is crumbling around me piece by piece.

"You are seven weeks pregnant."

"Keegan." I end it there. I feel like I'm dying a little. "Do you know what that means?"

"That the baby is Brody's and not Mason's? Yes, I know."

She's so deadpan, which is so unlike Keegan, and I know she's doing that for my benefit, but it doesn't help. I lose it. Fuck the ribs and fuck my face. There is no holding these tears and racking sobs back.

"I can't... I can't be... I can't be... I can't be pregnant... I can't be pregnant with Brody's..." I give up, no longer able to form words as physical and emotional pain consume me from head to toe. Thank God my boss gave me the rest of the week off. There's no way I could work with all of this weighing on me.

Keegan, who is blunt to an extreme, removes the probe, hands me some wipes, and rolls beside the bed I'm lying on. She takes my hand and holds it firmly, silently telling me she's here with me and that I'm not alone. I'm so glad it's her and not a stranger telling me this. I have the best family in the world.

"If you don't want to keep it, I can—"

"I'm going to keep it," I tell her. I'd already decided this. Granted, I assumed it was Mason's given the missed pill situation, but I'm thirty-five, I'm a doctor with a good income, not to mention the billionaire trust fund I carry, and I have a family full of support. My choice is far easier than for many women in my position.

She prints out images of my tiny baby moving around inside of me. There's a head and a heartbeat and the littlest arms and legs. It's mine now. But instead of being Mason's too, it's Brody's, and I don't know how to manage that.

"I have to tell him." I swallow a loud gulp. "Both of them." My tears come fresh and hard. I'm going to lose Mason. He'll run as far and as fast as he can, and I can't blame him for it. He may want me, but he didn't bargain on me being pregnant and definitely not with another man's kid. It's too new between us. I don't know any man who could handle that situation.

I don't relish the idea of Brody being forever in my life or the life of my child, but that'll be his choice to make. I just know I won't move back to New York, and I won't get back together with him.

On both of those, I'm firm.

My family is in Boston. My practice is in Boston.

This is my home now, and if Brody wants to be part of this, he can be, but I won't uproot my life or this baby's life for him. They say becoming a mother makes you stronger, and I'm starting to feel that. But Mason. Where does he enter into this?

Keegan comes in close to hug me, sensing I need that more than words. She does this for several minutes and lets me cry and cry and cry, and when my tears are all dried up, she helps me off the table.

"You need to make an appointment with my office, though I

should not be your regular OB. You'll need to find someone who is not related to you by blood. Not so easy in this hospital or even Brigham's, but it can be done. Katy loved the OB she used for Willow. I can get you her name if you'd like without mentioning anything to Katy."

I swallow and nod as I walk toward the exit while clutching the black-and-white image in my hand. "I'm thirty-five," I muse. "It's like Wren said to me when I was in Vegas. If not now, when?"

"Thirty-five isn't old by current standards to have a baby, but I know what you're saying."

"Thank you," I tell her. "You handled this exactly as I needed you to."

"I'm here for you no matter what. I mean that. This will stay between us, but whatever you need from me or any of us, you know you have it."

"Thank you," I repeat, turning into a broken record. I look at her. "Do you think he'll understand?"

"Mason?" she questions, pushing some of her long, red hair back over her shoulder. "I don't know. But if ever there was any guy who would, it's him. He knew the score with Brody when he took you to Vegas. Either way, Sorel, it'll be okay."

"Here's hoping."

I leave the office, clinging to that. I know I have to call Brody first. It's his baby. I wish it were Mason's, but it's not, and I can't change that. I can only hope what Keegan said about Mason is true, but if it's not, I'll understand.

I unblock Brody's number and find myself walking along the path that leads to the Charles River on the Mass Eye & Ear side of things. There are benches here, and the sun is just warming the eastern sky. I stare down at my still-flat stomach and touch it over my shirt as I sit down.

I'm going to have a baby.

For the first time since this all began, a smile touches my lips, and I place my hand over my stomach.

"I won't always be perfect. I won't always know the right thing to do or say. But I'll try. Okay?" At saying okay, my heart lurches, and a sob locks in my throat. Fresh tears well in my eyes, and I let them fall, allowing myself this moment of doubt and insecurity and fear.

"You'll be my priority, and you'll be so adored, born into a huge family who will dote on you and spoil you rotten. You don't have to be a doctor. I just want you to be happy. Whatever you do in this life, do it for yourself and no one else. I'm late to that game. I sacrificed a lot for other people, and now I'm learning how foolish that was. Always follow your instincts, ask for help when you need it, and remember there is pain in this life, but there's also beauty. Sometimes things don't turn out how we planned they would, but with any luck, the new version will be the right one, even if it doesn't always feel that way at the beginning."

With that thought lingering in my head, I pick up my phone and dial Brody. Everything hurts, but it's got nothing on my heart as he answers the phone. I'm calling him and not Mason, and I hate it.

He picks up after two rings with, "I didn't think I'd hear from you again, but I'm glad you're calling."

I can hear noise in the background, and I bet he's on the field. That's where Mason is.

"Can you go somewhere to talk?"

"Uh. Sure." He murmurs something to someone nearby, and a moment later, he says, "What's going on? Are you okay?"

My eyes close. "Brody..." My throat is impossibly dry, even out here in the humid air, and I try to swallow. "I'm... pregnant."

I'm greeted with silence for a minute or two, but I can't check the phone, and I don't open my eyes.

Finally, he clears his throat and utters, "It's mine?"

"Yes," I sob and quickly tamp it down. Tears won't help me with him.

Bitterness tints his voice when he asks, "How do I know that?"

I grit my teeth and ball up my fist in my lap. "God, you're such a bastard. I just had an ultrasound. I'm seven weeks along, and unlike you, I didn't cheat. The baby is yours."

"Shit, Sorel." That's all he says, and I can't tell what those two words mean because his voice is flat now. "You're keeping it?"

"Yes."

He huffs a breath.

"Come to New York."

I shake my head.

"No." Fortitude steels my spine and solidifies my nerves. "I'm going to stay in Boston. My family is here, and it's where I belong. It's where I want to be and where I want to raise this baby."

"And what about me? What about what I want?"

"What do you want?"

He hesitates. "I... I want you. That's all I know for sure. I hadn't thought about kids yet. Not really. I figured I had more time before that happened. I don't know. But if you came here, we could figure it out together."

"And what about my job here?"

He grunts. "Sorel, my job demands I stay in New York. Your job isn't like mine."

I smirk. That's what I wanted to hear from him. Still Brody. Still all about him and his needs and no one else's.

"Brody, I'm not moving back to New York, and we're not getting back together. I wasn't expecting this either, but if you decide that you want to be part of the baby's life, I welcome that. I'd like to do this amicably, but if you want to go through the courts or force me to do so, I will without hesitation."

More silence and then he shoots back with, "Is that what this is? You're after my money?"

I laugh because that's ridiculous. "Do you not remember the prenup *I* had *you* sign? I'm a Fritz, you moron. Money is the last thing I'm worried about with this. Regardless, if you want to support your child financially, that's your choice. I intend to raise this child on my own if necessary."

"This isn't the Sorel I knew. She was never this rough with me and was always willing to consider what others needed. Did you even think about how I'd feel about this?"

My eyes round as I stare out at the choppy water of the Charles as it flows by. "Are you for real with that? It's not like you asked how *I* feel about being pregnant with your baby or if I'm okay or anything. I understand your world revolves around you and no one else, but I'm tired of being a planet stuck in your orbit instead of my own sun."

He growls. "You call and tell me you're pregnant, but that you won't even try again with your child's father?"

"That's what I'm telling you." It makes me smile because I'm glad I'm no longer the Sorel he knew. The pushover. The one who was always too afraid to act. The one who put everyone above herself, even to her own detriment. "The Sorel you knew allowed herself to be blind to what was right in front of her for far too long. I won't make the same mistake twice. If you want to be part of your child's life, the choice is yours, Brody. If not, that's fine too. Think it over."

I disconnect the call. Maybe that was cold, but I don't care. I need to protect this child and myself. I'm not sure Brody is the best father for this baby, but I'm willing to give him the chance to prove me wrong.

Now I have to tell Mason.

25

MASON

Practice was grueling today, but it was also the first day I felt like the team came together as a unit. My offensive line was on point. My receivers and tight ends were exactly where I needed them to be. Maybe it's that I'm more focused than I have been in weeks. The mental turmoil I had been unable to see beyond is gone.

Sorel is mine. My arm feels great. The bullshit from the other day in the locker room has cleared. Everything right now is as it should be. It's perfect. And heading into our final preseason game, I'm ready. Excited.

And definitely anxious to get home to my girl.

Last night, she wasn't herself. She was quiet and missing some of her smile and spunk. She didn't want to talk about it, but I wonder if getting hit by that patient rattled her. It sure as hell rattled me, and I texted my uncle Callan, who isn't exactly my uncle, but as my dad's best friend and Katy's adoptive father, that's what I call him. He did his best to reassure me that what happened to Sorel isn't all that common and that he's never worried about having Layla work there.

It set some of my nerves at rest considering I know how

protective he is over his wife. But Sorel clung to me last night in a way she hasn't yet. I won't lie and say I didn't love it, but it also made me hesitant to leave her today. Oddly enough, she was up and out the door before I even woke up, so the choice was removed for me.

The lock disengages on the front door, and a smile instantly hits my face. I never used to look forward to coming home. I didn't dread it, but there was nothing sweet about coming home to an empty house. Having Sorel here, knowing I get to see her and talk to her and spend time with her fills me with a warmth I can't even begin to explain. It's the smell of food when she makes dinner or the sound of whatever 90s tune she's listening to or show she's watching. It's the scent of her perfume that lingers in the air, and now the feel of her in bed beside me.

It's home. She's made my house a home.

Only as I walk inside, something feels off. I can't even put my finger on what it is exactly—maybe it's the deafening silence when I know she's supposed to be home—but whatever it is, my pulse quickens, and the hairs at the back of my neck prickle. My strides grow long and urgent as I drop my bag and move to the great room to find it empty. She's not in the dining room either, but a faint sound in the kitchen draws me there, and when I cross the threshold, I find her sitting at the counter, a glass of water beside her, and a vacant expression on her face.

"Hey." I rush over to her and cup her face. I try not to wince. That cut and bruise set my teeth on edge, and I want to kiss it away so she doesn't feel an ounce of pain from it. She shakes my grip loose, but I can tell she's been crying by the red puffiness of her eyes, which are barely dry, and the stain of salt on her cheeks. "What's wrong?"

She pins me with a look that instantly has me stepping back and gripping the counter for support. My heart thunders at her turbulent expression. She's about to end this with me. I can tell.

"What is it?" I press when she doesn't speak. "Just tell me."

Her hands tremble in her lap and as she tries to hide them by knotting her fingers together. With a swallow, she says, "Mason, I'm pregnant, and the baby is Brody's."

Blood rushes through my ears, and I press into the counter. *Mason, I'm pregnant, and the baby is Brody's.* The words reverberate through my skull, angry and violent and making me fucking sick. The room spins, and all I can hear is *the baby is Brody's.*

My hands meet the back of my head only to tumble to my knees. It's like I just sprinted a marathon and can't get enough oxygen. How is this even... no. *Fucking no!*

I blow out a breath in an attempt to try and regain my control, only it's futile. My insides are being pummeled. Pulverized. My heart... God in hell, this hurts like a bitch.

Pregnant. Sorel is pregnant, but the baby isn't mine. That's what she's saying. Not only is it not mine, it's fucking Brody's.

My jaw clenches, my molars gnashing as jealousy like I've never felt before curls up my spine and hugs my shoulders. "How long have you..." My voice isn't my own. It's low and rough and mean with accusation. Goddammit! I clear my throat and try again. "How long have you known?"

She licks her lips and wipes her face. She's trying to be matter-of-fact and calm, but her tears betray her agony, and I break with her. A tidal wave of emotion knocks me sideways, and my anger and jealousy slip into heartbreak.

"I found out I was pregnant yesterday, but I didn't know how far along I was or whose baby it was until this morning."

I find myself nodding as I absorb her words. So, she knew she was pregnant yesterday and didn't tell me. That's not the most fun to hear, but then again, what was she going to tell me? I'm glad I didn't know it could have been mine. I would have gotten my hopes up, and that would have been a bigger blow than this. This is ripping the Band-Aid off, even if it still hurts like a motherfucker.

I turn and start to pace, my hands on top of my head as I'm unable to slow my thoughts down. It feels like my world is falling apart. Like the good thing I thought I had going, the thing I've wanted for so long, the best thing I've ever had is gone again. It's our pattern. I have her for a few days, and then she slips away from me.

Only this feels worse. More permanent.

My chest cracks open, my beating heart being ripped out of my body.

I stop pacing and face her. "Are you getting back together with Brody?"

She shakes her head adamantly. "No. Not ever."

"Are you moving back to New York?"

Another head shake because that's all she seems to be able to give me now.

I stare at her and I have to ask. I have to know. Even if it kills me. "Are you ending this with me?"

A sob wrenches from her chest. She's trying to stay strong and resolute, but it's not working, and she falls apart. "I don't want to." Her face meets her hands, and she loses it. Body-wrenching shudders consume her, and all I want to do is be there for her and comfort her, but I don't know how to process this.

I'm gutted too.

"You want to stay with me?"

She nods. "Yes, but..."

But she's pregnant. And that means it's not just her anymore. She'd be pregnant with another man's child and then a mother to it.

"It's a lot. I know it's a lot. It's a lot to take in and a lot to ask." She continues to cry into her hands, unable to look at me as she says, "But I'm asking you all the same."

I pry her hands from her face so she's forced to see mine. "Asking me what?"

She blinks at me, tears clinging to her eyelashes. "For what-ever you're willing to give me."

That hits me square in the chest and shakes my breath from my body.

"I'm so sorry, Mason," she wails. "I'm so sorry."

I shake my head. "You have nothing to be sorry for." I know that at least. "How far..." I choke and have to swallow past the thickness in my throat. "How far along..." I can't even finish that.

"Seven weeks."

I nod and start to pace again. She was pregnant with his kid this entire time. Every time I was inside her, his baby was there too. Fuck. *Fuck!* I'm so fucking furious right now. Not at her. Just at the world. At the universe. Why couldn't that baby be mine? I love this woman, and I just... I wanted a shot. That's all I wanted. I wanted my shot with her.

But how can that happen now?

"Is Brody... does he..."

With a steady breath and a calmer voice, she says, "He knows. I told him this morning."

My fist meets the counter with a hard thud when what I really want to do is punch straight through the stone. I want to feel bones crack and blood seep. Of course she had to tell him first. He's the father. But I hate that she told him before me. *I fucking hate that.*

She's mine.

My girl. My wife. All of this should be mine and not his. He threw her away. He took her for granted. Why does he get this and not me?

I'm starting to lose it too. I can feel it. And I don't want to lose it in front of her.

I need to calm down. I need to organize my thoughts. I need to get control of the bitter rage and jealousy I feel toward Brody.

But I can't. It's a snowball rolling down a mountain inside me. It's a fucking avalanche.

"I'm gonna go for a walk." I look at her and it hurts. "I'm sorry. I don't mean to leave you right now. I don't. I just, I need to because I can't think straight, and I need to think straight." I pause. "Okay?"

She nods, meeting my gaze. "Okay."

Okay. Our word of trust with each other. Something about that sends a current through me and lightens some of the heaviness in my chest.

"I'll be back in a bit."

26

MASON

I walk out the door, and I'm not proud of it. I'm not. But I can't stay in there another second. I'm too close to the edge, and Sorel needs and deserves better than that. I slam my fist into the button for the elevator and look toward Stone's door. I could go there, but I can't. It's too close to home. The elevator comes, and I climb on. The moment the doors close, I explode.

I kick the wall and scream and pull my hair. But nothing makes it better. Nothing takes this out-of-control feeling away. I keep cycling back to one thing. Why does Brody get this with her and not me?

The moment my feet hit the sidewalk, I take off at a full sprint. The press is long gone by this point, having already moved on to the next drama. People give me double takes and smiles and try to catch my attention, but I run and run and keep my head down. I debate running to Owen's. He's a dad and older than me and likely the wisest guy I know. But I don't want to interrupt his family time, and I don't want to see how happy he is with Estlin and Rory.

Rory is his.

That knocks Katy out of this too, because she has Bennett, and they have Willow.

Instead, I find myself running to my parents' place, my fist pounding on the door of their townhouse.

My mom opens the door and gasps when she sees me. "Are you okay? What happened?" She grabs me by my sweaty shirt and hauls me inside. "Asher!" she calls out. "Get down here."

I hear my dad's heavy footfalls on the stairs. My mom is standing before me, watching my face, but she's not pressing me for answers. Not yet. She knows me and can see that I can barely breathe, let alone speak, and that I need a minute. I may look almost identical to my father, but I'm like her in a lot of ways, and when things get overwhelming, sometimes we just need a moment before we can think rationally.

"Mason?" my dad asks and then signs, *What's wrong?*

My dad signs a lot with me. My mom does too. Growing up, I learned to speak both English and ASL simultaneously, and old habits die hard. No one knew what would happen with my hearing, but my deficit has been stable since I was about twelve or so. I wore hearing aids on and off through school, and even now I wear them on occasion. I have the most trouble hearing conversations in a loud space like a restaurant and with dialogue on the TV. I can't wear my aids in my helmet, and since I'm almost always in a helmet, I've gotten used to not wearing them.

"Sorel is pregnant, but the baby isn't mine. It's Brody's." The words tumble past my lips, but I don't feel any relief at setting them free. If anything, they burn worse now that they've passed my lips.

My parents are silent, and I can feel them exchanging looks with each other.

My dad takes me by the arm and leads me upstairs to his office. My mom says something about getting me some water, but she's giving me time alone with my dad. I know how they work. He sits in his chair, and I collapse on the sofa, dripping sweat everywhere, though he doesn't comment about that.

"Did she end it with you to be with him? Is that why you're so upset?"

I shake my head. "No, and she's not moving back to New York either. She told me she didn't want to end it with me."

He nods and rubs a hand along his smooth jaw. "How far along is she?"

"Seven weeks." My head falls into my hands, and I stare down at the floor.

"Explain to me what you're thinking."

I blow out a slow, even breath. "I'm thinking that I want that baby to be mine and not his."

My mom comes in with a towel for me and sets a glass of water on the coffee table. I wipe my face and head and take a sip of the water. It's cold and feels good, and I set it down instead of chucking it across the room because my mom is here, and I don't want to be the guy who is a loose cannon. That's not me. It's never me.

I hate feeling out of control.

"So you're not upset that she's pregnant, just that the baby isn't yours."

It's a statement and not a question, and I look up at him. "No. I mean, that part is a shock, yeah, but I love her, and I think once I got over that shock, I'd be happy. Really happy. We're technically married, and I didn't balk at that. Not for a second. I want this life with her, even if I didn't plan for it to start immediately. But that doesn't change the reality. The baby is not mine. It's Brody's."

My parents look at each other again, and part of me knows what they're thinking. My dad accidentally got my mom pregnant after a one-night stand, but neither knew who the other was, and my dad didn't know I existed until my mom moved up to Boston and accepted a job that put her as the Rebels' ortho-pedic surgeon. But I was his, not some other guy's.

"But she wants to stay with you?" my mom shoots back at me.

"Yes. She said she was asking for whatever I was willing to give her."

I pause as something hits me. Does it matter that it's not mine if she wants me regardless? Suddenly, I don't know.

As if answering my unspoken question, he says, "A lot of men choose to raise children who aren't theirs. Callan did it with Katy."

"Katy is his niece," I retort.

"Do you love Willow?"

"What?" That catches me by surprise, and I tilt my head at my dad. "What does Willow have to do with this? Katy is like my cousin."

"Ah, but she's not actually your cousin. She's not blood at all, and neither is Willow. But you were there for Katy when she was pregnant. Even before she got pregnant and was trying. You love them, right?"

"Of course," I answer easily.

"And Willow?" he persists. "If Katy came to you and said I need you to help me raise Willow and be a father to her, how would you respond?"

"I wouldn't hesitate to. But..." It's not the same thing. Is it? I loved baby Willow even before I knew she was baby Willow. I loved her when Katy was pregnant with her from the moment we found out she was pregnant. I loved feeling her move in Katy's stomach, and when I heard Katy was in premature labor, I dropped everything and ran to the hospital. And when Willow got sick and needed surgery, it was the same deal. No, she's not mine, but she's Katy's and—

"I know this hurts," my mother offers, placing her hand on

my forearm and drawing me out of that reverie. "I can't imagine it for you. But Sorel's giving you a choice, yes?"

"Yes. I think so. We didn't get that far. I left. But she said she didn't want to end what we have."

"You don't want to lose her?"

"No." I meet her gaze. "I don't want to lose her."

I get a soft smile in return. "Then I guess the only question is, can you love her baby because you love her?"

I blink at my mother and blow out a breath. Sweat continues to slide down my face, but I don't care. I hardly notice it. Can I love her baby because I love her? The way I love Willow because she's Katy's? Nice move, Mom and Dad.

My head falls to my knees, and I close my eyes, letting that question flow over me. I think about Sorel being pregnant. Going to doctor's appointments and getting ultrasounds. I think about her belly growing and buying furniture for a nursery.

I don't know what Brody said to her. I don't know if he's going to be involved or not. He'd be the dad. I'd be... I don't know what. What would I be? Sorel and I are barely together. It's been only a few days. We may be married, but she views it as fake and doesn't want us to stay that way. She said she'd try with me, and now this happened.

So what would I be to this child?

It's mother's boyfriend? That feels wrong. So inadequate. Not nearly enough for me. I'd want to be more. If I'm in something, I'm in it. I don't half-ass. I'd need to be more than that. Is that even what she wants from me? She didn't come right out and say that.

But she also didn't not say it.

Sorel isn't a single mom with a kid that I met and got to know after it was born. This is taking on everything from the start. Somehow that feels different. But is it? Being there is being there, and loving the child is loving the child.

Could I do that? Love her baby because I love her?

Hell, Sorel doesn't even know how I feel about her. Not fully anyway.

I sit up and look at my dad. "Would you have loved me if I hadn't been yours?" It's an impossible question to ask, but I do it anyway. "If Mom had shown up with a ten-month-old who wasn't yours, would you—"

"Yes, Mason. I would have loved you." He stares me down, not even a hint of reservation. He means it. "I would have been your stepfather and raised you as my son. Loving your mom meant loving all of her, and initially, I would have loved you for being a part of her. And then, I would have loved you for you."

I swallow and fall back against the couch, my fists digging into my eyes. Could I do that? Could I be part of this pregnancy, this child's life as its stepdad, or even as its dad if Brody doesn't want any part of it?

Yes. The word chimes through my head like a bell.

Yes, I could. What difference does it make if the baby is biologically mine? I'll love it because it's part of Sorel. I'll love it because she's mine, and that makes her baby mine. It's not what I would have wanted for us, but it's what's in front of me, and I don't quit. I don't give up. I don't fail, and I won't fail Sorel now. Not when she needs me. But more than that, I can't lose her. I can't walk away or let her go.

If Sorel wants me, she has me.

I stand and sign *I love you* to both of them and walk out. The front door slams behind me, and I sprint all the way home. By the time I reach the elevator, I feel like I've got this. That I can do it. It won't be easy, and I'll be jealous of Brody at every turn. I know I will be.

But Sorel doesn't want Brody.

She wants me.

And I want all of her, baby included.

I open the front door and go for the kitchen. It's empty, and the apartment is quiet. She wouldn't have left, right? Shit. She could have. She could have thought I was rejecting her. I told her I'd be back. That I just needed to think.

I jog from room to room. She's not in our bedroom or watching TV. She's not in the study, the gym, or the media room. I run down the hall and, without knocking, open the door to her old bedroom.

My lungs empty with relief when I find her sitting in her bed beneath the covers. She's holding her phone up in front of her face like she's watching something or FaceTiming someone. Her eyes well with more tears as she sees me, and I take a step toward her.

"I love you, and I want you, and I want the baby."

27

SOREL

For a moment, time stands still. I almost can't tell if I'm hallucinating at this point—it's been a hell of a day— or if he actually said every word I was hoping he would. Mason is young. He's a guy in his twenties and a football player at that. I didn't want or intend to saddle him with a pregnancy that's not even his, and in truth, I didn't think he'd want to be part of it, let alone burst in saying that.

He continues to surprise me in all the best ways.

Mason Reyes is the stuff of superhero fantasies and ultimate book boyfriends. I was friends with him for a year. How did I not see him until now?

"I'll call you later." Serena's voice comes through my phone, but I'm no longer paying attention to her. I can't pull my eyes off the large, sweaty, determined man filling up the doorway. *I love you, and I want you, and I want the baby.* My face falls into my hands, and I shake as more freaking tears start to pour out of my eyes. How I can still produce new ones is a marvel to me, and I'm positive I'm going to need an IV to rehydrate after all this.

But right now, I don't care.

I crawled into bed and called Serena the moment Mason left. I couldn't go into his room. It was his and definitely didn't feel like mine. For a moment, I thought about leaving, but he promised he'd be back, and I believed him. How could he not take time to think? Of course, he needed that.

So despite how painful and nerve-racking it was, I came in here to wait. I don't even know how long Mason was gone because Serena was next-level excited to become an aunt. She told me if Mason didn't come through, that she'd move back to Boston and the two of us would raise the baby like badass spinsters. She even started to plan the whole thing out for me, though I knew it was all to keep me distracted and make me laugh until Mason returned with a verdict.

Serena lives in Paris. Serena loves Paris. Lucky for her, it seems she's off the hook now.

Mason toes off his shoes and yanks his sweat-soaked shirt off before he climbs on the bed and pries my hands away from my face. "Is this good crying or bad crying?" he asks, hoisted up on his knees and hovering over me.

I gaze up at him, his green eyes light and sparkling with a smile on his lips that makes the dimple in his chin sink in enough to make him almost look amused.

"Did you mean it?"

He lowers to his haunches and holds my face in his hands as he stares deep into my eyes. "Every word."

"Good crying," I sob as tears fall like raindrops down my face.

"Shh, princess. No more tears." He practically chuckles as he gathers me into his arms.

I tuck myself against his chest, not even caring how sweaty he is. "I can't stop," I wail, feeling ridiculous and sublimely happy all at once. "You love me? Are you sure?"

Now he does chuckle. "I've never been so sure about anything. It's not new either. I realized it in Vegas." He lifts my chin. "Sorel, I've loved you for a year. You had me stuttering over my words the first time I met you, and no matter how hard I tried not to, I've wanted you like crazy every moment after that. I called you my instalove."

"What?" I pull back and look at him like he's crazy, my eyebrows folded together. "Your what?"

He smirks and smooths out the crease between my eyes. "My instalove. At first, it was more of a joke than anything. I haven't liked any woman as much as I liked you, and it was pretty immediate. It wasn't until we got married that I allowed myself to accept what it was and that I really was in love with you. It wasn't a crush or an infatuation as I had told myself. It was—*is*—love."

I wrap my arms around him and climb farther onto his lap until I'm straddling him. My face falls to his neck as gratitude like I've never experienced cascades over me. "Thank you," I whisper against his skin, keeping my face buried. "I was so afraid I was going to lose you and so heartbroken that the baby isn't yours. I still am." I pull back and meet his gaze so he knows. "I'd give anything for it to be yours."

He presses his lips softly to mine. "It will be mine, Sorel. I won't lie, that was a devastating blow, but I've thought about it, and I'll love it just as much as if it were biologically mine. I'll be its dad. If that's what you want from me."

Oh hell. Oh my hell. Oh my freaking hell.

My heart is racing so fast it explodes in my chest.

This man. I can't even with him. How is he real?

I hold him tighter and wrap myself around him like a vine, not even caring that he's next-level sweaty. "I don't know what I did to deserve you, but I'm so grateful for you. I think..." I swallow and lick my lips. "I think I love you too. In my head, it feels like it should be too soon for that, especially after everything I've been through over the last month, but in my heart, it doesn't feel that way. It feels right."

I sit back and wipe my face, but it's useless. These tears are persistent fuckers.

He kisses my cheeks, licking them off me. "Why are you still crying then?"

I laugh lightly. "I'm a broken faucet. I can't stop. But you know I'm going to get big and fat and be hormonal. More hormonal than this even. You know all of this, right? It's not the best way to start a new relationship. And there's that side of this too. This is so new for us."

"I don't care." He kisses me and kisses me and kisses me until I'm breathless. "You're going to get big and fat and I'm going to love every inch of it. Every curve. Every swell. Hell, I already love how big and sensitive your tits are. I'm going to have a fucking blast with those."

I laugh as he stares down and tries to squeeze one. I playfully smack his hand away, and he kisses my neck.

"As for the hormones?" He shrugs indifferently. "I'll do my best and try to be as supportive as I can. I'm not sure any guy can promise more than that. But if your hormones mean you cry, then that only means I get to hold you and kiss them away, so I've got no complaints there." A kiss to my nose. "Stop trying to scare me off. It won't work. I'm in this. For all of it. We're going to have a baby together. It'll be great."

"Stop!" I wail. "I want to stop crying and you're making me cry harder when you say perfect things like that."

"Are you okay with this? With me not just being a boyfriend or supportive? With me wanting to be part of all of it, including being a dad or stepdad or whatever I'll be. Because Sorel? I don't think I can just be there as a side character. If I'm in this, I need to be in this all the way."

"Am I okay with it?" Now it's my turn to laugh. "Yes. I'm more than okay with it. I mean, it's new and I'm scared. So much can happen between us at any time, but if that's what you want, it's what I want too. I hadn't even allowed myself to get that far with my thoughts. It's a dream I didn't think I'd have. I thought you'd run off, and I wouldn't have blamed you for it."

"It's a lot to process. I won't lie about that. And I'll have moments. Dark moments. Especially if I'm sharing this baby and you in any way with Brody."

I lean in and kiss his lips, shifting so my feet go on either side of his waist. "I don't know what Brody's going to be or not going to be. I told him this morning, and other than asking me to move to New York, he didn't commit or not commit. I'm sorry. I know that's not what you want to hear, but I'm going to be honest and tell you everything."

He swallows and nods. "I want you to. Even if it hurts to hear."

I gulp. "I told him if he wanted to be part of the baby's life, I'd welcome that. He's the father, and I'd never keep a willing parent out of my child's life. But I also told him I'd do this without him, and I'd be fine with that too."

"So the ball's in his hands now?"

My expression grows soft and contrite as I answer, "Yes."

He hisses out a breath and falls onto his back, staring up at the ceiling. It's an awkward angle, and I adjust myself.

"Stop moving like that. You're making me hard, and right now I have fucking Brody in my head."

I giggle. I don't even know why.

He pops his head up and glares at me. "That's funny?"

"That I'm making you hard while you're thinking about Brody? Kind of."

His lips twitch before his expression sobers again. "I don't know what I want to happen. I mean, I want him out of your life forever because that's the jealous, possessive guy in me, but for the baby... I don't know."

I collapse forward until I'm directly on top of him, my face right above his. Mason is intense. He's all gut reactions and strong feelings. Feelings he's not shy or afraid of. I admire that about him. In many ways, we're opposites like that. But right now, I'm trying. I'm trying to be more like that and less closed off. It's a fight. It's an internal struggle. But I owe it to him. That and so much more.

"I don't know either," I admit. "I think we need to prepare for either eventuality. But it doesn't change how I feel about you. It doesn't change that I'm with you and not him. I swear."

"I trust you."

I smile. Swallow. Lick my lips. And ignore the thrashing of my wary heart. "I trust you too. So don't do something stupid and fuck that up." I say it in jest, but he knows I mean it too.

"Yes, ma'am." He stretches his neck and kisses me. It's a promise. A bond. "When did he say he'd let you know?"

"He didn't." I pause. Hesitate. But if I'm doing this with Mason and he's doing this with me, it's what I'd do with the father of my baby. "I um. I have a picture."

"A picture?" he parrots.

"I had an ultrasound this morning. It's how I knew how far along I was." I bite into my lip but force myself to stop. I'm done questioning or waiting for Mason to run. He's here. He says he's in this, and I just told him I trusted him. "Do you want to see it?"

His green eyes glitter. "Can I?"

I climb off him and go over to the nightstand. The picture is sitting there because I showed Serena. "Serena says it looks like her," I quip, tossing back the same corny joke she threw at me. It did manage to make me laugh when she said it. Serena and I are mirror-image twins.

Mason rolls his eyes and sits up. I try to ignore the fact that he's sweaty and shirtless, but hell, that's not always so easy when it comes to him and his sexy man muscles. He takes the four-by-four square from my hand and holds it in his. He doesn't say anything, and for a few minutes, he simply stares at it, his expression unreadable.

"What are you singing?" he asks absently, his gaze still on the picture.

I hadn't realized I was singing aloud. "'Friday I'm In Love.'"

He squints. "Who sings that one?"

"The Cure."

A head bob and a quirked eyebrow. "You're going to raise my child on '90s music, aren't you?"

"Mason, stop!"

He laughs and nips at my neck, but his hand takes mine, and he threads our fingers together. "Nineties music and HGTV. That's a lot to grow up on."

"Oh, and your chick flicks, weird protein shakes, and peanut butter bomb things aren't? Let me guess, you won't let it eat sugar."

"Not during football season, I won't. If it's a boy, promise me you won't be one of those mothers who doesn't let him play football."

I grimace. "I'll think about it. But girls can play football too."

"True." He smirks. "That would be badass." He sets the picture down on the nightstand and pulls me back onto his lap until I'm straddling him.

"What are you doing?"

"Come on, princess. I need a shower, and you're taking one with me."

28

SOREL

He scoots us to the edge of the bed. Shifting me around on his lap, he stands and walks us into the bathroom.

"A shower?" I question, smiling at him because I have a feeling this smile is going to be glued to my face for a long time to come. None of this was expected with him. I figured even if he said he'd stay, it wouldn't be like this. It wouldn't be him talking about the baby as his or making plans for it and wanting to see the picture.

I didn't think he'd want to be a partner. Not after the last month and last few days we've had. He says he's loved me for a year, and I wish I had known it sooner. I wish I had left Brody for him back then.

"You're saying I don't need one?" he quips.

"You definitely do." I scrunch my nose and lean into his ear. "You smell."

"Good or bad?"

"I'm not answering that."

He laughs. "I probably stink. I ran about fifty miles after a full day of practice. It's a wonder I haven't passed out from dehydration."

"You? I'm the one who's been crying all day."

"Then we'll both shower, eat some dinner, and rehydrate. But right now, I'm not willing to let you go, so you're coming with me."

"A shower sounds pretty great," I admit. "So does dinner. Maybe pasta. Real pasta."

He groans. "Tease. I'll make you real pasta, but you have to try my plant-based one."

"I'll have a bite."

His eyes hold mine, and slowly he tilts his head to lean in and kiss me. His lips slide effortlessly with mine, and for a few minutes, we stand in the bathroom with me in his arms. Kissing. Tasting. Holding. Loving. Having a moment that's more than words with each other. It leaves me winded and my heart racing.

Setting me down on my feet, he then opens the shower door and starts up the water. He strips out of his track pants and boxer briefs. I get going on my own clothes, pulling my sweatshirt over my head, while he goes after my leggings. It's so surreal. All of this is.

"What a month," I muse, and Mason cracks up.

"No fucking joke." He glances up at me through his dark lashes. "But a really good one. A surprising one."

I drag my fingers through his sweat-dampened hair. "You're surprising. In the best of ways."

Once he has me naked, he scoops me back up into his arms and walks us into the shower. Warm water cascades over both of us as we stand beneath it, holding each other and enjoying the wet heat. I tilt my face to the stream and let it wash away the salt of my tears and the puffiness from my eyes. I don't know what it's going to happen with Brody. That's a massive uncertainty. One that will weigh on me until all of this is fully figured out.

But for now, I can't help but relax and enjoy this.

"You know, we're already married."

I drop my chin and narrow my gaze. "Your point?"

"My point is that we're married and now we're having a baby."

"Mason—"

"So you understand that even though I mentioned this the other night, we're not getting an annulment or a divorce."

I sigh. I wondered when this would come up.

"I'm more than capable of taking care of this baby both physically and financially and don't need the help of a husband for that. I want you, but we're skipping past all the stuff we shouldn't be skipping."

He holds the nape of my neck. "I know you can do it on your own. I never doubted that for a second. But you don't have to do it that way. You're not alone, and you don't have to do it alone. I'm in this with you."

"Mason, being pregnant is not a reason to stay married. Don't you think it's wise to take that extra piece of this off the table? The marriage wasn't real. It was a fuck you. I haven't done a lot of things right over the last month, but I don't see the benefit to staying in a marriage like that when we're trying to build something real."

"The marriage was real for me," he says plainly, and I find myself staring at him in shock. It's one thing to tell someone you love them and that you want to be with them, but marriage is next level. He went through that whole night... I glance down at my hand. At the princess-cut diamond eternity band.

My heart picks up its pace.

I feel sick. I had no idea. All the ways I've pushed him away. Would I even have been able to hear any of this a month ago?

"It doesn't have to mean everything. We can be together as

we are now. I can take you out on dates, and we can see where this thing is going between us the way any other couple would, but I love you, and you think you love me too." He grins tauntingly. "Besides, we still have about two months left on our three-month deal."

"Mason," I whisper, at a loss for words.

"I want us to stay married," he continues. "I want you to be my wife. I want to be the father of your children. Yes, this all got rushed and wasn't how I had planned to do it with you, but so what?" He shrugs and holds my chin. "That's life, right? We messed up the steps and did them all out of order, but what we have is as real as it gets."

I stare at him, utterly bewildered. "How are you like this? How are you wanting all of this with me? I keep waiting for the other shoe to drop with you, but you're like a shell game. Just when I think I know what cup the ball is under, I'm proven wrong, and you surprise me."

"You don't see it, do you? Maybe because you've been with the wrong people or because this thing between us is new for you, but it's not for me."

I look at the floor between us. "I've had a lot of incredible things in my life, but the only people who haven't betrayed me have been my family. My best friend in high school. My college best friend with Brody. It's hard to believe this won't turn into that too." I look back up at him. "You feel too good to be true, and it scares me. But I'll try to have faith and trust."

"Good. Because I couldn't breathe a day in this world without you. I need you like I need air." With that, he kisses me and steals mine. And in his kiss, I feel the truth behind his words. He could say a million things. Promise me whatever I want to hear. But it's empty, and he knows it. I don't need his verbal reassurance. I need this. I need him.

As if hearing my unspoken words, he walks me backward until I'm pressed against the shower wall. Pinning me in place with his large body, he deepens the kiss, his mouth devouring as his tongue holds me hostage. I'm so lost in the kiss, so lost in the feel of him that I twitch when his hand meets my breasts, only that surprised jolt quickly turns into a deep moan.

He smirks against my lips but doesn't say anything. He's too busy kissing me with no immediate plans to stop. His large hand lifts and shakes my breast, making the soft tissue jiggle. Another squeeze, and my eyes roll back in my head. I got a taste of how sensitive they are the other night, but god, if this is how it's going to be for the next seven months, I'll be attacking him constantly.

"You know that at some point I'm going to have to fuck these and then come on them, right?"

"Uh-huh. Whenever you want." I grab the back of his neck and turn my head the other way so I can kiss him from this angle.

"Oh, and nipple clamps. Those could be fun too. I want to make you come with just these." He uses both hands to squeeze them, and fuck, I could see how I could come from just that. It makes my clit pulse every time he does it like the two are now hardwired to each other.

"Sounds awesome," I murmur against his lips. "How about you get going on that making me come thing?"

"Needy little pregnant wife, aren't you?"

"Oh, god, yes," I cry out, my head falling back as he pinches my nipple at the same time he pinches my clit.

"With how responsive you are, you're going to be living on my cock, fingers, and mouth until you deliver this kid."

I can't reply. Not when he's rubbing my clit and kneading my tits, but I certainly have no objections. I need this. After everything that's happened in the last two days, I need it so badly. I don't even care if my ribs ache right now. They'll get over it, and a little pain never killed anyone.

"It's early still," I hum as he rubs circles on my clit and alternates that with running his finger up and down my slit. "We can do this all night. I don't have work tomorrow."

He grins against me. "Yes, but I do, and I need to not be sore or overworked."

"Ugh, your job sucks."

He laughs. "I'll make it up to you. I'll fuck you so good all night Sunday. You're a doctor. You're used to working on no sleep."

"True. But fuck me now. Please, Mason. Fuck me now."

"You have to be a good girl and come for me first."

"Yes, daddy."

He chokes on a wheezy laugh, his forehead falling to my shoulder. "If I weren't already married to you, I'd marry you again."

"Make me come, and I just might let you."

The way his fingers work only my clit makes my empty core desperate to be filled. With his cock, his fingers, I don't care. I'll take anything from him right now. I loop my leg up and around his hip and lean back against the wall. His mouth follows me, and he kisses me the way he's playing with my pussy, hard and rough with dizzying circles that make my head spin.

But the real killer is when he lifts my breast between us and tucks his chin so he can lick my nipple while still playing with my lips and tongue.

"Lick yourself with me," he commands.

My eyes snap open, and he's right there, watching me with a look so dark and hungry, I can't help but join him. My tongue rubs his and my nipple at the same time, twirling and flicking the same way he is. His eyes smolder, reaching new depths, and pleasure skyrockets through me. It's dirty and sexy, and what he's doing to my pussy feels so good I find myself grinding harder into his hand until I come.

My orgasm barrels through me, making it almost impossible to stand. As it is, I can't continue to lick him or my nipple because I'm now pressed into the wall, eyes closed as I ride wave after wave.

The moment a smile starts to curl my lips and my body relaxes, Mason lifts me and immediately thrusts straight inside of me. It's one of my favorite things he does. Not just the feel of him, but the impatience of him. The way he can't handle waiting for another second to be inside me. His cock fills me up so perfectly, and with how he's holding me and touching me and the words he's murmuring in my ear...

"I love you," slips right past my lips.

He pauses, our bodies tight and connected, his cock as deep as it can be.

"Open your eyes so I know you meant it," he orders, his voice unusually sharp.

My eyes spring open, and I stare straight into his fiery green gaze.

"I mean it," I promise him. "I love you."

"Wow." He breathes out a laugh. "You have no idea how many times I've thought about how those words would sound. It's pathetic how obsessed with you I am. I'm high. My dream girl loves me back."

I grab the back of his head and slam his lips back to me. With that, his mouth attacks mine, voraciously kissing me as he starts to fuck up into me, holding my weight with his hands and thighs. He's so strong and powerful and I gasp as he kisses and fucks me deeper.

It doesn't take him long before he's pounding into me. All I can do is hold on and breathe and feel. His body hits my clit with every powerful thrust, shooting sparks of electricity through me. I didn't know sex could be like this. I'd read about it. Even seen some of it in movies and shows, but I chalked that up to fantasy and spun fairy tales.

But the way Mason fucks me is unlike anything else. It's so much more than physical. It's visceral.

I kiss Mason's wet neck, tasting the remnants of the salt from his sweat. My hands fist in his hair as I get closer, lost in the loud smacking of our wet bodies. I can't help but move and squirm under his as he rams into me, fucking me with passion and fire and love and desperation. He grinds down on my clit, and I can't hold back.

"I'm so close."

"God, Sorel," he moans into me, nibbling on my lips and jaw and neck. "What are you doing to me?"

"Everything you're doing to me." I ride down onto him, trying to force him in until there is no space left that he's not filling.

His wet hand slides along my ass and straight in between my spread cheeks.

"Holy fuck, Mason!" I yell when he plays with my asshole for a moment before he digs his finger straight in.

"Ride me, princess. Ride my cock and my finger. Take me in both your holes."

Jesus hell. I quiver as he pumps both inside me, egging me on, urging me to take him just as he said. It's full like this. Tighter than it was before, and Mason is not a small man. Nothing on him is. Not his cock or his fingers. It burns in my ass a little, but not enough for me to want him to stop.

I gasp as he shifts and hikes me up higher so he can capture a nipple in his mouth. I'm dead. Gone. Holy freaking hell!

His finger continues to fuck my ass as his cock does the same, and he's getting close. So close his eyes are black, and his expression is glazed. He loves this. He loves taking me like this, and I've never been so turned on in my life.

"Tell me," I pant. "Tell me."

"Tell you what, princess? That your cunt feels so good. So tight. That I can't wait to feel my cock in your ass next. That you're my dirty slut who loves to take my cum from me."

Yes. That.

I nod, words failing me, my body trembling and spasming as my orgasm hits me like nothing ever has. A scream wrenches from my lungs, and my toes curl. He continues to pound me through it, the pulsing feel of my clit, the convulsions of my pussy, and the heaviness of my tits are euphoric.

With a heavy grunt and a low growl, he plants his face into my neck and comes, his teeth sinking into my shoulder as he does. With heavy pants, we hold each other, both of us still shaking and unable to speak. He slides his finger out of my ass but keeps his cock buried in me.

"I love you," I whisper, and I feel him smile against me.

It's true. Only someone with a heart like his could have pieced me back together and made me unafraid to fall and to trust. He was right in front of me for a year, and I didn't see it. Or didn't allow myself to. I'm so glad Brody cheated. I'm so glad Mason was outside the church when he was. I'm so glad I went to Vegas with him. I'm even glad I married him.

Undeniably, Mason's love is the best thing to ever happen to me.

And I'll do whatever I have to do to protect it. And him.

29

MASON

If nerves had a color, they'd be black. Or maybe vomit green. Definitely vomit green since I'm a bit sick to my stomach, and yet oddly turned on, so there's that. The sight of Sorel across the lawn of the Fritz compound talking to her parents and grandmother is triggering my dick. And my gag reflex.

And before you think that's gross or wrong, it's not my fault. She's throwing me coy, sexy looks every chance she gets. For the last few days, it's been nonstop sex every chance we get, and with each glance, memories of her naked and me coming all over her tits early this morning flash through my head. What's triggering my nerves is that Sorel is only eight weeks along, and with that, she's decided to keep things about her pregnancy quiet.

What's happening right now is complicated.

She's telling her parents and grandparents we're together. But she's not telling them she's pregnant. At least for now. And she asked that I keep that part of this a secret too.

Not so easy for me when surrounded by my best friends, whom I don't keep secrets from.

Compounding that, tomorrow I have my first regular-season game at one, and I just got here from our team walk-through, where things were a bit shaky. I have a lot on my mind. I need a win tomorrow. I feel like a dickhead for being here and having not yet told some of our people that Sorel and I are actually together, let alone pregnant. My main people know, but they don't know how serious it is because that's not the sort of thing you relay over text.

They think we're trying. Because that's what I had told them. Then everything else happened.

In fairness, I've been busy, and so have they. I texted that I needed to talk to them, and so far, it's been impossible to connect. Even with Stone, who lives next door. Tinsley left this morning for two months, so he's been completely focused on her like I've been completely focused on Sorel. And football. I've been focused on that too.

And the fact that my girl is pregnant.

Brody called her yesterday to say he needed more time to think. She said fine after being on the phone with him for more than twenty minutes. The two of them talked, and I didn't eavesdrop, though I was desperate to. She didn't tell him about me, and he didn't ask. I don't know what to make of any of this. Her reasoning for not saying anything was valid. She didn't want him to make a gut-check, emotional reaction based on jealousy or one-upping. This is a child, and Brody needs to be in it for the right reasons.

I get that.

Doesn't mean I like it.

Brody's indecision is another reason she wants to keep the situation on lockdown until she has a definitive decision from him.

At some point, Brody will need to know that I'm a package deal with Sorel and the baby. But being patient—as I've proven over the last five weeks—isn't exactly my fortitude. That's another thing. We're just about at the halfway to the end of our three-month bargain. What happens then? We didn't fully figure that out, and we haven't talked about it again since the shower.

It's weighing on me. I want Sorel only for myself as my wife. I don't want to have to share her or the baby with anyone else. I want them as mine and mine alone. But the baby isn't technically mine, and with that, there's a chance I'll always be second behind Brody.

"Hey, man. Glad you could make it." Owen comes in beside me with a slap to my back as he sips something I'm desperate to snatch from his hands and down in one gulp.

"Wouldn't have missed it."

Today is the annual Fritz end-of-summer bash. The massive lawn spread out before me is littered with children and adults dressed in wild colors running around since Rory requested a rainbow theme party, and Octavia Abbot-Fritz never half-asses anything. It looks like the most kickass gay pride party you've ever seen.

There are bouncy houses, clowns, balloon animal makers, cotton candy machines, crafts tables, and an ice cream truck. That's all in addition to the pool, waterslide, spread of food as far as the eye can see, and, of course, since it's a Fritz event, a large, fully stocked bar that I could use about now but don't get to indulge in.

"Rory seems to be having a great time," I note, watching Owen's daughter run around in her rainbow bathing suit. I try to focus on the fun around me, but like a magnet, my eyes skip over to Sorel and lock on Landon, who is staring at me with a look I can't read. She asked to talk to them alone about us being together. She told me I have nothing to be nervous about because they already love me, but the fact that I want to raise a baby that isn't mine as my own will thrust me up to superhero status.

When she tells them that part.

The jury is out on that. Her father already doesn't like me because I married his daughter in Vegas, and if ever there was a woman I want to make proud of me—other than my mother— it's Octavia. Plus, I think Stone and Owen might, well, I don't know what.

"She'll be throwing up by the end of the day for sure, but for now, she's enjoying herself. How are things going with—"

"Oh, my hell, take Willow from me." Katy shoves baby Willow directly into my arms before she proceeds to rip her shirt off right here in front of us.

"Speaking of throwing up." I gag. "What the hel—heck, Katy?" I correct my language since Katy doesn't like us swearing in front of baby Willow, who isn't exactly a tiny baby anymore. She's fifteen months old and walks or runs all the time. At the moment, she's in only a diaper, and I wrap one arm beneath her little butt and another around her back to hold her.

"She threw up all over my shirt. What else am I supposed to do?"

"Go into the bathroom?" Owen shoots back at her.

Katy rolls her eyes at us. "Grow up. It's a bra. They're boobs. You've both been around when I've breastfed her in the past, and you've both seen me in a bikini that shows way more than this. Besides, the bathroom is like fifteen miles away."

"Or a two-minute walk," Owen supplies, averting his gaze from his half-naked best friend.

"You try walking two minutes when you're covered in hot dog and ice cream vomit."

"Still..." He trails off. That's a difficult thing to argue.

"Mwaysn," Willow says, delight on her face as her slimy hands plaster themselves onto my cheeks.

"Hello, my darling girl. How's my favorite toddler? I haven't seen you in a bit."

"That's because you've been busy," Katy throws back at me

with a knowing lilt to her voice. "We should plan a movie night. Bennett is working nights for the next ten freaking days."

"Bummer. I bet you miss Daddy." I kiss her forehead. "Is your tummy okay?"

She gives me a wet, toothy smile, though her breath isn't fun. I can smell the throw-up on her, and unlike the two doctors on my right, I don't do so well with bodily fluids like that. I try not to gag. I try very hard.

"I guess I'm going to have to learn to get used to this baby vomit stuff," I muse only to freeze when both Katy and Owen do the same. Shit. I wasn't supposed to say that.

"What exactly do you mean by that?" Owen's eyes narrow on me.

"Um. Well." I don't lie to these people. I can't. Forget throwing up, my body revolts against it. It's like I've been programmed for truth and honesty.

"Tell me how I'm supposed to survive two months without my girl," Stone mercifully interrupts, only to scrunch his nose. "What's that smell?"

"And why are you half-naked?" Vander follows up.

Katy rolls her eyes at them too as she pulls a shirt out of her massive diaper bag and slips it over her head. "Happy now? You can all get over the panic of me in a bra. And for a pediatric emergency room attending, Stone, you'd think you'd know the aroma of baby vomit when you smell it."

"Right," Stone continues without missing a beat. "But I'm not at work, so I shouldn't have to smell vomit when I'm off the clock."

"Try living with Rory," Owen counters. "And you went two years without Tinsley. You can handle two months now."

Stone glowers. "You think it's a bad idea if I surprise her in London next month?"

"I told him it's clingy," Vander states with a shrug. "Tinsley already warned him that she'll be on a tight schedule with filming."

"Still, I think that's sweet," Katy tells him. "If you want to go to London, go to London, but she'll be busy, and you'll have to deal with that." She tries to steal Willow back from me, and I twist my body so she can't.

"Mine."

"Mwine," Willow repeats and I grin, bouncing my eyebrows at Katy.

"Ugh. Fine. Keep my kid."

"I will." I grin smugly. "My girl loves me. Right, baby rock star? You're getting so good with your words, sweetheart." I kiss her nose only to regret it when I get another whiff of puke.

"She is," Katy agrees. "And big. How is she already this big? I told Bennett we need to try for another. The world needs more babies."

"Can you have more babies?" Vander asks. Katy is a type 1 diabetic and has endometriosis. She had trouble with her pregnancy and ended up delivering early.

"I thought about a surrogate. Sorel once offered. Maybe I'll take her up on it."

I choke. On nothing. Then I cover it with a cough and a laugh because I don't think Katy was serious.

Owen is staring at me again. He's no fool. Not by a long stretch. As if to prove this point, Owen says, "You're keeping something from us."

"No," I answer quickly while averting my gaze and keeping it on Willow, who is now squirming because she wants to get down so she can run.

"That's why you just squeaked like a thirteen-year-old whose balls haven't yet dropped?" Stone jumps in, and now everyone's eyes are on me.

"Oh, my hell, Sorel is pregnant!" Katy practically screams.

"Shhh!" I hiss, glaring at her as I set her daughter

down so she can chase after the other kids. No one seems to care that she's only in a diaper, and Katy is too busy staring at me as if someone just branded her ass with an electric prod. "How could you even figure that out so quickly? What do you have, some sort of mind reading magic?"

"Wait!" Stone grabs my arm and twists me so I'm facing them. "Is that true?"

I sag a bit. "Yes. She's pregnant."

"Holy shit," Owen exclaims. "Why weren't you going to tell us?"

"I was. When the time was right. When she told me it was okay to. It's not simple." I glance around to make sure no one else is around. Oliver, Amelia, Layla, and Callan walk by, and I throw them an awkward wave. They look at me as if I'm nuts, and I turn back to my friends with my face in my hands.

"Why are you waving at my grandparents and parents like a six-year-old waving at Mickey Mouse?" Katy questions.

"Because I'm losing it," I cry, my hands flailing about "The baby isn't mine."

"The baby isn't yours?!"

"Jesus, Stone. Why don't you shout a little louder so the entire party can hear you?"

He grimaces sheepishly.

Owen holds up a hand. "Stop. Start from the beginning because nothing is making sense right now."

"The baby is Brody's," Vander states flatly, and I throw him a side-eye, though I shouldn't be surprised he already knows. "What? You have me checking up on him so I am. It's in his texts. Speaking of those—"

"Wait. Shut up for a second." Katy comes over and clasps my forearm, her eyes all over my face. "Are you okay?"

This is why I love her. "Yes. I'm okay now. It was a big shock and not a fun one to find out that the baby isn't mine, but Sorel and I are together, and I've made the decision to be part of the pregnancy and raise the baby like it's mine."

Katy climbs up onto her tiptoes and kisses my cheek. "I told her you're one of the best men I know, and you just proved that a million times over. I'm so proud of you, Mason. I mean it. That couldn't have been an easy decision."

"Shockingly enough, it's Baby Willow that made me realize I could do it. I love Willow like she's mine because you're mine." I shrug. "If you had ever asked me to raise her as my own, I wouldn't have hesitated. My dad pointed that out, and he was right."

Katy wraps her arms around me and hugs me tight. "I'm so happy for you."

"Thanks, babe. I am too. Sort of."

"What do you mean, sort of?" Stone pries as Katy steps back.

"I mean there's still a lot of uncertainty with Brody. He hasn't made a decision yet if he's in or out." I turn my focus to Vander. "Unless you know something I don't."

"He told his dad and Eloise that she's pregnant with his kid. His dad told him to be a man and step up, and Eloise told him that Sorel was lying and conniving and simply trying to hurt him. She told him to get a paternity test."

My eyes widen. "She said that?"

"Yes. Brody told her that Sorel sent an ultrasound picture that showed how far along she is and that he knows Sorel wouldn't lie and didn't cheat. He knows the baby is his."

My brows furrow, but Owen beats me to the question that is hovering on the tip of my tongue.

"Why would he tell Eloise about the baby?"

Vander shakes his head at a loss. "No clue. They hadn't talked in weeks. Not since Brody called it off between them after the wedding didn't happen. He asked if they could meet up to talk."

Weird. Okay. In truth, I hadn't thought much about Eloise. I don't think Sorel's had any contact with her, but I'll have to mention—

"They're all totally fine with it." A bump on my shoulder from Sorel drags me out of it. "Grandma and my mom especially love it. My dad is warming up to the idea." She beams at me. "See. All good. Like I told you."

I lean in and kiss the corner of her lips. "That's a relief. Um." I glance at my friends and then back at her. "So, I might have—"

"You're pregnant?" Katy practically tackles her with a full-body hug. "I can't believe you didn't tell us."

Sorel gives me a perturbed look. "You told them I'm pregnant without me?!"

"You're pregnant?!" comes two sets of voices from behind us.

All of us spin around at once.

"Grandma. Dad. Hi!"

30

MASON

Nothing has gone right this afternoon. And I mean fucking nothing. It's the second game of the season against a heavily favored team, the San Diego Storm, and so far, my center got hurt and carted off the field, my guys are dropping passes that straight-up hit them in the hands, and now my helmet mic isn't working. Oh, and we're down ten points.

I look over to my dad on the sidelines, who is talking into his headset. I shake my head and tap my helmet at my ears. He stops talking and signs, *You can't hear me?*

I shake my head again and sign back, *Headset not working.*

I read a curse slur across his lips.

He signs back. *Then run the play you want.*

Because there are people on the sidelines who watch coaches to try to read signs teams throw out. Except we're not using code. We're using American Sign Language, and that's not too difficult to decipher. This means until this issue can be fixed, the offense is mine to run.

I turn back to my guys in the huddle, my gaze flicking up toward the massive screen above the end zone. Fourteen seconds are left on the play clock, and I will not take a timeout or a delay of game penalty.

"We're flying solo, so I'm saying we fuck with them all and go deep." I meet each of their gazes. We're down and need a score since we only have seven minutes left in the fourth quarter. "Let's get into field goal range. Slant left, straight shot to Morris on three. And you will catch it. Ready, break!"

We separate and get into position. And with five seconds left on the play clock, I count down while surveying the defense, reading for a blitz or a defender set to come up the middle now that we have our backup center out here.

"Hike!" I draw back in the pocket and immediately have to run to my right instead of left because a defender is there just as I would have anticipated. I roll around him and shoot a quick glance up the field. Morris is getting into position, outrunning the corner, and I let my arm fly.

On my next breath, I get hit from behind, going straight down, but my eyes are still on the ball sailing through the air. Morris somehow manages to catch it, though it just barely misses the fingers of the other team. He makes it another ten yards before he's brought down, and fuck yeah, first down in field goal range.

Running up to the line, we huddle up again, and I can feel it. Some life is getting back into us. "We're not there yet, but I want to shove it down their throats. Let's run this right up the middle," I bark. "They won't expect it right now. I want all the blocks you can give on this one. Let's do it. We're playing for the fucking win tonight."

I get a round of raucous cries and helmet smacks as we get set and line up in formation. I shout out a bunch of hard counts and point out the defense when they look like they're going to blitz. Still, they're expecting another pass. I can see it. Sweat tickles the back of my neck, and my fingers hum with anticipation of the ball.

"Hike!" I yell and fall back the second the ball is snapped to me. I shift left and right and pump fake only to hand it off to our running back. And as I drew it up, he runs straight up the middle that isn't at all protected since the defense didn't think we'd rely heavily on the backup guy for a block.

Our running back stutters and pauses but then flies straight and doesn't stop, the ball tucked in his arm and against his chest as he sprints hard and fast.

"Go!" I cry, jumping up to see better and a moment later, he crosses the end zone. Touchdown! "Fuck yeah!" I run into the end zone and give him a headbutt. "Nice running! Let's win this!" I smack the helmet of a few other guys around us, all of us pumped beyond words.

I glance up toward the box and search until I make out my girl on her feet, jumping up and down. She's in my jersey, and I know my number is around her neck. I kiss two fingers and shoot them straight up to her and sign *I love you*. I get the same sign back, and my heart kicks up in my chest like a bull about to charge. If happiness were a color, it'd be the red and gold she's wearing with my number in white.

These two weeks since we found out she was pregnant have been the best of my life. She's in my bed. She's in my arms. She's on top of me and beneath me and on all fours for me. My girl is all smiles and sunshine again, and the moment I walk in the door, she's all over me. Her hormones aren't just tears, and I have no problems giving her everything she needs until she's so satisfied she all but passes out.

But it's more than that.

It's just having her back. It's us having dinner and watching TV or movies together. It's her singing and dancing along to whatever 90s song is playing in the kitchen if she's home before me and making dinner. It's her asking me this morning if I can come with her to her first official OB appointment—something I'd never miss.

Other than the shock to Landon and Octavia, we haven't told many people she's pregnant, just that we're together. She asked both of them to keep it quiet. My main people now obviously know, and she's told her sisters and mom as well as a few others, but that's it. She wants to wait until after that appointment, and she's closer to her second trimester.

I don't care. Now that my people know and I don't have to hide it from them, it's her show to run with that, and I'll follow her lead.

I thought her dad was going to kick my ass, but when she told him the baby was technically Brody's, and I still planned to be part of all of it, he didn't just shake my hand, he pulled me in for an unexpected man hug. Octavia too was near tears, and that woman doesn't show big emotions like that often.

The game continues, and with under thirty seconds left in the game, we hit a field goal to tie it and in overtime, we win. Covered in sweat and feeling like a champion because winning always feels that way, I come back onto the field to do postgame interviews. The reporters ask me questions, but suddenly, I catch a flash of that red and gold and adjust at the last minute to catch Sorel as she runs and leaps into my arms.

"Oh my gosh!" she exclaims. "That was amazing!" She kisses me, and I laugh.

"We're on TV."

"What?" Abruptly she pulls back, stunned and terrified, before she glances to her right at the reporter, who now looks like an eager beaver, practically shoving the camera in our faces. Sorel's hazel eyes go impossibly wide, and she scrambles out of my arms and tries to run off.

Instead, I grasp her hand and hold her still, keeping her tucked behind me and away from the cameras, but not allowing her to go far. I have no doubt we're being photographed anyway and that her in my arms will be all over the internet within seconds. Not even Vander could stop that.

The female reporter tries to bring Sorel back into her interview, but I make it clear, I won't engage. Two minutes later, it's done, and I hold Sorel's hand as we walk toward the tunnel.

"I feel so dumb," she mumbles self-deprecatingly. "I didn't even notice her or think about it. I was just excited to get on the field and tell you how amazing you were to come back and win like that."

"You know I don't care."

She glances up at me. "I suppose I shouldn't anymore either, right?" She shrugs. "I don't like the spotlight, and I don't like the attention, but you were incredible tonight. I was so proud. We all were." We stop before we reach the locker room. "I'm going to head home, but I'll listen to your conference in the car."

I lean down and kiss her lips. I don't care if we're still technically on the field or if cameras could catch us. I know she hates that side of this, but she's mine, and I want the world to know it.

"Did you know that Boston Sports Radio called me a cougar?" she remarks, a smile twisting her lips.

"Did they?" My lips bounce.

"You're a twenty-something-year-old stud, and I'm a woman past my prime in my mid-thirties," she mocks, sarcasm all over her. "No one can understand how we're together. They may think you're after my money."

I snort out a laugh at that and whisper in her ear. "I like that my wife is older than me. She's sexy as fuck. Those who can't see it are blind. And tonight, I plan to lick her tits until she comes and then fuck her until she comes again."

She moans and hip-checks me. "Behave." Another kiss, and I don't think happiness is a color anymore. It's just being near her. "I'll see you at home."

I head into the tunnel toward the locker room with another win on my shoulders and the woman of my dreams waiting for me in my bed. Everything feels perfect. And with that, much like Sorel, I suddenly find myself worried about the other shoe waiting to drop.

SOREL IS COMPLETELY OUT. Her body is tucked against mine, and her eyes flutter in a dream as she breathes heavily in her sleep. I came home, ate a light dinner, and we spent two hours watching TV and making out while stealing touches like a teenager before I convinced her to let me take her to bed, where I made her come until she all practically fell asleep in my arms.

I'm lying in bed beside her, but my mind is too active for sleep.

That's not all that uncommon after a game. I often go over everything I did wrong and everything I want to improve on for next week. It's nearing eleven and I'm watching the end of Sunday Night Football on my iPad with subtitles on when her phone rings on her nightstand. Sorel doesn't even stir, and I shift out from under her and crawl across the bed to make sure it's not her family or anything important given the late hour.

Brody. It's fucking Brody.

With a wry grin on my lips, I snag her phone from her nightstand and swipe my finger across the screen.

"Mrs. Fritz-Reyes's phone, her husband speaking."

Brody is silent for a beat. He expected Sorel to answer, but he should know that it's late, and Sorel isn't typically a late-night girl. Plus, she has work early tomorrow.

"She must not have told you then," he says quietly, almost smugly like he has the upper hand in this.

I grin. "You mean that she's pregnant? Yeah, she told me."

"How about that it's not yours. Did she tell you that it's mine?"

"Of course she told me. We don't hide things from each other." Now I grin smugly because that was a nice, cheap shot. "Besides, the baby is only biologically yours," I retort. "Otherwise, it's just as mine as she is."

"You motherfucker," he hisses angrily. "You don't even belong as part of this conversation."

I smirk and rub at my jaw, my gaze flicking over at Sorel, who is still out.

"You saw her with me tonight. Didn't you? That's why you're calling now. You saw us on TV. She told you she was pregnant with your kid more than two weeks ago, and other than that one call where you told her you needed more time, you haven't tried to contact her. Not one call. Not one text. She hasn't re-blocked you. Tonight, you see me with her and now you're calling."

"Fuck you, Reyes. You know nothing."

"You didn't think I'd stick around. You thought I'd bag out like a chump and Sorel would be alone to raise this baby. You didn't care so much about that part of it, just that you wanted me out of the picture. What kind of fucking man are you? Oh, wait. I already know. The kind who ruthlessly and unrepentantly screws around on his woman, knocks her up, and then doesn't even have the decency to try to do the right thing for her or the baby. But I guess I should be glad. Without you being a piece of shit, I wouldn't be in bed beside my sleeping wife."

"Sorel should be with me in New York. She's loved me for two years. She was set to marry me. You were nothing more than a friend to her. She told me so. She's just being stubborn and holding onto her anger, and I was giving her time to come to her senses with that. That's what I told her on the phone. Sorel needs the baby's *real* father, and I'm in New York."

"Jesus, man. How do you handle having an ego that big? I mean, I've met some narcissists in my life, but you might be the biggest. But you're correct. The baby does need a father, and with me, there's no moving required. I'm right here."

"Fuck you, asshole. You're nothing. She's using you to hurt me back. You're revenge and have been from the start. You're not real to her. Sorel never runs on the field. She never gets in front of cameras. She wanted me to see that. How stupid are you that you haven't figured that out yet? You're a goddamn bullshit rebound, and you don't even see it."

I can't lie, his words hit me below the belt if for no other reason than they're thoughts I've had before. She doesn't view this marriage as real, and I did start out as revenge and likely a rebound. Hell, she didn't even tell him I was still with her. She let him see it tonight on TV. But I'd rather cut off balls than let him know that.

"Aw, you're cute when you're jealous," I mock. "Funny thing about that, Brody? You have no clue all that Sorel and I have. And how sad is that for you? You threw away the best woman on this planet, and for what? A woman who you didn't even like beyond what she did with your dick?" I stop here, tempted to say something about how I know he's still talking to Eloise, but I don't. I can't reveal that I'm having him monitored.

"You're as dumb as you look and sound if you think you'll last with her. Soon enough, she'll be back in my bed, sleeping beside me, with our baby in her arms, right here in New York, and you'll be a thing of the past. You can bet on that."

"Hmm. Funny, because that sounds like a bit of a threat."

"Probably because it was."

"I don't take kindly to those. Especially when they include Sorel in the mix. But since we're passing threats back and forth, know this, I will fucking *kill* you if you mess with her. Point blank. You might not know me all that well, but I am the last person on this planet you want to fuck with."

He laughs. Actually laughs. Like I'm amusing him and shit. Legit, he has no clue. That's not even hyperbole. I will in fact kill the dude if he fucks with my woman and no one will find his body, and even if they do, there will be no evidence that points to me. I bet her dad will help. Hell, I bet all her uncles and cousins, and her brothers will help me.

But still. That might not be what's best for her.

I blow out a breath and drag a hand across my face to the top of my head as I get myself under control. I could keep fighting with him, but that won't help Sorel. I glance down at her, still fast asleep.

"Listen, Brody. Truth time? I'm not trying to be a dick. I love her. I've loved her for a long time, and I'm not going anywhere. She and I are in this for real, and I plan to raise the baby with her as mine. If you want to be a part of it, then I'll respect that and act accordingly. If that's not your game, then no one other than the three of us needs to know. But stop trying to fuck with her. Sorel deserves better than that. If you love her or ever loved her, think about your actions. She's been through enough. Let her be happy."

He makes a noise I can't quite decipher and hangs up.

Brody isn't done. I know that. He wouldn't have called her tonight if he were.

I play Brody's team in two weeks. I can only imagine how that'll go.

31

SOREL

Mmm. I sink a little lower under the blankets, feeling warm and soft and quite possibly having the best dream I've ever had. My eyes pinch closed, trying to chase it when I feel it momentarily slip away. A rush of cool air hits my wet clit, and I gasp. My eyes flash open, and I rip the covers up and peer beneath them.

Mason is between my spread thighs, a naughty smirk on his face as he blows cool air on me again. My lips part, and a moan slips out. "I thought it was a dream." My fingers rake through the thick strands of his hair, and I hum in pleasure.

"Not a dream," he promises. "Though I woke up hard just thinking about doing this. You have no idea how fucking good your pussy tastes right now."

"Is this what being with a younger man is like? If it is, I've been missing out all these years."

"Yes" is all he says as he rings my clit with the tip of his tongue.

"I want to see how hard you are."

The blankets slide down my body and get tossed away. Cool air tickles my skin, and I shiver ever so slightly.

"You want to see how hard you make me?"

"I was hoping I could feel how hard I make you. With my mouth."

He groans and shifts around to remove his boxer briefs and climbs up onto his knees, his hard cock smacking against his stomach. I lick my lips and reach out to run my hands up and down his firm abs before I grip his cock in my fist. He wheezes out a sharp breath, but his eyes are glued to my hand as I slowly jerk him.

"I love how that feels."

"You'll love how it feels more in my mouth."

He flashes up to me. "Lie back, and I'll feed it to you while I eat your cunt."

I swear, the mouth on this man is unlike any other. Sometimes it's just the things he says. Like he's not even trying to be dirty or get me off with it. It's just how his mind works, and I'm so here for it.

Speaking of...

I lie back, the Pixies', "Here Comes Your Man" pops into my head, and I giggle lightly.

Mason's face appears over mine with a questioning eyebrow raised.

"I have a weird mind," I explain.

He kisses my lips. "I love your weird mind. Share it with me."

"I had 'Here Comes Your Man' in my head."

He smirks. "Better that than 'Smells Like Teen Spirit.'"

I crack up. "Stop! I'll never get Nirvana out of my head now."

"Open your mouth, beautiful. I'll fill your head with something better."

Mason's thighs straddle my face, and I grab his dick in my hand and lick around his crown and into his slit. He hisses out a curse, but then I feel his hot breath on my skin, and I sigh in delight.

I've been doing everything I can not to think forward—something that is nearly impossible for me—and live in the moment with Mason. I'm ten weeks pregnant, I'm feeling good besides the occasional morning sickness and random bouts of dizziness, and other than when Brody called last week and spoke to Mason, I haven't heard from him. He didn't even bother to call back. He said he needed more time, but how much freaking time is more time? I want this baby to have a father, but more than that, I want it surrounded by love.

Brody is not love. Mason is.

A point he proves when he kisses my lower belly. He does it every time now before we get seriously physical. It's almost an apology to the baby, which never fails to make me smile. Like, *I'm sorry I'm about to do this to your mother, and please forgive me.*

It's so cute, and I eat it up with a spoon.

I'm not sure I've ever been this happy with anyone. With Brody, I always felt stressed and not good enough. I never felt comfortable being me or sharing my weird mind with him because he didn't get it, and he didn't try to. He expected me to accommodate him, and I did for reasons I can't even explain now. I shouldn't have had to change who I am. Not for anyone.

And with Mason, I don't even think about it. I'm me and he's him and it works. It's effortless. We like each other's weird. It's perfect, and it's what makes us perfect together. He's thoughtful and considerate and prioritizes me and my work and my needs, and in return, I do the same with him. Maybe it's true what they say, friends make the best lovers.

With my hand gripping his cock, I slide it all the way down my throat, past my comfort point until I start to gag. I try to swallow, but I haven't mastered the art yet, and it comes out sloppy. Mason doesn't care. He's licking my pussy like it's his favorite breakfast. His mouth and tongue devour me, and it's nearly impossible to give him anything resembling a halfway decent blow job with what he's doing. I want to blow his mind—literally. I want him to come straight down my throat. I want him to think this is the best blow job he's ever gotten. I want to suck his cock straight down my throat until his eyes fall back into his head.

But the way he's eating me makes that damn near impossible.

How can I focus on both things at once?

I attempt to center my attention on his dick. And his balls. I suck his cock like a prize whore—which, straight facts, turns me on. I lick and play and use my fingers to play with his balls, perineum, and even rectum. I may be boring, but I know enough to know that playing with a guy's ass or the space right behind his balls will have him lose his mind.

But all the while I work his hot, thick, large dick, he's all about my pussy. Or cunt as he likes to call it, and I think he only does that to catch me blushing at him.

Regardless of whether I'm focused or not, I can't help but moan and writhe and seek to take him deeper. His mouth. His fucking mouth! It's everything. And so good.

I grab the back of his upper thigh, hold on to his tight muscles, and go down on him. Or up in this case since his cock is above my mouth. The way he moans and pumps and fucks into me with renewed exuberance has me spinning. Two fingers slip straight inside of me and start to thrust right against my front wall while his tongue works my clit like a master violinist working his instrument.

"Princess. Fuck."

I can't even respond as I flatten my tongue and glide it up and down every veiny ridge and sensitive place. With my hand on his ass, I drive him in deeper, forcing my cheeks to hollow and my mouth to suck him as hard as I can the moment he hits the back of my throat. With that, the sounds coming from him are next level. It's such a power high. Such a trip. It doesn't matter that I'm gagging and drooling and fighting for air. I have tears streaming down my cheeks, and the back of my throat is on fire as he starts to pump faster into my mouth.

He's barely hanging on. His thighs are trembling, and his hands playing with me are unsure as his mouth gets lost with every deep pull I make. His cock grows thicker, longer, and I have to stretch my lips and throat to get him there while I do my best to breathe through my nose and not panic. I relax my throat and force a swallow.

A low groan vibrates from his lips straight into me. With his mouth and fingers working my pussy, sucking my clit, and fucking me, it makes me pliable, soft, and excited. My orgasm starts to build within me, and I moan.

"Fuck!" he hisses, and I do it again, moaning louder and increasing the timbre of my vibration every time he drives in deep between my lips. Especially with how he's now gripping my hip and pumping into my mouth like he can't help himself. His control is completely frayed. It's so freaking hot.

I bob my head up and down, increasing the suction in my mouth all the while his lips and tongue drive me up higher and higher. I swear, since I've become pregnant, there is no part of my body that isn't a live wire, and Mason knows exactly how to turn electricity into an explosion. His mouth devours me, thrusting up and into my pussy, fucking me in the same rhythm I'm sucking him, and I lose it.

I come so hard that it shocks me. My coordination is shot, and I find myself gasping for air, unable to keep his cock in my mouth. I grip it with my fist instead and jerk and jerk and jerk him so fast and hard he doesn't stand a chance. He comes with me on a roar, shooting straight onto my upper chest, neck, and face.

It surges my orgasm, and I'm so lost in the sensation of it all.

My eyes are closed, and I lie here in a happy stupor only to feel his lips against mine.

Reluctantly, I peek one eye open and find Mason's goofy, happy grin right above me. "You look so hot sprayed with my cum."

I smirk. "And you look so hot with my cum all over your lips."

He smiles and licks his lips. "Shower time, princess. We have an appointment soon."

~

"Can I ask you something?" Mason drawls as he holds my hand, and we head through the lobby of the hospital toward the elevators.

I'm quietly scanning around, hoping we don't run into anyone I know. I have a lot of family who works here at Brigham, but Katy told me her OB was amazing, and since I don't want to be part of my family's practice at my hospital, this seemed like the next best choice.

Other than my parents and grandparents knowing, I've sworn them to secrecy. Nothing is for sure with a pregnancy. A ton can go wrong at any given time—being a doctor sucks like that because we know too much—but I wanted to wait until I was a bit farther along to tell everyone as the risk of miscarriage goes down the closer you are to your second trimester.

"What's that?" I reply absently.

"Are you getting the NIPT test done today?"

That catches my attention and I turn to look at him. "How do you know what a NIPT test is?"

"I've been reading, Sorel," he says dismissively as if the answer should be obvious.

I stare at his profile, utterly bewildered. "You've been reading about pregnancy?"

"We are pregnant, are we not?"

My heart tugs in my chest. "Yes, we are." I reach up and kiss his cheek, but he's still not smiling, which isn't like Mason.

"So are you?" He presses the button for the elevator.

"Um, likely. They'll draw a bunch of blood to check for chromosomal abnormalities, and then around twelve weeks, I'll have an ultrasound with maternal-fetal medicine for further screening. Then, at twenty weeks, I'll have a complete fetal survey ultrasound."

He swallows and nods, but there's something else on his mind. Something he wants to ask but isn't for some reason.

"Do you have questions about that?" I query as we step onto the elevator and shuffle to the back. Mason is wearing a base-ball cap and is keeping his head down, but the man is six foot five or something insanely tall like that and is all muscle. He stands out in a crowd no matter what.

He leans down and whispers by my ear. "I was just wondering if you were planning to find out the baby's sex."

Oh. "I hadn't thought much about that yet." I glance up at him, but his eyes aren't on me. He's nervous, and I don't quite understand why. He's been a bit, I don't know, cautious with me over the last couple of weeks. He's still Mason, loving, sweet, affectionate, but there's been something lingering within him too. I haven't pressed it, figuring if he wanted to talk about it, he would. I know the stuff with Brody is heavy on his shoulders as well as his focus is on his football season.

"Did you want to know?" I whisper back.

He shifts his weight as the elevator comes to a stop. He's getting a few squinty-eyed looks, and this isn't the best place to talk about this. Especially since we haven't announced anything yet, and when we do, the questions and drama with it will be off the charts. I'm avoiding that. I'm actually dreading it like the plague. Mason suggested after this appointment that we schedule a meeting with his PR people to discuss what statement we plan to make publicly.

That all sounds good in theory, but it's going to be messy, and I don't know what to say about Brody being the father. I feel like I need to talk to him again about it and make sure he's folded his hand. I mean, that's how it feels since I haven't talked to him again after he told me he needed some more time, but Brody is strange. He's not always overt, and per Mason, he's waiting for me to come to my senses and move to New York.

I don't know.

It feels like something is brewing with him, and I don't like it. If he doesn't want the baby, I want him to relinquish his parental rights. I don't want him to come back out of spite or something and try to fight for the baby. I also don't want to call and nag for an answer. Being a father isn't a small undertaking, and the last time I spoke to him, I explained that if he wanted to be in the baby's life, that meant being a dad to it. Not just a distant person who was in and out of their life when it suited him.

A few people get off the elevator, and everyone shifts around. Mason wraps his arm around me and brings me in close. "I'd like to know, but ultimately it's your call."

Oh, Mason.

Our floor is next, so I wait until we're off the elevator, and I bring him down to the end of the hall where the stairs are instead of going toward the office. I place my hand on his chest and stare up at him.

"I think it's our decision, not just mine. Right?" I check. I don't think he's having second thoughts. The man is reading baby books and kissed my belly this morning before he went down on me. My gut says he's not. I think he's nervous about overstepping, and for about the millionth time in the last three weeks, I wish this baby were biologically his.

"You sure?"

My forehead scrunches. "Why are you asking that?"

He blusters out a sigh, his hand dragging through his hair in frustration. "Just some of the stuff Brody said to me."

"What did he say? More than what you told me?"

"Just shit talking about us. It's not important and I shouldn't let him get to me."

"No, you shouldn't." I step into him. "Do you want to find out the baby's sex?"

His lips bounce, and his green eyes brighten. "I'd like to know."

I reach up on the balls of my feet and place a kiss on his lips. "Then we'll find out. Either with the blood test or the ultrasound, but it won't be today. Today is blood work and the heartbeat, which is so cool."

He wraps his arms around me and drops his face to my neck. "I'm stupidly excited to hear the baby's heartbeat." He blows out a breath. "If Brody said he wanted to be the dad, would he be here instead of me?"

I hold the back of his head to me as I start to get choked up, and we're not even in there yet. Damn him and damn these hormones.

"It's yours, Mason. I meant it. I know going in there feels like this is all starting to happen for real, but if you're still in this with me, then I want and value your thoughts and input on everything. As for Brody, I don't know. I think we're both going to have to take that as it comes. *If* it comes. But regardless, you're the one I want in there with me. I don't know what he said to you, but I know that whatever it was, he was lying. I love you. Not him. He was a two-year mistake and you're the guy I wish I had seen all along."

He squeezes me tighter. "I love you. I love you so fucking much." His hand meets my lower belly. "Thank you for being perfect for me and for saying all of that. Let's go hear our baby's heartbeat."

His lips press to mine, and then he retakes my hand, and we go into the waiting room of the OB's office. Except this is Mason Reyes, and with his celebrity status, they immediately bring us back and put us in a room. I appreciate it more than I can say, and I can tell Mason does too.

I get changed, and a few minutes later, the doctor comes in and introduces herself to us. She gives Mason a quick double take, and I catch her cheeks flushing. I can't even blame her for it. Thank goodness for HIPAA, or this secret we're carrying would already be out there.

She morphs quickly into business mode and asks us a bunch of questions. This is where it gets tricky, and it's going to be the problem. I don't know a lot of Brody's family history. He has his dad, but his mom died when he was young of a rare stomach cancer. Other than that, I don't know much about his family history.

Then there's this...

"The baby's not actually mine," Mason supplies, and I can see it guts him to say it.

I have to hand it to our doctor. She simply nods and continues without missing a beat. But I can feel it sitting on Mason's chest, and I know he's hurting from it. We have a long way to go with this pregnancy and a lot of ways this relationship could go—after all, we've only been together a few weeks —but if it continues on this course, I think I have an idea that could help.

"Are you ready to hear your baby's heartbeat?" she asks, and Mason moves in closer to my head, wrapping himself partially around me. I'm starting to get a bump. Not a big one yet, more like I'm super bloated, but when I'm supine, I can really see it. Most of the time, the softness of my regular tummy hides it. Not right now.

"Definitely," I exclaim.

She squeezes a dollop of warm lubricant and pulls out her

doppler. Using the diaphragm of the probe, she presses it right into the lube, and immediately a loud, squeaky noise screeches through the room, making both Mason and me wince slightly.

"Sorry about that." She laughs. "Sometimes I forget to turn the sound back down."

The probe moves around. More of the scratchy noise taunts us, but then the sound of a hummingbird's wings, fast and fluttery, fills the room. Mentally, I start to count the beats even as the doctor says, "One hundred forty-eight. Sounds good. Nice and strong."

"Is it supposed to be that fast?"

I look at Mason, whose jaw is hanging open, his face filled with wonder. "Yep. Pretty incredible, right?"

Mason's eyes hold mine as his hand drags across my cheek. "Incredible. Like our baby's mom." He leans in and kisses me, and I sigh. I need to talk to Brody.

32

MASON

"It'll be fine," I reassure Sorel as I pull off my shirt and shuck out of my shorts, then toss both of them on the bed. I'm gross as fuck, but after that walkthrough, I could barely move, let alone shower, and I decided I'd rather shower in my room than in a locker room.

Besides, the less time I spend on the field or in any practice space here in New York, the better. I haven't seen Brody yet, but I have no doubt there will be an encounter between him and me at some point. Sorel and I told everyone we're pregnant— well, her family, as well as my dad's best friends who I consider to be my uncles and aunts—but we've decided to hold off on telling the world until we can no longer hide it, and we know Brody's deal.

She's been giving him space to figure it out for himself, but it's been a few weeks since they've talked, and he hasn't reached out to her with a decision. She told me she'd try calling him on Monday and proceed from there. That's her show. I don't want to tell her what to do with that side of things. I know it's weighing on her. It's weighing on me too. Hell, it's the first thing everyone asked us after we told them about the pregnancy.

"I know," she says with a heavy breath. "I wish I could be there with you."

"Except it's a late-night game, and since you can't travel back with me, there's no way you'd get home before tomorrow morning, and we want you to save as many days off as you can."

"What if he tries something?"

"Baby, there's not much he can do. We're on opposite teams. I'm on the field, and he's on the sidelines. Plus, cameras will be all over us after what happened in July. If you were there, the camera would be on you constantly."

"Ugh. Fine. Stop being such a voice of reason."

"Someone has to be. Your hormones are not to be trusted."

She giggles. "Facts. Speaking of, I'm going to go snack on junk since you're not here to stop me, and then I'm going to sleep. Go shower and think of me while you're in there."

I chuckle. "Yes, ma'am. I always think of my princess whenever I'm touching my dick."

"Good boy. Love you."

"Love you." I hit the red end button and walk with my phone into the bathroom, putting on Sorel's playlist as I go, and not even caring if it makes me a total pussy-whipped pansy-ass for my wife. My boxer briefs hit the floor, and the bathroom door partially closes behind me. I start the shower and face my reflection in the mirror.

I'm tight, and that's not a good thing going into a game tomorrow. A game I'm determined to win at all costs. No way in hell am I allowing Brody's team to beat me. Truthfully, I'm uneasy, though I'd never mention that to Sorel. Why hasn't he tried to call her again? Is he actually waiting for her to come to her senses and go to him, or has he moved on now that he knows I'm sticking around?

Either way, I would have thought he'd try to talk to her again.

It's not his style to lose or stay quiet. He likes the spotlight. He likes to look like the hero instead of the villain.

"WALK ON THE OCEAN" by Toad the Wet Sprocket comes on, and I find myself tilting my head toward my reflection and scrunching my nose. I love her, but fuck this. I hit next, and "Jane Says" by Jane's Addiction comes on, and this I can manage.

I step into the shower and groan at the feel of blazing hot water smashing into my muscles with ferocity. I did an ice bath at the stadium, but this I needed more than anything. Tomorrow night's game isn't going to be a picnic, and I'm too exhausted and burned out for a long jerk-off session, but I need a release—and then a full night of sleep after that—all the same.

Having an insatiable Sorel whenever I want her means I've been getting used to being inside her at least once a day. Her pussy is heaven, and just thinking about it makes my cock start to thicken and my balls ache. Sorel is always beautiful, but her belly is starting to round, and her tits are crazy full and sensitive—more than they were even a few weeks ago.

My hand grips my wet cock at the base, and I slowly slide it up to my tip. A groan slips out as I picture her on top of me, riding me, taking my cock as she bounces and sways, her tits heavy doing the same as she drags me in as deep as she can. I picture holding her tits in my hands and sucking on them as she rides me hard and fast.

Fuck, I wish she were here. I wish I could see her pretty, flushed face and those stunning hazel eyes, dark and hungry. My hand jerks faster, my grip firm, and far too soon, I'm groaning and grunting and shooting my load all over the shower walls.

My forehead falls to my forearm that's pressed against the tile, and I take a few deep breaths.

With a sated sigh, and feeling more relaxed than I did a few minutes ago, I take my time, enjoying the hot water, and wash up while I hum along to the next song that comes on, though I don't know who it's by or any of the lyrics. Sorel has been adding to her playlist, and some of the songs she has on here I've never heard before. She likes to tease me and say it's because she was born in the nineties and I wasn't. She's big on the fact that she's older than me, like that matters in the slightest.

Stepping out of the shower, I wrap a towel around my waist and open the door to the bathroom, letting some of the heavy steam out. Momentarily, I'm preoccupied, my head down as I turn off the music on my phone.

Which is why I don't notice the woman in my room until I look up and jump in shock.

"What the fuck?"

A woman wearing my goddamn shirt and what appears to be nothing else stands right outside my bathroom door. She's tall and skinny with long, blonde hair and an expression that's meant to be seductive. A phone dangles limply from her hand, which is a relief. At least it's not pointed at me.

She gives me a flirty smile that makes my blood run cold. "I have a key." She holds up the plastic rectangle in the same hand as her phone. "I've wanted to meet you for a long time," she purrs breathily. "I thought you might want some company tonight. I figured we could have some fun together."

"No. And fuck no. Get out. Now."

She pouts and shifts her weight. "Are you going to make me get naked to do that?" She plays with the short hem of my shirt that ends at her upper thighs. "I'll take it off right here if that's what you want."

"What I want is for you to leave. You had no right getting a key to my room."

She laughs lightly like what I just said is ridiculous. "Oh, like you haven't had women do that before. Come on. Don't be so rough. It'll just be tonight. No one has to know."

I snarl. "Grab your shit and get out of here before I call security."

"Shame." She gives me a long once-over. "I was hoping to ride that big dick of yours."

Horror blooms in my gut. How long has she been in my room? Did she hear me in the shower? I just jerked off to thoughts of Sorel doing the same thing to me. I feel like I'm about to throw up.

I fold my arms over my chest, wishing I were wearing a hell of a lot more than only a towel. "I'm married, and you need to leave."

She laughs with her head thrown back and everything. "Oh please. I think we all know your marriage isn't real. She was engaged to your former teammate the same day you married her."

"Out. Now." I point in the direction of the door. "This is your last chance before security escorts you out."

She huffs, displeased, but thankfully not crazy or aggressive. With an aggravated breath and some exaggerated movements, she snatches her clothes from the bed and storms for the door, tugging on her jeans as she goes.

The door to the room opens, but before she leaves, she turns her head over her shoulder and pins me with a disappointed and indignant scowl. "I'm not someone you want to kick out your door. You'll regret this."

"Somehow I doubt it."

With a sulk and a dramatic flip of her hair, she leaves, her clothes and shoes bunched up in her hands. The second the door is shut behind her, I flip the bolt—the one I should have had engaged the moment I got back—and run over to the hotel phone to call the concierge. I rip him a new asshole, something I'm not known for doing, but right now, I don't care. I don't even care when he apologizes and says he has no clue how she got up here or who gave her a key.

It doesn't matter.

She paid someone off, and they did it.

This is going to sound bad, but typically we get asked if we're cool with that sort of thing happening by a manager of the hotel. Women come and lurk in hotels when they know a sports team is here, and she was not the first to get up to my room. It was a question I never liked answering and one I rarely indulged in and only very early on in my career. The girls who show up in your room are the ones you can trust the least, and as I said before, I'm not stupid despite how people view me.

To come out of the shower and find a woman in my room is disconcerting, to say the least. I didn't want it or approve it, and no one asked me. I assumed it was because of the band on my finger, and I was fine with that.

More than fine. Hell, I didn't even think about it until she was standing there.

I flop down on my bed, my forearm over my eyes.

It's late, and I don't want to call Sorel back since she said she was going to bed. I don't want to wake her. Certainly not for that. Nothing happened anyway other than me kicking the woman out, but still. I feel dirty. I feel wrong. I'd go out of my mind if the roles were reversed.

Rolling over, I see it's now after eleven. Sorel goes to bed early and all but passes out. She's also a heavy sleeper and likely wouldn't hear the phone ring. This pregnancy has been a lot for her in terms of her need for extra sleep.

Shit.

If I call her now, it'll only upset her, and I don't want that.

I'll call her in the morning and tell her.

With a growl, I throw on a clean pair of briefs, brush my teeth, and climb into bed.

All I know is, I can't wait to get the hell out of New York and back to Boston.

Somehow, I fall asleep, and it isn't until the middle of the night that I wake up and realize, one, the woman had her phone in her hand the entire time. Why keep it on you if you're only there to seduce someone? And two, she left wearing my shirt.

∽

ALL GODDAMN DAY, I've been off. I slept like shit, tossing and turning most of the night, unable to fall back to sleep after I woke up with those turbulent thoughts. By the time I did fall back to sleep, it was just before dawn, and once I woke up and tried calling Sorel, she didn't pick up. When she tried to call me back, I couldn't answer.

I shouldn't feel guilty, but after everything she went through with Brody cheating, I want her to know everything. More than that, something feels off about that woman. I can't even put my finger on what. It might be that I'm paranoid about Brody. About Sorel's insistence that the other shoe will eventually drop.

But as game time draws closer, there isn't much I can do about it. I have to put it behind me, get my mental game ready, and transition into quarterback mode.

"Reyes, you're mic'd up tonight."

I growl a curse under my breath as the network rep comes over to me.

"Can't you pick someone else?" I hate being mic'd up. My speech is clear, but when you're a kid with a hearing deficit and have been in speech therapy your entire life and still rely on sign language on occasion, the last thing you want is a microphone capturing your every word. Especially for Sunday Night Football. More so when you've had a crappy day.

"Sorry, man." He shrugs, not sorry at all. "Network and the Rebels say it's you."

Of course they do. I'm a hot commodity tonight considering we're playing my wife's ex-fiancé's team. That's the stuff of prime-time and reality TV right there. Networks aren't fools. They know how to play the game and spin spice in their favor.

They're hoping I'll slip up and say something that'll go viral.

We go through our pregame stuff, many of us wearing our headphones and listening to whatever gets us game set. My dad does his standard speech, and after, I give mine.

"You know what this game is," I blaze in the center of a circle of men. "It's the difference between going home winners or losers. It's what makes us undefeated to start the season. It's any other game. It's nothing special. We kill games like these. It's a game on the road and a game against a good team. Let's show them who we are." I look at each of my guys, my voice and vigor climbing. "Let's show them how we play and that no one beats us. And let's fucking destroy them."

A ruckus of enthusiastic cries cracks through the air. The doors open, and we run as a team out of the locker room, past a series of cameras, through the tunnel, and onto the field. The stadium is juiced up for this game. The home team music and the roar of the crowd penetrate every corner of the outdoor stadium, filling the night sky. I'm directed over to the sidelines, and they get me wired up for sound. It's dark, and the air is cool. Football weather. And Sunday night is my favorite night to play.

I don't look across the field. I don't acknowledge the other team. I rev up my offensive line, encouraging and charging them up.

My dad comes over to me and, with a smirk, signs, *You good?*

With how loud the crowd is tonight and the fact that I'm mic'd up, I might end up signing more than the network and team owner would like.

I'm good. Ready, I sign in return.

"We're going to stuff it down their throats." He smacks the back of my helmet, and the game begins. We lose the coin toss and end up on offense first. The moment we line up in formation, I see it. The glares. The scathing looks. It's more than simple rivalry.

Brody ran his mouth, and he ran it good.

"Hey, Reyes," a defensive tackle calls out to me. "Prepare to eat grass all night long."

If I were still single, I'd reply with, *doesn't your wife shave her pussy?* But since I'm not, I go with, "We're on turf, you moron." I wink at him and start calling the play, but I can already tell it's going to be a long night.

"You know we're going to throw you a baby shower, right?" Katy tells me as she checks her blood sugar and then doses up her insulin pen.

"Stella kind of hinted at something," I admit. "I'm not really a baby shower girl."

Keegan shoots me a side-eye before returning to the menu. "It's more for us than for you. We need an excuse to eat tiny sandwiches and cake and drink alcohol you can't and purchase all the adorable baby things."

"It could be a Jack and Jill one if you want Mason there," Wren offers.

"No!" the rest of the women all shout at once. "Not a chance in hell. Do you remember Katy's?" Kenna questions with horror etched on her face.

Wren grimaces. "Oh. Right. Yeah, no forget that."

"What happened at Katy's?" I ask. I was invited, but I was in New York and didn't come home for it. I also haven't heard anything about it.

"It's been Fight Clubbed," Katy tells me. "We don't talk

about it. But let's just say there was an incident with a squirrel, fire, and Owen's pool."

I hold up my hand. "Stop there. I don't want to know more. Women only. Still, do you have any clue how big that'll be?" I throw back at her. "Like, I don't even have female friends, but with our family alone, it's well over a hundred women."

Keegan shrugs. "Grandma will do it at the compound. In fact, between Grandma, Stella, and your mom, you won't have a choice."

Shockingly, my grandmother has taken very well to the fact that the baby isn't my current husband's. After she and my dad got over the shock from hearing it how they did, both were very excited. I thought for sure that would tip her over the edge after all of this, but the woman didn't even bat an eye. She simply hugged me and gushed over having yet another great-grandchild.

My family is awesome. Overbearing. Always there. But awesome.

"Fine. I won't fight it."

I lean back in my chair and pick up the menu I've neglected to peruse. Everything looks incredible, and with how hungry I am—you'd think it has been days since I've eaten when it's only been a few hours—I wonder if it would be off-putting to get a few things. I can always bring home leftovers and eat them for breakfast.

"I'm totally getting the chicken gyro and the falafel with hummus thing. Both sound so good." My stomach growls as if to high-five me for that pick. I set my menu down and gaze about the restaurant. We've never eaten here, but Tinsley and Stone swear by this place, and it's just across the park from my apartment.

The door flies open, and Estlin, who is holding Rory's hand, rushes in. "I'm so sorry we're late," Estlin exclaims, slightly out of breath. "Owen got called into the hospital. There's some kind of big thing going on." She bobs her head down in Rory's direction. "I hope it's okay."

"Okay?" Katy questions playfully, turning fully in her seat to face them. "It's the best. I didn't know I was going to get to see my favorite mermaid. I would have brought Willow for you." Katy opens her arms, and Rory goes racing right into them. Katy is Rory's godmother, just like Owen is Willow's godfather.

"I wonder if Stone will get called in too if there's a big thing." Stone also works at Boston Children's Hospital. "He and I are supposed to watch the game together tonight."

"Oh," Estlin says, taking a seat beside me. "I don't know." She leans into me and whispers. "Owen said it was pretty bad. Some kind of school bus accident."

"On a Sunday?" I question.

She shrugs with a grimace. "That's all I know, and I didn't want to know more. I just hope everyone is okay."

I nod. "Same. How awful."

Rory comes bounding over to me. "Can I feel your baby?" she asks with a hopeful expression on her sweet face.

"Of course. But you won't be able to feel it move yet. It's still too early for that." I sit back, take her little hand, and place it over my growing bump.

"Daddy said you and Uncle Mason are going to have a baby like Katy and Bennett do, and after it's born, I can play with it like how I play with baby Willow."

I smile and kiss her cheek. "Definitely. You'll be her big cousin."

Rory jumps and squeals in delight.

My phone vibrates on the table beside me, and I pick it up, hoping it's Mason but not expecting it to be. We've played phone tag all day, but I know he's likely getting ready for the game that starts in a little more than an hour. Instead, it's Stone.

Stone: Got called into the ER, but it shouldn't be too long. It seems precautionary that they pulled us all in. I'll keep

you updated, but start without me and I'll join in progress if I need to.

Me: Sounds good. Hope it is just precautionary.

We order our dinner, and the discussion turns to the upcoming holidays as Rory explains to us that she's going to be a unicorn princess for Halloween, which we all agree is a perfect choice.

"Mason plays on Thanksgiving this year in Dallas, and I was thinking I'd take that time and go see Serena and maybe hop over to London to see my brothers. It might be my last chance to travel like that before I get too pregnant."

Keegan perks up at that. "For real? Would you want company?"

My brows pinch. "You want to come to Paris and London over Thanksgiving to see my siblings?"

"I wouldn't mind a little time in Europe this fall."

I squint at her. Keegan is blushing and trying to hide it in her wineglass. Keegan doesn't blush. "What's up? What am I missing?"

Kenna snickers. "Loomis Powell is going to be in England for the next few months. His mom broke her hip or something, so he's there taking care of her."

My head tilts, and the V between my brows deepens. "Loomis Powell? The actor? As in Tinsley's BFF? Isn't she in London filming with him now?"

"One and the same," Wren jumps in. "Keegan has a thing for him."

"I do not!" Keegan exclaims, throwing a piece of pita at her. "We're just friends."

"Ha!" Kenna explodes with laughter. "Dude, who are you talking to you right now? If by friends you mean fu—" She cuts herself off when Estlin throws her a sharp glare and swings her wide, intent eyes in Rory's direction. "Um. Right. Well, you know what kind of friends you are. You may not be together, but you're not *just* friends."

"Nothing has happened," Keegan grumbles under her breath.

Everyone pauses. Well, everyone except for me and Estlin, since I think we're a bit out of the loop on this one.

"Liar."

Keegan shakes her head. "No. Nothing has happened. You *assumed* something did," she emphasizes, pointing at Kenna, Katy, and Wren. "But nothing did. I went out to LA for that conference, and we legit just hung out. We're friends. That's it. Boring. Plain. Friends."

"Oh." Kenna sags. "Bummer. When you told us there were no details to tell, we thought you were being evasive."

"Nope." Keegan pops the P sound.

"And you want to come to Europe with me to see him?" I question, not trying to sound harsh, but I can't help but be a bit incredulous of that.

Keegan shrugs. "I don't know. It's dumb or weird, right?" She scrunches her nose. "Chasing a hot fling that isn't hot or even a fling."

"Hey, I ran away to Vegas with my friend and talked him into marrying me and now he's going to raise my child with me. I think dumb and weird don't apply when it comes to these things."

"Maybe not. Now we just have to figure out a way to get Wren and Jack together," Keegan quips, and Wren pretends to throw up.

"No thanks and not ever," she replies adamantly. "I'd rather set my hair on fire. He's the absolute worst on every level. Sorry, Estlin. I realize he's your brother, but I don't know how you tolerate him."

"He's different with me." She raises a shoulder as she takes a sip of her wine and bounces her eyebrows suggestively at

Wren as her voice turns taunting. "I believe I would have said the same thing to you once about Owen."

Wren scoffs. "Different. So different."

Inwardly I smirk but hold it in. Wren started last week in the ER, and Jack has been texting to complain about her nonstop. I need to take another shift down there just so I can watch the fireworks.

"Are you ever going to tell us why the two of you hate each other?" Katy questions.

"He's an arrogant butt face and always has been."

Katy snorts. "Oh, well, that explains it then."

Wren holds up her hand. "Trust me. It does. We're just... oil and water. We don't mix."

She leaves it there, and since our food is delivered, we drop the conversation in favor of eating. Afterward, I accept a ride home from Katy since it's dark and I'd rather not walk through the park alone.

"Have a good night," she calls to me with a wave as I open the door to step out. "We'll be watching Mason at home and cheering him on."

I give her a wave and head into the building, already tired. That's been the main thing this first trimester—other than my hormones—is the fatigue I've been experiencing. So far, at the beginning of my second trimester, that hasn't waned. I lean against the elevator and yawn my way up. I hope I can stay up for the entire game, but it likely won't end until almost midnight.

Stepping off the elevator, I come to an abrupt halt as I find myself blinking several times to make sure I'm seeing exactly what I'm seeing.

"How did you get up here?" I ask, my lips automatically pulling down into a frown.

Eloise pushes away from the wall she is leaning against. She offers me a smile, but it doesn't quite reach her eyes. "The doorman let me up. He wouldn't allow me in your apartment, but I told him I was your friend and showed him pictures of us to prove it. I explained how I wanted to surprise you."

And surprise me she did.

"Friend?" I scoff. "What do you want? Why are you here after all this time? Honestly, knowing you as I thought I did, I would have sworn you'd have come at me sooner. Then again, clearly, I didn't know you that well at all."

"I was hoping you'd join your fake husband in New York, but no such luck for me," she says, plowing past my comments and refusing to answer me. Part of me wondered if we'd have this moment eventually. I certainly wasn't going to seek it out.

"It's not fake," I tell her plainly. "What Mason and I have... it's the real deal."

"So you say and perhaps think. Maybe yes. Maybe no." She starts to crumple, her blonde hair all over the place, and she hastily shoves it back. "I miss you, Sorel. I've missed you so much," she cries, growing emotional. "You were my best friend."

"And then I learned you were screwing my fiancé!" I yell at her. "You weren't my best friend since friends don't do that to each other. Did you honestly expect I'd never find out? Did you think you could just continue to fuck him and all would be fine?"

She straightens her spine, but tears start to fall. Another step toward me and she catches sight of her reflection in the hall mirror, and annoyance flashes across her face. She wipes furiously at her cheeks and turns back to me.

"You're so self-righteous," she seethes. "You always have been. You threw me away without a second thought. I was such a good friend to you. You never saw it because you didn't let me explain. You just cut me off and cut me out. Just like that." She snaps her fingers. "As if I never meant anything to you at all."

I fold my arms, unimpressed, and lean my hip against the

console table. "By all means, explain." I pan a hand toward her and refold it against my chest. "But there is nothing you can say that will change my mind about our friendship."

She takes a settling breath. "I started sleeping with Brody long before you ever met him. A week before you did, I had decided to leave James for him. I was in love with Brody. I always was. I thought maybe if I wasn't attached to James anymore, my fling with Brody could finally turn into something real. Then he met you."

I shake my head and take a step back, shifting my weight as I think through what she's saying, though none of this makes sense. "You introduced me to him. Why do that if you loved him?"

"I was there with James, and it was his idea. When Brody saw you, he was all for it. What was I supposed to say?"

My hands fly out to my sides in frustration. "You never told me. You never said a word."

Her eyes glisten, and she grows equally aggravated. "What was I going to say? I was with another man, and you and Brody had hearts in your eyes from the moment you met. He didn't want me. Not like that."

"I still would have stepped back," I exalt. "Jesus, Eloise. I would have picked you over him, but not only did you not give me the chance, you picked him over me."

She stares down at the floor, and I do the same, my hands going to my hips.

I bluster out a breath, floored by this. There was nothing in her texts to indicate she loved him. Only that she loved fucking him. Still, she's an adult. She should have come to me and said something or made better choices. I don't know. I feel for her that she loved him, but that doesn't excuse what she did to me.

"That's the thing," I continue softly, lifting my chin and staring down at the top of her head. "I would have chosen you, and you never chose me. So that's it. That's all there is to it.

You're both single now, so have at it with him. I don't care, and I don't want to ever see you again. Honestly, I don't know why you bothered to come here or what you were expecting from me."

I go to move past her, but she slides in front of me to stop me, and there's a shift in her eyes. A hardening. A vitriol. A spitefulness I didn't see before as it was covered by her tearful, *but Daddy, I love him* bullshit.

"I was hoping you'd hear my side and understand. I was hoping you'd be my friend again."

"No such luck."

She smirks, and it makes my skin prickle with awareness. "That's a real shame, Sorel. I was hopeful this would come to a better outcome for us."

I narrow my gaze. "How do you mean?"

"He told me she's pregnant with his baby."

Ah. Now it's coming together, and it makes my heart pick up its pace. I don't trust Eloise, and I don't quite know what she's up to. But she didn't get what she wanted, and I can tell she's got another card up her sleeve. One I won't like.

"Yes," I admit warily, reflexively pulling my purse over my stomach to protect it from her.

"He also told me Mason was staying with you. I have to admit, that's a shock. I thought for sure it was all a lie." She flips back some of her long blonde hair from her face and glares at me. "Then again, I guess I shouldn't be surprised. Every fucking man who meets you falls for you. They see you as quirky, innocent, and sweet when you're actually frigid, callous, and unforgiving. You just proved that to me once again."

A nervous lump forms in my throat, and right now I want to get inside and lock the door. I don't like being out here with her. Especially when I don't know what she's up to. Other than she's not done with me yet.

"Eloise, get to the point of why you're here and go."

"Sure. I can do that for an old friend." She pulls out her phone. "I wasn't going to do this. You brought this on yourself. Remember that. You ruined my life, and I was still willing to give you a second chance."

"For real?" Sarcasm drips from my tongue even as my heart rate is going haywire. "How did *I* ruin your life?"

"Not only did you humiliate me publicly and then cast me aside like yesterday's trash, you took James and Brody from me as well. You made me look like the villain when I was only in love. You're not even heartsick over him. You moved on that night and didn't give two shits about me. Now you're pregnant with Brody's baby when it should be me who is. You have no idea how much that hurt me, Sorel." Her eyes brighten in triumph as she pulls something up on her phone. "Now I just wanted to return the favor."

Some sound comes from the speaker on her phone, though the screen is black. It's music. Jane's Addiction, but there's something behind it. Something that sounds like water. A shower running maybe? And... grunting. Groaning. Someone saying "fuck," in a low growl, and I know that voice. Those sound.

That's Mason. That's Mason having an orgasm.

After the audio cuts off, she swipes through a series of pictures and shows them to me one by one. His clothes on a rumpled hotel bed beside hers. A selfie of her only wearing his shirt, his hotel room behind her, reflected in the mirror she used for the picture. The last one is Mason coming out of the shower wrapped in only a towel, his head cast down and his focus trained on his phone.

"It's funny," she muses softly, though there isn't any humor in her voice or expression. "He didn't know who I was. Hell, he didn't even ask my name. He must have women up to his hotel room all the time for a quick fuck considering how fast he let me in. So you see, Sorel, sex can sometimes just be sex. Even when you're in love with someone else."

With that, she brushes past me and presses the button for the elevator. I'm too stunned to move. Too stunned to say anything. I'm trapped on repeat. Locked in a vicious loop of his moaning and groaning to my playlist. Her in his hotel room. The way the bed looked. Her only wearing his clothes. Him only wearing a towel.

"Oh, I almost forgot," she taunts as the elevator doors open. She pulls something from her purse and tosses it at me. It hits my side and falls to the floor. "I thought you might want this back."

It's his shirt. The shirt she's wearing in the picture.

She steps on, and the second the elevator doors close behind her, I fall apart right here in the hallway. My chest cracks open wide, and now I'm bleeding out everywhere.

No. No!

Scalding hot tears burn my cheeks, and I collapse against the wall and sink into a crouch. My hands cover my face, and I sob uncontrollably into them. Mason wouldn't do that. He wouldn't. He wouldn't cheat on me.

Pain as I've never experienced rips through me. I can't breathe. I can't think. I'm consumed. Broken. Betrayed. But it's so much worse than before. So much harder to bear.

For a few minutes, all I can do is cry as wrenching sadness and grief eviscerate me. I trusted him. I opened myself up. I let him in. I gave him everything that I am.

But no matter how hard I cry and how sick and angry and betrayed I feel, I keep coming back to one thing. Mason wouldn't do that. He wouldn't cheat. I wasn't shocked when I found out about Brody with Eloise. I was hurt and embarrassed and felt stupid and used. But I never had a *he wouldn't do this* moment because it didn't seem beyond his character to.

But Mason? It doesn't fit. It just doesn't.

Slowly, I stand and pick up his shirt from the ground. The soft fabric rolls through my fingers, and I can't bear to smell it because it'll smell like her. I know it will. She was in his hotel room. Then again, she was up here waiting for me, so clearly, she has some manipulation skills.

I lean against the wall and force myself to think this through rationally. I was on the phone with Mason as he walked into the hotel after his walk-through. We stayed on the phone as he went up to his room, and he told me he was going to shower. I teased him about it. I told him to think of me while he was in there.

I stare down at the Rebels red in my hand and close my eyes as those pictures flash to the forefront of my brain along with the video she made me listen to.

I go through them one by one. The bed. The clothes. Her selfie... wait! Her hair wasn't wet, and there was no one else behind her in that picture. He could have been beside her, but Mason is especially cautious about phones and cameras. He never would have let her take those pictures. Not knowingly.

And in the audio, it was only him moaning and groaning. No one else. No female accompaniment, and you'd think if she was fucking him to break us apart, she would have intentionally been loud so I could hear her.

The elevator dings, startling me, and when the doors open, I tense in anticipation of Eloise returning to stick it to me some more, but instead Stone walks out, casually glancing at his phone.

He halts when he spots me, surprised to find me out here and then concerned when he notes my face. "What happened?" He rushes over to me and takes my arm. "Is it the baby? Are you okay?"

"Mason wouldn't cheat," I utter, and he rears back, not having expected me to say that. I meet his eyes. "Tell me Mason wouldn't cheat."

"No," he promises adamantly. "He wouldn't. Not ever."

I swallow as more tears fall, and my forehead meets his shoulder. He wraps his arms around me and holds me for a moment. Stone is his best friend, but he's also my cousin. His assertion that Mason wouldn't cheat solidifies my own.

"Sorel, what happened?" he presses.

"Eloise was just here. She showed me an audio clip of Mason moaning and groaning in the shower and then pictures of her in his hotel room only wearing his shirt." I hold up the shirt I plan to burn later. "This shirt. And then a picture of Mason coming out of the shower only wearing a towel."

Stone drags my face up as if he's checking me to make sure I just said what I said. His lashes flutter in bewilderment for a beat before his expression grows hard. "Eloise had that on her phone, and she was just here?" he checks, his voice razor-sharp.

I nod slowly, not understanding his sudden shift.

"Fuck," he hisses and calls someone on his phone as he walks me to his place instead of mine. He unlocks the door just as whomever he calls answers. "Yeah, Van, Eloise was just here, and she has pictures and audio on her phone that need to be wiped ASAP, dude."

"Van?" I question. "As in Vander?"

Stone throws me a quick look, but he doesn't answer. Why is he calling Vander and asking him to wipe stuff on Eloise's phone? Then it hits me. Mason had mentioned that he was having a professional keep an eye on Brody's stuff, but he never said who.

"I don't know." He speaks into the phone. "I have no further details, but I'm guessing from last night." He checks with me, and I nod. "Wait. What?!"

Stone listens and then hisses out a curse before he runs over to the TV and turns it on to Sunday Night Football.

"Fuck," is all he says, and when I see the TV, I scream in horror. Fuck is right.

34

MASON

Sweat clings to my brow, and I lick my lips as I survey the field. Somehow, we've managed to eke our way down into their territory, small play by small play. They've been gunning for me this entire series, practically blitzing on every down. I've never had to run so much inside the pocket in my life. Good thing Stone and I work on my speed, or I'd have been sacked a dozen times already.

"Shove it down their throats." My father's voice rings through the speaker near my ears, and I grin. I'm tired of playing this their way—or should I say Brody's way. Wanting to throw the defense off, I go straight to the line instead of huddling up and call out the play to my guys on either side of me. I line up behind the center and bark out the hard count to try to draw these jumpy fuckers off-sides, but when that fails, I hike the ball.

It snaps into my hands, and I draw back and curl to the side. Time slows and my vision clears. Defenders are coming straight for me, but I can't let myself focus on that. They can go fuck themselves if they think they're going to scare me out of throwing.

I sidestep, spot my guy, and let my arm go. The ball sails through the air, and a moment later, I'm pummeled to the ground in a hit that instantly knocks the wind from my lungs. A helmet clips my face guard, and I go down hard, unable to stop it or slow my momentum, only to smack the back of my head on the turf.

Instead of climbing off me, the defender—the same asshole who was mouthing off to me about eating grass all night—presses his weight down, digging himself against my ribs, and growls, "That's for Brody, and if you're able to get up and walk after this hit, there'll be more coming for you. But here's a little message from him. Remember that threat he gave you because it's about to become your reality."

Whistles blow, and thankfully he's pulled off me. Absently, I note some of my guys pushing and shoving with the other team, but I can't quite get myself up yet. It was a dirty hit. No doubt about that. Helmet to helmet, yes, but I'd already released the ball, so there was no need for it other than to hurt me.

Yellow flags are scattered on the field for roughing the passer, and suddenly I have faces all over me.

"Mason, can you hear me?" It's my mother beside one of the athletic trainers and the team neurologist. She's not even supposed to be out here, since she's my mother and orthopedics, but no one was going to tell her that. Fuck, I wish she hadn't seen that hit.

I sign with my hands, *I can hear you.* Because I'm not sure I can talk yet. My chest feels like an elephant landed on it because essentially one did, and I need a second to wrap my muddled mind around that message. No, that threat. That was the word he used. It wasn't idle, and it wasn't about him making sure my clock got cleaned.

Something else is happening.

I just don't know what.

I catch my father standing behind my mother, the coach over his player, but his eyes are the eyes of a father.

"Don't move," the neurologist commands. "We need to check you out. Do you know where you are?"

"I'm fine," I manage. "I didn't hit my head." *Too hard.*

"No, we have to—"

"I'm good," I grit out, pushing his hand off me when he tries to keep me down. "I'm in New York, though it's technically New Jersey. I'm playing football, and no one is taking me out of this game. I'm not dizzy, I didn't lose consciousness, and I'm not hurt." *Too bad.* "I'm fucking fine. Dr. Reyes, tell them I'm fine," I demand from my mother.

She doesn't want to. Not even close, but she knows me enough to know I wouldn't say it to her if it weren't true. She's my mother and would kick my ass all over the city if I lied to her about that.

"If he says he's fine, he's fine."

Reluctantly the trainer and neurologist back off, and slowly I sit up. My chest hurts like a motherfucker, and I think he got my shoulder beneath my pads because now that I'm moving it, it stings something fierce. I glance to my left and catch Brody standing among the other coaches and players on his side of the field, a hint of a smirk subtly curling the corner of his lips.

"Reyes?" I snap back to my wide receiver who holds his hand out for me. "You good, man?"

I slap my hand in his and let him haul me up. I need a second after that, but I'll be damned if I let anyone know it or see it. "I'm good," I tell him, then look at my dad and the training staff again. "I'm good," I reiterate with more force.

"You still have to sit out one play," the trainer tells me.

I know this already. That's the rule if the training staff come on the field.

"One play," I agree.

Shouting and movement draw our attention over to the back and forth still going on between the players.

"Hey! Back it up," my dad yells since my guys are still shoving and we're a hot second from a physical fight breaking out. Referees are trying to get in the middle of the shoving and name-calling, and I strut my way over there and put my hand on an offensive lineman to hold him back.

"Not worth the penalty," I tell him, meeting his eyes. "Come on. We have a game to win. They're not worth it, man. I promise you, they're not."

"I said now!" my father yells, and heads back to the sidelines with my mother and the training staff following after him.

My guys step back, the skirmish cooling ever so slightly, but as the chief referee walks to the center of the field to announce the penalty and the fifteen yards and first down that asshole just graciously gave us, I head toward the sidelines of New York. Players and coaches run in toward me without stepping on the field of play. They have no clue what I'm up to and likely think I'm about to start a fight. Some of my guys surround me in case I need backup, only I'm not as stupid as that.

"Hey, Brody," I call out with a grin. "I'm mic'd up."

Everyone on the sidelines pauses, their heads swiveling in Brody's direction. And just as I predicted, that hint of a smug, fucking smirk falls.

"Maybe before you send an assassin to hurt me, you should tell him not to reveal who ordered the hit. Now everyone knows you're not just a dirty cheater but a dirty coach too. You tried to have him take me out of the game. No such luck for you tonight."

I don't address his message or the threat he sent my way. I can't. Not right now. Not even as I want to run off the field, call Sorel, and make sure she's okay. If she saw that hit, she'd be upset. But if somehow Brody did something or is trying to get to her, things could be much worse for me right now.

Then it hits me.

The woman. My shirt. Her phone in her hand.

Fuck!

Except I can't do anything about it right now.

Adrenaline flows through my system and brings my blood to a rapid boil. I want to pound his face in. I want to destroy him. And I will. My way.

With that, I head off the field, forced to sit out my one play. But that'll be all Brody gets from me.

I'm going to make him and his team pay for that.

"Mason."

"Mason."

"Mason!"

One reporter after the other shouts, vying for my attention as I walk into the post-game conference. After the game —or should I say after we destroyed them—I made a little thank you speech to my guys—something even Tony Clark was moved by as he gave me a fist pound after it—and then I was swept up by the neurology staff. I didn't even get to my locker.

My mother and the team ripped into me and demanded a full neuro and physical exam—for which my mother stepped out since, you know, she is my mom. After they deemed I wasn't concussed or broken—I did play the entire game and played it well after all—they let me shower. I'm bruised from the hit, and I won't lie and say I'm not already hurting from it, but no one needs to know that. The moment I stepped out, my dad was there, telling me that we had to do this conference on the quick because we were set to fly home after it.

I didn't get a chance to tell him about the woman last night or what Brody's threat meant if he's even heard the threat. I have no idea if the network will play any of the audio. I can only hope.

I haven't checked my phone.

I haven't checked the media to know what's happened.

I'm entering into this blind, and I'm not happy about it.

I give them all my patented cocky smile and address the podium and the sea of cameras and press beyond it.

"What a game," I start and get a small wave of chuckles that quickly turn into another barrage of my name being thrown at me.

"Mason, can you tell us what happened out there with the hit from Tweo?"

And this is why I wish I had been able to check my phone first.

"It was a hell of a hit."

That obviously doesn't satisfy anyone.

"It most certainly was," a guy from ESPN states. "We saw you address Brody Clear on the field. What was it you said to him? Is it your belief that the hit was orchestrated by him?"

So I'm assuming no one aired or leaked the recording. Awesome. If that stands, Brody is free to do as he pleases and won't be fired or fined. I don't know for sure if he hired that girl or if he was in on it, but my gut is telling me it's too coincidental and his message too well-timed and pointed for it not to be. Which also means he could send whatever he has to Sorel.

No sense in lying or beating around the bush. "Yes, I believe the hit was orchestrated by Brody Clear, as that's what Tweo said when he tackled me."

Murmurs rumble through the room.

"Can you elaborate on that?"

"They wanted to take me out of the game. Tweo bluntly stated that they were aiming to hurt me. He explained that the hit was from Brody, relayed a direct message from him, and informed me that I could expect more if that particular hit didn't knock me out of the game. It didn't. But given the final score, I'd say we had the last laugh with that."

Microphones are shoved closer to the podium, which feels ridiculous because the thing is airing on live TV as I speak, and I'm talking directly into a microphone.

"Do you believe that's because you're now married to Brody Clear's former fiancée?"

I shrug. "That would be my guess, but I can't speak directly to Mr. Clear's intentions and thoughts. I only know what was said to me, and my wife's name wasn't mentioned."

"Do you feel Brody was justified in his retaliation since you stole his fiancée?"

Nice. Real nice. Clearly a New York reporter.

"I don't think there is ever a justification for trying to hurt another player, and I didn't steal anyone. Brody cheated on her and she left him. Next question."

"Mason, are the reports that Sorel Fritz is pregnant true?"

Well then. At least they didn't ask if it was Brody's or mine.

I stare down at the reporter for a long moment before I dismiss them with my gaze and move on to the next.

"Mason, you and Dr. Fritz? Is it real or simply a publicity stunt?"

Jesus. What the fuck?

"Mason—"

I hold up my hand to stop them. "Listen, I love my wife. That's it. That's all there is to it. I don't care about publicity, and I never do anything as a stunt. I love my team, and I will fight for both them and my wife to my last breath. That's all anyone needs to know. Tonight, we played a hell of a game against a tough opponent. My guys showed up and played their hearts out, and I want to thank them again for the effort. If anyone has any questions about the game tonight, I'm happy to answer them. But I'm done answering questions about Brody Clear or my wife."

The room falls quiet for a moment, and I take that as my opportunity.

"Great. Thank you all. Have a wonderful rest of your night." I throw my hand up and get my ass out of this box of a room, even as the reporters start an encore of my name. I'm too anxious. I need to get to my phone. I need to call Sorel.

The team is already heading out of the stadium toward our bus, and my dad hands me my bag and phone.

You have about a dozen missed calls, he signs so no one hears or understands us. *What happened out there tonight?*

I explained everything from the woman last night to the hit from Tweo to what I said to Brody.

"Hmm. Does Vander know about this, or should I call Lenox?"

I smirk. "Give me ten minutes, and I'll let you know." I hold up my phone at him and jog onto the bus. It's quiet and dark. Most of the guys are tired and ready to go home to their families.

"Four and fucking O, motherfuckers!" I shout as I take my seat and receive a loud round of roars and cheers in reply.

With a fleeting smile on my lips, I check my phone to find a group chat with Vander and Stone. A few texts from Owen and even Katy, but nothing from Sorel. My gut sinks.

Stone: I came home from the hospital to find Sorel upset and crying in the hall. Eloise paid her a visit and returned your shirt to her. Eloise had pictures and audio, but before you fly off the handle, relax. We've sorted it out, and Sorel knows you didn't cheat.

Fuck. I drag a hand through my still slightly damp hair. So the woman was Eloise. I should have guessed that, but I'd never met her before, so I didn't know.

Vander: Face ID required to read this message.

I roll my eyes. Only freaking Vander.

I hit the link and have my phone scan my face for biometrics before his message shows for me.

Vander: I've wiped both Eloise's and Brody's phones, as well as their computers and other devices of any photographs, videos, and audio that star you. As far as I can tell, they haven't sold or released them to anyone. It was blackmail and to manipulate Sorel. Brody promised Eloise that if she fucked you or at least made it seem as though she did, it would be the revenge they both deserve and that they could start hooking up again. In another message from Brody to his dad, he stated that once Sorel learned you cheated on her, she'd come running back to him and all would be good.

Jesus hell. I read through the message again. Brody had this whole thing figured out, didn't he? A plan he was sure would work. At least Sorel knows the truth.

Me: I owe you each a case of something expensive. Thank you for taking care of that. I was mic'd up. Do we know where the audio is?

Vander: We know you were mic'd up. The broadcasters mentioned it, but they didn't play the audio on air. It's with the NFL as we speak.

Me: Perfect. How's my girl?

Stone: Sleeping. She was very upset about what happened, and then she saw you down on the field with a team of trainers and doctors around you. But she trusts you and believes that you didn't cheat. She knew you didn't even before I got there.

I blow out a relieved breath, but I won't feel settled until I have her in my arms and she doesn't push me away.

Vander: There's more, but we can discuss that in person in the morning.

Oh goodie. I always love it when Vander tells me stuff like that.

35

SOREL

I toss and turn, unable to fall asleep. All of this is my fault. I talked Mason into marrying me the same day I left Brody. I called out Brody and Eloise in front of a hell of a lot of people at the wedding that never happened. And because of me, tonight Mason got hurt. He got knocked down and knocked down hard. Add to that, he had to deal with Eloise showing up in his room and trying to seduce him. As it is, she heard him jerk off and recorded it.

Mason just finished his press conference and I watched it on my phone from bed as the press ripped him apart. I need to do something. I've been passive-aggressive with everything.

I married Mason to get back at Brody. I blocked both him and Eloise. Other than what I did in the church and our conversation in his apartment, I never held Brody responsible beyond that. Not with the pregnancy. Not with any of it. I've let him slide, and it's wrong.

It's somewhere just after midnight, but I roll over and find my phone. I don't know where Mason is or what his deal is, but I need to do something.

"What can I do for you, Dr. Fritz?" Vander's voice is even,

but I think I catch a hint of amusement on the tail end. I've never called him before. Hell, I hardly know the guy. He seems... I don't know. Quiet. Dark. Maybe even a little danger-ous. At least that's the vibe he gives off.

"I learned something about you tonight."

"And I assume this call is in the hopes that you can use your newfound knowledge of me to your benefit?"

"Not my benefit. Mason's."

"Go on," he says, his voice still low and flat. I tell him exactly what I'm thinking. And once that's done, he follows that up with, "Are you sure? Mason told me you don't relish the spotlight and try to hide from the press as much as you can. In fact, he wouldn't let me do this originally."

"But you have it?"

"I have it."

"And the audio? Is it enough?"

"I don't think so. Not without everything else."

"Then I'd like to use it all if it needs to be done."

"You must really love him."

I laugh. It's not even funny what he said, but it's been a long night. A long week. A long couple of months.

"I really love him. So can you help me do this or not?"

"You've got it."

Vander disconnects the call, and I dial the second number I need to reach tonight. I set it on speakerphone and place my phone on the pillow beside me. Mason's pillow.

"I figured I'd hear from you tonight," Brody says arrogantly as he answers, and how he can still be so cocky and surefire, I have no clue.

"Why? Because you tried to hurt Mason or because you thought I'd be stupid enough to believe Eloise got him to cheat?"

He's silent for a moment. "Listen, I don't know what Mason told you, but he's full of shit."

I roll onto my side and face my phone. "So you didn't have that player intentionally try to hurt him?"

He huffs into the phone. "Jesus, Sorel, can you blame me? The guy fucking stole everything from me and then had the audacity to throw it in my face. Of course I was going to retaliate. You were supposed to be my fucking wife. Not his!"

"And Eloise?" I ask calmly because he still doesn't get it. He thinks he's justified in what he's done. "What about what she tried to do?"

He laughs. "What did she do?"

"Oh, you don't know?" I question.

"No, I don't know."

Except I know he's lying. Stone told me about what Vander found, only I won't out Vander.

"Allow me to educate you then. She snuck into his hotel room, got naked, and put on his shirt while he was in the shower. Then she took pictures of herself like that and of him in only a towel. It sounds like stalking and harassment and a massive invasion of privacy and likely other illegal things to me. Personally, I think Mason should go to the police and file a complaint over it."

Brody clears his throat. "Sounds rather crafty of her."

Now I gleam. "It does. It didn't sound like something she'd think up all on her own, so I assumed you were her mastermind."

He clears his throat. "I might have been. Let me guess, he told you nothing happened between them."

"Actually, I haven't talked to him yet. I figured out that nothing happened on my own. You see, when Eloise showed up tonight to return the shirt she stole from Mason, I looked over her photos and listened to the audio she had. None of it added up. He was in the shower. Her hair was dry. Not to mention, there was no one else on that audio. Just him."

Displeasure colors his tone. "Hmm. Is that so?"

"Yep. But if Mason presses charges, the police will sort through her phone including her texts and call log as well as her pictures and audio. I'm sure they can tell me if I missed something."

"What do you want, Sorel?" he practically barks. "What are you looking for me to admit to here?"

"Here's what I know," I start, ramping up to deliver the kill, feeling like the bad cop in a TV drama. "You already admitted to sleeping with Eloise behind my back while we were together. You just admitted to trying to hurt Mason and to having him framed by Eloise. The NFL has the audio from the game tonight, and once they investigate, I have no doubt there will be repercussions for you."

"I heard the audio from the game tonight. They don't have a leg to stand on with that. It was Tweo making the hit *for* me. Not *from* me. Tweo was just being a loyal player to a coach and former teammate. He'll get fined for the hit. That's all. As for the threat, well, I don't know what he's referring to. Perhaps I might have mentioned at one point wanting to get back at Reyes, but that was all. I never said anything specific, and quarterbacks get hit all the time in the NFL."

Crafty. And unfortunately, true.

"What makes you think that's the only evidence out there?"

His voice comes through the speaker on my phone like gravel, coarse and unrefined. "Because it is. Nice try though. What game are you trying to play here? All I've done from the second I met you is love you."

I ignore that. "The way I see it, you have a few choices to make. But all of it hinges on your desire to be part of your child's life."

"What if I want you?"

"I'm not part of the bargain. I already told you that you and I are over. I'm married to Mason, and my possessive husband loves to tell me that he has no plans to change that. Not to mention, I love him like crazy."

There's a loud bang in the background, but that's it. Brody rarely loses his cool and never in front of others. Not even on our wedding day when I called him out on what he did.

But this call isn't about that. I need him to know that I know the truth. And I need to know where he stands on the baby.

"Brody, do you want to be a father to your child? I've given you plenty of time to make a decision. Take me out of the equation because that's done. This is about the baby. But you will have to understand that Mason will also be there as one of its fathers, and after what you did tonight, I have serious reservations about you. Can you be a father and all that entails in a healthy and positive way?"

He's quiet for a long moment. So long that I lift my phone to make sure he's still there and didn't hang up.

"Brody?" I prompt.

"Fuck," he hisses. "I really lost you? There's no chance for us?"

"No, there's not." I don't apologize for it either. How he thought there was one after all this time boggles my mind. Then again, I've never had an ego like his. "You lost me months ago."

"I thought for sure..." He trails off and curses again.

"The baby, Brody. I need to know where your head is with it."

"I... I don't know." For the first time, I hear dejection. Maybe even remorse. "I don't picture myself as a single dad. I'm not sure I ever wanted children. I mean, I guess I would have since I knew you wanted them, but I'm not an every-other-weekend, put-my-life-on-hold kind of guy. I don't know the first thing about children. Not without you there to raise it."

Meaning not without me being a stay-at-home mom and doing nothing else but raise our kids and have nothing for myself while he goes off and has his job and life. *So* glad I didn't marry him.

At least he's honest about that.

The irony of that? Mason has never once suggested I stop working after we have the baby. He knows what my job means to me just as I know what his means to him. Mason and I will figure it out, but it would never be one sacrificing everything for the other. It would be a partnership. It would be even since we're both the parents.

"I don't want to see you with Reyes," he continues. "I don't want to hand my kid back over to him. I'm not even sure how I'd be a father from New York with my schedule. Coaching is a year-round job. It's not like when I was a player. Football is my life, Sorel. You know that. If you want me in the child's life, you'd have to move back here."

"That's not going to happen, and I have no judgment with you not wanting to turn your life over for someone else. There's no shocker there to me. But I need to hear you say the words."

He sighs. It's deep and heavy because I know a part of him feels like shit for it. "I don't want to be a father to the baby. I'm sorry, but I don't."

"Okay. That's fine." I lick my lips and sit up, staring down at the phone on the pillow as I talk. My heart starts to pound, and my palms grow clammy with nerves as a sparkle of relief starts to glimmer inside me. "So here's the deal. You need to apologize publicly to Mason and admit that you were in the wrong and jealous and upset or whatever else you need to say to put the blame on yourself."

"No. Fuck that, I won't do it," he barks, and I go on as if he didn't speak.

"You will legally relinquish your parental rights to our child as well as sign a contract that prohibits you from ever publicly saying the child is yours."

"Why would I do that?" he says caustically. "What? And hand that over to him? Again, fuck that."

I had a feeling he'd be petty like this.

"If you do all that," I continue, "you won't pay a dime of child support. You won't be involved in the child's life at all. And I won't release the text stream between you and Eloise that I read on our wedding day or the one from the other night where you goaded her into seducing Mason to seek revenge on me and rekindle your affair with her. Plus, I won't release this phone conversation where you admit to taking Mason down and helping Eloise try to frame him."

"The fuck? Sorel, you're recording this?" he snarls.

I smirk. "I learned how to play dirty from you. Do you agree to my terms?"

His voice grows cold. Sardonic. "You won't go public with anything. You don't want the press to read those texts or see what we tried to do. You don't want anyone to know I'm the father of the baby either. You're much happier staying quiet. You'll do anything to continue to be a perfect Fritz princess, free of scandal and spotlight. So maybe there are a few things I want too."

"You could try to negotiate this," I admit. "Because you're right, in the past, I would have done anything to prevent things from being public. But now it's not just about me. It's about Mason and my child, and they're more important than my comfort." I pick up my phone and send Vander the text he's been waiting for. "You should be receiving an email now."

He makes a shrill noise as likely the email comes through from Vander—though it's untraceable and he'd never know it's from him—with our various elements of proof against him. The texts between him and Eloise, both from the wedding and over the last week, the pictures of Eloise in Mason's hotel room, and images from the hotel security of her bribing someone for the keycard and then leaving ten minutes later after Mason kicked her out.

"That, along with the audio of this call, are some pretty incriminating and damning evidence, don't you think? I mean, that's the sort of stuff that doesn't just lose people their jobs or blackball them in an industry. That could bring about some real prison time if Mason felt the need to press charges. It would be difficult to pay child support without a job, don't you think?"

"What the fuck are you doing, Sorel?!" he yells. "Goddammit!"

I brush my hair back from my face, sit cross-legged on my bed, and speak directly into the phone. "I want a public statement from you apologizing to Mason, signed legal documents that will stay confidential, and for you to leave us the fuck alone after that. That's it. That's your freedom, Brody. If you don't do that, I will go public with everything and sue you for child support. I think it's a nice deal, all things considered. Think it over. This time, you have twenty-four hours, or I go to the press with everything. And I think you know what as a Fritz I'm capable of."

"This is how you want to be?"

"Not even close. You brought us to this. But this is what I have to do to protect my husband and my child. Twenty-four hours, Brody. Let me know."

I disconnect the call and flop on my back. I hate playing dirty, but if I need to go public with everything, I will. If I have to put myself in the spotlight, I will. But I'm hoping Brody does what's right for Mason and for the baby. I think he will because, ultimately, it benefits him too. The next twenty-four hours will tell.

36

MASON

The plane lands sometime after two in the morning. By the time I walk into my apartment, it's close to three. I'm so much more than tired by this point, and those bruises I got during the game are angry and purple. A bath is in my future, and let's hope I can convince my princess to take it with me.

As it is, I don't know if she'll welcome me in our bed. If she'll even be in our bed when I walk through the door. My instinct says yes. If I follow what Stone and Vander said, then she's there waiting for me. But with Sorel, nothing is guaranteed. She's the water perpetually flowing through my fingers, but she's also what strengthens my veins and fills my heart.

Entering our bedroom, I find her sleeping on my side of the bed, her head on the pillow, her body curled up as it always is when she sleeps. She is my passion. My obsession. She is what I can no longer live without. My heart skips a beat, and my breathing turns shaky. The power this woman has over me. The miles I would walk for her. The mountains I would climb. The wars I would fight and the people I would destroy.

It's incredible how your life can change in an instant. How

simply arriving early to a restaurant would forever change mine. We were the only two there, and the moment I saw her, I knew I was never going to recover from the blow she had given me. But what I didn't realize in that second was that Sorel was it. The girl. The one under my skin and tattooed across each of my organs. I could have claimed I was simply scratching a year-long itch, but even I knew better than to believe in such bullshit.

Rules to live by: If you can't stop thinking about her, you sure as hell won't be able to fuck her once to get her out of your system.

She's the one I never knew I always wanted. I wasn't prepared when she came along. I hadn't signed up for her and all she came with. No, she blindsided me. She was a hit I never saw coming.

I even stumbled over my name when I introduced myself—something I had never done before. I sure as hell couldn't stop staring at her. I didn't hesitate to shamelessly flirt with her, but when I discovered she was dating my new teammate, it felt as though my legs had been cut off beneath me. I held back and played the friend card since I had no other one in my deck.

But the moment her eyes met mine outside the church that day, and she asked me to get her out of there, I knew it was finally my turn. I might have always been hers, but she was always meant to be mine.

I strip down and smile as I slide beneath the sheets and scooch in beside her. Sorel is the heaviest sleeper ever and she hardly stirs as I wrap her up in my arms, kiss her neck, and finally relax now that I'm beside her. My hand meets the small bump of her belly, and I smile. I don't know what will happen tomorrow. If she'll even want me here, or if I'll have a mountain of explaining to do, but for now, holding her like this... it's perfect.

My hand drags along her stomach, and my lips land in the crook of her neck.

"You don't get to touch the bump just yet."

I grin against her skin.

"What do I have to do to deserve rubbing my hand over my child, Dr. Fritz-Reyes?"

"I heard a story about you tonight?"

"Is that so?" I question and kiss a trail up to her ear and settle my body in tighter behind her. "I hope it was a good one. A steamy romance would be best. Was it the one where the sexy football player gets the girl of his dreams, fucks her till she can't see straight, and they live happily ever after?"

I can hear the sleepy smile in her voice as she asks, "How'd you know?"

"Because I'm a genius like that." I kiss up the soft, sweet skin of her neck as my hand glides along her stomach and under her shirt before I grow sober and serious. "I'm so sorry about tonight. I'm sorry about all of it. I'm sorry you were forced to have doubts. I'm sorry you had to hear about what happened in my room from Eloise and not from me because when I called you this morning, I intended to tell you everything. I'm sorry you had to see the hit on the field. I'm just so sorry, Sorel."

She reaches under her shirt and holds my hand against her ribs. "I know. I won't lie and say that wasn't an awful ten minutes because it was, but I believe you and I trust you. I knew in my gut you wouldn't cheat, and because of that, it allowed me to eventually think clearly about what I actually saw and heard in those pictures and video."

A shudder racks through me, and my face rests deeper against her as I begin to shake. The chokehold those words have over me, the power they wield...

"I love you," I breathe against her. "I love you so much."

"I hate that you're a football player."

I choke out a laugh. "Some moments are better than others."

She rolls over in my arms and pushes me back so she can scan my chest, and when her gaze snags on the large bruise from where Tweo's helmet slammed into my chest, followed by his shoulder pad, she gasps.

"Mason!"

Tentatively, she runs her fingers over it, being as ginger as she can be.

"I've had worse."

She glances up and scowls at me. "Statements like that won't get you laid. Did you hit your head too?"

"Not bad."

"Not bad?!" she parrots heatedly. "How am I supposed to watch you play again?"

I lean up and kiss her lips. "I'm not usually hit like that."

"That's another thing." She pushes me back, and her expression sobers. "You're not the only one who had a big night." She goes on to explain her conversation with Brody, where he stands on the pregnancy and the baby, and the ultimatum she left him with.

"You enlisted Vander to help you?" Now I understand why he said there was more, and we'd talk in the morning.

She shrugs. "Why not? You did."

Touché. "Sorel..." I trail off, at a bit of a loss. "You didn't need to do that for me, baby. I can more than handle him. The commissioner will review the tape, and Brody will get fined and probably fired."

She frowns lightly. "You haven't heard the audio, have you?"

Slowly I shake my head, feeling my face pinch up in confusion. "Not yet. But Tweo said—"

"Tweo said this is *for* Brody. And he never got specific with what the threat was. It doesn't actually implicate Brody in anything. Not fully. It could be construed that Tweo was acting on his own."

I blow out a breath. I had just gotten my bell rung a bit, so I didn't focus on the minutia of it. Just that he indicated it was a hit and a threat from Brody.

"By doing this, he won't be able to seek further revenge against you—because clearly he's spiteful like that—and I will have a guarantee that he won't try to come after us somehow with the baby. He could seek full custody or drag us through court just to be a dick. This removes him from our lives completely."

"Sorel, baby. If he doesn't say yes to your deal, if he takes his chances..."

"I'll do what I have to do, Mason. I'll do it for all of us. And I will hold to my word, but I think he'll do the smart thing and apologize so he can move on. He doesn't want to pay child support, he doesn't want his name tarnished more than it already has been, and he doesn't want to lose his job. If he's smart, he'll get over his pride on this. Honestly, it's more than he deserves."

It's impossible to argue with that, because no one wants him out of her life and away from the baby more than I do. I don't even care so much about the apology. It'll make him look like the wounded party still, but whatever. I don't care about that, so I say, "Okay."

She smiles. "Okay."

I pull her shirt over her head and roll us until I'm above her, settling my weight on my forearms so I don't press down on her. I stare into her eyes in the dark for a long moment before I dip and take her lips with mine. I want to sink into her, I want to feel her skin-to-skin, but that's not the best with her belly, so I roll us again until she's over me. My hands brush back her hair, and I cup her face so I can deepen the kiss.

This moment feels different. It's the calm after the storm,

and despite my exhaustion and the aching in my muscles, I'm relaxed in a way I haven't been in months. The tension and weight I've been carrying are lifted from my chest and shoulders. Because she's right. Brody will be smart enough to take the deal she offered him, which means he's gone from our lives. It means the baby is officially mine, and the only person I'll have to share it with is Sorel.

Her hips roll, and her pussy grinds against the hard length of my cock. It's late—or early—and she has to be up for work in only a few hours. I don't have time to savor her. Not right now anyway. I continue to kiss her as I tug my boxer briefs down followed by her underwear. My hand drags up her inner thigh, parting them over my own until she's straddling me. As always with her, she's fucking soaked, and without hesitation, I slide two fingers deep inside her.

She moans and arches her back, bringing her tits up closer to my mouth. I use my other hand to cup one of her breasts so I can get it the rest of the way there. Her nipple is sweet and tight, and I fucking love how this woman tastes. I give her a few more pumps with my fingers, just to make sure she's ready for my cock, and then I slide them out of her, grip my dick in my hand, and feed it to her inch by inch.

Her pussy is a tight glove and takes my cock so well. A harsh breath slips out of my lungs, and I find her lips again, needing to kiss her as I start to move. She's already panting, and I know it's because she's angled her body so the head of my cock hits her G-spot with every bounce and thrust.

"Fucking perfect," I rasp against her lips because she is. She's perfect in every way, but what makes her so is that she's perfect for me. We're perfect for each other. A match she never saw coming, and one that almost didn't happen.

I suppose that's fate.

I'm undeniably married to the love of my life, and we're going to have a baby together, but this marriage isn't real. Not in the sense I need it to be. Not in the way it counts. It's not how we should have done this, and eventually I'm going to have to do something about that.

But for now...

I roll us once more and link our hands together, stretching them above her head. My forehead meets hers, and with our eyes glued, I pump into her, angling my hips up so I hit her front wall with my cock and her clit with my pelvic bone. Planting my knees into the bed, I increase my pace, unable to slow down. The smooth, wet, hot slide of her pussy is magic.

"Ah, Mason."

I grunt, nearly coming on the spot just from that. "That's it. Say it again. Say my name again. Tell me who's fucking you. Tell me who's going to make you come."

"You. Oh god, Mason. Mason." Her face pinches up, and her eyes close as she teeters right on the edge.

"That's it, my pretty princess. Take it. Take all of me. Come for me."

She does almost instantly. Her pussy clenches my cock and milks me, drawing my own orgasm from me in a ripping, strangled roar I have no control over. I watch her face and come along with her, unable to believe the sight before me and my luck at having her as mine.

37

SOREL

Brody never called me back. And the midnight-ish deadline came and went. I was shocked. I thought he was going to do the right—and frankly, the smart—thing and move on with his life. First thing Monday morning, my attorney sent his attorney all the necessary legal documents I had mentioned to him on the phone. I'd already had them drafted just in case. The rest of the materials I had set to go in an email to my attorney as well as Mason's PR people. Mason is at practice all day, but when Brody missed the deadline, Mason asked me to take more time to think my decision over.

I'm not going to let Brody get away with what he did to Mason. Or me, for that matter. He didn't care about hurting either of us as long as his goal was met. Hell, he even used Eloise. The man didn't care who he messed with or how he did it. No one should get away with that. My plan is to send everything out this evening and go from there.

A knock raps on my office door just as I'm packing up to leave and head home.

I glance up to find Jack filling my doorway. "Hey!" I greet

him with a smile. "What brings you up to my neck of the woods?"

"I thought you'd want to see it."

My brows pinch. "See what?"

"You haven't checked your phone then, I take it?"

I shake my head. "No. I just finished with my last patient and was about to dictate and go home."

"Here." He walks in and comes around my desk, his phone in his hand. It's cued up to ESPN live streaming, and my heart skitters in my chest. His finger presses the sideways triangle, and the screen comes to life with Brody standing at a podium.

"What can I say other than these last few months have been an enormous struggle for me," Brody says, looking worn and beaten down. A look I'm positive is an act.

I roll my eyes derisively. "Always the fucking victim or hero."

"I never intended for things to get this far. Yes, I cheated on my fiancée. It was wrong, and to her, I apologize again. Sorel Fritz will always be someone I love and admire, and losing her because of my careless and callous actions will forever be one of my greatest regrets. With that, I owe Mason Reyes an apology. I know by now you've all heard the audio from Sunday night's game. A man has to take responsibility for his actions, and that's what I'm doing now. I was resentful of Mason's relationship with my ex, and I wasn't shy about making that known in the locker room and to close friends of mine. My words and sentiments were misconstrued because never, at any point, would I ever want a player injured at my hands."

"Wow," Jack muses. "He's throwing Tweo under the bus. I wonder how that will sit in the locker room."

"Brody doesn't care as long as his public image is still clean," I explain.

"That said, I take full responsibility for Tweo's actions and have decided to pay his fine."

I snicker. "Ah. There you go." I glance up at Jack with a smirk. "Feel better now?"

"Much," he replies sarcastically.

"I won't be taking any questions at this time. I simply want to apologize to my team, my players, my fellow coaches, the owner, Mr. Elmer, who has been endlessly supportive of me, the fans, who I love and appreciate so much, and most of all to Sorel and Mason. I hope we can all put this situation behind us now. Thank you for your time."

Brody walks out of the press room amid reporters shouting his name and random questions at him.

Well then. I suppose I won't be sending the email sitting in my drafts. That is if he signs the paperwork through his attorney.

Just as the thought hits my head, my phone vibrates on the side of my desk. I pick it up and see Brody's name flashing across my screen.

Jack smirks. "I'll let you get that."

"Thank you. And thank you for coming up to show me."

He gives me a wink and leaves my office, shutting the door behind him as I swipe my finger across the screen.

"I take it you saw my press conference?" Brody says into my ear, his voice low and even without even a hint of inflection.

"I did."

"Your attorney should be receiving the signed documents now. I had my attorney wait until after the press conference to send them."

A swell of relief rises up through me like a geyser.

"I don't want anyone to know I'm the father, Sorel," he continues before I can say anything.

"I have no plans to tell anyone, though eventually, when the child is old enough, they'll need to know and understand they're not biologically Mason's."

He swallows and clears his throat. "When that time comes,

please have the courtesy to speak to me before you speak to them."

"I will," I assure him. "Regardless, you have no liability, and I promise to keep it that way. That was in the documents in case you missed it."

"You think I'm a shitty person." It comes out as a statement and not a question.

"Honestly, at this point, I'm grateful for what you did with Eloise. It led me to Mason in a way I otherwise wouldn't have been. We all have demons, and we're all flawed. It doesn't matter what I think. You have to be able to live with yourself and your choices."

He's silent for a long moment before he says, "I meant what I said in there. Forgetting Reyes, I am sorry about everything that happened between us, and losing you will be the regret of my life. Without you, I think I'd be a shitty dad. Kids are, well, I don't know if they're for me."

I pick up a pen and twirl it around with my fingers. "Then you made the right choice, Brody. One I appreciate both for the child and for myself."

"Take care of yourself, Sorel. I hope you have everything in this life you deserve."

"Thank you, Brody. Take care." I disconnect the call and practically squeal in delight. It's done. It's over. Brody is gone and out of our lives for good.

~

"WHERE ARE YOU GOING TONIGHT?" Serena asks in my ear as I tuck my phone against my shoulder and brace against the frigid Boston wind.

"I don't know. He wouldn't tell me."

"He's going to propose."

That stops me short, and a man at my back nearly plows

straight into me. He snaps something I don't care enough about to hear at me and continues on. I'm too busy blinking at the ghoulish Halloween decorations that threw up all over the coffee shop on the corner from our building.

Speaking of throwing up... "What? Why would you say that?"

She snorts. "One, you told him a few weeks ago you had to figure out the marriage end of your relationship."

"So?"

"Two," she continues without missing a beat, "it's three months."

"What's three months?"

"This weekend marks three months since you got married, but he's traveling this weekend for a game. Wasn't that your deadline?"

"Yes, but we've only been together a short while," I protest. "He won't propose." I start to walk again, confident in that. "And when I said we have to figure out the marriage side of this, we do. I mean, the wedding wasn't real. How would we ever explain that to our kid? *Oh, Mom got wasted one night in Vegas and asked me to marry her so I could be her revenge against her cheating ex.* That doesn't exactly sound like the best story. I realize divorce is tricky, but I don't know. I don't like being married for the wrong reasons."

"And how does your doting, obsessed husband feel about that?"

I huff. "He agreed!" I exclaim.

"Uh-huh," she says dismissively, but thankfully she changes the subject. "Anyway, have you booked your flight yet?"

"Yes. Mom, Dad, and I are flying in the Monday before Thanksgiving."

"And Keegan?"

"She bagged out. I don't know what's up with her and this movie star guy, but she changed her mind."

"Poor Keegs. Still, I'm so excited you're coming. And you know I'm planning to fly in for the baby shower and stay through until after the baby is born. Aurelia and Zax agreed to temporarily move my position at Monroe Fashions to the Boston office."

I roll my eyes as I briskly head for the front door of our building. "That's because they're Mason's aunt and uncle of sorts. Do you think they could get away with not allowing you to move back here temporarily? Besides, maybe you'll take a fancy to Boston in the springtime and stay."

"Nope. Not a chance. But nice try."

"Fine. I won't push it. Yet. Listen, I just got home, and I need to take a shower before my date tonight."

"You mean before your engagement."

"Shut it, bitch. I love you."

"Love you too. Call me tomorrow and tell me everything."

"I will. Bye."

I slip my phone back into my purse and rush inside the building. It's annoyingly cold for it only being October.

"Oh, Mrs. Fritz-Reyes. Perfect timing." The doorman stops me before I can reach the elevator. "I was just about to deliver these up to your unit. I have a couple of packages for you and Mr. Reyes that were just delivered. The boxes on the bottom were sent by courier and required a signature."

A courier? Weird. "I can take them up."

He smiles and hands me three boxes and an envelope. I step onto the elevator, curious about the boxes that required a special signature, but my focus is quickly intercepted by the envelope sitting on top. The return address is from Eloise. What in the *Nightmare Before Christmas* could she be sending me? Sigh. When will this end?

The elevator doors open, and I head to my apartment, shifting and shuffling the boxes and the envelope so I can open the door. With my gaze still locked on the envelope, I don't notice or even comprehend the odd clacking sound until a bark makes me start and yelp. The packages fly out of my hands and crash to the floor while my feet skitter back as whatever made that sound jumps at me.

"Who are you?" I gasp as an adorable brown labradoodle puppy starts licking my hand. "Mason?!" I call out, only he's not home. I rub the puppy's head and catch its collar, twisting it so I can read the tag. "Vegas?" My face scrunches up. "Is that your name?"

"Shit," I hear Mason curse. "Vegas. Down!" The dog doesn't budge. It's very happy jumping and licking at me. "Down!"

Mason is scrambling toward me wearing a fluffy white bathrobe and what appears to be nothing else. His hair is wet and sticking up all over the place, and his feet slip and slide on the hardwood floors.

"You're home early," he almost snaps at me, irritated like somehow it's my fault there's a strange dog in our apartment.

"My last two patients of the day canceled. What is going on?" I cry out, laughing hysterically. There is a strange dog in my apartment jumping on me, and Mason is wearing the biggest bathrobe I've ever seen.

He rolls his eyes when he sees my expression, but his lips are twitching all the same. "Don't make fun of me. I wear this after I take a bath."

I shake my head. "I've never seen it."

"Because I don't usually take baths when you're home, princess."

I point down to the dog. "Who is this?"

He groans and grabs the dog by the collar to pull him off me. "This is Vegas. He was supposed to be a surprise, but clearly he's very smart as he somehow escaped his crate."

"A dog?" I'm incredulous. "A puppy at that? You didn't think that should be something we talk about first? Puppies are a lot of work."

"You told me in Vegas you wanted a dog. I got you a dog. Besides, I read that animals are good with children, and after Eloise randomly showed up here and with all that I travel, I wanted you to have a guard dog to protect you. I had to wait until he was big enough and ready to leave his mama or whatever."

I fall into a fit of laughter as the dog tries to come at me, its paws dancing in the air. "His mama?"

"Shush it, woman."

I'm dying. I legit have tears streaming down my cheeks. Mason just used the word mama while wearing a fluffy bathrobe. "Yeah. I can see how this affection bomb would be terrifying and scare everyone away." I rub its ears and face. "You're going to be trouble. I can tell." I glance up at Mason. "When did I say I wanted a dog?"

"When you were drunk right before you proposed to me."

Oh. Funny, I don't remember that one. "I love it. Him. Vegas is adorable."

Mason sighs. "Good. I'm glad because I think you were right about puppies being a lot of work. I didn't think about that."

"It'll be good practice for the baby."

"No! Vegas, stop!" Mason cries as the puppy starts to root and scratch at the boxes that flew out of my hands. I all but forgot about them with all the puppy excitement. Mason tries to beat me to them, but he's also trying to corral Vegas, so I get there first. Both of the boxes broke open when they hit the ground, and what I see spilling out of one of them stops my heart.

38

MASON

This is all going wrong. All of it. I had the entire night planned, and now it's gone to shit.

"Mason," Sorel breathes in a soft whisper as she sinks to her knees, ignoring the excited jumping and barking of our new crazy dog. I should have done more research, but this type came up as great with children, easily housebroken, playful, sweet, and protective. It felt like a no-brainer. Except for the puppy side of it.

And because of this wild thing, I can't get to the boxes that were supposed to be delivered straight up to me so she wouldn't see them. Now everything is a mess.

"What is this?" She picks up the silver frame and holds it in her hands.

"Give me a second. Don't move or touch anything else." I walk Vegas back into our bedroom and into his crate. He whimpers, and a pang of guilt hits me. "Sorry, buddy, but I have to go give Mommy her other surprise." This time I make sure the door is locked, then I quickly throw on a pair of jeans and a white T-shirt and fly back out to Sorel. She's still sitting on her haunches, staring at the picture.

Thankfully she didn't get farther than that. I skid onto my knees in front of her, and her watery eyes meet mine.

"You framed the ultrasound picture?" She sniffles and wipes her nose with the back of her hand. "I thought I lost it."

"After you initially showed it to me, I kept staring at it. I couldn't stop. I had it in my nightstand drawer, but it was starting to crinkle, and I didn't want it to get ruined."

"So you had it framed?"

I nod. "What about these other two spaces in the frame? What are they for?"

"You told me we'd have another ultrasound around twenty weeks." I tap the middle space. "That's what this one is for, and the third I figured we could put baby's first picture in there after it's born."

Sorel falls apart. "This is the sweetest..." She can't even finish her sentence, and I find myself chuckling. Her hormones are the best. I shift so my legs are stretched out in front of me, and I pull her onto my lap, removing her coat and tossing it behind me as I go.

"I wanted to surprise you."

"You did." Another sniffle. "The dog is crazy but adorable, and I love him already. And this... I have no words for this."

"Happy three-month anniversary."

"What?" she draws back, wiping the remaining tears from her face. "That's what this dinner tonight is?"

I shrug. "I won't be here on our actual anniversary so—"

"Mason, I, we, three months isn't, it's not a—"

I cut her off with a kiss. "Shh. I know what it is and what it's not. I know how you feel about it. Actually, I know how you feel about all of it. I don't care. I've decided I don't care."

"What do you mean you don't care?"

I go for the other box. The one she hadn't noticed because the picture frame caught her eye first. I pull out the small square box and drop it in her lap.

"I love you," I whisper. "I've loved you from the moment I met you. I just didn't realize it until I married you on that balcony. But when I said, I do, I meant it. I told you I'd give you three months, and I have. There will be no annulment, and there will be no divorce. I don't care if we did everything backward. What we have is real, it's binding, it's forever." I open the box to reveal the engagement ring I bought for her. "Sorel Fritz-Reyes, will you do me the incredible honor of marrying me again tonight? This time for real?"

She stares at me for the longest time, and finally, just when I think she's about to get up and run away, she throws her arms around my neck and says, "Yes. Yes, I'll marry you tonight."

My heart thunders, and I hug her back before I cup her face in my hands and kiss her.

The ring slides on her finger right beside her wedding band, and she sighs as she stares down at it. "You really don't half-ass anything, do you?"

I grin and kiss her neck. "Nope. Not my style."

She plays with the two rings on her finger. "Marrying you on that balcony was the best drunken decision of my life."

I smile and chuckle lightly. "Best *drunken* decision?"

Her head tilts, and her pretty hazel eyes meet mine. "The universe brought us together that day and to that moment. It brought me you. And you said yes when I asked. I think... I think my heart has always been yours. I just didn't know till you said yes."

"And now you said yes to me."

She leans in, her hand on my cheek, and she kisses me. "Do you actually have a wedding planned for us tonight?"

I grin like a bastard. "I do. I even have a gown for you, courtesy of your sister, Serena."

"What?" she squawks. "Serena is involved?! I just spoke to her, and she teased me that you were going to propose."

"Of course she did," I smart. "Because everything so far is starting off backward."

"Aw." She kisses me. "But that's what'll make a great story when we're a hundred and fifty. What's next?"

"Now we get married."

ORIGINALLY, Sorel was going to come home after I had everything set up. With the ring in my pocket, Vegas in his crate, and the frame in our room so I could show it to her later, my plan was to bring Sorel to Stella's for "dinner" and surprise her. None of that happened, but as we enter Stella's restaurant together, this might almost be better. Especially when she sees that everyone is here, including her brothers and Serena.

She gasps and immediately starts crying because that's pregnant Sorel.

I flew everyone in, not even knowing if she'd say yes. It was ballsy, but nothing ventured, nothing gained, and I wanted us to have tonight as it should have been. Sorel showed me the envelope from Eloise. It was an invitation to her and Brody's wedding, which made both of us grimace and laugh.

I told Sorel that I didn't return the favor for tonight.

Eloise and Brody deserve each other, but more importantly, Sorel and I deserve each other.

"I'll take her from here," Serena says to me as she whisks Sorel away from me. I didn't know how to plan this, but lucky for me, Serena did. Everything is how I think Sorel would want it. Candles and flowers and dim lighting and our people. It's quiet and casual and pretty and romantic.

It's our Vegas wedding, only multiplied and obviously without the covertly stolen picture and copious amounts of alcohol. Stone, Owen, Vander, and Bennett drag me toward the back where the makeshift altar is set up.

"Nice digs, man," Bennett says to me, giving me a fist pound. "You did a good job. Katy nearly started crying again when she put Willow in her little flower girl dress."

"You've got legit balls of steel doing it this way," Stone tells me, giving me a bro hug. "What if she hadn't said yes and you did all of this?" He pans his hand around the restaurant. Stella wouldn't let me buy it out for the night. She told me she was more than happy to give her sister her wedding.

"Actually, she said yes way before we got here." I launch into the story of what happened when she got home, including the bathrobe. My guys are splitting at the seams with hysterics, and I can't even blame them for it. No one was ever supposed to see that bathrobe, but last year Stone and Vander caught me in, and tonight, Sorel.

Whatever. The fucking thing is soft and cozy. Let them laugh.

An hour later, I'm nervously munching on shit I shouldn't be munching on. Tomorrow morning, the team flies to Florida. I likely should have waited. I don't get to spend much time with her tonight, and I'm essentially leaving her with a puppy, even if I did get a trainer and walker set up for him. But I couldn't wait any longer.

Our clock was ticking.

She said three months and then last week mentioned it again. I had to make this real for her.

With that though, something niggles at the back of my neck, and I turn around and nearly pass out standing.

Holy shit.

Sorel is in a white calf-length dress that hugs every curve, including her beautiful bump. Her full cleavage spills out of the cinched chest and sharp V of the neckline. But it's her pretty hair that's swept up with only her bangs on her face and her makeup that's shimmery and stunning. God. That's my girl.

I can't stop myself as I practically float across the room to her. I don't care if this isn't what it's supposed to be. "Princess," I greet her, smiling like a damn fool.

"Player," she says back, and I laugh. This fucking girl.

There is movement all around me and a tug on my arm that tells me I'm not supposed to be here. I'm supposed to be down at the end of the altar waiting for her, but I can't resist leaning in and whispering into her ear, "The moment the ceremony is over, I'm taking you into the bathroom and fucking you so hard, and I don't care who hears us."

My fingers glide along her neck before I wrap my hand around her. To anyone else, it looks like a loving caress. To my girl, it's a promise.

She shivers, and her cheeks bloom with color.

On a wink, I head down to where Stone, Owen, and Bennett are waiting. Her asshat brothers hoot and holler at me, and I flip them off. They're fucking ballbusters, but I've grown to like them more over the last couple of weeks that I've been planning this.

Vander gives me a shake of his head, either reading what my intention is with my wife—future wife? Wife redux? I don't know—or annoyed that I have him up at the altar about to do the service. He doesn't like being so out in the open. Even with this small, limited crew. I talked him into getting his minister's license, and his father, Lenox is having the best time with that. Then again, my dad married him and his wife, so I suppose it's full circle.

"Iris" by the Goo Goo Dolls starts to play, and Sorel instantly tears up as her parents, one on each arm, walk her to me. Did she honestly think I wouldn't play a 90s song for her? We had "Crash into Me" the first time, and now this one... I think this song is ours too.

Landon and Elle hand her over to me and I give them both

hugs. They were more than a little thrilled and excited when I proposed doing this wedding tonight.

Vander heaves in a breath, throws me yet another glare, and gets started.

I hold Sorel's hand and gaze into her eyes. This wedding is more of a reaffirmation of love and commitment since we're technically already married, so it doesn't require anything legal.

This is for her. This is so she knows how deep in this I am and never questions it. It's to erase all of her regrets and remind her that I'll always be her adventure.

That's what we do for each other. It's both of us. Never one-sided. And the moment I kiss her, one hand on the back of her neck and the other on her belly, my life finally feels like it's clicking into place, and all of the pieces I had scattered about come together into the most beautiful puzzle, complete with the picture Sorel always kept hidden from everyone but herself. It's mine now too.

I grin against her lips and swoop her up into my arms to carry her over to where the dance floor and food are. A song I don't know starts to play, and I draw her into me, our foreheads pressed as we slowly sway.

"Good surprise?" I ask softly.

"Incredible surprise. This is the wedding I always wanted. It's perfect, Mason. All of it is."

My chin drops and I kiss her, the rest of the room and the world fading away, leaving us in this bubble together.

"I'm sorry I have to leave you this weekend."

She smiles against me. "Serena and my brothers are here. I'll have plenty to keep me occupied and when you come home, we'll make our own honeymoon at home."

I'm already planning a trip for us during my bye week, but I don't tell her that. It'll be yet another surprise. The rest of the evening continues with us eating, dancing, and laughing with our family and friends. It's the perfect wedding with my dream girl. But when everyone's had a bit too much to drink and are having a bit too much fun on the dance floor, I wrap my arm around my bride and drag her toward the bathrooms.

"We can't!" She laughs as I swing her straight into the ladies' room since these places are always cleaner than men's rooms.

"We can," I assure her as I lock the door. "We're married times two." I push her back from me, and her hands fall to the counter behind her as she throws me the sexiest fucking look that legit makes my knees weak and my breath tumble from my chest. "Lift up your dress for me, Mrs. Reyes."

"It's Fritz-Reyes," she remarks.

I shake my head. "Not right now, it's not. You're mine." I jut my chin toward the bottom of her dress. "Show me what's under there but keep the top on. Your tits look unbelievably sensational in that."

One hand meets her knees, and she slides the dress up to reveal a white lacy garter and oh my fuck, those panties. They're going in my mouth. Right now. I hit the floor on my knees and take over, a man already past his limit, and my face goes straight into her pussy with a deep inhale. God. The way she smells. I groan, my grip on her upper thighs tightening as I nearly bust a nut. I swear, since she's been pregnant, her body is just...

I glance up at her. "I love you, and I know I'm supposed to be gentle and loving, but I need to do unholy things to you."

Her hazel eyes turn black, and she bites her white teeth into her plump, pink lip. "You've been such a good boy. Do it."

God. I'm so fucking done for.

"Come on, daddy." She smirks tauntingly. "Don't tell me you're afraid of getting caught."

I chuckle and nip her inner thigh. "I don't care if your entire family walks in right now. I won't be able to stop."

Her panties shred in my hands, and I cover her cunt with

my lips while instantly thrusting my tongue straight up in her. I drag her thigh up and onto my shoulder, and I go to town, eating her out like I never have before.

"Show me those rings, princess," I growl against her soaking wet flesh.

She wiggles her fingers in front of me before she runs her hand through my hair. My tongue flicks up and down, from side to side, and rings around her clit while I slip two fingers straight into her. My head tips back, and I watch her face, our eyes locked, as I tongue her pussy while finger fucking it. No. Finger banging it. I'm fucking her so hard and fast as my tongue licks and swirls and presses as hard as it can.

"Mason!"

"You're loud, baby." I reach up and grasp her neck. "Everyone is going to hear us. They're all going to hear you come."

I don't squeeze. She's pregnant. But I do give a tiny amount of pressure, so she feels it, and I continue to fuck her with my other hand and my tongue. Just as she's about to come, I flip her around so her hands are forced to plant onto the counter and her face is almost right up against the glass of the mirror.

On a gasp, I split her cheeks and ring her asshole with my tongue.

"Oh hell, Mason."

"They're going to hear you," I taunt, licking around her tight hole again before shoving my tongue inside and pumping it in and out. She moans, rocking forward, and I use my fingers to rub her clit while I continue to eat her ass.

"Oh my god! Then stop licking my ass with my family on the other side of the door. I can't believe you're doing that right now."

Me neither, honestly. I smile into her. "Not gonna stop."

I rub small, tight circles all over her clit and lick and tongue fuck her ass, and she comes, gripping the counter and watching her face in the reflection of the mirror with her tits half spilling out of her dress. Have I mentioned my wife is a goddess?

I don't even wait before I stand up, pull my dick out of my pants, and slam straight into her from behind. I want to watch her face in the mirror as I fuck her, and this is the perfect way to do it. With her tits everywhere and her makeup a little smeared and her hair a bit disheveled and her face magnificently radiant with my cock inside of her.

I start to fuck into her as I grab the side of her face and turn her so she's forced to kiss me. "Mine. My wife. Say it."

"Yes," she pants, barely able to catch her breath. "Yours. Your wife."

"My baby." I cup her belly. "All of this, it's all mine now."

"Yes," she cries, meeting me thrust for thrust, impaling herself down on my cock with a rapid ferocity I can hardly keep up with. We fuck and fuck, and it's noisy with our grunts and groans and moans and whimpers. It's deep and hot as I watch her and she watches me. There is nothing better this. I'd do anything for this woman. Anything.

Her body quivers and shakes, and her pussy clenches tight and hard to the point where I wheeze out a harsh breath. With her head back on my shoulder and her fists balled up on the counter, she starts to come all over me. The wet pulsing of her cunt is goddamn mind-blowing, and I can't hold back as I shoot my load straight into her, pushing and thrusting and fucking coming so goddamn hard.

My forehead plants into the center of her back, right against the top of her dress, and I breathe raggedly, feeling like I just ran sprints up a mountain.

"We're doing that again when I get you home."

She giggles. "You young men and your stamina."

I smirk. "I don't hear you complaining."

She slides off my dick, and I wince at the feel of losing her wet heat. She spins around but grabs a cloth towel from the counter. Men don't get such luxuries in our bathroom. We're forced to deal with rough paper.

She places the napkin between her legs and looks at me. "I love you, Mason. After we have this baby, I want you to adopt it. I want it to be legally yours, not just emotionally. I thought about this a while ago but wanted to wait for the right moment to bring it up. This is the right moment."

I hadn't thought about that, but I hold her face and kiss her lips so thoroughly, filled with so much love and gratitude, it makes my hands tremble.

"Thank you. Yes, I'd like to adopt the baby so it's all mine."

She nips at my lips. "And after we get used to it and it grows a little, I want you to get me pregnant again."

My dick twitches as if to say, *we're ready for our assignment.* "Just tell me when."

She smiles. It's the happiest smile I've seen on her yet, and it fills my chest with a warmth I can't even begin to comprehend.

Leaning in, she kisses my lips and then scoots into the stall to pee.

"Out, Mason."

"Yes, ma'am," I tease. I go to open the door and halt in my tracks at the people I find right on the other side. "Landon. Octavia. Hi!"

EPILOGUE
SOREL

The presents practically line an entire wall and are three tiers deep. This is what I was afraid of. Most of the women here are already on their second or third bubble baby bump, as they're calling the drink, which is champagne mixed with peach and blueberry puree. They have lemonade for me and the other non-alcohol drinkers, but it's giving me heartburn the way everything else right now does.

I don't mean to sound bitchy. I'm grateful. I'm just freaking exhausted, and with how sore my back is, I can't get into a comfortable position, no matter how many pillows I prop myself up with. I'm huge. I haven't seen my feet in I don't remember how long, and I needed Mason to put on my boots this morning for me.

I hit thirty-seven weeks yesterday, and in addition to reaching that milestone, I'm also officially on maternity leave for the next four months. That's also about the time Mason will start training camp, so we'll have plenty of time together when the baby is born. I'm excited. He's more than excited.

But the problem is the wall of presents and how I was told specifically not to set up the nursery until after I received all these presents. This means now that I'm exhausted, huge, and uncomfortable, I have to do all that too.

"You're cranky," Serena notes as she polishes off her bubble baby bump.

"I'm not. I'm happy." I smile. It's not a full smile because she's right, I'm cranky. I have a plate of finger foods balancing on my giant belly and my feet up on an ottoman because they're swollen and aching.

"I'm sorry," she says, refilling her flute from the drink dispenser. "It's my fault. I couldn't get away before now, and I wanted to be here for your shower. Deadline for spring fashion week is no joke."

I'm being cranky at my own baby shower, and now I feel guilty for it.

"You're fine. I'm glad you're here, and I wouldn't have been able to have this shower without you." I sigh and scrunch my nose at the presents. "You're going to help with those, right?"

"Yes, and I believe Dad and a crew of men are coming to transport everything to your place after. Mason and I already talked about the nursery, and we're taking care of everything. With his brawn and my design sense, it'll be perfection."

"Excellent." I toss a piece of cheese in my mouth. "Because it's going to take a forklift to get me out of this chair, and with my lack of design sense and brawn, I'm more or less useless."

Keegan snickers as she refills her drink. "Just be thankful it's not twins."

My mother snickers. "You're telling me. I had two sets."

"Yes, but at least you didn't have to birth me," Stella reminds her. "My poor mother's vagina. I was a big baby."

I wince. We're having a boy, and though I hate to say this, Brody is not a small man. This baby is weighing in at around eight pounds already, and I have another few weeks to go. To say my vagina is terrified is an understatement. No one knows yet that it's a boy. Mason and I have kept it a secret because he thought it would be fun for me to reveal it today to everyone in the color of the cake.

But speaking of Brody, last I heard, he married Eloise back in the fall and is already divorced. I haven't seen or spoken to either of them since that night last year, but Mason heard the gossip and spilled the tea for me. Rumor has it he cheated on her. Irony at its best.

Honestly, at this point, I don't care. They're both sad people, and I hope they find happiness and a less selfish and self-absorbed way of living. Conversely, being married to Mason these months—for real married—has been the best. During his bye week, he surprised me with a trip to Stone and Tinsley's private island for a few days. We ate, had sex, slept, swam, and lay on the beach. It was heaven.

The best part, it was just us and no one else around for miles and miles. He had gotten permission from my OB and everything, which is good because I was worried, but he assured me that if I needed it, we could be back in Miami by helicopter in under an hour. Thankfully, we didn't need it.

"Presents and dessert time, everyone!" my grandmother calls out, glee all over her face as tray after tray of desserts is set out on the long tables on the other side of the wall of gifts.

"Lord, Stella," Wren exclaims. "How much food did you make?"

"In case you missed it, we're sixty-plus women along with..." She trails off and pans her hand toward the door when there's a barrage of loud pops that sound like gunfire. I start, practically shooting out of my chair with a cry, when the confetti flies through the air and every freaking man from the Fritz and Central Square crews along with Jack and his friends and cousins, along with Mason is here.

"Surprise!" they all shout.

"Sorry," Katy whispers to me. "Mason wanted to be here so badly for the gender reveal that we didn't have the heart to tell him no, and we figured if he was going to be part of this, well..."

"Might as well include everyone," Tinsley finishes for her.

"Right. Wow." I glance down between my legs, my hand still covering my pounding heart. "Except, I just peed. Everywhere. In front of my entire family and my husband."

"Uh, that's not pee," Keegan tells me, staring down at the puddle on the floor.

My eyes round just as Mason comes over and surveys the leaking mess between my thighs. "Did you spill your water when we came in?" He chuckles. "Sorry. I didn't mean to scare you like that. I just wanted it to be a surprise because isn't that what today is all about?"

"Surprise, her water broke," Keegan deadpans.

"What?" half the room cries at once. "Her water broke." Those words murmur through the air, half-panicked, half-amused, half-excited, which I realize is too many halves, but whatever. My water just broke in front of every single human I know. My face flames, but at least I didn't pee. That's somewhat of a relief, except now I'm in labor and not only is nothing ready, but I didn't get a slice of cake.

"I broke your water?!" Mason shouts. "No. It's too soon." He grabs my hand in a panic and squeezes way too hard. "The room isn't set up, and I know we're technically full term, but it was supposed to bake in there for another few weeks."

"Breathe, Mason," my father tells him, placing his hand on his shoulder. "It'll all be fine. Babies come when they want."

"But I did this. It's all my fault."

Once again, I feel like I'm outside my body, watching the chaos and craziness of my family all around me.

"We should check her cervix," my aunt Grace demands, spilling half her drink as she rushes over to me. "I can do it. I have gloves in my purse."

"Mom, you're not checking her cervix," Owen states flatly

while holding Rory's hand and trying to pull her away from the frosting on the cake. "Rory, stop that. No fingers in the cake."

"Why is the inside blue?" she asks with a scrunched nose. "I wanted chocolate."

"Blue?!" That's my mother. "Oh my god! It's a boy!" And then she breaks down into tears, as do half of my drunk aunts.

"We were supposed to let you tell us when you sliced into it!" my aunt Rina whines as she hands Rory a fork and starts to dig into it herself.

Others join in, and now they're all attacking the cake with gusto, while my grandmother gets upset that it wasn't cut properly, and Rory is crying because she ruined the surprise. Meanwhile, Grace, Carter, and Keegan are going back and forth on who will check my cervix. Spoiler alert: None of them.

Jesus, this is getting out of hand fast.

I stick two fingers between my lips and blow out a sharp whistle. The room quiets, and all eyes turn to me.

"Here's the deal. Mason is going to take me to the hospital now because I'm starting to have contractions, and they're already not a lot of fun." My mother hands me a towel, and I shove it between my legs because I'm hot like that. She drops another on the floor and a third on the chair where I was just sitting to clean up my mess. "Thank you," I say to her and then go back to the room overstuffed with way too many people. "Yes, we're having a boy. We'll announce his name after he's born. Thank you all for coming and for the presents. I'll get to them after he's born, but if anyone purchased us a bassinet, a crib, newborn clothes, and gear, I'd appreciate you letting Serena know because she is now my point person for the nursery and making sure I have a space to bring my baby home to and that he won't be naked when I do that."

There's rumbling, and a few hands go up as if to say they're the ones who purchased those items. Awesome. Now we're getting somewhere.

I look at Mason as more discomfort rolls up my back, and the fact that I'm having back labor truly sucks. I've been uncomfortable all day, so who knows how long I was actually in labor before I realized it. If I wasn't in front of my entire family and they weren't all drunk, I might consider that cervix check after all.

"You ready?" I ask Mason, because yeah, it's time to go.

"Uh." He gulps, looking pale and a little lost. "Yes. Yeah. Of course."

"I'll drive you," my dad tells him, and Mason practically sags in relief. My dad and Mason have gotten very close over the last couple of months.

"Thanks, Dad." At least he's calm. No one else is. My mom is still sobbing that it's a boy and Stella is trying to calm her down.

Mason wraps his arms around me on one side, and Serena comes in on the other.

"My darling girl." My grandmother cups my face and kisses both my cheeks. "You take care and have a safe delivery of my great-grandson."

"I will." I kiss her back, and then we leave, getting to the hospital in under half an hour because my father knows all the back roads and drives like a total Masshole. Mason hasn't let go of my hand as we're brought into a room, and I'm helped into a gown and up onto a bed where they set me up with monitor strips. I can feel his hand trembling in mine. "Are you okay?"

"Yes. I just..." His eyes search mine. "I thought we had a few more weeks. The room isn't ready yet. We don't have a name. And I read... well, you know a lot can happen during delivery."

I lean in and kiss him. "You pick the name."

He shakes his head. "No way. I'm not living with you holding that over my head for the rest of our lives."

I giggle only to hiss out a breath when a contraction hits.

"Well," I pant. "I'm thinking we need to figure one out right about now. Where did we leave off?"

"N."

"Ugh." I focus on my breathing, my eyes closed, and my body centered like I learned in birthing class. "We didn't get very far."

"Nolan, Nixon, Nico, Noah, Neil—"

"Nolan?"

"Nolan Reyes," he says with a contemplative hum to his voice. I start to relax as the contraction wanes and open my eyes to see his smile. "I like it. Let's go with it."

"See." I smile. "Easy. Unlike labor."

The doctor comes in, and finally, my cervix is checked. Already at six centimeters, I'm the lucky recipient of an epidural. Hours pass. Contractions come and go along with some of our immediate family who pop in and out. Serena and my mom stay for a while, but when I start to have the urge to push, it's only me and Mason.

His head is beside mine as he whispers encouraging words and praise into my ear. I'm squeezing two of his fingers so I don't break his hand, but fuck does this hurt.

"Come on, Sorel," my OB commands. "You've got this. One more push. Come on. Give me one more big push."

The pressure is enormous, even with the epidural, and I can't breathe or think. I can only feel and I'm tired. I'm so tired. So freaking tired.

"Come on, princess. One more push and we get to meet him. You've got this. I'm so proud of you, baby. I love you. I love you so much. Push."

Fuck. Fuck! I bear down and push with everything I have left. I'm covered in sweat and pain, but I push and yell, and a second later, the doctor says, "Stop pushing. Stop pushing." More pressure, and then a tiny cry pierces the air.

"Mom, Dad, I'd like you to meet your son." A tiny naked

baby covered in vernix is placed right on my chest, and we're
both wrapped up in a warm blanket.

I stare down at the tiny, slimy baby and then up at Mason,
who has tears down his face. He leans in and kisses me before
he kisses the wet top of the baby's head.

"You did so good," he says to me. "Look at him, Sorel. He's
so perfect."

"He is."

I hold him for a few more minutes, keeping his little body
warm with mine. Mason cuts the cord, and then he's taken
from me to get weighed and measured. Mason goes with him as
they finish up with me, and by the time they're returned to me,
Nolan is swaddled tight in a blanket with a small cream-colored
hat on his head.

Mason climbs on the bed beside me, his large frame on his
side, and up against the railing still takes up most of it, but I
don't care. The nurse places Nolan back on my chest and helps
me start to nurse him. After he's latched on, starting to suckle
away, the room gets dark and quiet, and now it's just us.

Mason's hand is on Nolan's back, his eyes bouncing back
and forth between our nursing newborn and my face. "You're so
beautiful," he whispers reverently. "You both are." He leans in
and kisses me. "You're the loves of my life. I'm in awe of you.
Look what you made. Look at our sweet little man."

"I love you," I murmur, my body feeling heavy, even as I
can't stop watching my sleepy baby with his dark eyes and tiny
little face nurse from my body. I had no idea it would feel this
way. This consuming. This... perfect. Just as Mason said. I had
no idea I could love anything this much. Because with the three
of us like this, that's exactly what it is. Love. Perfection. Heaven.
Happiness. And I already know, come what may, it's what it'll
always be as long as we have each other.

BONUS EPILOGUE
MASON

"All right, little man, here's the deal." I hold his chest in the palm of my hand and thrust him up into the air, smiling along with him as he sucks in a deep breath and lets out his version of a giggle. "There's a few things you're gonna need to learn how to do." My elbow bends, and I bring him back down to me to kiss the tip of his nose this time before I thrust him back up into the air. "One is peeing in your diaper and not when we take it off." I drop him back to me and get his forehead before I repeat the motion. "Two is not puking up all the milk you drink."

As if to punctuate my point, he makes a noise, and before I can react, his little body jerks and he splatters my arm with hot, white, awful smelling milk vomit.

"Two needs some work, buddy. A lot of work." Gross. Though at this point, I should be used to it. It's why I'm shirtless half the time. Well, that and my woman loves me shirtless.

I bring him down and roll half on my side so I can lie him on his play mat and get myself cleaned up. The baby wipe is cold, and I shiver and make a noise I'd never want anyone else to hear me make—he's a baby, he's not telling anyone—and then swipe my shoulder with his burp cloth to finish the job.

I curl up next to him on the floor with a yawn. "Remind me next time to wait a full hour after you've eaten to bench press you. Thirty minutes is not sufficient. At least you didn't get your"—he turns red, tenses up, and an ominous noise comes from inside his onesie—"outfit," I finish with a sigh. "Who knew babies had so many... functions."

I scrunch my nose and lift Nolan off the mat so I can change his diaper.

"Now I mean it this time," I tell him as I set him down on the changing table in his playroom. "Real men pee in a diaper or, when you're older, a toilet or the woods when no one else can see. Not on the walls or on Mommy, and definitely not on Daddy. Got it?" I check as I start to unsnap him.

Slow, so slowly, I unpeel the tabs on either side of his little diaper and carefully peek in at what's waiting for me. Nothing good, that's what, but it's really more his waterworks I'm trying to avoid.

At the speed of light, I pull the diaper, clean him up, and get him into a new diaper.

"Phew!" I smile in relief. "We did it. Nice." I take his arm and bring my fist to his. "See? Isn't that better?"

I put him back in his onesie and carry us both down to the floor, keeping him on my chest as I lie back and close my eyes. I'm exhausted. Sorel is exhausted too, but my poor princess also has mastitis and a solid fever to go with it. She's been pumping and nursing, but I've been letting her rest as much as she can. Nolan isn't so interested in letting anyone rest. For three-and-a-half months old, the dude does not like sleep.

It's nearly seven in the morning, and I've been trying for the last two hours to tucker him out, but to no avail. I need caffeine. Serious fucking caffeine, but unfortunately with training camp starting in a little over a week, that's a no-go for me.

It's also my and Sorel's anniversary tonight. Well, our Vegas anniversary, and I had finally convinced her to let our parents watch the baby for one night so I could take her away—just to Cape Cod so we're not far—and then she got mastitis.

Still, despite the adjustments to life with a newborn over the last few months, they've been the best of my life. This last year has been the best of my life, and I wouldn't change any of it. I had a whole romantic—and sexy as fuck—night planned for my wife, but I'll happily take some snuggle time in front of the TV and a full night of sleep.

My hand rubs Nolan's back, and he emits a small burp and then snuggles in.

"Was that it, buddy? Was your tummy upset? Now that you've puked, pooped, and burped, maybe we can get a few hours of sleep. What do you think?" I roll my head and squint an eye open to find his closed. Hallelujah, praise Jesus.

Carefully, I curl to a sitting position, keeping him locked against my chest, and get myself up to my feet. I pad down the hall and into his room, where I deposit him gently into his crib. He stirs, his arms flailing up as he starts, but before he can utter a cry, he's back under, and I blow out the breath I had been holding.

Sleep. Oh, how I need you.

I rub the top of my head, yawning as I head into my room. The lights are out, and the air is still and dark with only a tiny stirring of Sorel's heavy breathing. Vegas is passed out beside Sorel as if he's been doing heavy baby lifting as well. Newsflash: he hasn't. He's just as much of an attention whore as our son is. I shove him down, and he moves to the end of the bed, giving me space to work with.

The cool sheets beckon me, and the moment my back hits them and the blanket swings over my body, I'm out like a light, only to wake up who knows how much later to warm, soft kisses on my neck.

"I'm dreaming," I hum and shift so I can sink deeper into the feel of Sorel's mouth.

"Yes," she purrs in my ear. "You're still asleep, and this is all a dream."

A smile curls up my lips. "Why does it sound like you're getting sexy with me?"

Fingers meet my chest and slowly walk down toward my hardening cock.

"Because this is your dream, not reality."

"Shit," I hiss when she grabs my dick over my briefs. "Fuck that feels good. This might be the best dream I've ever had."

"Mason," she sighs against my skin as her kisses continue to trail up my neck.

"Yes, baby."

"Mason, wake up. You're moaning in your sleep, and your parents will be here in ten minutes to pick up the baby."

"What?" My eyes snap open, and my head swivels frantically around. Sorel is standing on the other side of the bed, freshly showered with her shoulder-length hair still wet. She looks better though. I blink and blink again. "You're kidding me?"

"Kidding you about what? Your parents? No."

"No, that I was actually..." I shake my head and scrub my hands up and down my face, my cock painfully hard but starting to soften now that it's gotten the message and heard the word parents. "Never mind." I sit up and take in my beautiful wife. "How are you feeling?"

"Better," she says with a smile I haven't seen on her face in a few days. "The antibiotics are kicking in, and with my last feeding, I felt more of the clogged duct open up. God, it was better than an orgasm."

Hmm. Ha. My dick doesn't find that funny right now. That was the most realistic dream I've ever had, and over these last few months, we haven't exactly had a ton of sex. I mean, we have, but not nearly what we were having while she was pregnant, which was essentially marathon sex.

The doorbell rings, Vegas barks, a bit overexcited to see his grandparents, and she huffs. "They're early."

"They're always early when they come to pick him up."

"I know. I just wanted more time with him before they take him. We haven't left him overnight yet."

I climb out of bed and wrap my arms around her so I can breathe in the scent of her skin. "It'll be okay. He'll be fine, and it'll be good for us too."

"I know. I know all of this. It's just..."

"Tough. I want to and don't want to."

"Right. Exactly."

I kiss her neck, and she turns to hug me. "Get dressed. I'll let your parents in. They're heading straight over to my parents' place for dinner. I'd also bet money Stella and Delphine will be there."

"Then Nolan and Vegas will have plenty to keep themselves occupied, and I'll have plenty to keep you occupied now that you're feeling better."

Her eyes brighten. "Oh, like dinner and HGTV?" She's far too jazzed by that prospect.

"Uh-huh." Or, you know, hot, hot sexy sex.

With an excited squeal and a kiss on my cheek, she runs off, and I stare down at my poor dick.

"Looks like it could be a slow night for us."

I throw on some clothes and come out to say hi to my parents, who have no time or patience for me as they're all over Nolan, peppering my son with hugs and kisses and coos.

My dad signs, You look like shit. I laugh. I likely do. You better be ready next week.

I flip him off, and he chuckles.

"Go enjoy your night," my mother tells us, holding the baby

like she's never going to let go. "We've got him, and your parents have the dog. It'll be great. We promise."

Sorel looks like she's about to break into tears, and even I'm getting this pulling sensation to grab the baby and bring him back into our room. How do parents do this? If it's this bad now, he'll never be able to leave for college.

"Right. Um."

"Here."

My mother hands Sorel back the baby, and she tucks him straight against her, holding him tight and kissing him everywhere. I come in beside them and do the same, making him give me a fist pound because that's our thing.

"We're going to miss you, little man," I tell him. "You be good for your grandparents and let them sleep tonight. And remember the conversation we had this morning about peeing and throwing up."

Sorel throws me a side eye but doesn't ask questions. I talk to the baby a lot. She already knows this about me. And considering Nolan pukes on everyone he can, it was a conversation worth having.

Vegas barks up at me, and I bend down to give him some love, rubbing his head and ears the way he likes. "We'll miss you too."

Sorel and I pepper Nolan with more kisses, but then my parents take him and Vegas, and suddenly the door is closed, and it's just us. Alone. And it's quiet. Too quiet.

"Should I run after them?" I ask her, and she shakes her head, though her chin is quivering.

"It's one night."

I nod. "One night," I agree. "I miss him already. Is that lame?"

A tear hits her cheek. "No," she squeaks.

"Aw, princess." I gather her against me. "Come shower with me."

"I already showered." She pushes me away and wipes her face. "Go shower. You smell like Nolan's vomit. I'll order dinner for us from that place you like."

"This isn't the anniversary I had planned for us."

She waves that away. "It's fine. We'll do something for our next one in a few months."

I turn and head for the shower, feeling a little dejected. Maybe she's still not feeling well or maybe it's having the baby away from us for the first time. I don't know. But she seems... off. A little cold even.

I do my best to shrug it off and head for the shower, my heart heavy in a few ways. Still, it's nice to be able to take a shower without rushing through it, and I enjoy the hot water on my tired muscles. I didn't work out today, and it's not a good way to go into the season. Sorel's mom retired as a middle school teacher and has offered to be our nanny of sorts starting in a few weeks when Sorel returns to work.

I'm grateful for that, and hopefully, the extra set of regular hands makes a difference in everything.

Stepping out of the shower, I run the towel back and forth over my head before I wrap it around my waist. I suppose if we're staying in front of the TV tonight, I can wear sweats. I turn the corner out of the bathroom and stop dead in my tracks when I find Sorel on our bed. She's wearing... I have no clue what you call it, but I fucking love it.

Black lace. Straps. Full breasts, soft belly, pretty pussy, barely covered long legs.

Damn.

I lick my lips and take a step forward. "What's all this?"

She sits up a little, and the angle presses her huge tits together. Fuck, I need to squeeze those.

"You've been such a good boy while I was sick, I felt you needed a reward."

"You did?" Hope springs like my dick under my towel.

"I do."

She crooks a finger at me, and I practically fly across the room to the bed and jump on top of her. She giggles, sort of killing some of the sexy, dominatrix vibe she had going on, but I don't care. I need to kiss her, and I need to kiss her now.

My lips devour hers as my hands meet her tits. "Can I touch them?"

"Yes," she pants.

"I don't want to hurt you."

"It won't if you do it right, but don't squeeze too hard," she tells me, and I groan, kissing my way down her neck to them. I have to admit, I'm a lot obsessed with these.

"Fuck, princess, you are so goddamn hot right now, and I'm a second away from blowing my load."

"But I have toys."

My head springs up. "Toys?"

She bats her eyelashes playfully at me. "Doesn't Daddy want to play?"

And I die. My forehead falls to the bed, and I start laughing. "Oh, Daddy wants to play."

"Then tie me up already and be a good boy and make me come."

I pop my head up and roll us until she's straddling my thighs, and I can gaze up at her as my hands run up her sides. "You realize you're sort of mixing kinks up, right?"

"You realize I didn't know I had any kinks until last summer, right?"

Hmm. "Do you trust me?"

Her head tilts. "Of course I trust you."

And the ease in which she says that fucking nails me right in the chest. She trusts me. She means it. Fucking Sorl-I-trust-like-two-people-on-the-planet-Fritz trusts me. I am done. Not to be my wife, but "Turn It On" from the Flaming Lips hits my head, and I start to sing the chorus, making her crack up.

"Oh my god! Stop!"

I grab my sexy vixen wife and pull her up into my arms as I jackknife off the bed. "We're going outside."

Her eyes go globe round. "What?"

"I want everyone to hear how hard I get to fuck my wife."

"No!" She tries to climb out of my arms. "Mason, no."

I stop short and pull her face to mine. "Yes. You trust me. Remember?"

Her breath hitches. "I trust you."

Fuck, I will love this woman till my dying breath and beyond.

Without another word, I open our balcony. It's hot outside. It's over ninety with what feels like equal humidity, and the sun is high in the summer sky. But our balcony is high up. It's not completely blocked, but it's blocked enough. Sort of like the one we fucked on in Vegas. And legit, if someone from below hears us, they won't see us or know who is making those noises.

"Now, Mrs. Fritz-Reyes, let me see you in this outfit because fuck, you make me so hard." I grab her hand and rub it over my length, which is still somehow hidden beneath my towel that's managed to cling on for dear life. "How on earth did I get this lucky?"

Sometimes I honestly don't know.

It's not even simply her beauty. It's her heart and the way she loves and how she shares herself with me when it's the hardest thing in the world for her to do. I get this piece of her. I get every piece. They're all mine.

We don't have a lot of furniture out here. Shame. I'll have to change that, but for now I set her down in the chair and spread her thighs wide. I need to eat my wife's pussy because she never moans as loud with anything else. Especially since we've had our son. She's been self-conscious a bit because she's curvier than she was before she had him and has some stretch marks and whatever else women worry makes them less attractive to us.

She has no clue how gorgeous she is.

I start to play with some of the visible lines on her lower belly, and she tries to shove my hand away.

"Knock it off," I tell her, staring up into her eyes. "Don't ever push me away from what's mine. This is the body that grew our son. This is the body that pushed him out. I fucking love this body. It makes me hot like nothing else." I kiss the soft, slightly pink lines. "I love all of it." I get back onto my knees and show her a scar I have on my side. "I got this from a fight with my younger brother one day when I was being a shit. I deserved it. It was a rock, and it hurt. This." I point to my shoulder. "Is from falling out of a tree which made my mother nuts since she fell out of a tree when she was little and broke her arm the same way. Are my scars ugly?"

She puffs out a breath. "It's different."

I shake my head. "It's not. These scars tell your story as much as these tell mine, and I love your story because it's our story. Never hide yourself again. Okay?"

She gives me a soft grin. "Okay."

"My girl. Now spread your thighs wide. As you said, I've been a very good boy. I get to have my dessert before my dinner. Now show your world to me."

That earns me a smirk. Especially on our fake wedding anniversary.

I tug her nothing of a thong to the side and rim her clit with my tongue. She sighs, but that's not good enough. I suck it in between my lips and flick it with my tongue as my hand rubs up and down her pussy without entering it.

"Ah! Mason."

It's a start.

I spit on her pussy, right on her entrance. She doesn't need it. But I want to shock her. I want to get her head into dirty slut mode. I smack the wet flesh and shove two fingers straight into her.

"Fuck!" she cries, and there we go. Now we're in this.

My mouth consumes her cunt, licking her so good I'm likely going to be bald at the back of my head by the end of this as she rips and grinds and rolls and says a million incoherent things.

"They can't hear you yet, baby. I need my princess to be loud. I need everyone to know how good I eat your cunt."

"Oh. I... I can't." I suck her clit like I'm sucking an oyster down my throat. "Ah. Okay. Shit. Hell. Mason!"

There.

My fingers fuck up into her, rubbing her front wall with each thrust. I want her to come like a whore and a goddess. But her pussy tastes so good. She still has all these hormones and I swear they rile me like nothing else. I can't hold back. I can't stop myself. I'm a starved man. A man too in love and obsessed with his wife for it to be healthy.

She starts to come, and the feel of it on my lips and fingers is about to make me shoot everywhere, and I can't have that. I crawl up her body, and with my face inches above hers, I drive my cock straight inside her. My hand creeps up along her throat, and I give her a light squeeze as I start to fuck her right out here on the balcony for anyone to hear.

I smirk.

Because I can hear people, and I know she can too.

They won't be able to see us, but who wants to focus on that?

"Come on, princess. Fuck me like you mean it."

And she does.

She fucks up into me with those blazing emerald and chocolate eyes locked on mine. "Make me feel it," she says to me, so similar to what she said to me that night a year ago. So I do.

I fuck her so she has no choice but to feel it.

But to know people can hear her getting fucking hard on her patio...

"No one sees this pussy but me. No one gets these tits but me."

"No one," she promises, her body rocking and pumping with mine. "Not ever."

But now it's so much more than fucking. It's her body. It's mine. It's ours. It's us.

And when she starts to come, I can't help but let go and come with her. Knowing that it's only me who heard her, who has her, who owns her. And forever, it's her, my girl, my world, who owns all of me.

THANK you for taking the time to read Undeniably Married. I hope you enjoy Mason's and Sorel's story. I know it was an emotional one. If you're new to me or simply curious, uou can find all of my books on my website at http://jsamanbooks.com. XO

Made in the USA
Columbia, SC
09 December 2024

47624075R00224